PARTS ARE PARTS

A Kenny Carson Novel

John A. Wooden

Published by
JBOW Productions

ISBN – 10: 0-9767404-4-3
ISBN – 13: 978-0-9767404-4-5

Cover and Interior Design by: Jessica Tilles of TWA Solutions.com

PARTS ARE PARTS

A Kenny Carson Novel

The Beginning

THE MADNESS OF DEATH

ONE

IN DEATH AS IN LIFE WE KNOW WHY THE PIPER COMES CALLING.

With his pipes blasting loudly, as if it was time for a moment of exuberance, the pipes represented the evils of man. For the kiss of death, the prince of darkness, the prelude to eternity, it is a celebration. We can only *hope* it's good for life, and not a life of suffering. But the piper has never been a pursuer of a bright future.

Hope.

Sometimes it's just a four-letter word. A word many store in their back pockets, wishing that moment that required a dash of optimism never occurs.

Jimmie Claymore had a lot to live for, a lot to look forward to. After all, he was one of the biggest names in Hollywood. He had worked hard to get to this point in his life. Of course, having the *right* name and prestigious family influence always helped. His father, Regan Claymore, was a mainstay in Hollywood and had been for the past fifty years. From his humble beginnings as an extra on B movie sets to becoming the biggest name on the silver screen as a thespian, director and producer, Regan Claymore had established himself as the *Big Kahuna* on the Hollywood set.

Who would believe it had been thirty years since the younger Claymore had been in show business? Jimmie could remember his first role, playing Little Corky Hardway in his father's produced

1

television show, *Detective and Son*. He was a scene-stealer. Yes, that's how the TV critics described his acting ability. Of course he was . . . his father's son. And no way would the Big Kahuna's son be anything besides a scene-stealer.

Tears fell from his eyes as he thought about the old days. How, at age thirty-six, could he be thinking about the old days? That didn't compute to him or probably anyone else his age. In his mind, he knew no one should be considering old age or recalling golden moments before he was forty. In his wildest dreams he never thought he would live to see four decades. Unfortunately, his wildest dreams may be right.

He struggled to remember the good and bad times he had shared with his father. He was never much of a mama's boy. He was always his father's pride. Even with his father jumping from bed to bed or wife to wife, he endured it all. When people met and got to know him, their first compliment was always, "Damn, you're just like your father."

And he was.

Some would consider it an insult. But not Jimmie. Any comparison to Regan Claymore, good or bad, was a compliment. The elder Claymore was his hero. Who didn't want to be like their hero? He didn't care what others thought about him or his father as long as due respect came their way. And everyone knew—Claymores demanded respect. And he embodied the Claymore way.

Why now? It was only a thought. One he didn't want to harp on. It was already a trying day. Actually, he didn't know if it had been a day, two days or a week since his abduction. That's what it was—a kidnapping. Whoever kidnapped him knew his father would pay a pretty penny to get him back.

Why now? He screamed in his head again. This was the sixth or seventh time the same thought had resonated loudly in his thick skull. He had just shot the pilot for *The Streets of Gold.* This was his return to television and his breakthrough moment. This was his opportunity to do something without the Regan Claymore label attached to it. He was mono-e-mono on this one. It was *his baby.* His project. Detective, mystery and suspense genres had always been his bread and butter. From that first show as a child to his last movie, *The Kill Field,* where he played an L.A. detective in search of a killer who got his jollies from killing women and leaving them in various fields in Southern California.

What did one Hollywood reporter say about him? *"It is the most electrifying role Mr. Claymore has ever played. This is the role that allowed the talented Jimmie Claymore to make his own name in Hollywood. This is the performance the son stepped out of his father's shadow and became his own man."*

And that was so true. He loved his father and they had a great relationship, maybe too great. He was almost thirty-seven and his father was still there for him. He knew the reporter was right, he was out of his father's shadow.

But he wished his father were here now, with him at this very moment, at this very place—wherever this place was. He knew his father would find a way to overcome this little situation he was in.

A situation that really wasn't little at all.

A situation that smelled rotten with the piper's stench.

TWO

Even with his eyes closed, he could feel the powerful heat from the lights.

He assumed they were strobe lights, similar to the ones used on movie sets. If a person was stationary, and the strobe lights were in for a close-up, they were known to make that person feel as if they were being cooked. And, right now, it felt as if his face was baking. He was lying flat on his back, on a cot with a semi-hard cushion. He didn't know how wide it was. He speculated it was the size of a twin-sized mattress or smaller, but he had never slept on a twin-sized bed before. He was tied up tight, so tight he couldn't move.

No, I'm taped up, he thought again. He had tried screaming a couple of times, but his mouth wouldn't move. Whoever had kidnapped him had injected him with a drug that made it hard for him to speak. He was lethargic.

Then it hit him. What movie was it? *The Mind of the Demon.* It was his only horror movie. He was buried alive and in the scene his lines were, "If I shut up and shut down my thoughts, my hearing will increase and I will be able to hear everything. When you lose one sense, other senses are heightened."

Although it was only a movie, it worked.

He decided to reenact that scene.

He closed his eyes and shut down his thoughts. He was in another place, another time. He had been doing this for years. He loved meditating, drifting off in his own world—a world where he was the solitary figure.

He heard something. By the radiated sound, he couldn't tell if it was a radio or television.

It has been three days since the actor, Jimmie Claymore, was reported missing. Mr. Claymore failed to show up at a meeting he had scheduled with director, Brooks McLemore, in Chicago, and no one including his agent, Samuel Parsley, has heard from Mr. Claymore.

He is now the third member of the infamous teenage clique, the Jet Pack Eight, to come up missing. Singer and actress, Theresa Wenthill, disappeared nine days ago while on location in Santa Fe, New Mexico while shooting a music video. And, actor Wash Tunnell went missing six days ago at his home in Washington, D.C.

The Jet Pack Eight became famous almost twenty years ago when the eight child stars of Hollywood actors, directors and producers appeared in various teen movies and videos together. For several years in the nineties, the eight teenage stars were the hottest ticket in Hollywood.

I never put two and two together, Jimmie thought. He had heard the news of both Theresa and Wash, and hadn't had the time to check on either of them. That may very well been his downfall.

The burning suddenly went away. The light was turned off. He didn't know if he should open his eyes or not but he decided to open them. He realized he couldn't move his head or any part of his body for that matter. He moved his eyes. In his peripheral vision he didn't immediately see anyone or anything. With the strobe light turned off, the room was almost completely dark, with the exception of dim lights off in the distance. How far away, he didn't know for sure.

He looked down as much as his straining eyes would allow him to. He was bound by restraining straps or belts, or whatever they called them. From what he could see, it reminded him of restraining straps used in psych wards. He had been in a couple of movies that had a scene or two that took place in psych wards. His arms and wrists were bind against his sides. Although he couldn't completely see it, he could also feel the straps on his thighs, legs and ankles.

Isn't this ironic and original? he thought. If it wasn't for my schedule, I would have accepted the role of Dexter on Showtime. Now, I may be one of his victims.

He laughed inside at his thought. Not knowing it could be closer to the truth than he thought.

His attention was drawn to the television monitor that seemed to appear out of nowhere and was positioned directly above his head. He still didn't see anyone, so he assumed it was remotely operated.

The monitor blinked and a white screen appeared. What he saw next brought him to tears.

He'd recognize the flowing bleach white blonde mane anywhere. He had once been madly in love with the young lady nicknamed Terri. His heart ached as he looked at the monitor. He had seen Terri in numerous compromising situations. She wasn't always discreet about her private life. He had seen her in a drunken stupor and completely stoned out of her mind from various drugs. Hell, on several occasions, he had even physically carried her home and put her into her own bed. But he had never seen her in the state she was now. A state that made him physically sick.

He could feel the rumbling in his stomach. He knew he had to persevere. He had to. If he regurgitated now he would surely die. That's not how he wanted to die. He didn't want to die at all. Looking at the screen, dying from his own vomit may be the most humane death he could think of right now.

Theresa Wenthill, his Terri, was beaten up badly. Her face was twice the size he was used to seeing it. Her eyes were swollen shut and blackened. Her lips puffed up as if she had ten times too many collagen shots that were legally allowed by law. This was a different Terri than the one he had grew up with.

Terri's father, Thomas Wenthill, was the premier director and producer of fifteen television shows in the seventies and eighties. Ten stayed in the top ten for five years or more. Thomas Wenthill and Regan Claymore worked together on numerous projects, but more importantly, they were friends and closer than any two brothers, a relationship that was naturally passed down to their children.

Jimmie cringed on the cot as he looked at the monitor. He silently prayed this was a bad dream. *Or maybe, a bad movie.* Maybe someone had drugged him. Surely this had to be a bad dream. Terri was in a wheelchair, completely passed out. *Damn, I hope that doesn't happen to me.* It was a thought he immediately regretted thinking. But the reality was, Jimmie Claymore knew he couldn't do anything to help his friend, the woman he had known forever. She had always been a part of his life. *Please forgive me, Terri. Please forgive me.*

Then he saw them. Two men dressed in medical garb, lifting her up and putting her on an operating table. Next, he saw another man and woman, also dressed in hospital attire, join the other two.

His head was aching. For the life of him he didn't know why he was trying to think of what they called the hospital uniforms. His mind was taking a mental beating.

What is the damn name?

Scrubs! That's it, scrubs!

He felt a smile grace his face. *Weird,* was his thought. He was sure it was the drugs making him feel this way. Why else would he mentally beat himself up over the name of hospital garments? His friend was in a hospital with strange looking medical personnel and he was hoping whatever they did to her, they wouldn't do to him.

What in the hell is this about?

Then he saw it—the restraining devices, the straps.

Her ankles had been restrained, as he figured they had done to him. Simultaneously, her arms and thighs received the same treatment. Finally, her head.

Then the monitor got brighter. The lights in the room got brighter and the four were joined by one more—a man. Jimmie had to remember his surroundings and everything he witnessed on the monitor so that when the time came, he could tell the FBI, local authorities or whatever law enforcement agency that rescued him, what he saw. He knew he would make a good witness for the prosecution.

That was his meditation talking to him—positive thinking. He had to escape this situation he was in, and the first step in that escape was thinking he would survive this. Whatever this was?

Someone turned the volume up so he could hear. Yes, he wanted to hear.

"Today, we are performing a unique surgery," the voice began, "for a truly talented and lovely person. A person we all know and love. She is very Hollywood, a star, a headliner and very much so in the spotlight. And no, this is not plastic surgery."

The doctor laughed at his own joke. Jimmie Claymore didn't see the humor in anything he heard. Equally, he tried to catch the voice, but he couldn't. Meditation taught him to calm his nerves, and allow his senses to take over. He let his mind process the voice, while he listened as attentively as he could. He was starting to feel the drugs that lay foreign in his body.

This has to be a bad dream.

"But before we begin our procedure on the world famous Theresa Raquel Wenthill," the voice continued. "She is going to name the next person in our game to operate on."

Jimmie tried to zoom in on the man's eyes. He knew those eyes. He was sure he knew the voice too. *But from where? Who can it be?*

The camera zoomed in on his old friend, Terri, and Jimmie saw that she was awake. Her eyes were swollen but he could see a little white in each eye. She was definitely drugged. Confusion, disorientation and physical distortion crowded her face. Tears barely crept from her swollen and blackened eyes. Black and blue bruises dominated her once beautiful facial features. He recalled every positive review she had received over the years. *A sensual, thrilling voice. Best young talent with dynamic acting skills.*

She was the one of eight who made the easy transition from childhood star to young adult star. Terri made it look easy. After their Jet Pack years, she moved on and did it up big. She released three albums that immediately debuted on the top ten Billboard chart, won multiple music awards, and starred in two megahit movies before she was even twenty. And as her childhood friend, he kept up with it all. He was happy for her. Her success kept his drive and determination hyperactive.

As he continued to look at the monitor, the only thing Jimmie Claymore could do was feel bad.

Surgery, what damn surgery, it finally hit him.

"Remember, Theresa, we said," the commanding voice corroborated, "you have to name the next lucky person in your group to be operated on."

"W-W-Wash," she stuttered quietly, meekly.

"Wash Tunnell it is." The voice confirmed her selection. "I know you are wondering, Miss Wenthill, who I am. Well, wonder no more."

The camera was repositioned and Jimmie could see the entire scene, including all five members of the medical staff, and Theresa on the operating table. He was sure they weren't real doctors or nurses.

The camera zoomed in for a closer look at the man behind the commanding voice—the leader. The pseudo doctor looked directly at the camera, giving Jimmie or whoever else that viewed this in the future a very good look at his face. There was no doubt in Jimmie's mind, he knew this was the leader of the group. The man then pulled his medical mask off and Jimmie Claymore's eyes watered. The doctor smiled and Jimmie felt he was smiling for him.

It finally hit Jimmie and hit him hard. This wasn't about kidnapping, ransom or money.

It was about death, and at that moment, he knew he was a dead man.

THREE

JIMMIE CLAYMORE'S EYES WERE CLOSED.

If he could, he would keep them closed forever. He had definitely had better days. He couldn't really recall any at the moment. However, he could remember the most horrid, gruesome scene he had ever seen and that disturbed him. It should. He participated in the ghastly event.

It was on the grounds of the Herbert Brutus School for Gifted Students in Oxnard, California. The school was for promising young talent—future television or movie stars, singers, dancers or anything dealing with the entertainment industry. He and his seven friends attended the school when they weren't working, as in making movies or being regulars on television shows. At that time, the school was less than ten years old and it was gaining notoriety as being the best school in the world for young thespians. For some students, it was their home year round.

For Jimmie and his friends, it would be the last summer the Jet Pack would spend at Herbert Brutus School. They actually had graduated but that didn't make a difference at Herbert Brutus. Jimmie was sixteen, and although he wasn't the oldest of the group, he was one of their chosen leaders. Wash Tunnell was the other so-called leader and the oldest of the group. The school accepted students from ages ten to eighteen, but it wasn't unheard of for students over the age of eighteen to attend the summer sessions.

Wash took a late interest in acting, and his interest coincided with the interest of the Jet Pack.

Wash was the typical spoiled rich Hollywood kid. He was the fourth child and only son of Armstrong and Tippy Tunnell, one of the most successful acting duos in Hollywood history. Additionally, Armstrong was the chief executive officer of HD Films, one of the top four film industries in Hollywood during that time. Wash was not only his mother's son but his father's as well. The young Tunnell was a very decent athlete but was an even better actor. Some called him a natural. His friends attributed his natural acting ability to his greatest asset—his ability to lie and lie well. He had been in many scrapes but was able to lie his way out of each incident.

Wash loved trouble and he loved pushing the envelope. His parents blamed a morbid curiosity for his shortcoming. But his friends knew better. The old teenager just believed in trouble. And it was that shortcoming that led to the most grisly scene that the Jet Pack would ever witness. A scene they created, participated in, and executed.

Lights! Camera! Action!

Jimmie hadn't thought about that night in over a decade. It was an event he and the other members of their infamous group declared they would never mention. As much as Jimmie wished it were only a childish prank, he and the others knew when darkness fell over the valley in Oxnard, it would be a bad night for some of their classmates.

His eyes opened suddenly. The electrical surge shook his body. The jolt was terrible. The thought pervasive in his mind was *is this the day I meet my maker?*

He was no longer confined to a cot. He was sprawled on a cold, bare smooth concrete floor. His body was sore. From head to toe, he knew his body was black and blue like Terri's and Wash's before him. He couldn't physically see the bruises in the dark, dank, drafty room. But his body felt them. The aches and pains consumed his whole person except his face. He didn't understand.

Two people picked him up and put him back on his cot. He hated that—his cot. He didn't want to claim ownership of the cot or anything else in this place, wherever this place may be. It wasn't his haven. It was the hell he couldn't presently escape from.

The cot he was tied down on was more than a cot. With the push of a button, the small bed transformed into a casket-type apparatus, encasing him in a captive tomb. *His own private purgatory.* The so-called doctor and his four so-called medical colleagues looked on as the casket attacked him. He finally understood the cliché, *feel like I was hit by a sledgehammer.* Whatever electrical gadgets that were hooked up to the contraption hammered away at him worse than any five people.

The first electrical punch shot a pain so excruciating through his back he thought he would die on the spot. He heard himself scream, a horrifying cry he had never heard escape anyone's lips before.

Why now?

The punch was followed by electrical surges and charges throughout his torso and down his legs. Every blow was followed by an unimaginative squeal, yelp or scream that redefined his manhood. The stampede of currents gravely pulsated him both physically and mentally. His body was simultaneously invaded from every angle. The sledgehammer effect persisted repeatedly.

He wasn't one hundred percent positive, but he thought he had soiled himself twice over. In his short life span, he had never envisioned his death. And even if he did, he knew he wouldn't have thought about this form of death—not in a million years.

He couldn't calculate how long he was electronically beaten up. He was sure it had to be at least thirty minutes to an hour.

There was no way he could move his body. He was sure bones were broken, but he had no idea which ones. His manhood was tested. Unfortunately, his manhood had lost.

"Look at this pathetic asshole," he heard someone say. He didn't know if it was a man or woman's voice. Hell, he didn't even know if he heard what he thought he heard.

"Amazing! The great Jimmie Claymore could only take two fucking minutes of pain."

Jimmie didn't completely hear this comment. He was fading in and out. He felt the hot tears flow down his face.

He was defeated and *something* told him this was just the first phase.

Whatever that *something* was, he was right.

Part One
ACTION

CHAPTER 1

Millie dalbert loved coming to work every day.

This was her dream job. A job she didn't really dream about. It just happened. Hard work and dedication—those were the words her mother drilled in her head at least once a week when she was growing up. She literally couldn't remember a week that went by without hearing those words. Now, she wished she were here to see her success.

She was forty years old today, and she was celebrating her fifth anniversary as the manager of the Highland Post Office station on Highland and Summer Avenue in her adopted city of Memphis. She didn't surprise anyone when she came in with donuts and cupcakes. However, she was surprised when her staff threw the light switch causing the whole area to go dark, and thirty seconds later when she came out of her office and saw the cake with five candles. Then the lights came back on and balloons flowed from the ceiling. She was flabbergasted.

Tears flowed from her eyes. All because she wished her mother could be here today and enjoy this moment with her. *Hard work and dedication.* This was her doing.

She was on cloud nine and this was just the beginning of the day. They didn't open the doors of the station until eight o'clock and it was barely seven-thirty. Even after the doors opened, she stood around and goofed off with her employees. She actually had a select group of staff members. These were people who wanted to work for her. Many had transferred from other stations to the Highland station to work for the woman who believed in teamwork.

She didn't have to worry about any of her employees going postal. As high stressed as postal work could be, those who worked for Millie knew she would never allow her station to feel that pain. She hated the word *postal* and its dangerous implications. Therefore, she managed with a loving hand. Yes, the job got done, but not at the expense of browbeating her employees. If someone needed a few hours off to get their mind right, Millie didn't have a problem accommodating that need. After all, at the end of the day it was about surviving the same rat race they all ran forty plus hours a week.

Five years and counting.

It brought a smile to her face. It was going to be a great day, she could feel it in her bones. Her body shook with excitement. She couldn't wait to get home later that day to find out what her love had in store for her birthday.

When a package from WMT, the World Medical Transporters, arrived for her at nine-thirty, accompanied with specific instructions not to open until 10:00 a.m. Memphis time, she got even more excited. Of course, someone was playing a big, elaborate joke on her. Why would anyone send her a package via the world's largest carrier of medical supplies?

She smiled at the notion. She thought she actually knew whom the container had come from. It had to be her best friend, Sarah, who was a nurse and her doctor husband, Richard. She knew what the container was, a cryogenic freezer unit. Sarah and Richard were always doing crazy stuff like this. She could only imagine what crazy scheme they came up with this time.

The suspense ate at her but she did as instructed, she opened the metal container at the instructed time. She broke the numerous seals attached to the lid of the unit. As she lifted the lid, cold air and mist rose from the chilled unit. Two of Millie's subordinates had stepped in her office to see what she had received.

When the mist had cleared, Millie Dalbert looked into the cryogenic freezer unit, and all color left her face. Her eyes got big and the shock overwhelmed her. So much so, Millie hit the floor before her employees could catch her.

CHAPTER 2

The last shot in a gunfight doesn't denote the victor.

That thought occasionally resonated in my mind when I was faced with crazy situations like the one I was dealing with at the moment. What was supposed to be a show of support for my son, Stevie, at his school's field day activities, had turned into something worse—something deadly, something bloody.

For the past two years, I had been an instructor at the FBI Academy in Quantico, Virginia. Since my last major case, my life had changed. I had voluntarily removed myself from the field and Director Elliot Lucas convinced me to take an assignment at the Academy. The occasional investigations I worked were pending inactive cases, otherwise known as cold cases. The Bureau didn't believe in any cases being considered cold. Pending inactive sounded much better. These were cases I could also get students involved in. I made it a point to head up a case every class to keep my skills fresh.

The time away from the hustle and bustle of solving major cases had been a welcomed break. I had become a stronger family man, more in tune with my love for family. I had lost my mother, sister, brother and possibly, another brother and sister, whom my father didn't know if they were still living or dead. I was amazed it had taken me so long to know the true essence of family and love.

Today was another commitment to family. But life wasn't always about roses. Today was one of those sour moments. It wasn't life serving lemons and making lemonade. Hell, I loved lemonade. This was life serving death, and me trying to preserve the breathing.

"Come on, son, we don't need more people dying," my friend and one-time partner, Supervisory Special Agent Patrick Conroy, was saying to the assailant dressed in all black from head-to-toe.

He was a member of the cult, or gang, called *Code of Colors*. He was one of six members who attacked Stevie and his fellow schoolmates as they were playing soccer on three separate soccer fields on the school grounds. His other five co-assailants were shot. I wouldn't bank on any of them still being alive, but I wasn't sure. The assailant identified himself as *Mr. Code Black*. And at this moment he was holding a female teacher hostage at gunpoint. Either Patrick or I had time to check the status of the downed assailants.

Nor did we have time to check the status of the ten or more victims who had been shot by Code Black and his co-hordes.

Not much was known about the Code of Colors. They had been in the news lately, going on three similar killing sprees before this one. In the past, they had attacked high school and college-aged students. The motive behind their killing spree was unknown. The only communique they had released was an email sent to a freelance writer's blog. They described themselves as representing diversity of *madness and chaos*. Whatever in the hell that meant.

"These people that are dying are on you and the establishment," Mr. Code Black replied angrily. "You killed our code members and we're just settling the score."

I could tell by his voice inflection that we were dealing with a kid, probably late teens to early twenties. An overload of stress and fear dripped with every word he spoke—indeed a dangerous combination. What was supposed to be an easy assignment, and the possible death of hundreds, had been squashed by several unexpected agents, an eleven-year-old student and a spectator.

As much as we didn't want anyone else to die today, this kid was putting us in an untenable position—*die today or live to see another day.*

"Son—"

"I told you to stop calling me son!" the assailant interrupted Patrick. "My name is Code Black dammit. Mr. Code Black to you federal scum."

This was agitation we didn't need. I wanted to intervene but Patrick had established himself as the Alpha Dog. It was an intense situation and during moments like this, delicacy was the word of the day. His hostage was a blonde female. I was sure she was the physical education teacher. She stood about five seven. Her assailant was at least three or four inches taller than she was.

The other two guns pointed at him belonged to two younger FBI agents, Blane Taylor and Paula Coker. I had no idea why they were even here, but I was glad they were. Maybe they knew something about the attack on my son's school. But, right now, that wasn't important. There would be plenty of time to discuss that in the hot wash. Assuming we all got out of this thing alive.

"I'm sorry, Mr. Code Black," Patrick apologized to the kid. I knew he was hoping to diffuse the situation. The most important element in situations like this was to keep the assailant cool and calm. It sounded like a cliché, but it was true. The more stable the assailant, the better crazy situations like this ended in your favor—with no more deaths.

"You know what? I'm tired of talking," Mr. Code Black announced. Before he could pull the trigger of the gun he had against his hostage's head, Patrick and I both squeezed the trigger on our FBI-issued 9mm Glock 27s and blew half of Code Black's head off.

CHAPTER 3

THERE IS NOTHING MORE SPECIAL IN LIFE . . .

. . . than the birth of a child," I recalled my father, Howard Carson, saying to me as he held my sister, Alyse, in his arms. He would continue to tell me the joys of life always started with birth and outweighed everything else in the world. "How can you not love life when it is such a gift from God?" he had stated. I remember nodding my head as if I fully understood what he was saying, but at the age of ten, I didn't have a clue. I was sure my eyes were glassy with confusion—maybe incoherence.

Today, I knew the feeling well as the words resonated in my head. I was holding Stevie and my niece, Janessa, in my arms. She had come down to support Stevie's field day as well. I loved them both, but it was mixed with anger. I was pissed that both Janessa and Stevie had gone on the offensive when the six assailants came racing on motorcycles out of the mass of trees that sat maybe two hundred yards from the soccer field with automatic handguns and semi-automatic assault rifles.

I had taken a break from the job and had ridden with Patrick, who was at the Academy on business. We had just descended the hill and were probably fifty yards from the soccer fields when the attack occurred. I was immediately afraid for the kids and the school staff. Six riders, wearing different color outfits: white, burgundy, green, orange, blue and black.

Patrick and I sprinted to the field with guns in hand. I saw Stevie pick up a soccer ball, throw it at the rider in orange, and knock him off his bike. Janessa did the same damn thing her much younger cousin did and knocked the guy in burgundy off his bike. Before either could rebound, Patrick shot the rider in orange and I took out the rider in burgundy.

I didn't know where Agents Coker and Taylor came from, but I was glad they showed up. Although we had taken out five of the six assailants before the hostage situation with the rider in black, they still managed to kill six kids and two staff members, and seriously injured three other kids and two staff members. Thirteen dead or injured.

Now I was holding two of my loved ones tight and didn't want to let go. I was worshipping family even more—more than I ever had. Life was precious to me. I couldn't lose any more family members, even my father, whom I had an estranged relationship with for years.

When Stevie asked me to attend his field day, I was happy—no, honored he had asked. Normally, this was a Julia thing, my wife, Stevie's mom. However, Julia, like me, was an agent with the Bureau and she was away on a mission. I guess Stevie thought I was a good substitute. Internally, I smiled at the irony. I was sure I chose my mom over my dad as well when I was younger.

"Sir," Agent Coker interrupted my emotional moment. "I hate to interrupt, but Agent Taylor and I were sent here to retrieve you and take you to the J. Edgar Hoover Building."

"You guys okay?" I asked Janessa and Stevie. It was probably the tenth time I had asked them the same question. They both shook their heads.

"We are good Uncle Kenny," Janessa said. "Go take care of your business."

"No, I'm not leaving you guys," I replied. I looked at Agent Coker. "Tell whoever wants me at headquarters that I will shoot by later when this situation is stable."

"Sir, we were sent by Director Lucas," Coker responded. I was somewhat speechless. If Elliot wanted me, it had to be important. If it wasn't important, he would have called me or had his executive assistant call me. He sent two agents to retrieve me. That was big.

"If Uncle Elliot sent a team for you, I think you need to go," Janessa stated.

"Let me call the Director," I said more for myself than anyone else. "I'm sure he would under—"

Before I could complete my thought, Agent Coker was handing me her phone. "You still need a tan," I said to Paula Coker. She smiled. Which was few, and far between for Coker. Serious was her middle name.

"What's going on Director?" I asked as I walked away from Stevie, Janessa and Coker.

"You okay, Carson?' Elliot asked. It was a formality. He knew I wouldn't be on the phone if I wasn't.

"Doing well."

"And my family? Janessa? Stevie?" Elliot was Julia's uncle. Officially, on paper, that was the truth. In actuality, Julia's parents died when she was a young girl. Elliot and his wife, Portia, raised Julia as if she was their child. Her brother and sister were already grown and out of the house, but too young to raise a young girl. Elliot and Portia stepped in.

"They are doing as well as can be expected, but I prefer to stay with them. I hope whatever it is can wait."

"No. No it can't wait," Elliot stated matter-of-factly. "Sorry Carson, I have a case for you, a pressing matter. Your Bureau needs you."

I hated when Elliot went patriotic. That was his way of telling me to get my ass in. But I knew the case I wanted. "Elliot, I want the Code of Colors case. I think—"

"No," he cut me off before I could go farther. "Agent Coker will drive you in, while Agent Taylor will stay on the scene. There are other agents en route. As of ten minutes ago, Patrick is the lead on the Colors case. He can keep you abreast of what's going on with the case."

Before I could say another word, the phone went dead.

I was not happy.

CHAPTER 4

Special agent paula coker briefed me on what was going on.

Today at over thirty federal facilities throughout the United States, cryogenic freezer units were delivered to specific government locations, with instructions to open the units at a specific time, which was 11:00 Eastern time. To the dismay and surprise of all who opened the cryogenic units, the various sized units contained body parts.

Apparently, the body parts were from the three missing actors who had been reported as being abducted: Theresa Wenthill, Wash Tunnell and Jimmie Claymore. The three were part of an old teenage group of Hollywood friends who referred to themselves as the Jet Pack Eight. Many in the Los Angeles area referred to them as the Malibu Eight, a group of rich, spoiled teenage actors who thought they ruled the world. Rumor had it that they were the real, spoiled brats portrayed in movies like *Pretty in Pink, Breakfast Club* and the like.

The disappearance of the three actors had not only captivated America, but in some circles, many parts of the world. Three of the containers had been delivered to the J. Edgar Hoover Building and another couple to the Washington Field Office. The containers had been delivered by WMT, World Medical Transporters. It was the world's largest transporters of vital organs, body parts, cadavers, and medical supplies and equipment.

The use of cryogenic freezer units was an ingenious idea—the units were filled with liquid nitrogen or liquid carbon dioxide, both were great for preserving body parts. Basically, they acted as a pressurized storage container that prevented the loss of moisture from body parts. The concept was similar to that of body storage compartments in a morgue or medical examiner's office.

I could understand why Elliot was short with me now. Proper protocol for suspicious packages, boxes and yes, containers, was to be opened by a Bureau explosive ordnance disposal team. That protocol was applied to the freezer units sent to the Hoover Building and the WFO. However, the other units were sent to other federal buildings, such as several post offices, IRS and social security offices, and other similar offices. Whoever was behind this had played it right. And with the exception of the individuals in the D.C. area, every container was addressed to a person, with instructions to open the unit at an instructed time.

All of the body parts were already on their way to D.C. for processing via FBI transport. It was going to be a long night for the Bureau's medical forensics personnel.

It wasn't one o'clock in the afternoon yet, and I already had a bad feeling about this case. I made a mental note to check into WMT's invoices. Transporting over thirty cryogenic freezer units had to cost money, especially if all of the units were shipped overnight. Of course they were shipped overnight, that was WMT's moniker. They built their reputation on timely and quick service. In the past five years or more, they had exponentially grown every year by leaps and bounds. It was definitely worth having a conversation with someone up high in WMT.

Additionally, every person that a container was addressed to had to be interviewed. The mastermind behind this craziness evidently did their homework to know someone in each of those federal offices. I know Elliot already had the Information Technology section checking every name on the list. Was it really that easy to find every recipient of a container on the Internet or social media outlets? Even with modern technology, I still wasn't convinced every employee in America had an electronic footprint, especially federal government employees. It was scary to think Google, Bing or any other website had employee data on all Americans.

As important as this case was, I didn't want to be on it. I was even pissed at myself for being able to compartmentalize my overactive thoughts. As Paula briefed me, my mind was on the other case—the Code of Color, the case I should really be on.

I didn't get it. Jet Pack case had to trump the Code of Color. It was Hollywood and Hollywood was still powerful. Evidently, the Code of Color members were as psychotic as they came if they were trying to kill pre-teen children at a school in broad daylight.

No way should I be the lead on the Bureau's biggest case. Supposedly, Elliot wasn't deeply involved in the day-to-day operation as he used to be. I didn't believe that for one second. He was a master juggler and organizer. There was no doubt he still had his fingers in the pot of every investigation the Bureau was involved in, major or otherwise.

My mind was so preoccupied with Code of Color, I almost missed it when Paula briefed that a fourth victim was abducted yesterday. Derrick Paine, actor and director.

But more importantly, Derrick Paine was the son of Thurmond Paine, one of the biggest executives in Hollywood. He was a mover and shaker in Hollywood and the business world. Word on the street was not many things happened in America without Thurmond Paine's knowledge, and that included governmental decisions.

The disappearance of the first three members of the Jet Pack had already captivated America and in some circles, the world.

I could only imagine what the madness would be with a fourth abduction. I could only imagine the pressure Elliot would receive from the White House. The president had received a lot of support from the world of entertainment. If the containers truly were the body parts of the three actors, this would be a priority in the West Wing.

The more I thought about it, the more it really didn't make sense. I had been working cold cases with Academy students for the past two years. I could still do the job, but I knew Elliot had at least ten other agents on his go-to list for major cases such as this. I assumed I was no longer on that list.

"How long have you been on this case, Paula?"

"Actually, less than a week," she responded. "Both Special Agent Taylor and I were brought in four days ago for briefings. I think we were both surprised. This is a big case, and to get a call out of the blue to report to DC shook me to the core. At first, I thought it was WFO, but when I hit DC, I was directed to headquarters."

I smiled. "Alright Coker, this may be one of those be careful what you wish for scenarios."

"I know," she said. "I know oh so well." Although I was still smiling, Paula Coker was still the serious, no-nonsense person I knew her to be. She was the prototypical FBI agent that had been portrayed on TV for years.

"First, some clarity on Mr. Paine," she got back to her briefing. "We don't know his status yet. He was the director, filming his next movie on location in Santa Fe, New Mexico, when he failed to show up at the set at 2:00 a.m. He has a trailer on set as well as a hotel room in the local area and both locations have been searched upside down, inside out, to find the whereabouts of Mr. Paine.

"The Santa Fe Police Department and the New Mexico State Troopers were called in and neither had any success finding Mr.

Derrick Paine. Santa Fe Police don't want to call it an abduction for now for lack of evidence. And quite frankly, I agree. As we speak, we have two agents from the Albuquerque Field Office en route to check it out. Best case scenario, Mr. Paine got spooked and ran. He may have felt he was next in line for abduction."

I didn't say anything. My mind was still moving a mile a minute. *What was Code of Colors? Who was Code of Colors? And what did spoiled, super rich kids do to make someone want to slaughter them like livestock?*

CHAPTER 5

WORDS HAD A WAY OF FAILING ME WHEN IT CAME TO DESCRIBING DIRECTOR ELLIOT LUCAS.

Prior to Elliot becoming the Bureau's Director, bad news used to travel fast within the confines of the Capital Beltway. But those days seemed as if they were eons ago. That was probably one of the biggest complaints about Elliot; he ruled with an iron thumb and believed in being in the know. It was funny, or maybe ironic, he reminded older newsmen of another FBI Director whose name graced the FBI building. I guess control can do that.

Everyone in the Bureau, and throughout the federal government, didn't know how to take the man. I was convinced only two people truly knew him, and that was his wife, Portia, and his niece, Julia. He and I actually had a very good relationship but when he wanted to flex his muscles or fuck up my day, he knew how. As much as I wanted to dislike the man, I couldn't. He was more father than father-in-law or uncle to me, more big brother than friend, and definitely, more dictator than director the way he shrewdly wielded power and directed the Bureau.

There used to be a time you could turn on your radio and hear about whatever federal emergency was interrupting daily life in the Beltway. Elliot didn't believe in news stories dropping bombs before the Bureau wrapped its arms around the initial disharmony of bad news. It was unofficial, but the major newspapers, cable and network news stations didn't trump the Bureau. It was now a no-no to drop news bombs or potential news bombs without an okay from the Bureau's public relations office.

The cost of not complying with Elliot's mandate resulted in a non-relationship with the Bureau. Several reporters and networks had tried the man and lost. Some were still trying to re-open that door.

Many called it a dictatorship. Elliot called it *law enforcement*. For him, law enforcement meant having the opportunity to work a case without surprises from the media, or warnings or hints to unknown subjects, referred to as unsubs, or potential unsubs from news stories. The callousness of the media was put on noticed by the new Director.

Needless to say, he wasn't a media favorite.

I nodded my head to his executive assistant as I walked into his office. I was surprised the door was opened. I didn't need instructions. I closed the door as I entered, and walked directly in front of his desk and parked myself in one of two nice leather chairs. The other chair was already occupied by Maxwell Pack, the Chief of the Criminal Investigative Division.

"I want the Code of Colors case," I bluntly stated.

"Last I heard, people in hell wanted milkshakes, but they are just as disappointed as you," Elliot shot back. Maxwell Pack didn't say anything, but I could see all thirty-two of his teeth.

Like I couldn't describe Elliot Lucas the man, I certainly couldn't describe our relationship. I think on Mondays, Wednesdays and Fridays, and odd weekends he liked me. On Tuesdays and Thursdays, and even weekends, he could take me or leave me. As long as Julia brought his pseudo grandchildren around, he was happy.

"Maxwell, your show," Elliot stated.

Maxwell Pack was pure California. The man had probably spent the past thirty years in the Midwest or East Coast, and he still looked like he had just escaped a beach resort in sunny California. He had curly dirty blonde hair, with sideburns past his earlobes, a golden tan complexion and his suit fit him like he was a middleweight bodybuilder. Your first impression of the man was that he was in his late thirties, maybe early forties. But Pack was in his upper fifties and looked like he could still kick the asses of ten twenty-somethings.

"Well Carson, seems you were personally requested by Mr. Hollywood himself, Conrod Bach," Pack dropped the bombshell on me. It came as a shock to me.

"Why me?" were the only words I could muster up.

"To my understanding, you have history with the Malibu Eight kids," Pack replied. "You don't?"

I looked alternatively between Maxwell Pack and Elliot Lucas. History? My history was years ago. We used to party at the same clubs occasionally. Some would call it history. To me, it was happenstance. It was Los Angeles, and athletes and entertainers having a good time at the same locations. Something I hadn't thought about in years.

"Heather," Elliot said to his executive assistant via his speakerphone. "Have our two visitors come in."

When the two people walked through the door, I was sure my mouth was opened. Surprise would be an understatement. I was in another universe. Another time, another place.

The woman. The past. Evil reincarnate.

I didn't care about the man. It was the woman.

A nightmare from the past.

A past that could have changed my life forever.

I felt death in my heart.

And that wasn't a good thing.

CHAPTER 6

HAVING MERCY FOR THOSE WHO DO YOU HARM MAY ACTUALLY KILL YOU ONE DAY.

Those were the words I first heard in high school as our football coach lectured us on finishing our games strong. Never leave a team standing, because they will come back and bite you in the ass. "We call that the bitch who won't go away," he would say.

Calling Lydia Smithers a bitch or any other derogatory name would probably be a compliment to the woman. If the woman had her way, I would be rotting in a California prison for rape. And amazingly, I probably saved her life.

Every nerve in my body was on notice. I was suddenly on edge, the wick of a slow burning fuse on a stick of dynamite. I could feel the imaginary steam, similar to that of a cartoon character, shoot out of my ears. I felt the rage within. The pressure building. It scared me. It should. It was volatile. I was volatile. The hatred consuming me put fear in my heart.

If I had a hate list, Lydia Smithers would be at the top of it. And that was the easy part.

She had my complete attention. However, she couldn't look at me. I, on the other hand, couldn't take my eyes off her and I didn't like what I saw. Years ago, she almost turned my life upside down. I was a scapegoat because of the color of my skin. She painted me a rapist, and the Hollywood media tried to paint her a heroine.

It was the post-O. J. Simpson era. I was the big bad black athlete who had taken the blonde hair, blue eye princess back to my place and raped her. The creative, yet, untrue story was a reporter's dream . . . and there were enough reporters hoping this story would be their Watergate.

Truth is not an easy animal to hold. It rips hearts out and embattles souls.

The rage within me was festering and wanted release.

Lydia Smithers was a liar. She lied for a living. At the time, she was an up and coming publicist. She was a D-lister working for a mid-major Hollywood agency and a woman looking to make a name for herself.

She thought she was dating a teammate of mine, Tomas Hooper, one of the best wide receivers in the NFL during that time. We were teammates with the Raiders. The month was April. Spring training had just ended. Tomas was originally from Los Angeles and we shared a condominium in downtown L.A, just like we shared a condominium in the Bay Area during the season.

It was a great arrangement for us. I didn't always stay in California during the off-season. In the off-season, I usually stayed in DC or Las Vegas.

It was an early Saturday morning. I had been out all night. When I got back to the condo around four that morning, I found Lydia Smithers on the floor of the living room. Her clothes were ripped off and she smelled of alcohol and puke. Cocaine residue was on the coffee table, as well as on her face.

After trying to revive Lydia and doing a quick search of the condo, I immediately called the paramedics and the cops. I told them what had happened, as I knew it. The paramedics were able to bring Lydia out of her apparent drunken and drugged out stupor.

What happened next was my nightmare to bear.

Lydia told the LAPD I had assaulted and raped her. Though many of the cops recognized me, it didn't take them long to slap the handcuffs on me. I was still a black man in America and a white woman with bleached blonde fallen curls, a nice face with bruises and a nice figure had reported that she was raped by a black man. Although I was the one who called it in, I was the cops' number one suspect, only suspect. I had been accused.

Thanks to O. J., a black athlete and bruised white woman spelled trouble with the LAPD—then, the second most racist police department in America. New York was number one and would never relinquish that position. I actually thought my celebrity status meant something. I was an All-Pro defensive back with the nation's number one love/hate team. Walking out the door in handcuffs, I realized I wasn't much of a superstar. I was what I was, a black man in America, in the nineties, and learning that black and white in America was still a fact of life.

A fact of life many of us of color wanted to forget.

I was being slapped in the face in a hard and unforgiving way. *The American way.* It was the world we lived in, the world we tried to escape, but that barrier called reality kept us in the cage. There would be no escape. I had one thought on my mind as I was walked to the patrol car with undesired bracelets on my wrists, and that was rescue.

The ironic thing was I had never met or even seen Lydia Smithers before that day.

I refused to talk to the cops. It was a lesson my FBI brother, Steve, had taught me. However, I didn't call Steve with my one phone call. Instead, I called the FBI's Northern California regional field chief Elliot Lucas. After that phone call, everything moved fast. Elliot contacted Tomas, who was visiting family in Denver, and he jumped on a returning flight to L.A. Additionally, Elliot called one of the top attorneys in the area to represent me.

I never said a word while I sat and brewed in the LAPD's interrogation room. I listened to the threats and interrogative techniques of the detectives in charge and maintained my composure. I adhered to the advice I had received from Steve and others in case I was ever apprehended.

In interrogations, the purpose is to break you down using whatever method is best. With most people, whether they were guilty or not, the pure pressure of isolation could do the trick. For others, the combination of anxiety to escape the situation and possibly being locked up made the average person get diarrhea of the mouth. I wasn't an agent yet, but I knew the power of interrogation. I knew to shut the hell up until my attorney arrived. And those were the only words I eventually uttered, "I want an attorney."

My stay was only several hours. What followed was the truth and smear campaign against Lydia Smithers. This was the early days of DNA. Awaiting DNA results wasn't an option. But I had ammunition. First, Tomas informed the newspaper and not the district attorney that he and two other guys had ran a train on Lydia Smithers and this wasn't the first group sex session Miss Smithers had participated in. He provided photographs and a couple of recordings to back up his account of Lydia Smithers' lifestyle.

Elliot, with the blessings of several politicians he knew, would launch a quick and dirty investigation into crooked cops on the LAPD. It was an easy investigation. He knew the bad cops who were the focus of the investigation. It was something to get the LAPD's attention.

As fast as the case begun against me, the faster it ended. No apology. No "I'm sorry for falsely and wrongly arresting or accusing you of a crime you didn't commit."

I sued Lydia. We settled out of court for a measly one and a half million dollars. It was the principle . . . not the money. Her family had deep pockets as well as a name to preserve. This scandal was worse for them than me. I accepted the money in the hopes I never had to see the woman again. I realized now it was wishful thinking on my part.

She was back.

The ghost of the past was on my turf haunting my reality. Although I didn't know why she was here, I felt the invisible dagger in my heart.

The day was already long and getting longer by the minute . . .
It had just taken a hard left turn into the land of abyss.

CHAPTER 7

Lʏᴅɪᴀ's companion was lindsay barnes.

Barnes was an infamous attorney for Hollywood's biggest exec, Conrod Bach. He was tall and distinguished looking. The attorney stood at least six-four or six-five, with a thin and sleek frame. Under his two thousand dollar Italian suit, I doubt if the man had one muscle. He was naturally thin. I didn't know him personally, but during my days in the NFL, we had crossed paths at numerous social events. Back in those days, he had a head full of blonde locks and no facial hair. Nowadays, he only had facial hair, long silver sideburns to go with his silver eyebrows, mustache and beard.

"What can I do for you, LB," was the greeting by Elliot, as he stood to shake the lawyer's hand. And it didn't surprise me at all that the two powerful men knew each other.

"I need your help," Barnes replied while still holding Elliot's hand.

"No, you mean your boss, Conrod, needs my help."

The two men exchanged gazes before Elliot decided to sit down, which prompted everyone else to sit down. I stayed away from the immediate area of the conversation, around Elliot's desk. I sat at a small table off to the side and behind the official gathering.

I kept my eyes on the only female in the group, my enemy. Since the events in the park several hours ago, this was the first time my mind wasn't on the Code of Colors. If I thought about it, that probably would have bothered me. But Lydia Smithers had my attention now, which also meant for the time being, the Jet Pack Eight had my attention.

"Director, I'm representing the families of the missing actors in this matter, and I'm hoping we can work together on this," Barnes explained.

"Show me an official document, a letter or some type correspondence from the families stating that fact, LB," was the immediate response from Elliot.

Lindsay Barnes didn't say anything. From where I sat, I couldn't see his eyes, but something told me that he indeed was very familiar with Director Lucas, and regardless of how powerful he was in Hollywood or outside this office, his power was no match for the man behind the big cherry oak desk.

Elliot pushed a button on his desk phone and I think he surprised everyone who was in his office. No phone had rung and his executive assistant hadn't notified him of a phone call. "Conrod, what you expect to gain from sending your big guns to Washington?"

"Well, Mister Director, I think I deserve a little more respect than being kept on hold for over ten minutes," the gruff voice of Conrod Bach barked over the speakerphone.

"Conrod, I'm sorry you are feeling sensitive today, but I don't have time to give a damn about your feelings today," Elliot barked back with a smile on his face. No one seemed surprise by this exchange. The only one qualified to be surprised was probably me. But I knew Elliot knew people from all walks of life.

"How are you doing, my friend?" Bach asked.

"Doing great Conrod. But don't try to skirt the issue and feed me niceties, Mr. Hollywood, my plate is full. Fires are burning and unlike you, I have people above me that I answer to. Doing favors on this one is out of the question. I'm sorry, but LB and Ms. Smithers are wasting their time if you expect to get something out of the Bureau."

"Director, I think you should hear me out, or at least hear LB out. I know you don't believe it, but he really is representing the families of the actors on this one."

"Conrod, stop bullshitting me," Elliot stated as he leaned forward in his seat, with his face closer to the phone. "Everyone knows Lindsay Barnes has one client and represents one person, Conrod Jarrett Bach. I respect that. You know that. But I don't know what you want from me on this case. Possibly three are dead that we know of, a fourth may also be dead.

"If that is the case, that means there are four others we need to find and protect. If you can help me with any of that, Conrod, Maxwell and his guys will gladly accept the assistance. If not, my friend, once again, I say, I don't see why two of your top executives are in my office."

"Maybe I can explain that," Lydia intervened. Her voice was full of confidence. I don't know if she knew I hadn't taken my eyes off her since she walked in the room. If so, it didn't faze her. She stayed on point.

"Director Lucas, these were my friends . . . friends since we all were babies," she began. "Any information that comes out in your investigation, I could probably help with. As much as the eight individuals haven't kept in touch with each other over the years, they have kept in touch with me. I'm the common denominator. Not in terms of I'm the reason they were killed . . . but in terms of since we were small kids, I am the one who has talked to my eight friends every month, regardless of what was going on in their lives or mine."

If I were neutral or had indifferent feelings towards the woman, I would have had compassion for her. But I wasn't neutral. There was nothing indifferent about my feelings. However, I couldn't say the same for Elliot.

"Miss Smithers," Eliot began. "Considering I have lost loved ones and friends over the years, I feel your pain. However—"

Before he could complete his thought, I interrupted. "Why would someone or some persons want to kill your friends in such a heinous and violent manner?" I asked Lydia.

Everyone in the room directed their attention my way. All except one person. Lydia Smithers.

"I don't know," she stated, still looking at the Director.

"You must know something," I responded. "You come in here, to the office of the Director of the Federal Bureau of Investigation, and give us this spiel about you being *friends* with the Jet Pack Eight, and give us this story about communicating with every member of the group for years on a monthly basis.

"But you have no idea what was going on in their lives? If they had been threatened recently? Or if they had problems with someone from their past? Anything?"

Lydia didn't answer me immediately. All eyes were on her now. I took a glance at Elliot and Maxwell, and both knew my questions were legitimate. My tone may not have been, but my questions were on point. If you want to place yourself into an investigation, you'd better have viable information to barter with.

"Did you talk to any of *your friends* before any of them went missing, or did you talk to any of the others after anyone came up missing?"

After several seconds, Lydia finally stood and faced me. "No, I haven't." Her eyes were red. She was holding back the tears. I stood as well. I wanted her to see that I didn't buy what she was selling. Her last statement was a lie. I knew it. She knew it. My only question was why.

Lindsay Barnes also stood, which led to Maxwell Pack standing. The meeting was unofficially over. For them, not for me. I knew Conrod Bach was still on the phone.

I wasn't through with my questions for Lydia, but I think she was through with me. For now. I wasn't on a power trip, I needed information if I was going to be the lead on this case. "Can you at least provide us with contact information for the remaining members?"

Lydia looked at me. This was the first real eye contact we had made. As much as I would have liked for fear to be in her eyes, it wasn't. It was madness. If she could kill me at that moment, she probably would have.

"We don't have their information," Barnes volunteered. Before I could repeat what Lydia said about talking to her *friends* every month, he stopped me before I could even open my mouth. "As of today, the families agreed that the remaining friends should lay low, cut off communication with the world and only their parents would know of their whereabouts, and that includes cutting off Lydia and me as well."

I didn't believe this. Not one word. Looking at Maxwell and Elliot, I knew they didn't believe it either.

"Before we end this debacle of a meeting," I said with personality. "Mr. Bach, could you, Mr. Barnes or even Ms. Smithers, please explain to me why I was asked to be the lead on this investigation?"

CHAPTER 8

Four physical bodies and one on the phone...

... and silence overtook the tension in the room. Elliot dismissed Barnes and Lydia, and promptly got Bach off the phone. I was still standing, while Maxwell Pack had sat back down. For several moments, still no one spoke.

I had gotten myself in a bind. By speaking up, I had claimed the case as my own. That wasn't my intention. I wanted to kick myself. As much as I wanted to blame Lydia, I couldn't.

Life's a bitch. And then you die.

That was the saying. I don't know why the cliché occupied my mind. However, that's how I felt at that moment, that life was a bitch and for the first time in a couple of years, I had death on my mind. I knew everyone didn't endure hell before death as the cliché implied. But the members of the Jet Pack who had faced death, I'm sure the cliché more than applied.

In some ways, I deserved to be pissed off. This case was on my mind now, and not the case I really wanted to be on. So be it. For now.

I had just made Conrod Bach and Lydia Smithers's lives a bitch, and I was sure there would be a strategy session as soon as Lydia and Lindsay Barnes cleared the Hoover Building. Elliot had dismissed Barnes and Lydia with no concessions. Barnes made it a point to inform us that Lydia was staying in the city, while he was going back to California. I could only imagine the conversation between those two and Bach.

I was sure Bach wasn't happy. He and Elliot had history, I was sure of that. I wondered if that history included me.

"Are you going to answer my question, Director?" I directed my question to Elliot. I could still hear the personality in my voice.

"Carson, it's good to see you are engaged," he replied. Then he leaned forward in his seat and I knew I was probably in trouble. Normally, I would be intimidated. Lydia had given me liquid courage without the liquid. That always spelled trouble.

"You know why you were requested by Conrod Bach?" he continued. "When you and Ms. Smithers had your issues, I went to Conrod to smear Smithers's reputation. Before then, we had done business together. Since that day, we have also done business together. So this was not a return favor situation."

Elliot and I looked at each other. I wondered what was on his mind. The man was an enigma. You never really knew what he was thinking. He seemed different. He seemed off his game. But something told me, I was one of the very few in the world who could tell. I made it a point to log it in the back of my brain and ask Julia about it the next time we spoke.

"Smithers got a rise out of you, Carson. That's exactly what Conrod was hoping. He knows you are engaged and will see this case to ground. The man is an affable asshole, but he knows people, and what may inspire some people. Smithers got your attention. Run with it.

"You know, as I know, no way Patrick will leave you out of the Code of Colors case, regardless of what I tell him."

He was right on all accounts. I was engaged now. And I knew Patrick would keep me abreast of what was going on with his case.

I stood to leave.

"Not yet," Maxwell chided in. "You have a new team for this one KC. Special Agent Coker will be your partner, she is a helluva behavior analyst. Plus, we have provided two other agents who will provide support. Coker will introduce you to your team. They are in conference room three in my division."

"What about Special Agent Taylor? I would like him on my team as well."

"Taylor is on Conroy's team," Maxwell countered.

CHAPTER 9

Cɪᴅ's CONFERENCE ROOM THREE WAS A MEDIUM SIZED ROOM.

It was more a work area or situation room than a true conference room. A small, but nice mahogany table sat in the middle of the room. In each corner of the room was a workstation with an all-in-one computer/monitor and a printer. A sixty-inch flat screen television hung on a wall closest to the door of the conference room. On the opposite wall was a white projector for presentations. On the same wall as the door to the conference room were a couple of five-by-five white boards. That's where Special Agent Paula Coker was standing, looking at information written on the boards.

Sitting at the small table were two other agents, males. I knew one of the agents, Jonah Sanu, Jo Jo for short. Jo Jo was a behavioral analyst who had been with the Bureau for probably ten years or more. His father was Caucasian, American. His mother was born in Iran, but she had been raised in America. Jo Jo was one hundred percent American, but his dark complexion and shiny black curly hair made him look more Middle Eastern.

I liked Jo Jo, the man was a professional. I knew he had faced his share of ignorance within the walls of the Bureau, but he had dealt with it, and didn't allow it to prevent him from being a damn good agent. The man knew people and his analysis were usually on point. More importantly, Elliot considered him one of his top behavioral analysts, and I knew I was fortunate to have him on my team.

The other agent I didn't know. He was Caucasian. He had short blonde hair, a square jaw and a Kirk Douglas-like cleft in his chin. He was dressed in what some of us referred to as classic Bureau— black pants, white shirt, reddish color tie and his dark blue FBI windbreaker. Even dressed, I could tell he had an athletic build. I could also tell he was probably a future superstar with the Bureau, which meant he was probably a bureaucratic asshole. But that was me pre-judging. I hoped I was wrong.

"Special Agent Coker, talk to me, where are we?" I interrupted. Paula was deep into what she was doing. I hated to stop her train of thought, but I needed to engage, get my interest piqued. The Code of Colors was back in the forefront of my thoughts, but I had to compartmentalize and prioritize. Elliot and Maxwell Pack had made this my top priority for now.

I didn't like being requested for this case. I was realistic, the handwriting was on the wall, this would be an ever-changing case. The remaining potential victims didn't want to be protected by the Bureau. Plus, Conrod Bach was circling the wagons, he didn't want his world disturbed, or better yet, whatever funk was available to be spread, he didn't want any of it getting on him. And lastly, as an agent, I didn't need this case to shape my career.

I had been involved in several cases in the past that shaped my career with the Bureau. I wasn't trying to move up in the organization. I was in a good position. I could walk away anytime I wanted. I chose to remain a member of the Bureau, regardless of my financial status; therefore, I accepted the cases that were thrown my way.

Paula introduced me to my team, "Supervisory Special Agent Kenny Carson, Special Agent Jonah Sanu and Special Agent Montgomery Holt."

"Jo Jo, long time, brother," I stated as he and I embraced. "Looks like you lost a couple of pounds."

Jo Jo smiled. "KC, you are still full of shit," he replied jokingly. "I can't believe they give a great case like this to the likes of you."

We were still smiling when Special Agent Holt rudely stepped in front of Jo Jo with his hand extended. "Special Agent Montgomery Holt, sir, nice meeting you, looking forward to working with you," he volunteered in a serious, no-nonsense tone.

When I reached out, he squeezed my hand hard. Considering my day, I wasn't in the mood for who has the hardest grip or the biggest penis.

"Well, nice meeting you as well Monty, and looking forward to working with you."

While still holding my hand, he said the unexpected, "My name is Montgomery and you can either call me that, Holt or Special Agent Holt, but don't call me Monty. My parents didn't name me Monty, and frankly, I hate the name."

Well, I'll be damn. I had pegged this guy as an asshole and he wasn't disappointing me. I had dealt with Code of Colors trying to kill children at a school and a surprise visit from the last person I ever wanted to see, Lydia Smithers. Now I had this arrogant prick to deal with.

Wrong time to flex, Monty. Wrong time to flex.

We were still holding hands and had tense eye contact with each other. I wasn't in the mood for a contest. I didn't give a damn about whose penis was the biggest or hardest. Although I was sure I would have won that contest as well. However, I wanted him to get the gist of my words. I wanted him to know that today, he definitely crossed the wrong person.

"Special Agent Holt, I can accept that. Now you accept this. Go back to Chief Pack and ask him to reassign you to another team or another case. Unfortunately for you, I don't have the time or the patience to deal with the shit you are shoveling. I'd rather kick your pompous ass than share a space with you."

With that, he released my hand. His feet were clay. He didn't move. Something told me no one had ever been that direct with him. Why? I don't know. In less than two minutes, he became a member on my shit list.

"Talk to me, Paula, what you got?" I proceeded with business.

"SSA Carson, can we talk?" Special Agent Holt asked me. He was still in the same spot, facing towards the door. I was now behind him. I wasn't surprised he wasn't looking at me. As bad as I didn't want to be on this case, there were probably hundreds of agents in the Bureau who wished they were a part of this investigation. These were the type of investigations that made or jumpstarted careers.

"No, Special Agent Holt, you cannot. Please get your stuff and get out of my situation room."

He slowly turned and once again our eyes locked. I saw the disappointment and disdain in his blue eyes, and simultaneously the want and need to kick my ass.

I was still surprised when he grabbed his backpack, phone and writing pad off the table and walked out the door without conflict.

Assholes will rule the world, but only if we allow them.

CHAPTER 10

Seeing her in action, i understood why paula coker was involved in this case.

"Take it from the top, Paula," I stated as she, Jo Jo and I settled in. "Brief me on the abduction of the three actors."

Paula was calm and cool, and had a high level of confidence. "The abduction of each celebrity occurred three days apart," she began. "Unfortunately, what we have thus far is minuscule at best . . . actually, not much at all. We do know two weeks ago, Theresa Wenthill was shooting a music video on location in Santa Fe, New Mexico."

I intervened, "Hold on, Terri Wenthill and Derrick Paine were both abducted in the same off-the-beaten-path city?"

"Yes, it seems that way. Although, technically, Derrick Paine is not officially missing."

"Understand." And I did truly understand. Paine and the remaining members of the Jet Pack were probably all underground, keeping a low footprint. Visibiliy might mean death.

"Wenthill's video was supposed to be a two-day shoot and she had plans on visiting friends in Taos, New Mexico. However, on the second day of the shoot, she failed to show. Her room was dusted for prints, traces of blood, hair fibers or anything that could help us . . . and nothing. Once again the Albuquerque Field Office was called in. The only thing they were able to glean was that Miss

Wenthill had drinks with several members of the film crew the night she was abducted.

"Our boys interviewed the crew and got nothing. There were four crewmembers and they all had the same story. For the most part, they had a couple of drinks and they walked back to their rooms together. They all stayed on the same floor, and no one saw or heard anything suspicion. Her bed was unmade, and it's possible that's where she was. There's a good possibility her abductor was hiding out in her room before she returned from having drinks, waiting for the right time to make their move."

I was checking out the files we had on Terri Wenthill. As much as I was trying to stay neutral, I knew these knuckleheads did something to bring this on themselves. It was something I couldn't mention. It was early in the investigation. Unofficially, you couldn't speculate that the victims brought something upon themselves until you were two or three weeks into the investigation, and then, only if you had some type of hard evidence that they were involved in something cynical that made others seek retaliation.

"Three days after Miss Wenthill went missing, Wash Tunnell, was taken from his home in Gaithersburg, Maryland. Also, no visible clues. His girlfriend, a flight attendant, had been with him two days prior to her trek across the ocean. It appears she was the last one to see him.

"Mr. Tunnell was a renowned clean freak, very OCD, and had a housekeeper who worked twelve hour days, seven days a week. She last saw him the day before his disappearance, around two that afternoon. She claims to have left at eight that evening, and since Mr. Tunnell made it a habit to lock himself in his study for a day or two to rehearse his lines, she didn't think anything of it.

"However, he was a stickler about answering his cell phone, and the next day when the housekeeper arrived, his phone was ringing off the hook. She got suspicious, constantly knocked on the door and after no answer, she called the sheriff's office. She didn't have a key so they had to break into the study. They found the room *in complete disarray, like a struggle had occurred.* Those were the words of the deputy sheriff."

"Interesting," Jo Jo said. "The housekeeper had a key to the house, but not a master key to any of the rooms within the house?"

"No mention of that, but she was questioned by both the sheriff's department and agents from the Washington Field Office," Paula responded.

"How about Jimmie Claymore?" I said before Jo Jo continued down the road on Wash Tunnell. I wanted to see the similarities between the three abductions, if there were any similarities.

"Jimmie Claymore was a different story. We have more information to work with. The same M.O. as far as time, three days after Mr. Tunnell was abducted, Mr. Claymore arrived in Chicago at eleven fifteen for a meeting with film director, Brooks McLemore. The limousine picked him up at eleven thirty at O'Hare International for his noon meeting. Needless to say, he never made it to the meeting."

I paid close attention to Paula's every word. I was amazed at how far Paula had come since her training days. She was efficient and good at her job. From her time at the Academy, I knew she would be doing good things. She was studious and meticulous, and very well at reading situations. She didn't jump in haphazardly and make rash decisions. I was glad she was a part of the investigation.

"However, we have procured airport videos from his debarkation from the gate security area to the limousine. He stopped on several occasions to sign autographs. No incident. Very straightforward. Once outside, he walked directly to the limousine parked at the curbside and that's when things got strange. The driver was dressed in uniform, got of the car, walked around to the other side and opened the door for Jimmie Claymore. When Claymore was halfway in, the driver pushed Claymore the rest of the way in and proceeded in behind him. As soon as the door closed, the limousine sped off.

"Detectives with the Chicago PD interviewed the owner, manager and dispatcher on duty at the limousine rental company and Carlton Dayton, the driver, was the regular driver that usually picked up celebrities and top executives. He has been with the company for fifteen years and they had never had a problem with him. He checked in when he arrived at the airport at exactly eleven fifteen.

"Mr. Dayton had a stellar record, great credit, always paid his bills on time, has a wife, two kids, nice car and they live modestly in the suburbs of Harvey. The Chicago PD faxed us a photo of Mr. Dayton. Size, height, weight and nationality, unfortunately, did not match up with our limousine driver. Our driver is Caucasian, while Mr. Dayton is African-American.

"There is no sign of Mr. Dayton. His family hasn't heard from him and his cell appears to be turned off. Also, the GPS on the limousine was disabled, so the car hasn't been found."

I was impressed with how she laid out the information they had gathered thus far. I was ahead of her, recalling what I knew about each member of the Jet Pack. Information I planned on sharing after Paula briefed us on the owners of the cryogenic freezer units, WMT. The company had delivered the cryogenic containers to various locations this morning. This was the information I was most interested in.

Paula turned our attention to the screen as she began her presentation. I don't know where she found the time to put together any presentation, let alone one with so many details.

"The information is still coming in on the company's drivers," she explained. "Some of the interviews are still being conducted as we speak. Those we have received have been sent to your e-mail. So far, no glaring admissions or relevant information."

"We are interviewing all the drivers who delivered the containers, right?" I asked.

Paula and Jo Jo looked at each other, and then turned their attention back to me. "KC, we don't know anything about the drivers who delivered the containers," Jo Jo stated. "Nor do we know where the containers were shipped from. And we also don't have invoices. All of the delivery receipts we have received from those who received the cryogenic units are fake. Basically, we don't have any official paperwork for these deliveries, to include the drivers of the delivery trucks."

"Can you pull up the information on the company?" I asked with exasperation in my voice. This was disappointing and upsetting. However, it was stupid to cry over spilled milk. This plan was well thought out.

Paula immediately started typing on her keyboard and within seconds, the website for WMT was on the overhead screen. It was an interactive home page with a slideshow of the various functions the company performed. Judging from the photographs, they did everything from transporting passengers and body parts to delivering pharmaceuticals and medical supplies. They also transported doctors to perform emergency surgeries. Another portion of the slideshow showed a partial list of their customers, which included hospitals and corporations worldwide, major pharmaceutical companies and even the federal government.

"How about management, the corporate staff?" I asked.

Paula hit the icon that said *Staff.* Then another site appeared with two rows of personnel. I wasn't sure, but the first face looked familiar to me. He was the chief executive officer and founder of World Medical Transporters.

"Click on the CEO, Brian Dye."

A bigger photograph of Brian Dye appeared, along with a biography. While I was reading his bio, Paula jumped in with her comments. Like I said, the woman was efficient.

"Brian Dye is an interesting character," she began. "If you think you know him, it could be from a number of places. Believe it or not, he actually started out as a DJ, in the California area. He went by the moniker White Sexual Chocolate."

I smiled. Yes, he did go by that moniker as well as several other nicknames such as KFD for King Freak Daddy and GGW, God's Gift to Women.

"I guess Mr. Dye thinks a lot of himself with a handle like that," Jo Jo weighed in.

I smiled even more. "No, believe it or not, Mr. DJ White Sexual Chocolate was a shy, mild mannered guy of Irish descent except when he was drinking and behind the turntable. His nickname actually came from the fact he loved women of color back in those days. Believe me, he didn't discriminate. If I remember right, I think he actually hooked up with our female victim, Theresa Wenthill. He was the first one to start spinning her records, even before she received her first major singing contract. Hell, he's probably the reason she got that contract."

I was still looking at Brian's bio, which of course, didn't have any of the information I had just volunteered. Out of my peripheral vision, I could see Paula watching me.

"Needless to say, you know Mr. Dye," she finally added.

"Yep, I do. But it's been a while. A long while. We lost contact when I quit football and joined the Bureau. If I remember right, I think Brian was putting himself through college by being a DJ. I think he majored in safety or industrial hygiene, or something like that. He was a pretty smart guy."

"I would say," Jo Jo chided in. "From his bio, he started Union Safety and Health Group as a small business, sold it five years later to a big defense contract company for two hundred million dollars, then started World Medical Transporters."

"And in less than five years, WMT was a billion dollar company," Paula picked it up as if they were tagging this portion of the briefing. "The company has only been up and running for seven years and last reported, it was worth over two billion dollars. Not bad for a DJ."

"Not bad at all," I said under my breath, "not bad at all." I re-read Dye's biography three times and thought about him and Terri Wenthill. I also thought about the other members of the Jet Pack Eight and soon memories of old times in California were flooding my mind.

"While it's on my mind, let me brief you on the remaining members of the Jet Pack Eight," I volunteered. "At least, the information I can remember, which may or may not have made it to the official record."

Both Jo Jo and Paula bucked up. I think the simple fact that I knew these Hollywood types had piqued their interest. Yes, it was about the case, but it was also about me knowing Hollywood royalty.

That was the craziness of the world we lived in, even for agents. We were enamored with the lives of the rich and famous. In many instances, we didn't see them as real people. We didn't want to see them as real people.

Even with all of the crazy antics we heard or read about, to us, they were mysterious and mythical creatures.

CHAPTER 11

THE PAST HAS A WAY OF SNEAKING INTO THE PRESENT.

I was a rookie defensive back playing for the Raiders when I met former child stars, Drake Devlin and River Gillard. The two were the best of friends, and they allowed me to be in their small circle. We were all around the same age. Drake was a super genius or something. His IQ was out of this world, and the man had done more in his twenty years of living than most people in their sixties or seventies. He was a man of all seasons—graduating from college in three years, then traveling the world and attending medical school.

His best friend, River, was super cool and one of the best damn screenwriters in Hollywood—and he wasn't even twenty-five yet. He was the lead writer on three TV shows, two dramas and a comedy, as well as writing scripts for two movies per year. Both amazed me. Plus, they were funny. They were known as Ebony and Ivory, River's ebony to Drake's ivory.

They were truly magnets for some of California's most beautiful women. But what really impressed me was the famous people they knew. From athletes to entertainers to politicians and businesspeople, they were in the know and people wanted to know them.

My first, and continued, association with the Jet Pack was with Drake and River.

"Let me begin with our recent missing actor, Derrick Paine. I really don't know how to describe Mr. Paine. If both of you are familiar with his work as a child, he always played the nerdy, geeky kid, who always seemed a little weird. After meeting and speaking to Derrick, I realized his roles weren't too far from the truth. He was an odd and strange guy. Smart as hell, but he always seemed to be on edge. When he began his directing career, I got it. I got the horror flicks, the supernatural genre. That was him. And as crazy as it sounded, I always thought his movies represented his life. There was an element of truth in his tales of horror."

"How so?" Paula asked.

"Good example. In his movie, *Dark Heart,* a corporate executive has a dark side and goes on a killing spree, chopping off the heads of his victims and burying the corpses with their shoulders showing but missing their head. In the end, he gets off while someone else is implicated in the crimes. The movie ends with him closing another business deal, while the alleged killer is killed in prison."

"You think he actually killed in that manner and made a movie about it?" Jo Jo asked facetiously.

"It's not something I can prove," I stated. "Just a passing thought."

I saw the look on both of my fellow agents' faces. I decided to continue my brief. "Mitzy York. Mitzy was a bitch . . . and believe me, I'm being complimentary when I say that. She was the youngest of the group and probably the nastiest, in terms of mouth, personality and actions. She was privileged and she didn't hesitate letting you know she was privileged. On screen, she comes across as being the sweetest, nicest person in the world, but in the real world, she doesn't have a problem letting you know that you are not on the same scale as her."

I was happy to see both Jo Jo and Paula taking notes. "Terrence Parkins is another asshole," I added. "Rumors around LA were that the man was narcissistic and self-absorbed. Even with the twenty-four hour media cycle, many rumors that never made it to the media included Terrence's alleged rapes of minor-aged females. The thought that the Jet Pack was protected by someone big really centered around Terrence Parkins and Wash Tunnell. Both were rumored to be the face of illegal activity, from excessive speeding to rumors of abuse and special privilege."

"You don't sound like you're a fan of the Jet Pack," Paula commented.

"Before I answer that Paula, let me finish my take on the other two actors, then I will give you my thoughts or feelings, or whatever you want to call them." She nodded and I proceeded with my impromptu briefing. "Dyson Ryker. I like him." I looked at Paula Coker and smiled. She smiled back.

"Dyson was real . . . what you saw was what you got. He didn't give you the pretense or Hollywood version of himself. I wouldn't call him a friend, but we got to know each other. He was the one the other members of the group went to when they had a problem or issue to deal with. He loved people and I don't know how or why, but he loved the other members of the Jet Pack. He was clearly a different sort than the rest."

"Maybe you liked him because he loved sports and played in the NFL like you," Paula noted.

I smiled. "No, Paula. Did it help that we had commonality? Sure. But we also had commonality in our nationality as well. Dyson was half-black, half-white. He is a better actor now, than he was as a child. I think his biggest issue back then was that he loved sports more than acting. After playing the sport he loved, he was able to move on. I liked him because he was real . . . acting initially paid the bills for his family, but his athleticism allowed him to follow his dreams. Acting was once his profession, and then football, then acting became his third act. But being a good human being was always first . . . unlike most of the other Jet Pack."

I was surprised. I thought Paula would come back with something else. She didn't. So I moved on. "Trinidad Capture." I took a moment before continuing. It was intentional. Trinidad had a place in my heart. At one point, she was a true friend. But she was more than a friend. I had to come up with the right words and get certain thoughts out of my head.

"Trinidad was the oldest of the Jet Pack. Unbeknownst to many, she was a nurturer. It seemed like it was her job to keep the rest out of trouble. I'm not sure if she did a great job of that. I think she and Dyson, working hand-in-hand, tried their best. During that time, we were cordial. I knew she wanted to just live her life, be her own person. Unfortunately for her, the Jet Pack Eight was called that for a reason—they were automatically lumped together for whatever reason."

"So, what are your overall feelings of the Jet Pack?" Jo Jo asked.

"In relation to this case, I think they seriously hurt or offended someone in their past. Who? I have no idea. What they could have possibly done? I also have no idea. If I'm right, I think it was bad, seriously bad. You don't chop up a specific group of people for nothing. Of course, in our business, we know there are plenty of crazies out there. However, I think if this was a case of killing the Jet Pack Eight because of what they stand for, then this would have happened years ago when they were news, when they were the *it* thing. Since it's happening now, I can only assume it was something that happened years ago."

"Carson, with me," Maxwell Pack stuck his head in the door and said to me. He completely caught us off guard.

Before I departed the room, I said to Paula, "Contact WMT's public relations office. Tell them on behalf of FBI Director Elliot

Lucas, Supervisory Special Agent Kenny Carson is requesting the presence of Mr. Dye at the J. Edgar Hoover Building at his earliest convenience, preferably within the next forty-eight hours."

"What if he says no?" she responded.

"Trust me, he won't."

My confidence sounded genuine. Truth be told, I was hoping the billionaire remembered the times we used to hang out and act a fool together—the times before he became a billionaire.

CHAPTER 12

MAXWELL PACK WAS THE EPITOME OF CLANDESTINE.

I had the feeling he was probably at the door for a minute or two during our discussion on the Jet Pack. I wasn't sure if Paula Coker had seen him there or not. He didn't have the presence of an Elliot Lucas, but he still demanded attention in any room he entered.

According to Julia, Pack had been a minion of Elliot for at least fifteen years. He had worked for Elliot as his deputy regional chief on two occasions, at two different regions, and his moving up the ranks in the Bureau was all Elliot's doing. To be fair, Pack had deserved his promotions. Elliot put him in a position to succeed, and that's what Pack did—succeed. He had a grocery list of successes—from organized crime to kidnapping to bank robberies and antiterrorism, the man had successfully spearheaded many operations.

The rumor was Elliot was grooming him to be the next Director of the FBI. But no one was convinced Elliot would ever give up his current position. The call sign for the Director was Raven, and I don't think anyone who knew the man could picture anyone else being called Raven. However, if that day ever occurred, Maxwell Pack would probably be a natural to wear his shoes.

"So what's the issue with you and young Montgomery Holt?" The question was stated in a mild and calm tone with a lot of hidden meaning behind it. Holt's father was a senior executive with the Bureau. Like any executive's offspring within the three letter agencies, there were many eyes interested in the career of one of their own.

"He's a prick and I don't have the time or inclination to coddle him," I replied without hesitation.

A slight laugh escaped Maxwell's lips. "Yeah, he is a little snot-nose asshole, but his father is Nicholas Holt, Chief of the Counterterrorism Division."

Now it was my time to laugh a little. "Like father, like son," I stated.

Nicholas and I had history, but it didn't make a difference. Most of the Bureau's personnel disliked the older Holt. It wasn't a secret he thought he should have been the next director, instead of Elliot. Then he was even more pissed off when he was passed over for the deputy director's position. There had been many questions about the legality of investigations conducted by his division. So much so, several major newspapers and magazines had run exposes on the Counterterrorism Division. However, the man had survived those rumors and even a congressional hearing.

"Yes, like father, like son," Maxwell repeated, as we stopped in front of Conference Room 1, at the end of the hallway. Looking in the room, I could see at least ten to fifteen bodies spread throughout the room. This room was much bigger than Conference Room 3. It took up at least half of the space on this side of the floor. When I saw Patrick Conroy and Blane Taylor walking towards the door, I realized this was the situation room for the Code of Colors investigation.

"Agent Taylor, I take it you have been briefed on your new assignment by SSA Conroy?" Maxwell asked as soon as both were within earshot of us.

"Yes sir."

"Sounds good. Conference Room 3. And thanks Agent Taylor for your professionalism."

Maxwell was a hard man to dislike. On the grand scale of things, he was many layers below the director. On the other hand, he truly was the next calling of Elliot Lucas. I understood why Elliot called on Maxwell for advice and counsel. On paper, Maxwell worked for the Executive Assistant Director for Criminal, Cyber, Response and Services Branch. However, in theory, everyone throughout the building knew he worked directly for Elliot Lucas.

"So, Conroy, I hope you are good with Special Agent Holt being on your team." It wasn't a question. The statement dripped with facetiousness as Maxwell had a smile on his face.

"It's not a big problem, Chief," Patrick replied. "We have a lot going on and enough work to keep everyone busy. He should get lost in the shuffle." The glance Patrick gave me, I knew he wanted to kick my ass for sending the little shit his way.

"Don't bank on it," Maxwell stated as we followed him to his office, which was across from Conference Room 1.

His secretary had left for the day and it made me realize that I was unaware of the time of day. So much had occurred today that time was irrelevant. It was laughable that this morning I had taught a class before being involved in a shootout with the Code of Colors, then being summoned to the Hoover, being assigned a case I didn't want and receiving a helluva shock from the past in the form of Lydia Smithers. I should have been running on fumes, but my adrenaline was up and I was as alert as I had been all day. I knew whenever I sat down for the day I would probably be sleep within seconds.

I was in for a welcome surprise walking through the door of Maxwell Pack's office. Sitting at the small office table was Dr.

Melvin Clayton. In the world of modern jargon, Clay was one of my BFFs, best friends forever. We were two years apart, with me being the oldest, and we grew up in the same neighborhood in Memphis, Tennessee. We played high school sports together. During those days, I was best friend with Clay's older brother. He and I reconnected when I moved to DC years later to be an agent for the Bureau.

Quentin Morales, also a special agent with the Bureau, was my other BFF. The three of us were like brothers, or better yet, the Three Musketeers. All for one, one for all. Quentin was now assigned to the Las Vegas Field Office as the special agent in charge. It was a good assignment for him. He needed the time away from DC, and it helped that the love of his life was also in Vegas.

As we shook hands, I was curious why Clay was in the Chief's office. "This has to be big for the great DC homicide detective, Dr. Melvin Clayton, to be in the house," I joked.

"It is good, Carson," Maxwell chided in. "Believe me, it's very good."

We all sat and Clay jumped immediately into his briefing. "Gentlemen, three months ago I was approached by the Bureau of Alcohol, Tobacco, Firearms and Explosives to consult on an investigation that possibly involved gang-related activity."

Clay was a lead homicide detective with the DC Police Department, but that was just a title for him. He was involved in many departmental activities, including a top liaison of the gang activity unit. That told me the ATF thought the Code of Colors was affiliated with gang-related activity. And when it came to knowing gang-related activity, Clay was a virtuoso.

"In February, a Jolson Electronics semi-trailer was hijacked and robbed of its cargo." Clay paused for effect.

I didn't need the pause and effect. And I was pretty sure the same applied to Maxwell and Patrick. Jolson Electronics specialized in electronics such as computers, games, videos, televisions and stereo equipment. That was the dummy business, the side of the business that brought in average returns on investment. The true source of income for the company was their development of military weaponry for the Armed Forces.

Before he could proceed, Patrick intervened. "So, you are saying this is not the first we have heard of the Code of Colors?"

"That's true," Patrick answered. "If you guys let me get through this, I will be briefing both occurrences." Patrick nodded his head. Maxwell and I were both in receptive mode.

"The hijacked cargo consisted of weaponry en route to Fort Bragg Army installation in North Carolina," Clay continued. "The robbery occurred off I-40 East, at the Tennessee – North Carolina border in the middle of the night. Surprisingly, no one was killed.

"None of this was released to the media. However, the hijackers did record a video and uploaded it on the Internet. Unfortunately, ATF responded quickly in deleting the video before it had widespread dissemination. But here is it for your perusal."

Clay turned his laptop around after hitting the play icon on the screen. Five men or boys of various heights and sizes appeared on the computer screen dressed in different color garb from head to toe.

Code of Colors.

The one in front, which we assumed was the leader of this operation, was dressed in all-white. He was approximately six feet tall, medium build. I could tell he worked out, probably daily. He was flanked on his right side by a guy, maybe two to three inches shorter than him, dressed in red garb, and on his left side was another guy matching his height dressed in burgundy. All three men had their arms folded on their chest. It looked more like a fashion statement.

The last two were both dressed in black and both stood about six-four, six-five. The one on the right had an M-16 rifle in his right hand pointed towards the sky. The one on the left had a similar pose with an M-16 in his left hand. Even with black hoods on, these two looked intimidating as compared to the three other guys, who looked somewhat comical.

Then the one in front, dressed in all-white, got animated, bending his knees and talking with his hands as well as his mouth, trying to put emphasis to his words. "Hey boyyyyy, Code of Colors in the house. Striking fear in the hearts of men."

It really did sound more like a comedy skit than real world. The assailant mimicked the voice of Flavor Flav of the nineties rap group Public Enemy. And just as fast as he was animated, he became serious. The problem was, I didn't think any of us took him seriously after that performance.

"I know, I know," Clay began. "America's funniest videos, right? The hijackers transferred the stolen weapons to a mid-sized rental truck. Well, guess what? Three days later we found the abandoned truck with three men in the back, dead from multiple gunshots."

"Let me guess," I interrupted. "Clothes missing and it was probably the three shorter guys from the video?"

"We are thinking the same thing, but we can't be for sure," Clay responded. "Their hands and feet were removed."

CHAPTER 13

SAY WHAT?

Patrick said aloud what we were all thinking. What the hell? Any other time I would say what a coincidence, but I don't think any alphabet agency believed in coincidence, especially in the Bureau. First, Hollywood actors turned up missing, then dismembered— now members of Code of Colors were turning up dismembered as well.

Clay didn't allow our surprise to interrupt his briefing. "Two weeks later, another Jolson Electronics shipment destined for Fort Drum in New York was hijacked. It was the same situation, except this time, the video displayed five people with the same mentality. Guys out to kill and make a point."

Clay showed us the next video and I understood what he meant. The hijackers were dressed in the same garb as their predecessors, but this video was no joke. It displayed some very serious assailants out to deliver a message.

This time around, they had killed three couriers delivering weapons to Fort Drum. The incident happened five miles from a military installation. That was a message within itself. The Code of Colors wanted those in authority to know they meant business. They were stockpiling weapons to start their own little war.

Unfortunately, they still didn't relay what message they were really trying to convey. We didn't know why they were staging battle, and truthfully, who they were staging battle with. Initially, I'm sure ATF and everyone else thought it was the military or federal government. But attacking and killing kids could mean they had something against education, schools or students. Or maybe these were just soft targets.

Then Clay briefed us on three other events regarding the Code of Colors. Events we were already aware of. "A month ago, the Code of Colors appeared again, but this time on the national stage. At Wilmington Baptist, a private college that sits on the outskirt of Wilmington, Delaware, eight assailants, each dressed in different color garb, attacked students in the courtyard of the campus. Most of the students were transitioning from one class to another. Initially, they killed twelve and wounded another fifteen. Unfortunately, five of the fifteen later died from their injuries."

"Why didn't someone report the freaks dressed as buffoons before they started shooting?" Patrick inquired. It was more a frustrated thought than an actual question. Regardless of how long you had been in this business and how much you had seen over the years, craziness like this still got to you.

"Three armed security guards were a party to this madness," Clay responded. "Unfortunately, the only guard who survived thought he was about to see a demonstration or at worse, a protest. They thought it could be anything except what it ended up being."

"In other words, they were caught off guard just like the students were," Maxwell pointed out.

The best the four of us could do were look at each other with a certain internal sadness. This was the world we lived in now. The only exception, this world had cell phones with cameras, camcorders, Instragram, Facebook and other means of media. Six members of the group carried out the shootings, while the other two recorded the incident. The world saw their versions of what happened. Some students recorded the initial sighting and from what little conversations we pieced together, many thought it was funny. That is, until the group pulled out weapons and opened fire.

Courtesy of YouTube and every cable news network, we saw every piece of footage recorded. Every bloody detail, every shot fired.

Soon after, there was a shooting at a strip mall in Lexington, Kentucky. The small plaza was a hangout for local high school and college kids. The good thing is once the shooters were spotted, the teenagers dispersed. Three were killed, which included a security guard, and another four were injured with gunshot wounds.

"The last shooting happened in upstate New York," Clay explained as we were now looking at the Code of Colors video version of what happened. "On the first two floors of an in-residence alternative school for wayward youths. Eleven killed. No one else hurt. Six other missing. However, three of the bodies from your guys confrontation this morning have been identified as students of the school."

I looked at Patrick, who said, "I didn't know that. We identified the six bodies earlier and only two came back with any kind of criminal activity in their past."

"Yeah, the three students were bad actors in school," Clay added. "But just school offenses, no juvenile records or felonies or anything like that. We think they may have been recruited via the Internet, but we don't have credible evidence of that. No one has been able to track any kind of computer-based activity from the group. And that includes the NSA."

"So you guys brought the big guns into this?" I joked, referring to the National Security Agency.

"Yeah, with the Code stealing weapons slated for the Army, the first thing the ATF and Director Lucas thought was terrorist group.

ATF reached out to the NSA and a couple of other agencies for assistance. Unfortunately, there hasn't been any chatter about the group over any communication means. It's as if the group doesn't exist, except when they appear.

"Everyone is reaching out to confidential informants and other contacts, and no one knows anything about the group. We hoped someone would have come up with something before they attacked again . . . but that didn't happen."

"What is it I'm missing?" I questioned. "I know there's something. If not, we wouldn't be having this conversation." I looked at both Clay and Maxwell. Maxwell had that smug look that I was used to seeing on Elliot. My brain was working overtime. My thoughts were running wild. I needed something to latch on to.

Maxwell was the first to speak up. "We're thinking that there's a connection between both of your cases."

The comment didn't surprise me, and I doubted it surprised Patrick. Dismemberment in two cases, occurring around the same time wasn't much of a stretch. In the Code case, it had only happened one time, but that once was enough.

"What makes you think so?" I asked.

"First, the obvious, of course, was the dismemberment of body parts," Maxwell spoke up. "However, there is a distinct difference in the cuts. From what we've been able to determine thus far, the Jet Pack's cuts are precise, surgical cuts . . . definitely from a doctor or someone who has had experience with medical procedures, and each body part looks as if it was removed by a laser. Whereas, the body parts of the three Code members were chopped off by an ax or hatchet. The blade was definitely sharp. One chop on each hand or foot."

Maxwell let that point sink in. dismemberment in both cases, but different procedures. Maybe coincidence. I didn't think so.

"Although each cut was clean, I think the person doing the chopping was rushed," Maxwell elaborated. "I think it was based on the situation. The leader of the group wanted to get rid of the three clowns. As you noticed in the recording, they came across as being a sideshow. They got rid of the bodies fast, making sure they took the hands and feet for identification purposes. Which was a smart idea.

"Unfortunately, it took a while to make an identification of the three dead Code members. DNA came back negative. And it took a while to finally get some kind of face recognition hit. But, believe it or not, the three were all low-rent, no-name actors. "

What the hell? Low rent or not, this had me scratching my head. Even connecting the dots or puzzle pieces, this was stupid. If I was the mastermind behind this madness, no way I would hire dumbass actors to carry out my demands.

"What else?" Patrick asked.

Patrick was antsy. I wasn't sure what was going on. Maybe it was the simple fact Maxwell Pack had information that he didn't have. I think we both understood why Maxwell wanted joint investigations with separate agents-in-charge. However, as agents, we live off information. The lack of or delayed information can be frustrating as well as throw off your momentum. Leading an investigation was similar to being a hot shooter on a basketball court or a hot quarterback on the gridiron, you wanted to be in a zone where everything flowed and fell in place. However, perfect cases didn't exist for us.

Maxwell was in control now, the lead briefer. I didn't like the look he and Patrick exchanged. It was a known fact that both Maxwell and Patrick were considered to be Elliot's guys. I had heard the two weren't fond of each other. This was my first time viewing it up close and personal.

"The three shooting sprees occurred on the same day a member of the Jet Pack Eight went missing."

CHAPTER 14

...AND SO IT BEGINS.

He remembered the first time he had a shot of Hennessy Ellipse Cognac. He was a disc jockey at Saint Amos Gin & Sin in Los Angeles. It was the biggest and hottest nightclub in L.A. He was one of a hundred or more DJs who had applied for a job at Saint Amos. Exclusive couldn't begin to describe how private and how exclusive the membership was at the club. It was at the top of the list of the top five clubs in America, and on the list of the top ten clubs in the world.

What was more surprising was when the phone call came in. He would learn later that Saint Amos didn't peruse applications. Job offers were on a by-name basis. *He was a by-name.* He had no idea who recommended him. During those days, he didn't have the confidence he had today. He knew he was the best disc jockey in the city, probably in the whole state of California. When he looked down on the crowd at any nightclub and spun his vinyl, that was his confidence. He was transformed to another world.

He had the beat and the sound, and it all began in his head. Regardless of genre, his fingers were magical. He knew the right music to play, the right order and at the right time. He could never explain the transformation he went through. He was the real mix-a-lot and he had the best hook, the best story in the world – he was a white DJ conquering the world of rap and hip-hop, as well as pop, rock-and-roll and top forty. He owned the world of music during that period in L.A.

He was a by-name request.

Saint Amos really was different. They didn't negotiate. He was given a salary, a benefit package and a schedule. His schedule was built around his school schedule. A school schedule only those in his inner circle knew about. He was surprised they gave him that one concession. He wasn't sure his reputation preceded him, he was just happy he could go to school and have his dream job.

Then it happened . . . on his third week on the job. Ladies' night. It was Wednesday night back in those days. They liked his music . . . liked the way he mixed. He didn't get it. He was hesitant. He was holding back. It was a different crowd. A crowd he should have been comfortable around. Young white starlets, black athletes, musicians, actors and entertainers, superstars, the rich and famous, the super wealthy and even the not-so-famous and wealthy.

This was different.

He was used to spinning for a mostly African-American and Hispanic audience and the people who looked like him stood out. But it was cool. It was a symbiotic crowd. They were one. The music brought them together.

But now, he was where he wanted to be, where he thought he always would be. The big league.

He was at the bar, between sets, waiting to get a drink. The place was packed, which was nothing new. It was always packed. Every place he worked, he got drinks free. It was a part of the DJ package. He was also used to the club patrons hooking him up with drinks.

This night was different. He was waiting at the bar. He wasn't a priority. He was just another DJ.

"Ray, a drink for Mr. DJ White Sexual Chocolate," the man said to the bartender, the same bartender who could care less about who he was. Regardless of him being a DJ at the club, he had been invisible. But this black man, this smooth, silky gentleman with the velvety voice, he had priority.

"And give him the good stuff, cognac, H.E."

"Yes sir," was the bartender's response.

The DJ just shook his head. "Kenny Carson. They call me KC," the black man introduced himself. "I play for the Raiders. DB, kick returner. You need to stop playing and do what you do Lil' Guy. Be DJ White Sexual Chocolate. Be what you are."

"What am I?" the DJ asked.

"You're Brian Dye. Mr. DJ White Sexual Chocolate. King Freak Daddy. The best DJ in America. Brian, I don't know you personally. I have checked you out spinning records and your interaction with women. You got something dude. Use it."

The two men looked at each other. The man named KC smiled . . . while the DJ was still at a loss for words. His name *was* Brian Dye, deejay and college student. Kenny "KC" Carson was a star defensive back with the Raiders. Two men in reversed roles. The black man helping the white man. And for one reason—because he liked the way the DJ spun records.

"Be yourself Brian. Be White Sexual Chocolate. Be what you are. Be the best, Lil' Guy . . . because that's what you are—the best." KC raised his glass and Brian did the same. "To you White Sexual Chocolate. Bottoms up."

The cognac was smooth. Warm. Velvety. The best fucking alcohol he had ever drunk. Liquid orgasm. He couldn't help but smile. Hell, he knew who the man was before he ever introduced himself. He could probably tell KC his statistics, the amount of tackles and interceptions he had, his kickoff and punt return averages, and how much he meant to the team. He was crazy about the man. He smiled.

Then it happened.

KC bought him another one.

Hennessy Ellipse Cognac.

He was reborn that day. His confidence increased a thousand percent. That night he turned the place out. His best gig ever. He had reclaimed his mojo.

And at the end of the night, the bartender signaled him over. Waiting on the top of the bar was a bottle of cognac, H.E.

"You know how much that goes for?" the bartender asked, referring to the cognac.

"No, how much?" Brian replied.

"Well, the shots were five bills each. That bottle retail is probably eight grand. We sell it for twelve."

The blood drained from the deejay's face. Five hundred for a shot of cognac. He didn't get it. Besides seeing the man on the football field, he didn't know anything about Kenny Carson. This had to be a gimmick. "What's the deal?" he asked the bartender.

"Don't worry, dude. KC is cool. He's not gay or no shit like that. He believes in you. If not, he never would have recommended you."

. . . and so it begins.

CHAPTER 15

. . . And the sun rises in the morning.

"It must be nice to have money," said the muscle of the three men in this auspicious meeting. He stood six foot one with a full mustache and goatee. His body was chiseled from daily workouts and training sessions. His blonde, naturally curly locks were pulled backed in a ponytail. He had tried, on several occasions, to cut, wash and perm the curly locks out, but they always came back. So he decided to just pull it back and wear a ponytail. His hair was his vanity.

He wasn't as refined as his two cohorts, and that was okay. They were friends first, and business associates second. They had been friends for what seemed like forever. At least fifteen years.

"That's a dumbass statement for a millionaire," Brian Dye, the richest of the three men responded. He was the also founder and chief executive officer of the world's largest medical transport company, World Medical Transporters.

"Well, Mr. Dye, I have millions compared to your billions and Doc's hundreds of millions," the muscle retorted. His name was Ray Reynolds. He didn't have a claim to fame. He was once the best bartender in L.A. However, that was years ago and only one of the many jobs he had held over the years. His greatest asset was reading and knowing people.

From the first day he met Brian Dye, he knew the man would be successful. He hitched his wagon to a newfound friendship and it had made him a millionaire. But Brian was more than his meal ticket. First and foremost, he was his friend. Brian had tolerated and even encouraged his jack-of-all-trades mentality—and he really was a man of all seasons. It had benefitted him well, and more importantly, it had been advantageous to his friend over the years. So when Brian told him what he needed on this task, there was only one reply, "When do we start?"

Secondly, Brian was indeed his benefactor. Ray was never good with money. He remembers his grandfather always joking with him, "What you doing with your money, boy, selling it?" He always had responsibility and for him, a penny earned was not a penny saved. It was a penny used to help the family, or to have a little fun in an effort to forget about the stress of not having money.

"Ironic." The two men looked at their third friend, their business associate. In many ways, he was the leader of the pack—the Alpha Dog. Those who knew him like his two friends, considered him to be a renaissance man. He was the leader of his own rock band, a part-time actor—mostly theatrical stage productions, a producer, screenwriter, a world-renowned shootist . . . and the title that fit him best, a neurosurgeon.

"Care to elaborate."

"Well, Brian, it was KC who introduced you to Hennessy Ellipse Cognac as well as the person who, in your mind, gave you your big break," the doctor explained. "Now, he wants you in D.C. tomorrow to discuss WMT's role in all of the madness that occurred today. Ironic, a man you once idolized, who turned you on to your favorite drink, could be the one who sinks your battleship."

"Doc, you are too damn dramatic, as always," Brian replied. "Yeah, I like KC for setting things in motion for me. He didn't have to. Hell, he didn't know me, but he gave me a break. A break those who actually knew me wouldn't have given me. So, yes, I respect the man and appreciate him for doing what he did for me.

"Would I be here if he hadn't given me a break? Hell, who knows? I think I would have been successful, but the gig at Saint Amos opened a ton of doors for me, you know that Doc."

"Doc, I still don't get why you wanted Agent Carson involved?" Ray weighed in.

"Because, like everything else, the good doctor wanted to be in control," Brian explained in his most cynic tone. "Chose his own investigator and throw in the madness of Code of Colors to distract him from his true mission. As long as the events coincide, KC's true conviction will be focused on the Code of Colors, and the decapitation of young superstars he once partied with, who almost took his comfortable life away. Truth me, our case will take a backseat."

"Lydia did that to him, not the Jet Pack," Ray countered.

"One and the same, Ray, one and the same."

The immediate silence was deafening. No words were spoken, but the man referred to as Doc and the CEO reflected on another time and place, an older time and place. Both knew Lydia Smithers' role in almost imprisoning Kenny Carson for life. Equally, they knew her role as a great friend to the actors known as the Jet Pack Eight, and how his innocence blackballed the woman and put her life on hold for ten years.

"Anyway, some of what you say may be partially true Brian," Doc responded. "We still need to stay on script and stop ad-libbing so damn much. We never mentioned anything about killing kids."

"You wanted to get the attention of the FBI and more importantly, one Agent Kenny Carson," Ray quickly retorted. "This was the best way to get his attention, the best way to distract him. I don't know how you knew he would get assigned to the killed actors' case . . . and maybe I don't need to know. But stay out of my lane, Doc, and I will stay out of yours.

"You and Brian have your secrets. I respect that. I don't remember you saying anything about not involving kids or even killing anyone. We each have our own little piece of the pie and I, for one, like it that way. You guys keep your secrets. But don't step on my toes and I won't step on yours."

Again, no one spoke. Two men eyed each other. The third took in the minor drama. He was used to the abrasive and aggressive personalities of both men. He was the conduit between the two. He did the initial introduction of both men. One, he had known since they were knee-high to a jackrabbit, the other since he started working at the Saint Amos Gin & Sin. He knew they would be able to tolerate each other, but he also knew they would have their moments. This was one of those moments. And he loved it.

"You forget one thing, KC is a damn good agent, and we may be hedging our bet betting against him," Brian said to Doc, but his comment was really meant for Ray. He knew both men well, and knew how best to approach each. Doc would immediately get his methodology, while hearing his words and take heed at some point. The man would just be happy they weren't directly meant for him.

"From here on out, we need to be extra careful and calculating," Brian continued, still looking at Doc. "You know I love my three sons, but Ray made a good decision to keep them guessing on the true motive of Code of Colors. Thus far, Code has been a good mislead for us. Eventually . . . hopefully, later than sooner, the FBI will realize what we are doing. Then, as they say, the shit will hit the fan."

"That's true, Brian." The doctor couldn't let it die. He knew what Brian was doing with Ray, but he wanted to have the last word. After all, he was the Alpha Dog. He wasn't the touchy, feely type. Just like his surgeries, he wanted it understood by all of his staff members, what his objectives were before he picked up his first medical instrument.

"But Ray, you fucked up when you selected the three dumbass actors in the beginning. Then you fucked up again taking the kids from the alternative school and throwing them into action before they were fully trained."

If looks could kill, Doc would have dropped dead with a massive heart attack. Ray Reynolds' complexion and attitude had turned darker. But the Alpha Dog didn't care. His oration was condescending, it was also the truth as he knew it. It was the way he wanted his operation ran.

"You don't have to worry about me entering your lane, Ray. But make damn sure your ride stays on the road, or we will . . . have a problem."

Before Ray Reynolds could respond, Brian did what he was best at doing when it came to his two friends—keeping the peace. "Ok, Doc, Ray gets it. This will be another successful venture, just like all of our business ventures. Let's do what we always do."

They raised their glasses and clinked them together in a ceremonious toast.

Brian had a smile on his face. He was good at outward appearances. He knew this was a long ways away from a business venture. This was a venture both he and his best friend couldn't walk away from—a path they had been destined to take since one bad night years ago. But he had a smile on his face. And that smile didn't represent the fear he had in his heart.

While his friends, his business associates, had a look of hopeful doubt on their faces.

CHAPTER 16

RESTLESS WAS NOT THE BEST DESCRIPTION.

Derrick Paine was sure there was a better adjective for what he was feeling. In many ways, he was like a young kid with ADHD. He hated the acronym. He wished he didn't know the term or meaning of *attention deficit hyperactivity disorder.* But that was him. That had always been him. As a small child growing up in Hollywood, and now, years later, that term still haunted him. Hell, he hated the term even more since his two boys also suffered from ADHD.

After further thought, restless was the best description for him. He was tired of hiding out like he was a criminal on the run from the law or bounty hunters out to collect a fee on his head.

In this case, it may be my severed head.

Derrick wanted to laugh at his lighthearted thought, but he couldn't. He didn't see the humor in decapitation—especially his decapitation. Plus, Terri, Wash and Jimmie were his friends. They grew up together. He always hoped they would grow old together. Even after that bad night, he hoped life would return to normal and they would be sharing their grandchildren's pictures one day. Instead, they were being cut up like chickens being prepared for the frozen meat section.

It was hard for Derrick to focus. Some of it may have been the ADHD. He knew it was more than that. He was tired of his disappearing act . . . the isolation . . . and the fear.

The phone call in the middle of the night had scared the shit out of him. And that was the best way he could put it. It was a computer voice-box. *Our friends are not missing, they are dead. Their bodies cut in pieces, in sections. Get the fuck out of there. Instructions are in the usual place.*

It could only be one of two people who knew about the cabins in Ruidoso, New Mexico. Unfortunately, he knew the drill. He just wished he never had to accomplish the drill for real. And this was real. Too fucking real. This was life and death. Survival.

And why? Because six prestige kids had overstepped their status in life, and committed the ultimate mistake. No, the ultimate crime. He knew he could call it a stupid mistake. A stupid mistake that could have, and should have, cost them their freedom. Everything about that night was about panicking and overreacting. One misstep led to another misstep, which led to another. They had crossed the lines of sanity. And it begged the question, *were they ever sane that night?*

Derrick Paine refused to answer that question. *He* knew the answer. *They* all knew the answer. They were Hollywood royalty and if they committed any other crime, they probably could have walked away—*unscathed.* But this wasn't any other crime. This was gruesome, heinous . . . and something you didn't walk away from.

However, they were able to walk away. That was the day he realized the power of status. It was the status he and the rest of the Jet Pack hoped to have one day. Unspeakable became the word of choice. And they didn't talk about it—not one single day, or one single mention. In their minds, regardless what their hearts knew, that day, and night, never existed. Not acknowledging that day ever existed, meant it never happened.

Are we reaping what we sowed? He wasn't sure he wanted to know the answer.

Instructions are in the usual place. That was the code. Without hesitation, he followed the instructions. The usual place was under the floor mat in his car. Even though he had a rental car, there was no doubt in his mind the instructions would be there.

He was directed to drive towards Albuquerque on I-25 South and stop at the Out Post ten miles outside of Santa Fe. There would be a lone car in the parking lot, the keys would be on the ground, behind the front tire on the passenger side. When he got in the car, he lifted up the floor mat and the instructions simply stated, *Ruidoso. Albert Lane Lodge, Cabin 33.*

Derrick didn't need directions. He knew them by heart: I-25 South to Highway 380, east to NM Highway 48. He jumped back on the Interstate and drove the hundred and ninety miles to his destination, not stopping to take a piss or get a drink or anything.

That was four days ago. He had heard the reports of his disappearance. He also heard the reports of his three friends' body parts being shipped to various federal facilities. He wondered if he had stayed in Santa Fe, would that have happened to him. He hadn't thought about it, but Terri was abducted, kidnapped, taken or whatever from Santa Fe as well.

Derrick wanted to shed a tear for Terri. But he had already cried for his friends. They all hoped they would never see these days. However, they were forewarned. He didn't want to say that they deserved it—in his heart, he knew they did.

They committed the crimes.

He told them that night that he would get his vengeance. *Whether it be a year, ten years or a hundred years from now, vengeance will be mine, punk-ass motherfuckers.*

Those were the words, the thought that had been with him for two decades now. He and his friends had misstep. Now they were being punished for a mistake. In his mind, it wasn't right. However, that was how his mind worked—status trumped everything.

Years ago, they all uncomfortably laughed and smiled at their accuser and his rants and raves about vengeance. Internally, he knew. Several others knew the same thing. This wasn't an idle threat. They knew the man. Like he had grown up with the others, he had grown up with him. Although they were still teenagers, he was a man of his word—and his word dripped blood that night.

Derrick poured himself a drink. He looked at the bottle. Like the other five bottles in the trashcan, this one was now just as empty.

Yep, we were able to walk away. But we didn't walk away unscathed.

CHAPTER 17

SOMETIMES YOU DON'T KNOW, WHAT YOU DON'T KNOW.

It was past midnight when I dragged myself into Janessa's penthouse. She lived on the thirtieth floor of the CarsonOne Productions building, which was located in the downtown area of the nation's capital. The top two floors were residential areas. Julia and I had a similar residence on the twenty-ninth floor.

It took a keycard and a six-digit code to access the elevator to her penthouse. I was always amazed at the size and luxuriousness of the place. It took up the entire floor, and it was probably the biggest penthouse in America.

The elevator led to a huge sunken living room, accessible by three steps that led down into the space. The flooring in the foyer was white marble. The living room floor was hardwood. The dining room set off from the living room, which also connected to an overly large kitchen. There were six other rooms that were accessible by two separate hallways, three rooms per hallway. There were two bedrooms and a bathroom down one hallway, and an office, family room and bathroom down the other hallway. Each bedroom could have easily passed for an oversized master bedroom in an above average house. And this was just the first floor.

The master bedroom and two other huge guest bedrooms presided on the second floor, which was half the side of the first floor. Each bedroom had its own bathroom.

Janessa was a collector of African and Egyptian art, statues and figurines of various sizes, and other art pieces. One piece of art that sat in the living room consisted of a three feet by four feet picturesque painting of a log cabin sitting in the middle of a beautiful dark green pasture. Two wooden rocking chairs sat on the porch of the cabin. In the background was a body of flowing bluish-green water and on the other side of the water was a beautiful mountainous area.

Janessa said it was an actual cabin in the countryside of a province in Mozambique. She had taken a picture of the cabin and its beautiful backdrop and paid an artist handsomely to paint it upon her return.

She was sitting on a posh, large white sofa, sipping on a glass of red wine. As I approached her, she got up and gave me a hug. It was a tight hug.

"I love you, Uncle Kenny."

I didn't immediately speak. I wanted to take it all in. Truth be told, tears had formed in my eyes. As a family, we had had our share of losses—from my mother to my brother, who was Janessa's father, to my youngest sister. Hell, I even had a brother and sister of whom I had no idea were alive or dead.

"I love you more, my lil angel." Those were the first words I said when I first laid eyes on my niece. Although she was no longer a baby or little girl, she was still my little angel. CarsonOne Productions was Julia's and my company, but Janessa was the everyday CEO. She was the one who took the company from an eight-figure company to the two hundred plus million dollar company it was today.

We sat down on the sofa with Janessa in my arms. "Where are the boys?"

"You know where they are, in their room." They were my sons, Stevie and Devin. Devin was actually my nephew, my sister,

Alyse's son. Unfortunately, she had killed herself several years ago. I became father, instead of uncle to my nephew.

"They're playing video games. I just checked on them," Janessa stated.

"How is Stevie doing?"

"Doing great. He is an amazing kid. He is a true Carson. He reminds me so much of you and dad."

I had to take it in. I was never sure if Stevie and I were anything alike. In Janessa's eyes, we were. I had heard the same thing from my dad, my wife and several friends. But this was the first time I bought into the comparison. Still, I didn't know how I felt about Stevie being anything like us.

"That was dumb what you two did today. I'm just glad you two didn't get hurt," I said as I kissed her on the top of her head.

"It was dumb and stupid in your eyes, but we are Carsons, that's how we roll," she said with gleefulness in her voice. "Shoo, if I had my handbag with me, I would have had my own gun. I saw Stevie throw the soccer ball and I did the same thing. We weren't going down without a fight."

I didn't say anything. I didn't know what to say. I have always worried about my family—my wife, sons, niece and nephews. My father and I were estranged but we had a better relationship now than when I was growing up. Julia was my life. However, she knew and accepted my love for my biological family. And equally, she accepted and loved my family as well.

"Elliot is arranging for a Bureau psychologist to come over tomorrow to talk to Stevie . . . and you, too, if you think you need it. She specializes in the treatment and well-being of children."

"I know, he gave me a call."

"Of course he did." I had to smile as I thought about the Director of the FBI. I knew he loved my boys and Janessa's twin brothers, but his true loves were the women in his life—his wife Portia, niece Julia and Janessa.

"Really, how are you doing, Unc?"

"I have a massive headache, but I think it's just because of the long, eventful day," I said. I heard the concern in her voice and I wanted to quiet her soul. If I was being truthful, I would have told her that this day was more than just eventful, it was trying. Code of Colors, Lydia Smithers, Jet Pack Eight and Trinidad Capture all had a place in my mind. My racing mind.

My brain was working overtime, thoughts jumping in and out like a championship ping pong match. I was tired and my biggest issue was trying to control the thoughts from overwhelming me. I couldn't connect the dots, how all of the ingredients mixed and created the chaos that had ruled the day.

I kissed Janessa on the top of her head again as I got up to go check on the boys.

"Hey dad," the boys said in unison as I walked in their room. Both were focused on the video game they were playing. It was so funny saying their room, since this was Janessa's place. Our primary place of residence was in a Virginia suburb called Gainesville—the same location the Code of Colors had attacked today. But Stevie and Devin spent half their time with Janessa at her place. I think they liked the fact they had rooms in Gainesville and in downtown D.C., especially since we also had the penthouse on the twenty-ninth floor.

Looking around the room, I realized Janessa had redecorated since the last time I was here. There were two full-size beds in the room with a dresser and armoire. An entertainment center sat against the wall with a 55-inch flat screen television, X-box and PlayStation. There were also two large recliner chairs that sat on each side of the room, at the end of each bed. The boys were sitting in the chairs while they played their game.

As much as I wanted to talk to Stevie to ensure he was okay, I just took it all in. The contrast between the boys was interesting to me. Stevie sat forward in his chair, tongue sticking out, very intense and focused. The tongue sticking out was definitely a family trait. Devin's tongue was also out, but he was sitting back in his chair with the recliner up to rest his legs. He was just as intense and focused, but in a relaxing way.

I lay down on Devin's bed and watched the boys play their game. I don't remember how long it took me to fall asleep. I was exhausted. I do remember closing my eyes. I just don't know how long it took before I actually fell asleep and put the world at bay for several hours.

CHAPTER 18

NOTHING LIKE THE LOVE OF A CHILD!

It was even nice sharing a bed with Devin. I was still laughing at the thought of Stevie declaring he was too big to sleep with his old man now. I could remember the time when I had to kick him out of our. Life was crazy that way—kids grew up fast today. I wasn't sure if they grew up as fast as my generation or not.

I woke up early. As much as I wanted to give credit for being hyped for the investigation, I couldn't. It was a part of my DNA now. And of all things, I had to have a cup of coffee to get me going. It was ironic. For over forty damn years, I didn't dare touch a cup of coffee. Then they made me an instructor, and coffee and donuts became a part of my routine. I hated it. But I couldn't resist it.

I was just happy I still worked out like a beast, like I still played in the NFL. And just that thought got me thinking about the case again—the Jet Pack Eight. Specifically, about Trinidad Capture. Even today, I couldn't describe our relationship.

I first met Trinidad at a nightclub in Santa Monica. "You could have had four interceptions if you stop playing to hit someone," the autumn hair, dark complexion woman said to me. From what I knew of her, she was part Native American, part Spanish and part Caucasian. She always referred to herself as a mutt. As she put it, her Caucasian father was mixed with something as well, so she could represent several nationalities. Her voice was partially hoarse, partially silky and all Northeastern.

"Is that right?" I said with a smile in my voice. I was at the bar by myself, nursing a bourbon and Coke, my favorite drink in those days. "So, were you a defensive backs coach before you became a super hot actress?"

She sat in the empty barstool next to me as I continued to stand. "So, needless to say, you know who I am," she stated.

"Yeah, Ms. Capture, I watch movies like most of the world," I tried being facetious. "And evidently, you know me as well."

"Of course, Mr. Carson, you are probably the ninth best defensive back in the NFL." I laughed hard. The interesting thing is she didn't. She had a serious look on her face. I continued to smile.

"Damn, that's just like calling me a bum," I said. "You really think there are eight DBs in the league better than me?"

She finally cracked a smile.

"Break of dawn to you, SSA Carson," Patrick greeted me, breaking up thoughts down memory lane, as I was invading his conference room, aka work area, to find out what was going on with the Code of Colors investigation.

"Top of the morning to you as well Supervisory Special Agent Conroy," I returned the greeting. Patrick poured me coffee as he was refilling his own cup.

"Damn, KC, I remember a time when if it wasn't water, you didn't drink it," he stated. "Now, you drink coffee and eat donuts and still look like a fucking Greek god . . . asshole."

We both smiled. "Patrick, you know your skinny ass can't talk," I retorted. "I don't think you have gained a good two pounds since we have known each other. And that sucks."

We made some more small talk about the so-called good old days, which was a mere ten years or so ago. Patrick was my fourth partner with the Bureau, but the first I had a long-term partnership with. We were close. He had my back and I had his. I knew what was going on in his world, and he had an idea of what was going on in my mine. Those things we disagreed on, we never brought up. He was a favorite agent of Elliot's, and used to provide information to our boss on our investigations and things regarding other agents and investigations. I never mentioned anything to Patrick about that practice. That was his call, his decision, not mine. Equally, I was an unorthodox agent, sometimes using intimidation or stepping outside the law, and he never turned me in or told me I was crossing the line.

Part of it was partnership, the other part was friendship. It was all built around mutual trust and respect. The man had my back and, in turn, I was there for him.

We were looking at the four white boards in front of the room, with information from the investigation. There was plenty of information written in various colors of erasable ink. It had to be erasable, because none of it was worth a damn.

I stated, "Hard go of it, I see."

"Very hard, KC. These motherfuckers are invisible and believe it or not, smart as hell. We don't have anything on them. I reached out to U. S. Cyber Command to see if they could help in some way."

USCYBERCOM, as it was called, was a sub-unified command that fell under the U. S. Strategic Command, which meant its top boss was a four-star general or admiral at USSTRATCOM. The Navy and Air Force alternated commanders, meaning for two years it was manned by a four-star Air Force general, and the next two years it was a four-star Navy admiral.

However, USCYBERCOM was made up of military and civilian personnel from every branch of the military, including the Army and Marine Corp. Of course, the easy part was to say they were responsible for everything computer or cyberspace related. The hard part was that included a ton of information and operations. From what I knew, USCYBERCOM consisted of at least ten various locations stateside and overseas. And if I knew about those locations, that meant there were probably another ten to twenty locations I didn't have a clue about.

"I see you are calling in the big dogs, Patrick. Is CYBER any help?"

"Not yet, but we will see as time goes on. You know as I know, our window is small. It's only a matter of time before both Code and Jet Pack strike again."

I shook my head in agreement. We were stating the obvious. We both knew it. "I wish we had some cooperation from Hollywood, but no such luck."

"Don't worry, you will when someone else comes up missing from the Jet Pack and they realize this hiding shit is not worth a damn."

I knew Patrick was right, but it still gave me a feeling of uselessness. The Jet Pack were no longer kids, but I knew the delusion that occurred in Hollywood. Regardless of how realistic or how much they got it right on TV or in a movie, the stars who portrayed the characters didn't believe in reality. They didn't, per se, believe that they were above the law—they just felt the law didn't apply to them.

"Ironic thing, KC, every damn agent in the Bureau thinks they want to be on one of these investigations and they don't have a clue of the headaches involved with cases like them."

"You are so right, Patrick . . . you are so right."

Fifteen minutes later, I was in my own work area, my own designated conference room. My mind was on both cases, and the possible connection. I felt as if I was playing the role of yo-yo for the assailants in both cases.

"KC, you alright?" Paula asked me, snapping me out of my trance. I was surprised I wasn't the first and only person in the office. It was Saturday. Paula had beaten me in and I wondered if she spent the night here. As much as I was tempted to ask the question, she had a change of clothes and looked fresher than me.

We exchanged greetings. More like exchanged mutters. Then I looked at the files she had placed at the head of the table, my designated area in the conference room. I should say stacks of files. And next to the files were coffee and a chocolate donut. I smiled when I took a swallow of the coffee and it was to my liking. I didn't know how she knew and I wasn't asking.

She really was a smart lady, the making of a damn good agent. "Paula, what time did you go home?" I asked. At the Academy, she was in the best shape of any of her classmates and very competitive. She often wondered if she made friends with any of her classmates. At the Academy, because of the group exercises and drills, such as working cases together, classmates often times do get close. However, occasionally, there was the one, two or three students every class who didn't connect with anyone. Something told me Paula could have been one of those students in her class.

"Who said I went home, sir?" she replied playfully.

"I did."

"Eleven. And before you asked, I have been here since four."

It was six-thirty now. I had been in a good hour and I was astounded at the work this woman had done in such a short time. Blane Taylor and Jo Jo Sanu were racking up miles traveling the United States to every location that received a container with a body part. They were conducting interviews with every recipient of a container.

I was impressed with the unsub or unsubs ability to put together the list of recipients. Some of the names were damn near impossible to find, especially on a website, such as the little known chief of the technical writing and editing department of the Pantex Plant, a little known site of the Department of Energy located in Amarillo, Texas, and a branch manager of a small post office site in Memphis, Tennessee.

I looked at the initial interviews of each recipient as well as the interviews of everyone who came in contact with the containers, from those who initially signed for the containers to everyone who touched or transferred the container to the actual recipient. There were interviews from the WMT driver and delivery person in every location. Details took time and patience to review. Blane and Jo Jo were responsible for conducting more detailed interviews.

This was my world. *Investigating 101.* I conducted classes at Quantico on how to properly investigate a case. I was responsible for two things: teaching trainees the A to Z of investigating and actually assigning students a cold case to investigate. I was good at what I did. It was my badge of self-satisfaction. During my two years, my students had a success rate of forty percent of solving cold cases. That was an insanely good.

I was known as the *revenge seeker, the master of vengeance* throughout the halls of the Hoover. It wasn't a good reputation. I could solve the cases that dripped with vengeance. At least, that was the word around the building. I went with it. In some ways, it bothered me, in other ways, it didn't.

My last two big cases were all about vengeance. The last one specifically was very personal to me. I revenged the group, the man who was responsible for killing my brother over a decade ago. It supposed was to be my last case. But I was hooked on the Bureau. It was my adrenaline rush.

And though I didn't like the names, revenge seeker or master of vengeance, I liked that I had an appetite for solving these types of cases.

I didn't know what Wash Tunnell, Terrie Wenthill, Jimmie Claymore, Derrick Paine or the rest of the Jet Pack had done, but I knew they had done something in their past. It wasn't the way a normal agent should think. But that was why Elliot liked me, the reason he put me on these type of cases—I didn't think the victim was always innocent or didn't deserve the pain inflicted on their life.

I couldn't say if they deserved to die. I wasn't judge or jury. I was just realistic in a morbid type of way. Life wasn't as cut and dry or black and white as the justice system wanted it to be. I knew the feeling of sadness due to the loss of family members. I equally knew the taste of vengeance. The difference—death of a loved one was a dirt sandwich, whereas, vengeance was a juicy steak dinner with all the fixings. Meaning, death in any normal circumstance, be it by natural causes or even accidental tasted bad going down. But there was usually no one that could be blamed. Life and death happens. However, death at the hands of others, and knowing and being able to take some vengeance on those who caused the pain could be sweet and satisfying. And those who thought otherwise, had never been placed in that situations and felt the taste of revenge.

Everyone had a life not yet told. Everyone also had secrets. For many of us, we didn't want that life told or those secrets revealed. Some lives not yet told included the death of someone significant in their lives. Too often, secrets included a taste of vengeance.

I was the agent assigned to decipher and tell the story, as well as bring the avenger to justice.

I had files in front of me that told the stories of all three victims and a fourth potential victim, assuming Paine was a victim, as well as the other members of the Jet Pack. I was hoping something would jump out at me and bite me in the ass—something that told me why someone wanted these kids dead in a gruesome way.

Paula Coker had put together some very complete files. I wasn't surprised. I had police reports, information from the Internet, hospital records, newspaper clippings, magazine articles and various other miscellaneous files. I smiled. Paula was good, but I knew she had help. I wouldn't dare mention it to her. She was using her resources. It was an easy sale. Every agent and their mother wanted to be on this case.

It was almost evening. Brian Dye, the founder and CEO of World Medical Transporters, had rescheduled his interview for the beginning of the week. I had mixed in reviewing files with viewing videos of the Jet Pack. Private videos, public displays, indecent dalliances, anything I thought could help me in solving this case.

I remembered the Jet Pack from my days in California. Often times, they could all be seen together. Most times, it was a mixture of three or four. There was never a time when there was just one or two. They were wild. They were rich. They thought they owned the world.

I was about to return to my WMT files when Paula slid some other files to me and said, "Found something."

Those two words were telling.

"Look at these," she continued. "These are WMT's financial files. We hacked their system, went back a year. You are not going to believe this, but every one of the shipments was free of charge. We can't figure out what every transaction was, as in what was shipped. But of their invoices, the cheapest charge was twenty thousand. The highest was over three million.

"But guess what? When you look at the transactions from the shipments in question, the invoices included company names that were made up, as in non-existence companies, and no financial information. Additionally, six of the transactions had no information at all."

Paula was excited. Hell, I was excited. Someone at WMT was deeply involved in this madness. Things were finally looking up.

On the other hand, this was the lie we were telling ourselves.

CHAPTER 19

My secret weapon, my Mr. Everything.

That was the nickname bestowed on him by Coach Patty Mitchell. Patty was a redheaded, freckled faced, light complexioned African-American, mixed with Irish. He often stated he was a different kind of mutation. But his unusual mixed heritage didn't bother him. The coach stood six foot five and could easily lift three hundred fifty pounds without breaking a sweat or a grunt. He was the head football and basketball coach at Mercury Heights High School in tiny Mercury Heights, South Carolina, on the outskirts of the state capitol, Columbia.

On a football team of less than thirty players, Coach Mitchell's secret weapon, Ray Reynolds, played six positions and wore two jerseys. His regular number was number 44 as the starting tight end and linebacker, the same number he wore when he played safety, running back and wide receiver. Occasionally, he switched jerseys to number 63 to play center or guard.

During his playing days, his six foot one frame carried two hundred thirty pounds. The weight served him well on the football field and basketball court. Mr. Everything—that was him.

Coach Mitchell was his mentor and actually, *his* Mr. Everything. The man taught Ray how to do it all, from yard work to building a house to managing and supervising people. Whatever Ray wanted to learn, Coach Mitchell taught him.

When North Carolina State offered him a football scholarship, it was the happiest day of his life. He couldn't wait to tell his mom and younger brother and sister that Coach had delivered on his promise to take care of him. His first two years of college were great, then came the summer after his sophomore year. The summer his world would change, the summer his mother, brother and sister would become the victims of a head-on collision on I-85.

He was devastated. He thought his life was over. The reason he had worked so hard to achieve what he once thought was the unachievable was now gone.

He was his family's savior. The two bedroom, five room house he had grew up in barely stood on its own foundation. He was the one who was going to make it right. The one who would rescue his mother from the five-and-dime store job she had worked for minimum wages ever since he could remember. The one who was going to ensure his brother and sister received a college education.

He knew if it wasn't for Coach Mitchell, he would have probably killed himself. He was in a state of depression that whole summer. He decided he would take a year off from college. That's the lie he told his coach anyway. And Ray knew in his heart the coach knew he was lying.

As always, Patty Mitchell didn't give up on him. He moved Ray in with his wife and their three kids, and Patty convinced Ray to become an unpaid assistant coach during his so-called break from college. Ray had new life. Then within six months, another loved one died on him. Coach Mitchell suddenly died on the sideline of the state football championship game—the first ever for Mercury Heights. Aneurysm. He didn't know what the fuck an aneurysm was until that day. He had lost the four closest people in his life, the four people he loved most in life.

Patty's wife, Joyce, gave Ray her husband's vintage 1968 Ford Mustang. He thanked and hugged her. Then he jumped in his classic ride and set out to see the world.

His Mr. Everything had taught him to be a jack-of-all-trades, which also prepared him for a myriad of situations. Wherever the wind blew him, would be the place he'd call home.

Patty didn't give up on him.

Now, Ray Reynolds couldn't give up on himself.

CHAPTER 20

MAN IS THE MOST DANGEROUS THING KNOWN TO THE UNIVERSE.

Guns, knives, clubbing and many other things can cause death. But man is the initiator, the facilitator in so many different ways. I was addicted to the job. I had plenty of reasons to walk away. However, both Julia and I were drawn to the madness and dangers of being FBI agents. We enjoyed our financial riches, Stevie and Devin as well as the rest of the family, but we couldn't walk away from the Bureau.

Protect and serve was a nice cliché. Defending our country against foreign and domestic enemies was another good one. But the reality was for us was that we couldn't abandon Elliot, regardless of what he'd advised us to do. On a quarterly basis, he always posed the question to us, "Why are you here?" And our answer was always the same, "Because we want to be."

For Julia, he represented the father she lost. For me, he was the pseudo big brother.

I think both Julia and I were idealists. Thinking we could make a difference in the world, at least in America. And we owed it to Elliot to be there, to serve him, and to protect the masses from the many fools and maniacs in the world, which was a part of our mantra. Of course, the fools and maniacs were a part of the masses. Sometimes the realistic and unfortunate thing for every law enforcement person in the world was the fact the fools and maniacs multiplied each and every day of the calendar year.

It was Tuesday night. The investigation was still less than a week old. I was tired of looking at the files and records of the Jet Pack. I knew every element of everything that had happened with the containers that were shipped to federal buildings. I knew which body part was sent to which federal facility. Hell, I even knew every movement of the Code of Colors.

Yes, I was beyond tired of looking at paperwork or computer screens or video recordings of shooting sprees. The frustrating thing was none of it had led anywhere. It was disheartening. I was still caught between a rock and a hard place—my personal hell of thinking more about the Code case versus thinking about my primary case.

Out of both cases, I had only written one note worth investigating further. Were the heads of the three actors sent to specific people for a reason? I didn't know if it was just as random as the other parts being sent to federal agencies throughout the United States. The conspiracy theorist in me wanted to believe the body parts were a smoke screen. I wasn't doubting myself, I just wasn't sure. Truthfully, whoever was behind this madness could have killed the actors and hid or buried the bodies. This was about letting the world know what they were doing and eventually, why they felt they had to do it.

Frustration. It was killing me. For the past several days, I was popping two three-hundred twenty-five milligram aspirins every four hours to subside the pestering headache that was kicking my ass.

I was equally laughing at myself. I could recall Elliot, my brother and I sitting around years ago, and Steve and Elliot talking about how frustrating investigating a case could be. I always thanked God that wasn't my life. I was thankful the Good Lord had blessed me with the athletic prowess to play professional football. I didn't want the headaches of solving cases and looking for bad guys who had done bad things.

I smiled at the memory. I was the one now with the headaches. In my mind, I could imagine Steve looking down from heaven laughing at his little brother doing what he used to do and getting just as frustrated.

Who chooses to be an FBI agent?

I did.

And that was funny to me. I was equally frustrated because Brian Dye had constantly postponed and rescheduled our interview, plus I couldn't focus on my primary investigation. The fact Patrick and his team as well as Clay, the ATF or the NSA had no traction on the whereabouts of the Code of Colors wasn't sitting well with me. They also had no clue who the Code was or what their true purpose was. And of course, the fact there was speculation both the Code and Jet Pack investigations were connected was another sledgehammer pounding my head.

However, the biggest frustration was probably sexually. Julia had been gone for a month. It didn't seem long, but we had an active and great sex life. It was doused in love, but hell, we probably had sex just as much as we made love. That thought made me feel good and recall a time when I walked in on Julia telling one of her girlfriends that if she didn't know the difference, then she probably has never made love before. Truth be told, I didn't know the difference, but I would never tell Julia that.

We weren't sex addicts. At least, I didn't think we were. And truthfully, there had been plenty of times we had gone a month or longer without sex. But I didn't do frustration. I didn't because our lovemaking or sexual sessions removed tension for me. I didn't have that right now. Julia wasn't here. I hadn't had a major case in over two years. This wasn't a pending inactive case, this was the real deal. And the real deal was kicking my ass.

I don't remember falling asleep. I do remember the eight hundred pound gorilla in the room. Her name was Trinidad Capture. Before Julia, there was the woman I called TC. I don't know if we ever loved each other. Actually, I don't know how we felt about each other at all. We had a great friendship, we had a great relationship based on conversation, movies, drinking, eating and yes, sex. Sex and then some.

In the world of Hollywood, the sex life of actresses and female entertainers are taboo, unless they make it an issue or topic of conversation. Of course, Kim Kardashian, Paris Hilton and others had made their name and reputation via sex, but most starlets didn't advertise their sexual activity—especially if that sexual activity included other females, multiple men or group sex, like orgies.

That was Trinidad.

She had a sex drive that matched the biggest porn stars. It wasn't a well-known thing. It wasn't a topic of conversation. I was an athlete, the stereotypical athlete. The worse and ugliest football player could get laid on any night of the week, especially in the big cities of California. That went tenfold for a player who played a sexy position like defensive back, wide receiver, running back or quarterback. I played defensive back. Additionally, I was an All-Pro and a halfway decent looking guy, which made finding women a non-issue. Or better yet, women finding me.

However, TC introduced me to another world. It was her secret world. We were regular sex partners, but sometimes, other women joined us. The great actress, Trinidad Capture, loved women just as much as she loved men. Our relationship was genuine. We loved spending time together, being together, having sex and more importantly, having conversations. We could talk for days about nothing or get into semi-heated conversations about sports, relationships, politics or just about anything.

In so many ways, we were one. We were more than friends. We probably could have a future together.

Then Lydia Smithers happened.

We didn't have a formal parting of the ways, a formal goodbye. Our relationship was based on friendship, and it was also based on uncertainty. After that day, whatever we had was no more. From that day until I met the woman named Julia McEntyre, Trinidad Capture stayed on my mind.

And that was the bad thing.

She was back on my mind.

CHAPTER 21

WHO KNOWS WHAT TOMORROW MAY BRING?

Send body parts to different federal facilities—what a genius plan.
It wasn't something I would have thought of, but I wasn't a psycho. I didn't know if the mastermind or masterminds behind this plan was psychotic. I didn't really know what we were dealing with, or better yet, who we were dealing with. That was always troubling in any case.

For whatever reason, I didn't consider our assailant or assailants to be psychotic or have any kind of off kilter mental faculties. I also didn't think we were dealing with just one assailant. I thought this was a cooperative effort. I didn't know what craziness the Jet Pack had gotten into, but whatever it was it was bad. That was just my thought. I didn't have anything to back up my theory—no evidence, no reasons.

Another frustration kicking my butt was the lack of cooperation from the camps of the remaining actors of the Jet Pack. Our job was to keep them alive. But how could we? We didn't know if Derrick Paine was abducted or a disappearing act. We didn't know the location of the other four actors and how secure they were. It was troubling. Nothing had happened and that was a good thing. I knew our clock was ticking and I didn't know how much time we had before the next actor was abducted or killed. I didn't know if we would have a repeat of medical containers being shipped to federal buildings. Or, if this was a one-time thing and the assailants had decided enough was enough.

I highly doubt that.

The one member of Jet Pack we didn't have to worry about was Trinidad Capture. She was now the wife of Brian Dye and I knew she was the one member not hiding out. I was sure Brian had more than an adequate amount of guards keeping her safe.

Regardless of how tired I was looking at files of the Jet Pack case, my team had been busy and productive. We had discovered information about WMT that was disappointing at best. I was happy the CEO of WMT had postponed our discussion until today. The postponements and rescheduling was probably a power move. Good old Brian. In his world, he was big shit and I was less than a small turd. But I knew the CEO in another life, a world that seemed like it was so many eons ago.

Brian and I were once very good acquaintances, if not friends. I still had respect for him. I just didn't know how much he had changed over the years. Walking into the interview room, he still had a youthful look, even with the mustache and goatee. Back in the day, he was a man of a thousand hairdos. You never knew what you would get from Brian. One day his hair may have been pulled back in a ponytail, another day it would be free flowing, the next day it could be a damn mullet. The guy was funny and completely off his rocker sometimes, but two things you knew about him—he could spin some music and he loved himself some women.

Back in those days, he had several nicknames. My favorite was DJ White Sexual Chocolate for his love of black women. The other nickname was Lil' Guy. He stood around five-ten, but he was skinny as a rail. He probably weighted a hundred and twenty pounds with wet bricks in his pockets. The CEO of WMT was shy back then. His deejaying and a few drinks brought out the confidence and wildness he held within. With his baby-face looks, women were naturally drawn to him. Now he was a billionaire with a famous actress wife. I was expecting him to be a completely different man than the man I knew years ago.

"How you doing, Mr. Dye?" I stated as I entered the room. Brian stayed in his seat. I was impressed. His suit was navy blue, probably Italian fabric, worth about three thousand dollars, if not more, with an off-white shirt that complemented his suit well. No tie.

I could immediately tell he had definitely picked up weight. His face and his belly were fuller, and he was no longer the string bean he used to be. He still had his head of hair, but he was thinning at top.

"We are doing well, Agent Carson," his mouthpiece, attorney Seth McClane, responded to my greeting. He stood up to introduce himself. Although I had never met the man in person, I knew who he was. He was the lead man at the McClane, McClane & Taybor Law Firm. The other McClane was his wife. Seth was a corporate attorney as well as a criminal defense attorney. The organizations he represented were worth at least fifty billion dollars combined. He only dealt with senior leadership of these organizations. Lead executives such as Brian Dye, who, by Internet standards, was worth three plus billion dollars.

"I will be speaking for Mr. Dye today, agent, so please direct your questions to me," McClane stated. The attorney looked distinguished with his full head of salt and pepper hair, slicked back but very professional. He was only five-seven or five-eight but his slender frame made him look taller. There was no doubt in my mind that the man was great at his job.

I didn't wait on Brian to stand or even acknowledge me. He was playing the lead dog role. I could either acquiesce or make his snobbish ass talk to me. I chose the latter.

"No offense, Mr. McClane, but I knew this asshole when he was spinning records, paying his way through college," I said with a smile on my face. "Now, he is a successful businessman, with a great company, and trying too hard to act the part of an asshole."

"I take offense to that, agent, and we are here of our own accord, to assist in your investigation, and the disrespect is not appreciated," McClane responded in a professional but forceful tone as Brian stared hard at me.

I didn't say anything. There was no need to reply to Seth McClane or even hear anything else he had to say.

"You're still an asshole, you know that," Brian stated in a mild, but even voice.

I like to think my smile was infectious, as one formed across his face. "Hey, DJ WSC, just trying to draw you out of your shell. Welcome back."

Laughing, he replied, "Yeah, your ass was always trying to draw me out of my shell, even when I was already out my shell."

To the dismay of his attorney, we talked a few minutes about life after L.A., our families and our business success. It was nice just having a talk with an old acquaintance. I think we both knew that it was only a matter of time before the conversation turned to business. Brian told me how he came up with the idea for World Medical Transporters.

I already knew the Internet version of his story, how he rose in business to his two marriages and three sons to his philanthropy ventures. But I wanted to hear his version, see the pride and ownership of his success. I wanted him as an ally, and not an adversary. Someone in his organization had betrayed the trust of the company or gone rogue. I needed his cooperation and possible assistance in finding out who was behind the betrayal.

Our few minutes turned into about thirty minutes. The last of the casual conversation took a turn I didn't expect.

"You remember Venice?" he asked me.

"Of course I remember Venice," I replied. "Hell, I introduced you guys. Heard you two got married."

Venice Lyons was a beautiful woman. To look at her, you would think she was Caucasian. However, she was very fair skinned. Her parents were African-American as well, but both of their complexions were fairer than Venice. She had beautiful red hair and that was Brian's favorite. And *she* was Brian's favorite.

She was a few years younger than me. Although she was a Raiders cheerleader, we had connected because she was originally from Clarksville, Tennessee, which was about sixty miles north of Nashville, and I had attended college at Tennessee State University. Trinidad had introduced us. We became friends with benefits. When I wasn't hanging with TC, I was hanging with Venice. One day while hanging out at a club in Los Angeles, where Brian was deejaying, I introduced the two of them, and before you knew it, they were a couple.

"Well, after you left for the FBI, we got married," Brian volunteered. "Unfortunately, she was killed on the Santa Monica Freeway one foggy morning. She died along with seven others in a thirty-car pileup."

"I'm sorry to hear that Brian." He was somber, borderline sad. I knew the story. I was shocked when I heard the news. Truthfully, before then, I didn't know they had gotten married and had kids. I felt bad for him then, and for whatever reason, I felt bad for him now. I didn't know why. I knew he and TC were married now, and I knew she was also a good woman.

"Terrible fucking way to die," he said.

I didn't say anything in return. I didn't want to overplay my hand. As much as I wanted him as an ally, I didn't need him to be down. And the Brian I once knew, when he got down, he went to a place in his mind that kept him down for a while.

I was happy Seth McClane knew his client as well as I did. "Agent Carson, you have questions for us?" It was a great transition.

"Yes, Mr. McClane, I do. Primarily about the company's standard operating procedures and shipping protocols."

"What exactly are you asking, Agent Carson?"

"He wants to know how we do things at WMT in terms of shipping," Brian clarified as he leaned forward in his chair and rested his hands and elbows on the table.

Good, I didn't lose him. Yeah, I could have requested the chief operating officer or vice president of shipping and transport, but neither person would have the passion to talk about the company like the person who created and developed the processes, and made the company a success. I needed Brian Dye to be engaged, and he was.

"My goal, and the success of WMT, was to make the shipping process easy for all medical agencies," Brian explained. "Be it hospitals, medical suppliers, research and development organizations, doctors outside hospital networks, you name it, we wanted the process to be easy. We made it easy to create an account, gave one month discounts, one-time use discounts, and we made it easy to package products.

"When it comes to body parts, which is what you want to know, we actually provide free training to organizations on packing body parts, or they can opt to have us pack items for them. We show them how to use our containers and how to set the temperatures. And if need be, we provide organizations who have an account with their own containers."

"Interesting," I said. "I would think you would still want your payment in advance?"

Brian didn't say anything. He had a perplexed look on his innocent face. His attorney leaned forward and put his hand on Brian's arm.

"W-W-W-What you mean KC," Brian was finally able to open his mouth. "If you have an account with us, you pay us an initial fee or half, if your account is less than a year old, and the balance is due within thirty days. If you have been a customer for more than a year, your initial payment is only twenty-five percent, and the balance is due within sixty days."

"What if I told you almost thirty shipments were billed to bogus companies and your company didn't receive a cent from these numerous transactions." Brian didn't say anything. He leaned back in his chair. I wanted to say his eyes were dead, but they weren't dead. Shocked? Confused? Maybe. I couldn't put my hands on it.

"Most of the transactions were billed to four companies. Companies that didn't have an account with WMT. And from our financial forensics, there was never an official transaction of any type made for pickup or shipment. It looks as if everything your people did was free of charge for these fictitious companies. And worse, six of the shipments had no company or return address in your ledger or database on these transactions."

Brian still had a mystified look on his face. And I still wasn't sure of the meaning behind the look. He was the founder and CEO of the company. He was perched on top of the food chain. This was possibly someone at the lowest level of that same chain taking advantage of an apparent blind spot in the company. But researching the company's protocol, at least a couple of personnel in management had to sign off on all shipments.

This was surprising and shocking news for Brian. I was sure of that. I actually thought that was maybe Brian's issue with this. Although all of the shipments were within the continental United States, something told me that Mr. Dye had lost anywhere from a half million to a million dollars.

"We will research this information and get back with you immediately," Seth McClane stated.

I wondered if Brian would sleep well tonight. Someone within his business was cheating him. Brian had changed over the years. I could tell he had more confidence and he didn't need alcohol to bring that confidence to the forefront. He always had smarts and intelligence. His lack of confidence held him back. Somewhere, somehow, he got an influx of confidence that made the boy a man, and turned the deejay into a billionaire.

"Brian, the remaining members of the Jet Pack, do you ever hear from them or know how we can get in touch with them?"

"With the exception of Trinidad, you mean?"

"Of course."

"No, KC, I haven't heard from any of that bunch in several years," he answered. "Even Trini doesn't keep in touch with any of them. They were always bad news. You know that. Trini and I made a deal, I would stop my whoremongering if she wouldn't deal with those misguided assholes."

Brian tried to laugh it off. I didn't say anything. I knew there was an element of truth to what he said. His whole persona had changed at the mention of the Jet Pack. It was ironic. Years ago, it was normal for the eight kids from Malibu to piss someone off. Trinidad and Dyson Ryker were the two who tried to keep the others out of trouble. The more I thought about it, the more I was amazed someone hadn't harmed them before now.

"Let me guess, their representatives are not cooperating with the FBI and you guys have no idea where the remaining eight are hiding out? And if you do have any digits on them, I'm sure the numbers you have go directly to voicemail or have been turned off."

"You know the rich and famous well," I joked. "You mind if I reach out to Mrs. Dye?"

"Yeah, I do mind," Brian replied. "She is well protected and as I stated, she doesn't have anything to do with her old crowd."

I don't know if the question caught him by surprise or he was being overly protected, but I could hear the angst and anguish in his voice. He really didn't want me to speak to Trinidad. I had to wonder why. That was my job to wonder why. However, I couldn't help think that he knew about me and Trinidad's past history.

I watched as Brian and his attorney departed the room. Paula Coker escorted both out the building. Something was going on with the man once known as DJ White Sexual Chocolate. He was always the jealous type. It was one of his major faults.

I didn't know what tomorrow would bring, but something told me that even in a company as big as World Medical Transporters, the founder and owner of the company was not as in the dark as he pretended.

I could only think to myself, *please don't be mixed up in this madness, Brian.*

CHAPTER 22

WHEN I'M SUCCESSFUL, YOU WILL BE TOO.

That was the promise Brian made to him. He was the exceptional bartender. They made an impeccable team. Like a marriage, they formed a union of one. When one got a gig, it meant a job for both. Brian being the deejay, he got the majority of their gigs.

A smile spread across Ray Reynolds's face as he recalled their days of old, when Brian would pick his nickname based on the venue. DJ White Sexual Chocolate was the most notorious and well-known. His favorite was when they did bachelorette parties or female only events, and Brian's moniker would be DJ Whup Dat Ass. Ray actually burst out in laughter as he thought about the different events they worked—he as the bartender and Brian as DJ Whup Dat Ass, the deejaying stripper.

Ray couldn't help himself as he laughed louder. It was always fun because Brian would oil himself up and only wear a pair of tight briefs or swimming trunks. And amazingly, regardless of what social status the women came from, they all ate it up. The things those women did to him were crazy. Brian didn't complain or push anyone away. From the beautiful to the oversized, from the homely to the thin, from the rich to the low income, the man was pure magic with women. Of course, it took a half bottle of whatever spirit he was drinking to increase his courage or make him numb, but he pulled it off—each and every time.

Ray was amazed when the man made his money. First millions, then billions. He gave his best friend a ton of credit. He remembered how Brian used to go to school for undergraduate and graduate degrees Monday thru Thursday, and even took some classes on Saturday morning, but Thursday night thru Sunday night, he belonged to spinning records and chasing booty. He often wondered how in the hell the man could party to four, five or six in the morning and be in class two hours later on a Saturday morning. But he did it. And he would be full of energy Saturday night for another round of fun.

He knew he owed Brian a lot. He had done right by Ray and, equally, he knew he had to return the love and do right by Brian. He was once a poor kid, now he had an eight-figure bank account, a two-million dollar house and four luxurious cars. Yes, he owed his best friend and owed him big.

He didn't know the inflictions Brian and Doc went through at the hands of the spoiled actors known as the Jet Pack. They asked for his help. It took him all of two seconds to say yes. Now he was driving a three-year old Kia Optima from New York to Clarice, South Carolina, the site of his next attack. The car was owned by WMT, but it wasn't on their official listing. The car was registered to his alias, in case law enforcement types stopped him. Additionally, all his transactions were completed with cash. He didn't need to leave a paper trail of any kind.

The drive gave him plenty of time to think of the past, the present and the future. He never foresaw his present life. The more he thought about it, he never thought Brian would be the success he was. His friend had a determination he wasn't used to. Even being the athlete he used to be, Brian took the cake. He was making what he considered to be great money as a deejay, but the man kept grinding with his schooling. Then after he finally got his undergraduate degree, he took a job as a safety and industrial hygiene specialist versus being a deejay, which was the higher paying gig.

Ray didn't understand initially. As much as Brian kept telling him he had a plan, Ray thought the friendship had ended as the former deejay was always working. Then after rarely seeing each other over a three and a half year period, Brian came to his job, gave him a twenty-five thousand dollar check, and told him he worked for him now.

Since that day, he never looked back. He was the *guy*. Whatever his friend needed, he did.

Even when his friend asked him to do something illegal, his answer was simply, "What you need me to do?"

When Brian answered, "Kill people."

It was a simple reply for Ray, "Kill who?"

CHAPTER 23

How do you define that your finest hour matters?

Clarice, South Carolina was a small town in the southwestern portion of the state, approximately forty miles from the South Carolina – Georgia state line. The town's population was around ten thousand, but four thousand of the residents resided at the Clarice School of Academia, better known as the Clarice Monarchs. The school was the state's best preparatory high school for some of the smartest teenagers in a three state area—North Carolina, South Carolina and Georgia. But most importantly, for South Carolinians, the school was the victor of over twenty athletic championships the past ten years, including six Class 5A football championships.

For Ray Reynolds, it was a school of dread for him. His mentor, Coach Patty Mitchell, was coaching in his hometown school, Mercury Heights, only football championship game when Patty had an aneurysm and died. The game was cancelled, postponed or rescheduled. The Monarchs won their first football championship that year. That was almost twenty years ago. Ray knew it wasn't Clarice School of Academia's fault for killing his mentor. But it left a foul taste in his mouth. Over the years, he occasionally had dreams about blowing up the school. It was only a dream.

Then his role as the leader of the Code of Colors fell in his lap. At some point, he knew he would be paying the town of Clarice, and its famous school a visit. He was mad at himself for thinking about Patty Mitchell. He was sure the man was looking down on him from heaven. And he knew he wouldn't approve of his actions. But he hoped his pseudo father, his mentor would understand why he was doing what he was doing. Brian Dye was not only his friend, but the closet thing he had to family now.

He was doing what he had to do.

"How do, boss?" the teenager said to the man. The boy was an eighteen-year-old African-American. He stood six foot three, weighted all of two hundred sixty pounds, pure muscles, less than five percent body fat. By political correct and age standards, the boy was a man, but his baby face, love for video games and conversation usually gave him away. Even so, the teenage man had been buying alcoholic beverages for five years now, without anyone asking him for any form of identification. Size and color could do that for you. He had a dark complexion, what other African-Americans would call midnight. He wore his hair in a tall, wild afro that stood on his head, with no sense of neatness or structure.

"White, I be good, how you be?" Ray returned the greeting. The teenage man's name wasn't officially White. On every job, Ray called the leader of the job White. Ray thought it cut down on confusion. For him, everything was paperless. No identification of any form. When they went on a job, none of the eight assailants would carry cell phones or anything else. They would don their clothing and no two team members wore the same colors.

"Where are the other playas?" Ray asked.

"The other gangstas are sharing three other rooms . . . and I have a room to myself," White explained. As with the other operations, the team consisted of eight members.

"So, one room probably has three guys in it and you have a room to yourself," Ray repeated. "And no one complained about that?"

"If they did, it wasn't to me," the teenage man replied in a nonchalant, I-don't-give-a-damn tone.

"Cool," was Ray Reynolds acceptance.

The men focused turned to the television that sat on the combination dresser, refrigerator holder and TV stand. A news channel out of Hilton Head/Savannah was discussing upcoming events in the local areas, to include Clarice, South Carolina and the Clarice School of Academia.

Ray never liked the school's name: School of Academia. He thought it made all other schools seem like they were full of dumbasses, or second and third class students. He recalled playing them in both football and basketball. During one football game, his small team in numbers injured at least twenty Monarchs. And what did the Monarchs do? Just have another twenty players take their place. It was discouraging and disheartening. Clarice had to dress at least a hundred players. His school, Mercury Heights, barely had a second string, while Clarice fielded a team with five or six strings. And the sad part for Ray—he knew their third and fourth string was probably better than Mercury's first string.

"So, let me guess, two days?"

"No, Mr. White, let's say four or five days," Ray corrected his subordinate's assumptions. "Do you have everything I detailed?"

"Yessirree," White replied. "But why so long?"

"I still have things to do and the date coincides with the school's athletic banquet."

They continued to watch the newscast, before White stated, "It's gonna be spectacular."

Ray Reynolds smiled. It was an internal thing. A thought that always stayed with him. "That's funny."

"What's that boss?" White asked.

Ray didn't immediately answer. He wanted to gather his thoughts. "My old coach asked me once," he finally said. "How do you define that your finest hour matters?"

The kid turned his head and gave Ray his undivided attention, trying his best not to display the confusion he was feeling at the moment. He often felt Ray talked over his head. To hide his ignorance, he wouldn't say anything, just pretend to be interested. And, in most cases, he did have an interest. For the teenage man called White, it was another opportunity to learn something new.

"When I asked him 'what,' he stated, 'by a spectacular event that will define your life forever.'"

The kid didn't say anything.

"White, this will be . . .

. . . *your finest hour.*"

CHAPTER 24

THE TOTALITY OF YOUR EXPERIENCES CAN KILL YOU.

And that's how Mitzy felt, like she was beating on death's door. By her standards, she was the least successful of the infamous Jet Pack Eight and her failures haunted her existence. They made her do stupid things, such as overdose on her drug of choice at that time. She was weak when it came to living and dealing with life. Her three near-death adventures had been captured by every media outlet in the world. That's how she felt anyway.

Every time she did something stupid, it always ended with her feeling worse. And she was tired of the media always mentioning what she considered to be the lie—*Mitzy York has proven to be the actor of the infamous Malibu Eight.* She had heard that line a lot over the years and still, she didn't believe it.

On her own, she kept the Malibu Eight or Jet Pack Eight in the limelight. She had always wondered where in the hell the media got Malibu Eight from anyway. Only three of the eight of them lived in Malibu or even had ties to Malibu.

Hell, what difference did it all make?

She didn't like the media blitz now, especially considering the recent events. Her failures were once classified as legendary and the last thing she wanted was for them to be back in the forefront of everyone's mind. She wasn't doing anything—now. And that was her luck, even when she wasn't acting crazy or committing career suicide, the bad in the world still found her. She was sure she was jinxed that way.

Her latest escapade was getting drunk and high with her favorite rock-and-roll band. Unfortunately, that wasn't the worse thing. The worse was later when she had sex with all four members of the band, and their lewd acts were caught on video. Of course, video in this case included cell phones, the chosen destroyer of lives these days.

This time, her mother didn't say anything. She was tired of chastising her. *Tired of dealing with her mess.*

Her mother's words always hurt her. Hell, just thinking about her mother hurt her.

"Mitzy, it's your life," her mother said to her in the calmest voice she had ever heard the woman speak to her. "You are my baby. I love you so much and that may be the problem. But no more, Mitzy, it's your life and I'm going to let you live it."

She looked at her mother. She didn't believe it was the same woman she had known all of her life. Her mother was giving up on her and as many times as they had fought, and yelled and screamed at each other, she was at a loss for words. As much as her mother's words and pure presence had hurt her, this hurt her more.

Initially, she didn't believe it. Then her mother said, "You know what, you are, and have always been one of the best actors I have seen on the screen. It hurts me to let you go. But Mitzy, you will always be my baby. And if the time comes, I will eulogize you like no other."

Then Mrs. Gloria York opened the door to her daughter's Brentwood, California home and walked away without looking back. Mitzy cried that day. And it was the first time she truly cried from sadness and defeat since that dreaded day twenty years ago. She knew that was the problem—that dreaded day. The day she and her friends chose to never speak about, to never mention. They chose to press on with life and live. Unfortunately, what she and a few others didn't realize, choosing to live life doesn't mean that regrets and consequences would easily dissipate.

Regrets and consequences.

However, things were different now. Maybe it was her mother walking away. Maybe it was the life she was living. Whatever it was, she hoped it was different now. She hoped she was safe from the madness. She wished she could say the same for her friends. *But fuck them!* They abandoned her.

All but Dyson.

He was always the good one. The sweet one. The fucking oddball in the land of misogyny, narcissistic assholes. He was always the fucking decent one.

In her mind, it was his fault. Instead of saving them from themselves, he was trying to get busy with Trinidad. That's why she did the things she did that night. Dyson was supposed to be there—to stop them from their own stupidity—to stop them from stepping over the line.

In her mind, she knew Dyson was the one to blame.

That night happened because of his absence.

Mitzy York was tired of living. But that was more than an occasional thought. She had a drug problem. She had a drinking problem. She had a slut problem. In essence, her life hadn't worked out the way she wanted it. The fact she was the most talented of the Jet Pack didn't help either. Her downfall had always been due to her lack of self-confidence and her strive for perfection.

Unfortunately, even when she had reached perfection, it wasn't good enough.

That one night.

She did reach perfection.

And it cost lives.

Regrets and consequences.

Yes, she had them. They were kicking her square in the ass twenty-four hours a day, three-hundred and sixty-five days a year.

She and her friends had once committed heinous and gruesome crimes. Now they were the victims.

If only she could reverse time.

CHAPTER 25

HE DIDN'T LIKE HIS WORLD BEING UNDER ATTACK.

But there wasn't much he could do about it. He understood.
He lived it. No rest for the wicked . . . and once upon a time, he
was one of the *wicked*. He never truly understood that saying until
today. One event, actually, one mad night placed that unspoken
title on his doorstep – *the wicked*.

He was one of eight. Now, one of four. The land he grew up,
the culture he was born into, they were his world. The world he
would trade his left testicle for. *His world*. Now he was trying to
wrap his arms around the moment at hand. He didn't know what
or how he should feel.

Although he didn't know the fate of Derrick, he was sure he
had been captured or kidnapped or abducted or whatever law
enforcement was calling it. Derrick was always a weak link. His
thought was that the killers wouldn't ship body parts to the Feds
until they had he and Mitzy York as well. That pissed him off.
Trinidad and Dyson would escape because they weren't around.

How fucked up is that?

His thoughts went back to the weakling, Derrick Paine. He
didn't consider himself a conspiracy theorist, but he couldn't help
himself when he thought about Derrick. He was considered to be
one of the top five directors in demand, but Derrick was in the top
three. His former friend was now his nemesis. *His weak, scary ass
was actually good . . . no, great at something.*

He didn't wish Derrick any harm. However, he did wish he had been kidnapped before his best friend, Wash Tunnell. Wash was a man's man. He knew how to have fun. They knew how to have fun. He wished his friend was still alive. Hell, he wished he was there to save the day. No, to save him. He felt miserable that Wash had died a terrible and painful death. It had to be painful to have your limbs and head cut off. He hoped his friend was already dead before the cutting began.

When they had conducted similar type crimes years before, their subjects were dead. Maybe barely dead. But dead all the same.

He wasn't sure who the exact killers were, but he did know they didn't have mercy for Jimmie, Wash and Terri, and he knew for certain they wouldn't have mercy for the likes of him, Mitzy and Derrick. He wanted to speculate who the killers were, but he couldn't get his mind off the two who weren't there—Dyson and Trinidad. It was a stupid thought. Maybe because he wanted them dead. He needed them dead.

Why not them?

His time was running out. He hoped not. In his mind, he was just getting started. It was only a matter of time before he became the film industry's top director. It wasn't an overnight process. He had done his grind, paid his dues, kissed more ass in a few years than anyone should kiss in a lifetime—now this.

He was known around Hollywood as the Creator. One reporter wrote, *"We have finally found the man from Midas, the director with the Hollywood and Midas touch. He led us by the hand and teased us with Death By Computer. Then dropped the bomb on us with one of the most intriguing characters and storylines we have seen in years. The Code Breaker, Thornton McGill, has been a welcomed change to the mundane, one-dimensional characters that have flooded the big screen the past decade or so. Finally, we have our new John Ford, Alfred*

Hitchcock and Steven Spielberg rolled into one. From childhood star to teen idol to mature director and producer, we have our Creator."

As much as he wanted to smile, he couldn't. He felt sick. He felt like a phony. Thornton McGill wasn't his creation. Dyson Ryker and Derrick Paine came up with the character, Thornton McGill, years ago while making up stories off the cusp. His past three movies weren't his idea. He wished that they were. Dyson and Derrick were that good. Their abilities to make up shit on the run pissed him off, but Dyson and Derrick not only gave him permission to use the character, they actually wrote the three scripts that made him a superstar. Now he despised both men. Why? He wasn't truly sure why. But officially, in his mind, Derrick Paine was his nemesis, the one keeping him from becoming the director in demand.

He suddenly felt empty.

No.

A case of melancholy had fallen over him—similar to a mother covering her stillborn with a blanket. He didn't feel as secure as the dead baby. Sadness owned him. A glum he hid well from others.

His stepfather always told him he had delusions of grandeur. He wanted to be the big man. He hated himself. He couldn't do it on his own and that bothered him. *Delusions of grandeur.* He hated that bastard. If he was alive today, he knew he would be enjoying this moment.

He searched his mind, trying to remember the last time he was stable. That small element eluded him. The funk called his name before he reached his twentieth birthday and camped out at his doorstep for two years. On good days, he wanted to kill himself. Those were the days he remembered most. On bad days, he wanted to kill others. Something he had done before. It was the guilty pleasure that ate at him every day.

Dyson Ryker.

He needed Dyson, the one who cared and brought him out of his funk. In so many ways, the so-called odd guy out was his savior. Dyson was his true friend. From the age of five, the black kid with success written all over him had been there. When the others tried picking on him, Dyson was there. When his stepfather was being a dick, he ran a quarter mile to the house next door, the Rykers, and slept in his childhood best friend's room. When school kicked his butt or he forgot his line or needed someone to talk to, Dyson Ryker provided the support he needed. No. The support he required.

If only he had arrived earlier. Only if Dyson had saved him one more time. One ghastly, awful night. A dreadful, abysmal night that would define his life forever. Even today, it sickened him to think about what they did. What he did. Even that night Dyson was his savior. And he still wished he had never gotten Dyson involved. Thanks to him, they were no longer best friends, but Dyson was one of them—the Malibu Eight, the Jet Pack, the Gang.

If only Dyson had shown up earlier and saved him. No. Saved them. If only he and Trinidad had done what they'd always done—be the grownups.

Ten hours. It was ten hours that changed his life. That changed their lives. *The infamous Jet Pack Eight.* His eyes stayed focused, looking straight ahead. At nothing. The way he felt about his life.

Nothing.

Emptiness.

Void of a soul. That's what his stepfather said.

That became the last straw with the fat man. Pure instinct took over as he grabbed the man and tried to choke the life out of him. Strength he didn't know he had surged through his body. Every internal fiber that composed the teenager found its way to his hands—the same hands that gripped his bastard stepfather's size nineteen and a half neck. The overweight man wasn't going easy. He grabbed his stepson's wrists and threw the kid off. When the heavy man regrouped and decided to attack, the overpriced ten thousand dollar sterling silver candle holder met his head and stopped the man in his tracks.

That happened on a Sunday afternoon when his mom was vacationing in the Bahamas. The teenager didn't panic. In fact, he went directly to the medicine cabinet in his parents' master bathroom, grabbed three aspirins and washed them down with a can of beer. Then he fixed a sandwich, watched TV until midnight and finally called his childhood best friend, Dyson, to come over and help him. "I have an emergency situation," came out of his mouth when Dyson objected.

Dyson came in, accessed the situation and with the calmness of someone thrice his age, he devised a plan and the two of them methodically executed every step. They were precise in their actions. By the time the first bell rung for school, the two of them had buried the body east of Los Angeles, on a desolate road near San Bernardino.

"Mr. Parkins, you need anything?" the man asked the director/producer as he peered around the door.

Terrence Parkins didn't look up from his seated position in the living room of his stash house. He flicked the light on that set next to the reclining chair that he had occupied for the past couple of hours.

"Mr. Parkins?"

"I'm okay, Thomas. Thank you for asking."

The man servant closed the door behind him.

Terrence thought about his current situation. He knew he had outsmarted his potential kidnappers. No one would even think to look for him in his current location. Like so many people, he had driven on numerous highways and interstates, and seen the houses in the middle of nowhere sitting off the interstate. Several years ago he bought one of those houses. Savory, Georgia. Sixty miles north of Savannah, off Interstate-16 between Savannah and Macon. It was a big beautiful white house trimmed in blue-green paint that sat a half mile from I-16. However, exiting the interstate, taking the side roads took three miles and twenty minutes to reach the house.

His man servant, Thomas, was the only person who knew he stayed here, occasionally, when he wanted quiet time. He paid Thomas a very fair salary to tend to the place in his absence and be his servant when he stayed at the house.

Yes, he was convinced he was safe—secure. He would let this whole thing play out. As much as he loved and cared about his old friends, he preferred to live. He hoped the FBI would capture the murderers before they killed anyone else. If not, he would ride out the storm.

And live to make another movie—and many more after that.

Terrence Parkins turned the light back off and continued to look straight ahead in darkness.

His environment matching his mood.

Part Two

FANTASY IS REALITY

CHAPTER 26

AND THE WICKEDNESS SHOULD END – VIOLENTLY.

Conrod Bach remembered when he came up with that line. It was for his third television show, the drama, *The Wicked Detective*. Terri Wenthill's dad, Howard, was the star of the show. He laughed at that reference, *dad*. He was *dad* to the young stars and starlets—in more ways than one.

He never thought such a statement could be true as it was today. *And the wickedness should end—violently.* His children were dying violent deaths at the hands of madmen. He knew there was more than one. He had been around long enough and crafted enough stories to know this was not the work of one person, one man. Someone was challenging his authority. He was being bypassed. His children were being slaughtered, like they were cattle in a meat factory. And he could only imagine why.

He turned his attention to the show on the television. The TV was tuned in to one of the weekly news shows. The title of the show may have made his stomach churn if he truly gave a damn: *From Superstardom to Lunch Meat!*

I can't remember a time when Jimmie Claymore, Terri Wenthill, Wash Tunnell and Derrick Paine weren't in our lives. I can remember begging my parents to stay up late to watch little Jimmie Claymore and his father in the top rated TV show The Detective and Son. Jimmie sparkled as Corky Hardway, playing next to his father, who also produced the successful television show.

And how can we not bask in the successes, and ups and downs of the eight teenagers who went by the moniker, the Jet Pack Eight. For the past two plus decades, we have marveled at Terri Wenthill going from child star to a successful singer and actress with the one-name recognition—Terri. Equally, Wash Tunnell went through his troubles transitioning from child star to young adult, but when he finally figured out the transition, oh what an actor he became.

And for Derrick Paine, ask any thespian in the business today, who would they love to work with, and the answer is simple, Derrick Paine. Known as a perfectionist with meticulous attention to detail, Mr. Paine had become one of the top three or four directors and producers in Hollywood.

Tonight on Seeker of Truth, we will examine each of these celebrities' lives, and see if we can figure out how these perceived beautiful souls' body pats ended up in metal containers, officially referred to as cryogenic medical freezer units, and shipped to federal facilities.

Bach turned the TV off. Even before they delved into how ghastly or gruesome their deaths were compared to the saintly lives they lived, he was already fed up. Maybe he was being too much of a cynic. He was judging again and he knew that was wrong. But anyone who knew his children, the so-called Jet Pack, knew his children were everything except saints and angels. They could raise hell with the best of them.

The man couldn't help himself. He turned the TV back on. The broadcast went on to relay how the scene at each location was something out of a sophisticated horror film. Several body parts were described in detail. Fortunately, the nation's thirst for breaking news didn't translate into the news stations showing photographs of the body parts. But the show reported that each body part was in pristine shape and each cut was every clean, no blood, no mess.

Thank God for small miracles.

As Conrod flipped through the channels, one newscaster even mentioned, "Out of respect for the victims' families, we won't be showing any photographs of the contents of the containers." He made it a point to write down the name of the reporter and his producer, the network would be hearing from him.

Of course, he was trying to glean whatever he could from the broadcast. He heard about the unbelievable number of government locations that broke protocol and opened the metal containers with unknown contents. He didn't laugh at this. He and Director Lucas went back years and he knew the man would be chopping off many heads for that goof-up.

He was hoping to learn something from the broadcast. Thus far, Lydia had struck out in her attempt to extract any information from the Bureau. He was hoping she could have made amends with the lead investigator, Kenny Carson, and maybe doing an apology session, he would work with the woman who lied about him years ago. *Unfortunately, forgiveness is not for everyone.* Conrod laughed at this.

He then picked up the brown file that sat on his desk. He had opened it before, but only took a quick glance. It was a thick file. He was mad at himself for not being man enough to open it—while he was sober. He wasn't big on drinking, but today . . . his code went out the window.

Crown Royal. That was his liquor of choice. He didn't know how many shots he had taken before he finally mustered up the nerve to open the file and view its contents. The news show was still playing in the background. He tried to keep an ear to what was being said, but his attention was now on the big brown file with the numerous photographs.

Tears started to roll down his face as he looked at, in detail, the first three photographs. *Terri. Jimmie. Wash.* His heart was broken. In so many ways, these were his children. He raised them. Maybe that was the problem. He raised them.

The tears continued to fall.

He continued to drink.

His heart grew heavier with each photograph.

Memories flooded his mind . . . ate at his soul . . . made him realize he wasn't the man he once was.

In so many ways, he did this. He was culpable.

Parenting was the hardest thing in the world. He knew that. He remembered his friend, Elliot Lucas, telling him once, "If parenting wasn't the hardest thing you've ever done, you didn't do it right."

He knew that to be true. Because he didn't do it right. It took the murder of his loved ones to come to that realization.

The more he looked at the photographs, the sadder he got. He was now oblivious to the TV. He was trying his best not to get any tears on the photographs. Then he saw it. He didn't know if it was meant for him or not.

CB,

> *I will never forget how you used to open up the summer session, "I am the father of you all." And like any parent, you had your favorites. They could do no wrong. Even if that meant killing six people, for no other reason than they had the backing of Hollywood's most powerful man, then why not?*

> *Bravo to you, CB, if you are reading this.*

> *And know, we don't hate you, Mr. Bach. I can't say we feel sorry for you either. You are not to blame for what your chosen kids did. You are to blame for them not receiving*

the justice they should. Look at it this way, we are cleaning up the mess you left behind.

Three down, five more to go. Stop us if you can, CB. Stop us if you can!

And to make the game fair. Just for you, Mitzy is next, followed by Terrence, then your favorite son, the one who shares the blood of both parents, Derrick Brutus Bach, or his Hollywood name, Derrick Paine. Then, the last two bastards—Trinidad & Dyson.

You used to like games, CB. Well, this is a game of Stop Us If You Can.

Love you DAD

And – in your words - Once upon time, when the darkness turned to light and the light turned to darkness, and evil succumbed to goodness and goodness smiled upon evil – I indeed – love you!

Conrod Bach took another shot of his Crown Royal, while he just stared at the letter that seemed to stare back at him. The tears had stopped running.

He then picked up the .357 Magnum automatic weapon that sat on his desk.

Unfortunately, he knew he wasn't man enough to pull the trigger.

Not today anyway.

CHAPTER 27

ANXIETY WILL BE THE DEATH OF ME.

That's how I felt the whole day. I had been bugging the hell out of Patrick, trying to get information on the Code of Color case. His frustration and discord was just as bad as mine. As a lead agent, these were the types of cases you loathed. It could take a while to get some traction. You were always waiting on the next shoe to drop, hoping that would be the shoe that left a trail of clues in its wake.

Many didn't get investigative work. On TV shows, it was always as clear as the nose on your face who committed the crime. Within that hour show, the whole investigation was over, case solved, bad people killed or arrested. Even if the show depicted a four or five day investigation, as an agent, you wished all of your investigations took four or five days. I didn't know an agent who could magically work that fast on some of the simple cases, let alone one that involved crimes in multiple states.

Criminals were on their own schedule, with no regards to your time. I laughed at the thought. Sure, criminals are thinking about the agents or cops who are trying to put them behind bars. I could still hear Elliot telling the media, "We have agents who have the ability to think like the criminals they pursue." Then a couple days later, telling me that for the most part, no law enforcement type could really think like the damn fools who commit crimes.

For both Patrick and I, we were approaching a week on our perspective cases. I decided to take my team of Paula Coker, Blane Taylor and Jo Jo Sanu out for dinner. Since day two of the Jet Pack investigation, Blane and Jo Jo had been jet-setting across the country, interviewing federal employees who received cryogenic freezer units with body parts of the dead actors. They had touched down three or four hours ago, and like damn good agents, they came directly to the office.

Unfortunately, they hadn't shared anything that jumped out to Paula or I, which only added to my frustration and anxiety.

"So, why did you choose the FBI over the NFL?"

The inquiry from Paula was probably a good question for another venue. That was my first thought anyway. I wasn't sure dinner at the Downtown Monster, a small diner within walking distance of the Hoover Building, was the place for this conversation. Or maybe it was me and not wanting to answer the question was the issue. I became an agent for one reason, and one reason only—to avenge my brother's death. It took ten years to get the opportunity to accomplish that feat. And I knew I was one of the lucky ones. Many law enforcement types put on the uniform for that very reason, to avenge the death of a loved one. But less than one percent probably got fortunate enough to get the opportunity to accomplish that act.

The interesting thing was the Downtown Monster was one of the first diners I frequented when we used to play the Redskins during my NFL days. From the outside, the place looked like a dive, but the ambiance inside was borderline sports bar and a Mom and Pops joint, and the food was heavenly. Plus, even in the middle of Redskins country, it was a great place to check out games on Thursday or Monday nights. Sunday was a day to stay home and watch NFL games.

"Long story, Agent Coker," I finally replied, "but one day I will share it with you." She shook her head and that was that . . . or so I thought.

"You heard about the Just Cause case?" Jo Jo threw it out there, the not-so-fast fastball ready to be knocked out of the park, into the Potomac.

"Yeah, big case for the Bureau two years ago," Paula replied.

"KC was the lead agent on the case," Jo Jo provided. "Since then he has been the Bureau's darling." I shook my head as he laughed his butt off. Jo Jo could be a playful ass sometimes. He was a good agent, and definitely good people. I rolled with the conversation.

"Sometimes on the job, you get lucky Coker," I stated. "Just Cause, I guess, fell onto my lap. Right place, right time."

"That's not what I heard," Paula replied. "The word around the Bureau is that you were a regular lead agent on Director Lucas's desktop cases when he was the deputy director."

The waitress came over to take our drink and appetizer order, which was a welcome relief. Desktop cases was the term given to cases that the deputy director or director took direct interest in. The short of it was, when Elliot was the deputy director, he had his own investigative personnel who reported directly to him. No one was sure how many personnel reported directly to Elliot, but Patrick and I were members of his unit. The former director didn't have any desktop teams, but it was thought Elliot had enough personnel to handle five or six major investigations simultaneously. Often times, I was a lead agent on many of those investigations. Now, as director, Elliot still had his desktop teams and his deputy director had none.

Ironic how that worked out.

"Yeah, I was one of the director's lead agents, Coker," I commented when the waitress walked away. "It was a big responsibility and I loved being one of the so-called chosen ones. I was just happy I was given the opportunity. I worked some big cases, put some bad guys away, saved some lives. It was a good gig Coker."

"Many say you were chosen because of your wife," Paula said with plenty of skepticism in her voice.

"What's your deal Coker?" Jo Jo intervened. Before Paula could answer, Jo Jo continued, "Speaking of opportunities, you have an incredible opportunity now, and you are more worried about busting your lead agent's balls. One, that's stupid to throw away an opportunity like this.

"Two—"

"I'm not throwing away this opportunity," Paula countered. "I was just asking questions. I guess being an analyst, I just got carried away."

"Agent Coker, either the director or Chief Pack selected you to be on this team," I stepped in. "For one, I'm a very upfront and frank person, no sense in pulling punches. Up until now, I had the utmost trust in you. Now, I will be watching my back."

"SSA Carson, I didn't mean anything by my questions or comments."

"Oh, I know you didn't, Coker," I replied. "If the Chief of the Counterterrorism Division came to me as a young impressionable agent, trying to make a name for myself, I would probably fall for the company line as well. But really, Coker, what's the smart move, pissing off Nicholas Holt or pissing off the Director of the Federal Bureau of Investigation."

CHAPTER 28

YOUR NIGHTMARE COULD BE MY DREAM.

I couldn't recall who said that me, but it was very appropriate in this investigation. The Jet Pack had everything, but evidently it wasn't enough or maybe, it was too much. Having success and dealing with success are definitely two distinct items on opposite ends of the spectrum. I was sure the victims of the Code of Colors wouldn't mind exchanging lives with any member of the Jet Pack when they were at the pinnacle of their young careers.

Too often, I don't think enough people realized how jaded life could be. Which was another way of saying how fucked up life could be.

Equally, I don't think enough people realized how good they had it. I wished my fellow Americans realized that happiness really did initiate in the heart.

My thinking was off. I really was thinking like a dreamer. No two people are alike, just like no two situations are alike. Many of us made the poison we ingested. And sometimes we had to distinguish our poison from our kool-aid.

Was Paula Coker my poison? Would she drop this or continue to work with Nicholas Holt? Should I get her kicked off the team?

All valid questions. The biggest issue was dealing with Nicholas Holt or let sleeping dogs lie. Thoughts were swimming in my head. As much as anyone could know Elliot, I thought I knew him a little bit more. If I took Paula's betrayal to Elliot, not only would she be off the team, he would probably kick her out of the Bureau. He was a man of loyalty. You broke that code of trust, you were of no use to him. It was a career ender in the Bureau.

I thought I would play it close to the vest. It was best to keep it to myself for now and try to make heads or tails of this situation. I didn't owe Paula Coker anything, but I didn't want her to ruin her career before it really got started. If she was selected to be a part of Elliot's special teams, then she was good at her job.

This was the last thing I needed. I didn't need the distraction. I also didn't want to overthink this whole thing. I was pissed more than anything else. The betrayal was kicking my ass. I also had to deal with Jo Jo and Blane. There was no promise either would trust Coker. She was my problem, which meant her interactions would be with me. I was now in a situation where the members of my team would be looking over their shoulder.

It was late and my headache was returning thinking about Special Agent Paula Coker and her betrayal.

I was back at Janessa's place. She and the boys were sleep. They were back in school, with personal bodyguards from our company taking them to school and even sitting in their classrooms. Janessa also had a team of ten bodyguards stationed around the school, without the school's knowledge. There was no way another incident would be happening at the school again. It had to be the safest school in America now.

But that mindset brought me back to the Code of Colors. If the Code was targeting schools, what school would be next? And what was the best strategy to glean information on their future plans? If there was a pending attack, did that really mean there was a pending abduction of the next member of the Jet Pack? Were the cases really that connected, if they were connected at all?

All were good questions, but tough to gauge. I was fighting the constant thought that kept recurring or playing in my head. Lydia Smithers may know the answers to my questions. I hated that thought. I was pissed at myself that the thought kept replaying in my head. I had been thinking that way for a couple of days now. I knew she was still in the D.C. area, staying at a nearby hotel.

I was lying in bed with my eyes wide open. As much as I was wanted to see the future, get a glimpse of solving both cases, my mind kept doing a rewind to being arrested, riding in the back of a cop car and sitting in an interrogation room.

I grew up in the 'hood, and every black teenager and young black man had the same thought at some point in their young lives—never see the inside of a cop's car or jail cell. I was fortunate. I only saw the inside of a cop's car and interrogation room. But it did scar me—made me leery of white women as well as white America. And that thought pissed me off.

Of course I had gone to school, played ball and worked with whites who didn't like me simply because of the color of my skin. But I always tried to stay above the fray, be the better man. At that point in my life, the Raiders' staff was mostly white, a third of our team was white and I partied with people of all nationalities, especially in California. It was the land of milk and honey, the true melting pot of America. Unfortunately, O. J.'s case had changed that dynamic.

I had gotten past that point in my life and over two decades later, being leery of race or a person based on skin color had returned. I didn't want to be around Lydia in any capacity. Although I knew in my heart she could probably blow this case wide open for us, I couldn't bring myself to do it.

I could always meet her in person with Paula Coker present, but I was cautious of her as well. I realized I had to get out of my head. If I didn't, I would kick Coker off the team, which would result in her being kicked out of the Bureau. As much as I wanted to laugh at all of the irony flooding my existence, I couldn't. I really wanted to just close my eyes, get some sleep, wake up and press on with life without the drama of Lydia Smithers and Paula Coker.

I was living in a nightmare and I knew how to downgrade it to a dream.

If only I could catch a few winks of sleep.

CHAPTER 29

THE BUSINESS OF BUSINESS IS TO MAKE A PROFIT.

He didn't know why that thought popped into his head. He was in a luxury hotel room, completely nude. Well, not completely. He did have a blindfold on. He was sitting on the sofa, legs spread wide, a half smile on his face and his nature ready for his action. It was a pseudonym replay of the first time he engaged in sex. He was sixteen then.

And just like that first night, the same woman, who was a fourteen-year-old girl then, was on her hands and knees slowly approaching her prey. Reenacting the same scene that occurred when they were teenagers . . . she the experienced sexual one and he the pure virgin.

As much as he didn't want to be with the woman, she was his weakness. Since that night at Herbert Brutus School for Gifted Students, he had been drawn to the woman like a dog to a steak. He had heard stories about men being pussy-whipped . . . and these tales were followed by details of men having the best sex they ever had. Sex so great that the men didn't have a choice but to keep coming back. But those stories were followed by phrases such as I wish I knew where that woman was today, or I wish she never got married, or damn, I wish she was still in my life.

Brian Dye hoped like hell that what was done in the dark stayed in the dark as Lydia Smithers wrapped her mouth around his nature. The first time they hooked up years ago, he didn't have a clue it was Lydia pleasing him. He actually didn't find out until a couple of months later. Now, even with him knowing it was Lydia, he still liked the feel and mystery of the blindfold.

The suite consisted of two bedrooms, a large living area and two bathrooms. And Brian's idea of a good time was christening every room. He loved his wife. Trinidad was the love of his life. He had loved the woman since he was an adolescent and she was a teenager. Regardless of the love and children, the relationship was based on convenience. From day one, that was the status of their relationship. She was the reason he was a billionaire, the reason he was a man of confidence. She really was the woman behind the man.

He knew he could never complain about sex or lovemaking with Trinidad. She was an animal, the best in bed. But Lydia was on a different level. The woman was pure sexual gratification. As much as he loved burying his face between her legs, Lydia was the alpha in this union, and she dictated the action.

After thirty minutes in the spare bedroom, they had made their way to the master bedroom. She was on top and riding him like a stallion. It was rough and he loved it. Occasionally, she would grab him by the back of his head and make him suck her breasts, or she would kiss him hard and even eat his lower lip.

Their commonality was their sexual deviance. He loved the craziness and spontaneity she brought to the table.

While Lydia loved the danger of being bad or getting caught. She was afraid of Trinidad. She knew her friend didn't care what her husband did. But Lydia knew Trinidad believed strongly in the power of friendship. Yeah, if she found out, Lydia knew she would be dead. And the danger of it all made her hornier.

It also helped that she loved the man. If she had to guess how many men . . . or women, she had had sex with over the years, she knew she wouldn't be anywhere close to getting the number right. It didn't make a difference though. Brian was the one. If it had to be secretive sex encounters, she didn't give a damn. He was worth it. He was her one.

They were now lying on their side and Brian was behind her, thrusting hard. Her right leg was in the air and intermittently, they would tongue and kiss, as Brian smacked her ass at her request. Both were immersed in sweat and the smell of sex turned both man and woman on. She called his name repeatedly, begging Brian to fuck her. With every mention of his name, he thrust harder, pulling her hair and biting her nipple hard.

Then he yelled out he was coming and Lydia did something she had never done before, she pulled off his blindfold and told him she loved him. Brian couldn't believe what happened next. After he came, his penis stayed semi-rigid. He can't recall the last time that happened. Then a tear fell from his eye.

He understood why. No one had told him they loved him in a very long time. Not his wife. Not his sons.

The business of business is to make a profit.

Whether intentional or spur of the moment, unbeknownst to Lydia Smithers, she had just saved her life.

CHAPTER 30

LOYALTY WITHIN GOVERNMENT IS LIKE LOVE ON A ONE-WAY—
NON-EXISTENCE.

I was running late this morning. I was walking into the Bureau
at seven-thirty. I was operating on maybe a good three hours of
decent sleep. I had spent the night eyeing the ceiling. When I tried
to really get some sleep, I tossed and turned until I finally fell into a
stupor. Now I had to confront my challenge—Paula Coker.

"Look at what the cows dragged in," Jo Jo bantered at my
expense.

Everyone was in the conference room and I shouldn't have
been surprised. I actually told Blane and Jo Jo they didn't have to
be in until nine. I expected Paula to be here. I was really hoping she
was here by herself so we could talk. That would have to wait now.

"I would say good morning but that would be a lie," I said. "So
far there is nothing good about this morning."

"Maybe I can help you with that," Paula stated.

I was getting coffee from our small coffee table. A better
statement would be I was preparing my coffee. Many joked that I
liked a little coffee with my cream and sugar. As funny as it sounded,
my coffee did consist of a lot of creamer and sugar, sometimes a
mixture of French vanilla creamer and regular creamer. The heat is
what I desired, more so than coffee.

I was still in tuned with what Paula was saying. "I thought about
what we may be missing," she continued. "I did a comprehensive

background check on all of the personnel who received the cryogenic freezer units, and you wouldn't believe what I found."

"Their lives date back to several years before their work history began, and any high school or college information you have on them don't add up," I stole Paula's thunder.

"How did you know that?" she asked.

"I didn't," I replied. "Jo Jo and Blane told me last night as we were leaving the restaurant. Evidently, they are pretty good at their jobs as well Paula." I couldn't help myself with the dig. But I did want to hear what else she had, if she had anything else.

She didn't say anything. The expression on her face said a lot. She didn't know where she stood with the team. The biggest issue was I wasn't willing to let her off the hook yet. I wanted her to earn our trust back.

I think my constant gazing at her made her realized she needed to say something. "Can we talk about this and then get back to business?" she asked.

"No, let's focus on the investigation," I replied. "I know you have more, enlighten us."

She didn't hesitate. "I ran the photographs of all of the personnel and, of course, all came back with their current identifies. However, I was sure I recognized four of the personnel. Those four reminded me child actors, so I surfed the net and those same four actors don't have a technological footprint since they left the limelight years ago."

I looked at Jo Jo and Blane, and the three of us all looked at each other, before we all returned our gaze to Paula. "You may actually be on to something, Special Agent Coker . . . now tell me, where do we go from here?"

"I think we should personally hit the field and interview all four, throwing out the data that we know who they are."

Everyone was quiet. We were all taking it in. I already knew the answer. Paula was right. We had to interview the four federal personnel she thought were once child actors. If they were once different people, why did they change their identities? But more importantly, how was it possible for over thirty people to get federal jobs with bullshit histories? To do that, it took power—plenty of power.

The conversation I had with Blane and Jo Jo the night before was actually a thirty-minute conversation. It took five interviews before they decided to really do a more in-depth search on their candidates. That's when they found the information. They didn't act on the information, or lack of information they found. They thought it was something they should bring back to D.C. for discussion. I agreed with their logic, it was now my job to take this to Maxwell Pack and possibly, Elliot Lucas, to see what was going on.

"I agree Special Agent Coker, let me run this by Chief Pack and we'll take it from there."

"Now, can we talk about the eight-hundred pound gorilla in the room?" Paula asked.

This was opportunity for another quiet moment. But I didn't want that. "I wanted to do this one-on-one Special Agent Coker, but since you want to do this in front of the group, let's dance."

"I made a mistake Supervisory Special Agent Carson. I know we have an issue because we are using official titles. You don't trust me now . . . and it doesn't take much to see that Special Agents Taylor or Sanu don't trust me as well. I want to be on this team, but if you don't think I'm worthy, I probably to go back to my previous assignment."

"Do you want to be an agent with the Bureau?" Jo Jo asked Paula.

"Of course I do," she replied. "I know I screwed up and I'm willing to make my amends."

"Well, that's all and good, agent. However, I'm sure if KC told Chief Pack or Director Lucas he doesn't want you on the team, both will want to know why. If KC was being honest and told them how you betrayed the team, I'm sure you would be looking for another job altogether. And Paula, the bottom line, and this is me being nice, Director Lucas would blackball your ass from getting any law enforcement or even security job anywhere in the United States."

Paula looked stunned. But she was also being tough. I saw her fighting back the tears. There was no way she would allowed three male agents see her shed a tear. I admired that.

"Paula, what trust we had in you is gone," I began. She stayed tough. "But it's up to you now to earn back that trust. Jo Jo is right. If I kicked you off the team, you would be out of the Bureau and believe what he said about the Director. Your family can be the wealthiest in the country and still not yield the power of Director Lucas.

"You fucked up. I don't know if you thought you had the Montgomery Holt lucky charm behind you . . . but if you thought that, you are wrong. Monty, nor his dad can help you. Believe me when I say that. Just do your job Paula. Let your work do your talking. And get away from the politics and drama. Because I guarantee you, I'm the one who has your back. And no one else. If you want to be a politician within the Bureau, learn it first, then play it. But not before."

I saw a certain calm cross Paula Coker's face. I think she finally got it.

I had planned to talk to Maxwell and Elliot, but not to ask permission. It was my case. I didn't want to leave this area because I had to stay abreast of the Code of Colors case.

But duty called. It was time to direct my attention on solving one case at a time—my case. Which would lead me to the unsubs I coveted.

CHAPTER 31

Sometimes life is a game worth contemplating.

I felt like a knight at the roundtable as Patrick Conroy, Maxwell Pack and I were gathered around the small conference room table in Director Elliot Lucas's office, as we waited for the big man to get off the phone and join us. The meeting was a spur of the minute thing. I had caught up with Maxwell when he summoned both Patrick and I into Elliot's office.

"That was Lindsay Barnes," Elliot stated after he hung up the phone. "It seems show business's top executive, Conrod Bach, is anxious and running scared."

"Scared of what?" Patrick asked.

"Secrets, truth, lies and speculation," Elliot replied. "As we all know, in the world of big business, powerful men have powerful troubles. If those troubles ever saw the light of day, empires would crumble, Patrick."

Elliot's voice trailed off at the end of that statement. Something told me he was probably thinking about his secrets. He was a powerful man who ran the most powerful investigation agency in the world. The Bureau's secrets could probably crumble the U. S. federal government if they got out.

"Barnes will be providing us with more information sometime within the next couple of days regarding his Jet Pack brats," Elliot volunteered. "I know it's been a week and no doubt we haven't made much movement on either case. I made it a point to call Barnes and let him know enough was enough. I want information that will point us in some direction. I know about covering your ass, but I don't like being in the middle of the ocean in a patchwork lifeboat with tape over the holes.

"Additionally, I've just learned something disturbing. Neither Bach nor Barnes has a clue of the whereabouts of their missing actors. Unbeknownst to you Carson, I had Maxwell provide agents to sit on the homes of Ryker, Capture, York and Parkins. An hour ago, I had teams serve bullshit federal search warrants on the home of each. We found nothing. I expect the media to be all over this tonight."

What the hell? Needless to say, I was shocked. I didn't immediately understand the strategy, and knowing Elliot, this was a part of a strategy. It may have been a strategy he thought up on the fly, but that wasn't his modus operandi. Elliot was spontaneous but only to a certain degree. He was one who always had a plan. In this instance, I wished he had shared that plan before I found out this way.

"I don't get it," I spoke up. "I don't get the strategy Sir."

"That's easy Carson. It's time to shit or get off the pot. This is minor pressure, but enough to get everyone to thinking. And by everyone, I mean the remaining members of the Jet Pack, Conrod Bach, if he is involved, and those abducting the actors as well as the Code of Colors."

"So we wait to see what happens or when the next shoe drops?" Patrick asked.

Elliot replied, "If you want good chili or stew, you have to stir the pot. We have done our due diligence by press release, which states the actors are not suspects. We received information that they may be in danger and we are diligently searching for them. We served the warrants at two locations, and the other two locations, we did break down the doors to ensure no one was hurt, dead or being held captive.

"To answer your question Patrick, the next shoe will be dropping soon. The question is, will we be prepared to catch it when it drops?"

CHAPTER 32

THE BOGEY MAN CAN BE A WOMAN.

Julia Carson was a liar and she knew it. She lied to herself every day. She loved being an agent just as much as she loved her husband and boys. It was the lie she lived with every moment of her life. When she heard about the attack on Stevie's school, her heart skipped several beats and she actually had an anxiety attack. She wanted to make a beeline back to D.C., but she was assured everyone was safe.

She was mad at herself for not making the decision to go home. After all, the case she was on was her own self-appointed mission. Her mission was important. Her family was more important. She did what she thought she had to do. Her mission was on hold. It would be there when she got back.

She heard the door open. The tall blonde would be shocked when she walked in the master bedroom of the two-bedroom hotel suite and saw her. That was the plan. She loved the element of surprise. She was so good at it.

And it always worked like a charm.

The color faded from Lydia Smithers' pink skin as soon as she saw Julia sitting at the small table in her bedroom.

Or maybe it was the gun with a silencer and the serrated knife that sat on the table.

"I promise you, I can put a hole in the front or back of your head or put this knife in your throat before you take a step," Julia stated in a calm demeanor. "And believe me, I don't have a problem shooting you, knifing you or even gutting you. That's how much I despise you and love my husband."

"Y-Y-Y-You're KC's wife?" If Lydia could kill herself, she probably would have. Her fear was ten times that of her worse day. Yes, she had had fearful moments. However, looking at the woman that sat at the small table in her hotel room, she knew this might actually be the day she died.

"You know who I am, Ms. Smithers. And I don't take it lightly when people play stupid with me. We understand each other?"

"Yes, I guess we do," Lydia responded with obvious fear in her voice.

"Have a seat."

Lydia made her way to the table and sat across from Julia. The fear was unmistakable. She really wasn't sure she would see another day. Of course she knew Mrs. Carson. She knew everything about Kenny Carson and his life. She hated the man just as much as he hated her. She made a mistake when she blamed the man for raping her. But her life changed for the worse. She became a pariah. Her family and friends distanced themselves from her. And she equally distanced herself from others.

She originally traveled to Europe for a six-month getaway. Six months actually turned into ten years, before she was summoned back to her native Los Angeles. During her stay in Europe, she lived in Spain, England, France and Italy. She missed those days, she missed Europe. Timing was everything. Being so far away from her hometown, she was completely shocked when an Italian suitor asked her why she lied about Kenny Carson raping her, when he clearly was trying to help her. She didn't have an answer. However, it made her realized America was home and where she belonged.

She knew it would take time for her life to get back to normal. But years later, she still didn't know what normal looked like.

"You obviously have information for Agent Carson, so talk." Julia was terse, straight to the point. She knew the woman was afraid. She couldn't blame her. If she didn't have the nerves of steel and the shoe was on the other foot, she would be nervous and afraid as well.

"I wanted to talk to KC."

"Ms. Smithers, let's get something straight, I don't like you. I really would prefer to gut you, than talk to you. But I try my best not to disrespect anyone. The single fact I don't like you is making it hard for me when you call my husband KC and not Agent Carson, or Special Agent Carson, or anything official.

"You understand what I'm saying?"

The fear that already permeated her body overtook Lydia as she pushed the chair back and attempted to get up. She almost fainted when the hand gripped her neck. She had never known anyone to move so fast. Julia's snakelike striking movement froze her, and whatever blood she had possessed in her body, felt as if it had completely drained from head to toe.

Fear can be debilitating. In Lydia's case, it was downright paralyzing. Her body didn't belong to her. She couldn't will her body to move. This was the most fear she had ever felt in her life. She had been through a lot in her life. She had dealt with fear before, on numerous occasions. But this was the first time she felt true fear—the fear of death.

And the real dilemma was—her fear was coming from another woman. Before today, it was something she could never fathom.

The scary monster in her life, possibly the one who might take her life, had breasts and a vagina like she did. She had seen movies and read books about badass women. All of that was fiction. Fictional women doing dangerous, manly acts. Hell, she was in Hollywood. The land of fiction.

But right here, right now, *her bogey man was a woman.*

"Please. Don't. Kill. Me," she managed to stutter. She could feel tears rolling down her cheeks. *What have I gotten myself into?*

"I'm not going to kill you, Ms. Smithers," Julia replied in the mildest of tones. She was struggling with her self-control. Usually, she was the epitome of control, but internally, she really did want to hurt the woman. She settled on receiving whatever information the woman had to share.

"But don't disrespect my husband . . . and tell me what I came here to hear."

"I-I-I-I don't have any information," Lydia lied.

"Try again," Julia said as she tightened her grip on Lydia's neck with her right hand, while the knife's tip in her left hand settled on the base of Lydia's jugular, something Lydia had missed before.

Julia said, "Life is not a fairy tale or a Hollywood movie, woman. Life is real. Sometimes people die walking across the street or in their sleep or worse, at the hands of a deranged person like me."

She let that sink in. She was growing weary of Lydia Smithers. She knew if she stayed around the woman too much longer, she really would kill her. And that wasn't her plan. That wasn't her mission.

"This is what we're going to do," Julia continued. "First, you are going to get a clean pair of panties out of your drawer. Then we are going into the restroom and you can change. Next, you will sit on the toilet and tell me everything I need to know about the remaining members of the Jet Pack. And if you don't, I promise you, the restroom will be your final resting place.

"And that, I promise."

CHAPTER 33

Every dog eat dog day appears normal to the broken spirit or misguided soul.

Cleaning herself in the restroom of the master bedroom, she recalled Trinidad introducing her to the football player. He was enthralled in conversation with her friend and two other females, and of all things, they were talking sports. He was cordial, even nice. However, Lydia didn't like the man introduced as KC. He didn't do what other men would do—make eye contact, look her up and down, and compliment her on her beauty. Instead, he continued on with his conversation.

She was younger then, certainly self-absorbed. Dumber. Hungry for attention. Clueless.

She didn't know if that was the day she knew she would make him pay for not showing her attention. For not being mesmerized by her beauty, her sexiness. That morning. It wasn't planned. The man she hated. He saved her that morning. She was pissed. She wanted to die that day. She blamed him. If only she would have died that day.

If only . . .

She was sitting on the toilet. She only had on a bra and panties. She'd soiled her previous panties. She was happy Julia Carson, who she looked at as a crazy, out of control agent, made her change her underwear. She was just hoping she survived the day. She didn't know what she was thinking when she tried to get away from the mad agent. The woman could have killed her.

Real fear is actually seeing your own death, the realism, the finality.

She remembered the movie, remembered the line—hated both the movie and the line. She got it though, she finally understood.

She was a black belt in karate and Taekwondo and the thought of attacking the agent made a temporary visit to her mind. She considered herself as the cat backed in the corner by the dog. The cat always came out fighting, always came out the victor. However, she wasn't stupid enough to believe this was true in the real world. She knew the agent had left the gun and knife on the table.

"It's moments like this," Julia began. "That people motivate themselves to do something stupid. They want to replace the mouse in their heart with a roaring lion." Her voice was slow, deliberate. With every word, there was meaning. And Lydia Smithers knew the meaning.

"We think about movies we have seen," Julia continued. "And a bolt of lightning hits us in the ass and it's like we've drunk a gallon of liquid courage. Then we do something stupid, something that gets us hurt . . . something that may even kill us.

"I know your life Ms. Smithers. From being banished to Europe by your best friend, Trinidad Capture, to you being the face of your father's company in the international market to—"

"My father is dead," Lydia interrupted.

"No," Julia retorted. "Your dad is Conrod Bach. Probably the best kept secret in Hollywood. I'm surprised no one has ever leaked the information, or smart journalists never made the connection."

"How do you know that?"

"Because I'm good at my job, Ms. Smithers."

"How did you know about Trinidad?"

"Because Trinidad was in love. And you tried to have the man she loved put away on bogus rape charges."

Lydia's head dropped. Tears flowed from their ducts. Thoughts of years past dominated her mind, contributing to her headache. A moment in her life she never wanted to relive, she was doing just that. Trinidad was like a big sister to her. Although KC didn't know how Trinidad felt about him, she knew. And she betrayed Trinidad's love and trust. That was the part she never understood. Why was she so jealous of her best friend, the woman she looked to, the lady she would have fell on a sword for. These were thoughts she had already cried over, thoughts that haunted her existence for so many years and she had exiled. Now she was reliving those dreaded days.

"When we were younger, teenagers . . . something happened," Lydia suddenly stated. "It included six of my friends . . . six members of the infamous Jet Pack Eight. The exceptions were Dyson and Trinidad. I think there was an accident or something, but people died. And don't hold me to this, but I think it was swept under the carpet."

Lydia paused. She was nervous. But Agent Carson was correct, she did have courage, mixed with a certain amount of fear. "I-I-I have newspaper clippings," Lydia muttered.

"Clippings of what?"

Lydia replied, "I can show you. I have them in the bedroom."

"Tell me about them, give me the cliff notes version." Julia did have an interest in the clippings. But this was a game of the mind as well. She didn't know Lydia's sexual orientation, however, she did know that some women were uncomfortable undressing in front of other women. It was an element of embarrassment. Even with Lydia still wearing a blouse and bra, and a clean pair of panties, there was another element of embarrassment and fear sitting on a toilet, feeling vulnerable and helpless to defend herself.

"The clippings are from various locations throughout the country . . . and some from other countries as well. The clippings are from locations where the Jet Pack Eight were shooting movies."

"Hold on," Julia intervened. "Take me back to the beginning."

"What do you mean?"

"Something led you to the clippings, so basically, tell me everything from the beginning. What made these clippings necessary and important?"

"While I was overseas, the best way I could keep up with my friends was via the internet. Whenever I looked up anyone, it seemed as if there was a killing at every location. If it was New York, Chicago, Los Angeles or any other large city it wouldn't have been a problem. But some of these places were small towns, or in some cases, big towns that didn't experienced crimes like bigger cities experienced.

"And interestingly, law enforcement never looked at the movie crew as possible suspects. So over the years, I just kept collecting the clippings."

"You never approached any of your friends about what you were doing or questioned them about any of the crimes?"

"No, I didn't."

"You tell anyone?"

"No . . . but I did make it a point to go to some of the sets after I returned from Europe. I was hoping it would help. And it did . . . in a way."

"How so?"

"The frequency of the crimes decreased. And I don't think it was because of me. I think the crimes just happened. I think it was something that just happened. Plus, I don't think any of the crimes were connected. I think because they had maybe killed someone years ago, that they thought they could get away with murder . . . literally."

Julia was trying to take it all in. What the hell? Her uncle, Elliot Lucas, had told her about KC's thought that the actors had done something very bad in their past to make someone want revenge. But this was unbelievable on many levels—major actors killing random people. If it was true, then the list of people wanting revenge could be unlimited.

"Why do you suspect your friends? Maybe it was a member or members of the production crews."

Lydia said, "If only that were true. Different production crews. Some of the crewmembers were on multiple sets, but for some of the crimes, it was never the same crew or crewmembers. In other words, the commonality was my friends."

"Give me an example of a killing . . . actually one each by the remaining three actors who are still living—Derrick Paine, Mitzy York and Terrence Parkins."

"About four years ago, in Merced, Illinois, five people, three men and two women, were shot and brutally chopped up at a motel on the outskirts of town. Terrence was shooting a movie there. It happened the night they completed shooting a three-day scene in Merced.

"A couple of years ago, in Pattison, Washington, a redheaded woman was caught on video leaving the house of a man who had his throat cut. He was completely nude and tied up spread eagle on his bed. Mitzy was doing a movie there.

"And lastly, a year ago, Derrick was shooting a movie in Banksfield, Maryland. And—"

"Eight people died from being poisoned at a party," Julia intervened. "All the deaths were attributed to someone spiking the punch. The party was at the town's convention center, which included another seventy-five people. And every victim died at least a good thirty minutes after they digested whatever poison they were administered."

"That's right."

"Ms. Smithers, these are serious charges. If we do find your friends, from the information you have, we will be charging them for these crimes. Assuming we can prove all you have said."

"I know."

"Ok, I need those clippings."

They went into the master bedroom of the hotel suite, and Lydia got the clippings from her luggage, while Julia retrieved her weapons. When Lydia gave Julia the big yellow envelope with the clippings, Julia, in turn, gave Lydia a small baggie with listening devices.

"You know what these are?" Julia asked.

"Not really," was Lydia's weak and barely audible reply.

"Listening devices. I did a sweep of your suite. There are at least ten devices in the bag. I'm sure you know who bugged you. Something tells me it wasn't your dad."

Lydia didn't say anything. The two women gazed at each other. Julia turned to walk away, and then she stopped, and turned back around.

"My dad told me to stay clear of you," Lydia said. "He said he met you once. You didn't speak. But he noticed you. You gave him a vibe of a very dangerous person. He said you were introduced as a your uncle's executive assistant. But Conrod knew you were dangerous. You were the one to watch out for."

Julia didn't respond. She just gave a half nod.

"You mind if I ask a question?" Julia said.

Lydia didn't say anything. But the look on her face was agreeable.

"I know that professional athletes, actors and entertainers have sex with so many women, they forget all they did have sex with. Tell me, did you and my husband ever have sex and maybe he forgot?"

Lydia didn't immediately reply. Julia saw the look in her eyes. She knew the answer even before Lydia responded. "No, no we didn't."

The women continued to exchange gazes. Both knowing history is the past, but a stone throw from the future.

As Julia departed the room, Lydia Smithers sighed a sigh of relieve. For a couple of days in a row, she had somehow cheated death. With Brian, it was being totally honest. With the agent, she told three quarters of the truth. She knew it was a big chance. She rolled the dice that the agent wanted information and wasn't out to kill her. She was right.

The bugs throughout the suite told her Brian didn't trust her. That was dangerous.

Brian Dye was more dangerous.

CHAPTER 34

TIME.

Who can define what's an adequate amount of time? During our relationship, I had probably spent about ten percent of our time together discussing my cases with Julia. In turn, she had probably spent less than five percent discussing her cases with me. However, we had spent one hundred percent of the time loving each other. When I opened my eyes and she was snuggled up next to me, I didn't question it. She was there, I was happy. Sometimes in life, that's the only thing that mattered—being there.

She was snoring, which told me she was tired. She was usually a very sound sleeper. Something told me hearing about Stevie had completely messed up her mojo . . . which also meant she couldn't adequately concentrate on her case until she physically laid eyes on her son. Hell, I didn't know what case she was on or if the investigation was even over. I knew Julia. Family was priority one.

I had gotten in late, which meant I was dirt tired as well since I didn't hear her come in. The alarm wouldn't have gone off if the code was inputted correctly on the elevator code pad. However, I should have at least heard the elevator doors opening.

When she rolled over into my arms, it was a natural instinct to ensure she had a space to roll into. That was us—this was as natural as we got as a couple. Everything fit—from captured to awkward moments, from good times to bad, we always found a way to make it fit us. And at the end of the day, it was about being together. Loving each other. Taking care of family.

Damn. I loved this woman. And I knew she loved me. Something told me she also came here to help me get myself together. I was off kilter on this case. I needed to focus. The simple fact Julia was gracing my presence would fix that. I could never explain it, but our pure presence did that for each other.

Synchronization.

As if on cue, she was nibbling at my neck and her hand was rubbing my johnson. She was a maestro. She knew how to stimulate me. She could play me like a fiddle, stroke my instrument, and get me in the mood. Hell, I was a man and that's wasn't hard to do. The miracle was making me want her more and more as each day passed.

"Well, hello Mrs. Carson."

"Hello yourself," she said back in a sexy and subtle tone as her lips met my lips. My instrument had already gone from soft to super hard in less than five seconds. This woman was truly remarkable. No, it didn't take much. Her presence alone was an aphrodisiac for me. She was the love of my life, my heaven and earth, my virtuous woman. She made our magic work.

Of all things, a soft sensual kiss put me over the edge. Our tongues meeting put me in a frenzy. Natural. My whole body had gone through ten phases of stimulation. From goosebumps to hard nipples, which Julia was teasing with her tongue to occasionally sucking on, to being sexually hot and everything in between. The woman got me, knew me. Tonight, she was the doctor and the conductor. Our bodies were on the verge of being one. And as always, I liked the process of our bodies merging as one.

She was kissing my body in all of the right places. I could feel the symbiotic effects as she crawled over me, moving in a snake like fashion, going from one part of my body to another with the grace of an eagle sizing up its prey. For me, this was the exciting part. The way her fingers exploded my body, light at times, sensual all the time. She had worked herself from my head to my toes at least two times, placing soft kisses and sweet bites in all the right places. I was the ripe fruit ready to be picked and suckled, and the lady of my dreams didn't let me down. When her hot, wet mouth finally engrossed my engorged fluke, it really was heaven on earth. Damn, this was the life.

Julia was a woman on a mission. My body was tingling with excitement. I couldn't wait until the next act, which I didn't have to wait long for. She crawled up my body again, this time resting on top of me. She leaned over and my mouth met her breasts, her perky nipples as she grabbed my fluke and led it to her wet insides. Her internal warmth got me more aroused and I think I even grew another inch or so.

We really were synchronized. Her rhythm met my rhythm, or my rhythm met her rhythm. Regardless of who was in control, we had this thing about multiple positions. It was our thing. It wasn't often our lovemaking consisted of one sexual position. Maybe it was the freak in us. I couldn't tell how long we were engaged in the act. We ended up in a spoon position.

"Damn, I love when your cases stress you out and you need a sexual energizer," I joked. My breath was short. I was spent. This was a helluva workout. I felt good, very good.

Julia said, "I came home to be with my boys." She slid back towards me. We were already close. I didn't think our bodies could be any closer. Evidently, Julia disagreed.

"Talk to me, what's wrong woman?"

"Tired. Worried." I didn't say anything. I was sure she wasn't through talking. "I just needed a break. The case I'm on is mentally draining."

Julia didn't talk about her cases. When we first met, she was the executive assistant for her uncle, Elliot Lucas. He was the regional chief in Baltimore at that time. As Elliot moved up, so did Julia. I would learn later that she was much more than an executive assistant. She had analytical and field agent experience. But her true skills were as an assassin. Julia didn't tell me that information. We had actually worked on a case together, where those skills were very helpful. Additionally, from seeking her analytical advice on numerous investigations, her counsel came from a different perspective—the perspective of an assassin.

I didn't judge. Especially the woman I loved. She was an asset to the Bureau and the country. But more importantly, she was my wife. The woman I loved. Hell, I didn't give a damn if she was the country's number one assassin, she was the person I trusted most in the world.

If she needed me to be her intermission from her case, I was down for that. Her world was different from my world. Being exposed to the secretive life of three alphabet agencies, agents and clandestine operations, the woman knew what she could deal with, what she could take.

I just wished she took more breaks like this.

"I talked to Lydia Smithers," she said before she fell asleep with her head on my bare chest.

I didn't try to wake her . . . this was something that could wait until morning.

CHAPTER 35

THE ESSENTIALITY OF MOM.

I woke up to the smell of bacon, ham and eggs, and an empty bed. Even in Janessa's place, Julia was the woman of the house. It didn't take long before Devin did what Devin loves to do—come running into the room and jump on the bed. He was my little man. The kid was always full of energy. In title, he was still my nephew. However, in my heart he was my son just as much as Stevie.

"Why. Are. You. Jumping. In. My. Bed." I said as I grabbed Devin and ticked him. As he moved and wiggled from my tickling, his hearty laugh was loud. He actually made me feel good.

"Stop, daddy, stop!" he screamed out several times, but I kept going. When I finally stopped, he was exhausted, and so was I. The only difference, he would be reenergized in mere minutes, while it would take me longer.

We lay on the bed as he grabbed the television remote and flipped through the cartoon channels. "Time to get up, dad, momma said breakfast is almost ready."

I smiled. "Devin, that was five minutes ago. How come you didn't say that when you came in?"

"Because you were tickling me." I laughed when he said that and tickled him some more. From the mouths of babes. At this age, kids keep you young.

I often referred to Julia as the All-American girl. There was nothing she couldn't do. From being a good niece to a low-maintenance wife to an extraordinary executive assistant and super-agent, she could do it all. And that included being a superb cook. The only problem was she didn't know when to stop. On the island counter and dining room table was a buffet breakfast—pancakes, waffles, scrambled eggs, grits, ham and cheese omelets, bacon and ham. I could only shake my head. Remarkable. Amazing.

"You know when I'm uneasy, I have to cook," she said.

I said, "I didn't say anything."

"You didn't have to, I know that look."

I didn't question her. In the beginning of our relationship, I was the atypical male, always trying to solve a problem whenever she discussed an issue. She never told me not to solve the issue, but I slowly realized that this woman was ten times smarter than me. She tolerated my attempts of being a problem solver for her.

I was good with that. I realized that if I needed someone to discuss issues with, I had a great one to do it with. After all, many considered her to be one of the top analysts in the Bureau. That was why I was happy when the boys were finished eating and left the kitchen.

"I guess I'm on cleanup duty," Janessa said. "Unless I need to leave." I think she got the feeling I needed to talk to Julia about my case." I was probably antsy and doing a bad job of hiding it.

"You can stay," I responded. "I don't mind if Julia doesn't."

"You're the one who needs to talk," Julia countered. Janessa got up and started cleaning the table. I think we all had smiles painted across our faces. I was pretty sure my smile was the uncomfortable one.

"Tell me about the case," Julia said matter-of-factly, in a calm, let's do it tone.

I smiled more. "Am I that transparent or are you that good?"

"Both," Janessa jumped in. "You are very transparent when it comes to needing your wife's help and she reads you better than anyone I know . . . with the exception of me, that is." We all had a good laugh at my expense.

"What's going on?" Julia asked as she took a sip of coffee.

"It's me," I stated. "I don't have a feel for the case. Can't focus. My mind is elsewhere."

"On the Code of Colors investigation?" she suggested.

"Of course it is."

"You trust Patrick?" she asked, already knowing the answer.

I gave a half-assed smile. "Of course I do. You know I do. That's not the point. The point is I can care less about the rich and famous of Hollywood. I care about assholes who tried to kill my family."

"So passionate," was Julia smartass remark.

She was right though. I was passionate. I wanted revenge in the worse way. Whoever the Code of Colors was, they were my enemies now. I knew the two cases were connected. I was fucking up. I didn't need Julia to tell me that. I needed her to listen, to let me voice my concern. And after the words left my mouth, I knew I was being an ass. But I needed to hear that for myself. It would help me press forward with the investigation I was assigned to. Additionally, since she talked to Lydia, she probably had information I needed.

"Yeah, so passionate," I repeated her statement. "You don't have to say anymore. I get it."

"Yes and no, SSA Carson," she joked. "The Director thinks you are missing a couple of elements of the case that could possibly break everything open."

"Such as?"

"First, you are a field agent. You investigate. But you are best being in control, talking to people of interest. Not staying in one place. Not just working out of a conference room."

"And secondly?"

"Secondly, I took control and handled the other issue for you."

Janessa was still cleaning with ears wide open on our conversation. Sometimes I wondered what she thought of her uncle, what the thought of me. She had done a lot in her young years, way more than anyone in our family had done. She had always been a responsible kid, being the parent to her younger twin brothers when she was just a teenager. I think taking over our company when she was barely out of college was the second biggest thing she had accomplished.

"Tell me about Lydia Smithers."

Julia told me about the conversation they had. I knew my wife. I was sure there were things she left out. I asked her a couple of times if she had done anything to Lydia. The first time she smiled. The second time she gave me a look that said I shouldn't ask that question again. I took in what she told me. And what she conveyed to me was beyond crazy to me.

"What you think the deal is with the listening devices?" I asked.

"Her boyfriend doesn't trust her," Julia replied.

"What boyfriend?"

"Brian Dye."

I didn't blink. Nor did I say anything. If I did say something, it would have been, "What the hell?" I couldn't lie, Lydia was a beautiful woman. But she wasn't a Trinidad Capture. From class to natural beauty to great in the sack, Trinidad could be classified as a woman in her own category, just one class below my wife.

"How do you know that?"

"There was also a hidden camcorder in the ceiling of the master bedroom. Only thing of interest was Brian and Lydia knocking boots. He has feelings for her. She loves him."

My thinking cap was on. I couldn't imagine what these folks did when they were younger to get to this point. Equally, I didn't have a clue who would kill these idiots. And they were idiots to me.

These were folks who had it all from the day they were born and it still wasn't enough. My job was suddenly tougher, harder to get my arms around. I had put myself behind the power curve.

Brian and Lydia could just be items and victims of circumstances. However, I wasn't buying it. First, WMT was deeply involved in this investigation, followed by Lydia showing up in D.C., then a somewhat awkward interview with Brian, and lastly, Brian and Lydia were an item.

I would be jumping on a plane the next day. It was time to get back in the game.

Elliot was right. I was in my own way. I had take control. *Be me.* The *me* who solved cases, who compartmentalized issues and challenges.

Julia and I didn't speak anymore about the investigation. The woman knew me, she knew what made me tick. This was her way of winding me up. And I wasn't stupid . . . Elliot planted the seed, Julia took the information, analyzed it, made an assessment and took action.

I was just hoping Lydia Smithers was still in one piece.

CHAPTER 36

The darkness in hearts beats the drums of doom.

We had an early morning flight to Memphis to have a sit down talk with Ms. Millie Dalbert, the post office manager who had the unfortunate luck of opening a cryogenic freezer unit that contained the head of Wash Tunnell. I had read the report from the Memphis Field Office interview with the manager. Evidently, their video equipment was malfunctioning so they didn't get a chance to record the session. In my mind, the agent's interview from the MFO was incomplete, lacked substance. The questions were generic and short on details. Even when asked a simple question such as "Tell me in your own words, what happened?" Ms. Dalbert's answer was less than twenty words.

We didn't have a set time to interview Ms. Dalbert. We were actually still sitting on the tarmac at the Memphis International Airport, in a parking space reserved for privately owned aircraft. We took one of my company's Gulfstream G550 aircraft. It was always funny to me when I referred to anything as being mine when it came to CarsonOne Productions. Janessa was the CEO and overseer of the company. She had done a marvelous job of making the company way more than I had ever envisioned.

During Elliot's confirmation hearing as director, the question had been raised on whether the company presented a conflict of interest for Elliot. After all, Julia was his niece, co-owner of our company, we both worked for the Bureau and we had multiple contracts within government circles. Both Julia and I were ready to turn in our letters of resignation if it came to that. However, Elliot dutifully deflected the issue. He pointed out that he had no stock or interest in CarsonOne and we were dedicated agents who didn't mix our business with Bureau business. I was surprised that argument worked. Elliot had used our aircraft to travel, especially during clandestine operations and that included transporting agents to various locations. Additionally, when Julia or I traveled on Bureau business, we always traveled using our own aircraft. It was a luxury for us and truthfully, for the Bureau as well.

Conflict of interest? Hell yes it was a conflict.

The media predicted Elliot would have a hard time being confirmed by the Senate. Surprisingly, for the first African-American director of the FBI it only took two weeks from the beginning of hearings to the end. The rumors about Elliot having files on members of the senate ran rampant, which helped his quick confirmation. Knowing the man as I did, I wouldn't be surprised if the rumors were true.

I had shared the clippings and information on the Jet Pack I had received from Julia with Paula Coker. From the moment we sat down on the aircraft until now we had been going over locations of crimes and locations of film shoots of the various members of the Jet Pack. It was hard to believe that six of America's favorite teenagers had grown up to be successful actors and directors, and coldblooded killers.

Unfortunately, even the unbelievable is almost too fucking unbelievable to believe.

From Lydia's clippings, Wash Tunnell was the worst of the three dead actors. He had killed seven people in five states and two overseas locations, Germany and Turkey. Bodies had been buried in open fields or on farmers' properties. The graves were very visible. The latest killing was only three months ago. I remember seeing something on cable news about the death. Ironically, it wasn't a Bureau case. Probably because the first murder was committed almost fifteen years ago, the killings were years apart and in various locations. It was my thought that no one in the Bureau picked up the murders. The Bureau's Behavior Analysis Division was the best in the world and good at identifying similar patterns in investigations, but some things slipped by even the best crime fighters.

Jimmie Claymore was the saint of the group. He had killed only one person, a female, and I was sure it was a situation that had gotten out of hand. It was at a hotel in Dallas, Texas. From the information we had, the young woman was an ad executive who was in town for a few days—she had picked up a man for the night. The police report even stated, initially, the sex seemed consensual, but the man evidently got carried away. From all indications, they were in the doggie style position, playing a game of asphyxiation, and he actually stroked her to death. The hotel cameras caught the man on video, but his face or likeness wasn't visible. That was six years ago.

I didn't want to see or even think of Terri Wenthill as a murderer. Her voice was golden and she was born to act. That thought made me realize that killing may have been a part for her, an out of body experience. If everything we had was true, Terri, like Wash, had also had her first kill some fifteen years ago. Julia told me Lydia didn't think any of the actors knew of the others misgivings, but it was hard for me to believe that. Terri's first kill was approximately two months to the day from Wash's first kill.

It took place in Chicago, while Terri was completing a two-day performance. Being a singer and actress, if she was a killer, she had tons of venues and victims to choose from. The person she killed was a guy in his thirties. He was found in his car with his pants pulled down. From the old police report we had, it was confirmed the man had indeed had sex before he died. A used condom was found at the scene, still on his dismembered penis. He was shot three times above the base of his penis. The ammo slugs were compatible with a .380 semiautomatic handgun.

What made this even more unbelievable were the various methods of death. Supposedly, Terri had killed five times over the years. Two years after the Chicago incident, a young man was killed inside his father's hardware store, beaten to death with a hammer. That was in Nashville, Tennessee. The next crime wouldn't happen for another six years, in New York, a young couple was killed in their home, both shot after they had sex. The police report also mentioned it was possible a third person was involved in their sexual act. The weapon of choice was also a .380. However, there was no reason to connect the New York case with the Chicago case, especially since the cases were eight years apart.

She had killed again that same year, this time in Wichita Falls, Texas, an Air Force captain stationed at Sheppard Air Force Base. He was found dead in his bathtub. Detectives had deduced that he had been hit with a Taser first, while he was in the bathroom, and probably fell in. Looking at the photographs of his death, his body was at a very awkward angle. It looked as if his head had hit the hot water knob, forcing his head to twist. His legs were dangling over the side of the tub. And a box of three unopened condoms was thrown on his body. I didn't know what that signified, but it wasn't good.

"Wow, this is so damn . . ." Paula had trouble finding the right word to describe what she was feeling.

"Bizarre, remarkable, crazy, freakish," I tried helping.

"I don't know what to say," she replied.

We were working on killing number five in regards to possible murders committed by Terri Wenthill. I kept using the word *if* in relation to all of the clippings and information we had. We began the process last night, reaching out to various police departments throughout the country as well as surfing the internet, trying to correlate the Jet Pack members to the locations of crimes committed per Lydia's clippings. She had also made notes related to each crime and actor, and why she thought the actor was responsible.

Her work was very detailed and thought out. She was a true public relations goddess. From what we were reading, she would have made an excellent attorney. Hell, from her meticulous attention to detail I wanted to hire her at CarsonOne as our PR person.

Everything was still so unbelievable. I was still having a hard time wrapping my head around any of this. The troubling part for us as a Bureau was twofold—one, proving any of this in court, if we ever got to court, and two, trying to boil down a no-shit list of suspects for these killings.

"I don't know if I told you this or not, but I'm a big Terri Wenthill fan," Paula said out of the blue. Our coordinated effort consisted of me checking out a specific crime via the internet and Paula checking out police reports. Some of the reports we had received faxed information. Other reports were accessed via email or access to various databases.

"So am I," I replied. "Actually, I'm a movie and TV buff when I get the time. Plus, I love music."

"Yeah, I love music as well."

"What kind of music?" I asked. "Let me guess, you like country and western, but not at the same time."

She laughed. "Funny. I'm a jazz lover, especially piano tunes, and classic rock and roll."

"Really?" I am surprised.

I was expecting Paula to come back with something else, but she didn't. We were sitting across from each other on the plane. I looked over and she was as white as a sheet.

"KC, do you see who victim number five is?" she asked me.

I hadn't checked out the name. When I did, I understood why Paula had gotten quiet.

Victim number five was Hendrix Merry. He was found outside Columbia, South Carolina, in the backseat of his Ford Sedan naked from the waist down. There was a knife in the back of his neck, where he had been stabbed three times, and once in the middle of his back. The report stated he had also had sex before he died.

The investigation was still fresh. It had occurred nine months ago and a wave of shock had spread throughout the Bureau.

And he had died on the job.

Hendrix Merry was an FBI special agent on an undercover assignment when he was killed.

This was a game changer.

CHAPTER 37

THERE ARE MOMENTS WHEN THE WORLD TRULY DOESN'T MAKE SENSE.

Dr. Lazarus Rossey remembered when deoxyribonucleic acid became the lay of the land with the Bureau. He had been a doctor for six years, working for the Air Force Research Laboratory when he applied for a job with the FBI's infamous Crime Laboratory, or the Lab, as it was called throughout the halls of the Bureau. That was around 1986. Two years later, he was one of many personnel assigned to the research and development team to research the use of DNA analysis to solve crimes.

Since those days, the use of DNA had blown up exponentially. He had held numerous positions throughout the lab over the years, to include opening multiple satellite or regional offices in the U. S. When one of his team chiefs called and asked him if he and his team members could come for a meeting, he didn't think anything of it. He was sure they had run into a situation that either doctor had experienced before.

They knew, as he knew, there wasn't a situation he had never experienced before.

He was in the office of the Director now, which was a place he was use to. He was also used to the man himself. He and Director Lucas had a long history. Once upon a time, he was the team chief on all of Elliot's investigations. He knew the man and the man knew him. Also present was Maxwell Pack and his team chief, Dr. Bobby Padgett, who had brought this issue to his attention.

"Talk to me, Old Man," Elliot initiated the conversation, referring to Dr. Rossey. That was his handle for the doctor he considered a friend and valued colleague.

"Well, Top Dog, you know how we always laughed that one day there would truly be something I had never seen before?" Elliot shook his head. Dr. Rossey got up from his seat and put a twenty-dollar bill on Elliot's desk. The director didn't like where this was going. He had known the man for over two decades and he knew this couldn't be good.

"I finally won the bet, even though it took over ten or fifteen years, huh?" Elliot replied.

"Yes you did, Top Dog, yes you did." Dr. Rossey sat back down and the two exchanged gazes. "Director, the damnedest thing occurred in the Jet Pack case. You know we have three bodies now. You are now going to believe this shit, because it is truly remarkable and un-fucking-believable."

Elliot was fascinated by the excitement and confusion in his friend's voice. "What you got, Old Man?"

"Top Dog, we've run tests ten times, and every time, we've received the same results. All three DNA results from the Jet Pack members we have . . . have the same biological father."

Elliot leaned forward in his chair. The interest of Maxwell Pack was also piqued. The men looked at each other. For several moments the room was filled with silence.

"You sure about that Old Man?" Elliot asked.

"Yes, sir," Dr. Padgett intervened. "For paternity, every marker on all three victims matched. We had our two closest locations accomplish their own tests, without us providing them any information of our findings. This is highly unusual, sir, but they are all related. They all have the same father."

"Dr. Rossey, did you write me up a one-page narrative?" Elliot asked.

"As always, Top Dog, as always."

"Also, Old Man, I have a project for you and your people," Elliot added.

"Anything Director."

"I need you to pull everything you have on the Special Agent Hendrix Merry investigation and run the foreign DNA tests again. I remember we couldn't match some female hair particles with anything in the national database. See if those hair particles match Theresa Wenthill's."

"What? Seriously sir?" Dr. Padgett asked.

"No problem, Tog Dog, I'm on it," Dr. Rossey responded. The two doctors departed the room. Once again, silence dominated the room. Maxwell didn't want to interfere with the director while he was in thought.

"What do you think?"

"On which issue sir?" Maxwell replied.

"On the craziness of this damn case," Elliot clarified.

Maxwell said, "My experience is very minimal with these people sir. You know them. You have broken bread with them, spent time with them. In other words, you know better than anyone if these kids were capable of doing what Lydia Smithers is saying they did, and as far as the whole one father issue, you probably know who the father is."

"That's the thing, Max, I do know. And it's not one of those three, I guarantee you. And if those three members of the Jet Pack are related, there is a good possibility the others may be related as well."

"The others, as in the remainder of the Jet Pack?"

"Exactly. And it may shed some light on what's what in this damn case."

It was the first time Maxwell had heard any type of frustration in Elliot's voice in a very long time. The man wasn't human. He didn't stress or get flustered over investigations or nuances of investigations. He knew it was the murder of Special Agent Merry. Any fellow agent hated losing another agent, especially to something this senseless. Ever since Carson shared the news, Elliot had been in another place.

"Hollywood is a suck ass business," Elliot stated. "The likes of Thomas Wenthill, Regan Claymore and Armstrong Tunnell would sleep around, but none of them were stupid enough or had the ego to father multiple kids and set them up to be the top actors in the business.

"Only one man had that kind of ego and that kind of power. Only one man would set these events in motion years ago and wouldn't have the foresight to see the disaster it would bring years later."

"I will jump on the horn and notify Carson of this information."

"No. Not a good idea, Max. Get with the Old Man and let him know that information stays within the lab and with you and me. Let Carson and his team stay the course. I have faith in he and Jo Jo, but Taylor and Coker may let the information slip.

"No. Stay the course. Carson needed to regain his legs, become the KC of old. He's back, which means we are in a good position. This is not information he needs to complete his investigation. But I do want him to find out what started this whole mess. If these kids are truly killers, what set them down this path? It had to be an event so devastating and mind-bending, that it turned decent kids into lifetime murderers. I want to know what it was."

CHAPTER 38

Memories stay with us for a lifetime.

Memphis and I had a love/hate relationship. It was my hometown and still had a place in my heart. I just wasn't sure what place it held—the light or the darkness. Regardless of how much death I had encountered in my life, my mother's death was the hardest. And when she died, a part of my heart had died as well. My sister, Alyse, and I had moved to Nashville with our brother, Steve, during my sophomore year in high school. My father, Howard Carson, was too distraught to raise us, coupled with him and I having an estranged relationship, it was a good decision for Steve to raise us.

Whenever I returned to the city, my mom was always my first thought. Then, it was Howard Carson and our turbulent history. I was sure, as a baby, I probably peed on him every opportunity I got and I was equally sure he probably found reasons to spank my butt every chance he got. He was a son-of-a-bitch when I was younger and very mean to my mother. He and my mom fought a lot and I would learn years later that my mom could be a handful as well. I never saw that part of my mom, nor did I want to believe it. But evidently I was the only one who didn't see it.

I'd like to think my mother didn't have a choice. Steve was really my half-brother. We shared Howard's blood, but we had different mothers. I also had two other siblings Howard fathered by another woman. A brother and sister no one had heard from in over two decades. Both were bastards who made my life a living hell. The rumor was they were dead. I didn't know, nor did I give a damn.

Unfortunately, I would lose both Steve and Alyse to death. Those deaths weren't attributed to Memphis. However, the city represented both good and bad times for me. Deep in my heart, as long as my mother was buried here, I would consider it my hometown.

It took us probably a good thirty minutes to get from the airport to the Highland Street post office. We already had a car waiting on us when we landed. The post office was actually on the outskirts of the neighborhood where I grew up. We had also touched base with the Memphis Field Office prior to leaving D.C. and had an agent meet us at the post office just in case we needed assistance. He stayed in the car as conducted our interview.

Julia was right. I was a field agent. I did my best work in the field conducting my own investigation. I could sit in a situation room, look at other agents work, but it wouldn't feel like my investigation. Julia made me realize that was the problem with this investigation, I didn't feel like it was mine. They say ownership is nine tenth of the law, but not if you don't feel like you have ownership.

I felt right. I had ownership.

It was around eleven in the morning on a Friday when we arrived, lunchtime for some, pre-lunch for others. In my mind, I was envisioning workers throughout America clock watching, waiting on eleven-thirty or twelve o'clock to go to lunch. For many in the workplace, lunchtime was an everyday milestone. It began the countdown to the end of the workday. I couldn't help but wonder if Millie Dalbert was one of those people.

The Highland post office was small. It looked small on the outside, but was bigger internally. The manager's office was in the back of the post office. I thought the clerk was going to have a heart attack when he looked at our badges and we asked to see his manager. I didn't know if he was just normally nervous, or if he had actually done something illegal and wondered if we were coming for him.

Another male worker escorted us to the manager's office. Interestingly, even with cluster of mail bins and mailbags, the post office looked even larger in the back area. There were four individual rooms and a break room, with two sets of lockers on opposite walls. Ironically, the place had a French vanilla smell to it. I wondered if it smelled that way because there was a female manager. Looking at the wall outside of the manager's office, there were pictures of the employees who worked at the post office. Of the twelve employees, five were females.

Our escort told the manager we were outside her door and she summoned us in. I hadn't read much about Millie Dalbert. I knew she was African-American, originally from Kansas City, Kansas. She had worked for the post office for almost fifteen years and was one of the youngest employees to become a post office manager.

Millie Dalbert walked around her desk and shook our hands. She was dressed in her post office blues, light blue short-sleeved shirt with the post office emblem above her left breast and dull blue pants.

"Hey, I'm Millie Dalbert, manager of the Highland station," she introduced herself.

I pulled out my ID and badge, "Supervisory Special Agent Carson, and my partner, Agent Coker." As we shook hands, I looked at Millie. She had soft features, stood about five six, medium build, with an athletic statute. She had a short hairdo and burgundy rimmed glasses that went great with her walnut brown complexion. Even from the front, I could tell she made the ugly and dull uniform fit her just right. She wasn't exactly busty, nor was she anywhere near small.

"Do we know each other, Ms. Dalbert?" I asked out of curiosity. She looked very familiar, but I couldn't put my finger on it, I couldn't place where we had met or encountered each other. I had a great memory, terrific recall, but I was off. I was trying my best to regain my focus or at least keep my primary focus on this one case.

"No, Agent Carson, I don't think so," she replied in a soft voice. "Have a seat," she stated, as she led us to a small circular table. "What can I do to help? What can I tell you that I didn't tell your last agent?"

"We are just trying to be thorough, Ms. Dalbert," Paula answered. She and I had discussed her taking the lead in interviewing Millie Dalbert. I wanted to observe Millie as well as let Paula gain more experience. "As you can probably imagine, this whole situation is unnerving. Of course, everyone looked at these actors as the Jet Pack Eight, but they were also sons and daughter, brothers and sister, and in the case of Wash Tunnell, a father who had children, a boy and girl. So we want to make sure we turn over every rock."

Millie didn't flinch. Her demeanor was calm. No signs of nervousness. Maybe it was my imagination. Maybe I was trying to convince myself this woman had something to hide. I was getting a feeling something wasn't right. It was as if she was holding back something, and that something could be gas, a smirk or even laughter. I don't know what I expected, but I expected something more besides a woman forcing herself not to react. And the more I looked at her, the more I got that feeling we knew each other. Or maybe the simple fact that her clerk was so nervous and she was a hundred and eighty degrees different from him was throwing me off.

"I understand," she finally responded awkwardly. I think her reaction had totally stumped Paula Coker.

"Can you please go through everything that transpired that day, from your first time seeing the cryogenic freezer unit to actually opening the unit, and your subsequent actions afterwards?"

Millie went through everything that transpired that day. She told us that day was her birthday and the package arrived around nine-thirty that morning, with instructions to open at ten. She thought the unit was a gag gift from her sister, Sarah, and her doctor husband. That's why she didn't panic when she saw World Medical Transporters stenciled on two sides of the containment unit. She remembered the smokey vapors emerging from the freezing cold unit when she opened it. Then she saw the severed head of Wash Tunnell, with his eyes still open. The next thing she remembered was waking up on the floor with her employees squatting and standing over her.

Her mannerism was direct and to the point. There were no emotions behind her words. She told us the A, B and C of what happened. A man's head was in a freezer unit, she passed out. That's an emotional reaction to a person she didn't know personally. That was nothing new. It was a dramatic event, a scary moment. A severed head would freak the hell out of anyone.

But now, giving us her account of what happened, Millie Dalbert showed no emotions. When I read the report, although it didn't state the same, I got the feeling she gave the agent the same information she gave us. If the agent had videotaped the interview, I was sure she would have had the same emotionless look on her face.

As soon as she quit talking, Paula wasted no time with her first question. "Did you know Mr. Tunnell?"

"Only from his movies and TV appearances."

"So you immediately recognized the severed head as Wash Tunnell?" Paula quickly retorted.

However, Millie Dalbert didn't answer as quick. In her eyes, I could see her mind searching for an answer. I didn't expect this.

"Of course not. Where would I have met a movie star like Wash Tunnell?" She tried her best to laugh it off. I was impressed with Paula Coker. I wanted to see how this whole thing played out.

"Ms. Dalbert, you told the other agent you recognized the head as Wash Tunnell immediately," I intervened. "When I read that I thought it was strange."

"Why so?" she asked.

"Because when a head is severed from its body, it tends to lose its natural look," I stated. "Some heads may actually swell— cheeks and eyes getting a little puffier. While other faces may get a little darker as crazy as that may sound since the flow of blood is terminated. In other words, Ms. Dalbert, when trying to identify a loved one, it's hard to recognize a severed head, let alone a person who is not familiar to them.

"So are you sure you didn't know Mr. Tunnell? Maybe when you were younger or maybe in your travels, you met Mr. Tunnell?"

"I don't know what you are implying, agent, but I don't sleep around, and I certainly don't have one night stands. Not when I was younger and not now. I wish I knew why someone would send me Wash's head. But I don't know why I was selected."

Millie Dalbert looked at me as if I was the wicked witch stealing her child. Actually, I think she was looking through me, trying to find an answer. "I really don't know if I like your implications," she stated.

The room was filled with tension. I'm sure the three of us had various thoughts occupying our minds. For me, I thought about something Elliot Lucas had taught me years ago. If you ever wanted to make an interview awkward, put the interviewee on the defensive. You just had to know what would rattle their chain.

For Millie Dalbert, it was the idea of sleeping around—the thought of her being an easy lay.

The next thought on my mind was Paula Coker had missed it. Millie Dalbert did know Wash Tunnell. She made it personal when she mentioned *Wash's head.* There was a gleam in her eye when she said that. An ounce of familiarity. She definitely knew Wash Tunnell.

"Ms. Dalbert, we looked up your employment history and the only job you have ever had is the one you are currently in," Paula said. "By official records, you have never been married. The house you live in, you bought it as soon as you moved to Memphis, and you paid three hundred thousand for it. Additionally, the two addresses we have for you in Kansas City, Missouri were apartments that are no longer there, and the realty offices are no longer in existent, so we cannot verify you ever lived at these addresses.

"Also, by official government records, you didn't exist until fifteen years ago."

The two women exchanged gazes. I was proud of Paula. She was in control, and once again, the wheels were turning in Millie's brain. *We were in her head.*

"And? What's your point, Agent Coker?"

"Can you tell us where you got the money to buy a house worth three hundred thousand dollars with no prior work history?" I chimed in. It was the double barrel effect, and it was working.

"I came from a well to do family and didn't have to work. I am the youngest of three kids and I was my mother's baby girl. One day, I woke up unhappy with my life and decided it was time for a change. So I moved here to start fresh. If that's a crime, evidently someone forgot to tell the United States Postal Service."

The woman was lying about something or holding something back, but what, we had no idea. What was her involvement in this mess? This was one of a thousand and one thoughts swimming around in my head.

"Millie," I said, "how do you know Wash Tunnell?"

Once again, she was uneasy. But this time, she didn't hesitate. "I do not know Wash Tunnell," she stated. "Never met the man in person. Only seen him on TV."

The attitude in her voice was obvious. The first interview she was prepared for. This one, not so much. Rehearsed versus spur of the moment.

"Officially, this interview is over, Ms. Dalbert," I stated. "For now, we will let you be. However, we are coming back. In the meantime, I want you to call your attorney, if you have one. If not, you may want to invest in one. Complete your shift today, but I want you to think about one thing."

I signaled Paula to get up. Coming to Memphis was a matter of convenience and to get me more focused on this case, my investigation. I never expected this. I didn't know what it meant. Millie Dalbert knew Wash Tunnell. That may have been why his severed head was sent to her. How she knew him was the mystery. Why she was lying was probably a bigger mystery.

She was on my radar, and for good reason.

"Pardon me, Agent Carson," she said as we turned to depart her office. The tension in her voice was very pronounced. As much as she was trying to mask the stress, she couldn't. "What one thing?"

"To be honest."

CHAPTER 39

THE SPEED OF LIGHT HAS NEVER BEATEN THE SPEED OF BAD NEWS.

Conrod Bach didn't think there was anything more majestic than the view from his penthouse balcony. He had a view of Los Angeles and on a clear, smog-free day he could see the city come alive. He could take in the hustle and bustle of the immediate downtown area—which was the location of his company and penthouse—to the mountains that sat on the outskirts of the city. To his west, he could take in the breathtaking view of the blue-green waters of the Pacific Ocean. The building was approaching thirty years old. Over the past five years, he could count the number of times on his fingers and toes he had been out of this building.

He considered himself to be a blessed man. Regardless of how fucked up and jaded he had been in life, for whatever reason, the Good Lord had taken care of him. He didn't completely understand it. He was convinced his shortcomings outweighed the good he had done in life by a country mile. And he had done a lot of good . . . which meant he had done his share of bad, and then some. He wasn't as spry as he once was. He used to be a man of action, a man on the move.

He had just lit up his favorite Cuban cigar when his son, Sylvester, joined him on the balcony, which was the size of half a football field.

"We need to talk," Sylvester announced. He was his father's son as far as looks went. Like his father, he had a full head of black hair, slim face and baby blue eyes that sat wide on his face. The only issue Conrod Bach had with his son was his height. He didn't have his father's stature. Conrod was all of six -foot four, while Sylvester barely stood five-feet-eight.

"Have a seat Sly," father said to son. Conrod was lying back on a row of loungers that were close to the patio doors. The area was covered with green turf that was soft to the touch.

Conrod also saw the big manila folder in his son's hand. He knew some things you couldn't run away from forever. As much as he had tried to run away from his past, he knew one day it would seek him out and find him.

This was that day.

If he could, he would have laughed at the moment. However, it would have been rude to find the humor in his actions. As much as he wouldn't acknowledge it publicly, he knew his past was an embarrassment, something the offspring he openly accepted as his blood would have to live down. The fact he had billions would ease the blow, and in his world, money always made the pain fade faster.

But this day was finally upon him, and he had to be man enough to face the music.

"Damn, life can be great some days," he said to Sylvester, who actually preferred his God-given name. However, his father was the only one who called him Sly. "I wish I could say to hell with it all, son, and just move to a tropical island and enjoy life."

He took another puff of his Cuban and blew out three rings of smoke. "My father taught me that. I ever tell you that?"

"No sir, you didn't," Sylvester answered.

The two men looked over the horizon and continued to take in the view. No words were exchanged. As much as Sylvester wanted to further the discussion, for now he was content. He loved the man others knew as the King of Hollywood, but he was hard to talk to. Unfortunately, this was the day he had to gather up the strength and get the words out. This was business as well as pleasure. When they had their best talks, they were always surrounded by business. The pleasure part was few and far between.

"I ever tell you about my old man, your grandfather?" Conrod asked. Even before his son could reply, he kept talking. "Brutus Baxter Barron, King Son of a Bitch."

"What? Brutus Barron? The billionaire, the oil baron?" a surprised Sylvester shockingly expressed.

"And one in the same. My father, my old man. Love that old motherfucker." Conrod took a shot of his cognac, followed by another pull of his Cuban. "Yep, I was the second oldest son, the fifth oldest child. The first four kids were my three sisters, then my oldest brother, and then me. After me, my parents had more four children—two girls and two boys. These were all the kids my father claimed . . . those who came from his wife, my mother. Growing up, there were two farm hands and a house-girl, the young daughter of our housekeeper.

"The two farm hands were my half-brothers, sons my father had with other women. The house-girl was my half-sister. I didn't know this until years later, but my mom knew about them all. But the rumor was my father had over twenty damned kids, but still, he only claimed nine, me and my brothers and sisters who came out of my mother's womb."

"Damn, Conrod, why in the fuck are you telling me this now?"

"Because I can, son . . . because I can. Plus, this is the end of the road for your old man. And somebody needs to know my story. At some point and time, you can sit around with your brothers and sisters and share the story. That is, if you choose to do so. But at least one of my kids will know my story and will know the stories being told about me are real, are true. And Sly, it will be up to you to decide if you want to respond to the rhetoric, say a comment or defend my legacy in court."

Sylvester Bach walked the few feet to the outdoor bar, grabbed a shot glass, along with another bottle of cognac. It was midday in L.A., and he wasn't a drinker. When he did drink, it was usually at night, in the comfort of his home. He was a family man with a beautiful wife and three equally beautiful daughters. He felt his life and career had been guided by his father.

All the rumors and stories he had always heard, he was about to hear from the man himself.

This would be . . .

. . . the rest of the story.

CHAPTER 40

THE GOLDEN GOOSE SOMETIMES LAID TAINTED EGGS.

"I'm not sure exactly how old I was when my father sat my brother and me down," Conrod began. "I was somewhere north of twenty and south of twenty-five." He took another swig of his cognac, followed by another pull on his cigar. "My brother, Arnold, was truly the good son. Dad had sent him to college to be a business major and CPA. And that sonofabitch was great with numbers.

"But Dad sat us down to do what I'm doing now, tell us about his life. Son, I should tell you first, I was a pistol back in those days. If it walked and it looked good, I was trying to jump on it. Hell, I looked like John Wayne or Gary Cooper, with my slender and muscular physique, plus I had the Barron name, which meant I came from money. And Sly, regardless of what anyone tells you, money improves your looks tenfold."

Conrod Bach had to laugh at his own joke. Sylvester had had several shots and was now lying back on his lounger. He was taking it all in. He definitely had an interest. His father was a private person. His privacy was like a chest of gold he hid from others. Even if the conversation only lasted ten minutes, he wanted to hear it. He had to hear it, before he broke his own news—news he was sure his father already knew was coming.

"Dad was pissed at me because I had slept with this golden haired filly in Midwest City, on the outskirts of Oklahoma City, not far from the Air Force base. Evidently, she and I shared the same father." He turned his face to look at Sylvester, who had a look of surprise on his face.

"Dad wasn't too happy with me," he continued talking. "He began telling me about all of the dirt he knew about me. Then he broke the news that his daughter, the golden haired filly in Midwest City, was having an abortion and another girl I had impregnated in the area was also having an abortion.

"I couldn't say shit, son. My old man made the decisions in the family and we didn't object. Hell, I could have objected but he probably would have kicked my ass. He was six-foot three, two hundred sixty pounds of pure muscle and probably in his early to mid-fifties at that time, and he still had the venom of a viper mixed with a cobra. I had personally seen him kick younger guys' asses on numerous occasions.

"One of the big differences between us, I was a lot nicer son. Your grandfather could and would kick someone's ass at the drop of a dime. His temper was short, his bite hard and strong. He often said he had a low tolerance for bullshit, and he never lied. Hell, I thought he was going to kick my ass that day. But no, he gave me a reprieve. Sort of anyway."

Conrod rose and put both his feet on the ground, taking a seated position on his lounger. Sylvester kept lying down, but he turned his body to face his father.

"Sly, sometimes we really don't know what we don't know. I didn't know that one of the best things in the world is having your old man to talk to you. Whether it's about life or fucking up, just the act of a father conveying knowledge and wisdom to his son is priceless. Dad telling us about his life was gold. Priceless."

Sylvester was speechless. Out of all of his father's children, he probably had the closest relationship with the old man. This wasn't a first and now he understood why his father always bent his ear—it was something he inherited from his father.

"When he told us about everything he owned, and how wealthy he really was, I think my brother and I nearly passed out. Sly, we didn't have a clue. Hell, I don't think my mother even knew everything Dad was into. The man loved Western movies, so he owned prime land in the Dakotas, Montana and Wyoming, and many Western movies during the sixties were filmed on his properties. In Dallas, Little Rock, Pittsburgh and several other cities he owned office buildings that were also used for movie and televsion sets. The man owed storage facilities, parking lots, apartment buildings and furniture stores. And all of this was on top of his oil and cattle companies.

"When I tell you your grandfather was one of the first billionaires in the world, it's not an exaggeration, the fucking man was loaded."

Like a sudden strike of lightning, Sylvester saw the excitement fade from his father's face. His eyes were glassy and Sylvester was sure he was forming tears. Then Conrod gave a half-assed smile, but his face still possessed a somber gaze.

"Then he told my brother and me about all of the illegitimate kids he had." Conrod's delivery was slow and deliberate, and filled with emotion. "The old geezer told us he had over thirty fucking kids, and that didn't include us. And he was an equal opportunity fucker—white, black, Mexican, Asian, he didn't give a damn. Hell, I think he even had some European kids."

Conrod shook his head, and grabbed the bottle of cognac that sat on the ground between the two men. This time, he preferred the bottle over the small glass he had previously used. He took a long swallow. Brought the bottle down and took another one.

"My punishment Sly, for impregnating my half-sister—a woman I didn't know was my sister—and the other girl, was pulling up stakes and moving to California. Son, I almost shit on myself when he told me that. But he told me it was time I used my degree and have some fun at the same time. So, to California I came with a new surname, Bach, my mother's maiden name. And my first job outside the family was working for HD Films, or Hoover Dam Films."

He looked out at the horizon and threw both his arms up and forward. "I built this son. Every single brick. I worked at HD for three years writing screenplays for movies and TV shows. And, my dick of a boss, the CEO of HD, Harry Tunnell, threw every one of them in the trash. One day I called my father, told him I wanted to branch out on my own and he told me no. He ordered me to meet him in the boardroom of HD a couple of days afterwards.

"Two days later, Sly, I was the first one in the room for the weekly staff meeting. Mr. Tunnell wanted to know why in the fuck I was there. Before I could say anything, my father walked in and told Tunnell I was now the CEO of the company.

"Sly, I looked at my father like he was fucking crazy, like he was on drugs. Harry Tunnell had this look like someone had just fucked his wife right in front of him or something. My father told him to get the fuck out of the building and told me to take a seat at the head of the table. Then security guards escorted Tunnell out the building.

"It was then my father explained to everyone in that room that HD Films was a subordinate company of B&B Productions, another company my father owned—lot, stock and barrel. That sonofabitch Tunnell wasn't worth a damn. Every TV show the company had was doing bad in the ratings, every movie produced was a flop. I took over and everything changed. We became a success almost overnight. I did everything—from writing scripts to movies, selecting casts, marketing our products, the whole nine yards.

"Sly, I took the business by storm. But son, I had the same problem my father had. I was screwing everything, and like my dad, I was procreating. I couldn't get enough of pussy. And it seemed like every woman I had sex with got pregnant."

"Dad, what are you really trying to tell me?" Sylvester's impatience was shining through. He didn't like the direction of the conversation. He felt as if his father was trying to tell him something really bad, maybe borderline catastrophe. He wasn't sure, but that was his mindset at the moment. Maybe the cognac was getting to him. After all, he was drinking with no food on his stomach.

"I guess, in a way, I am somewhat rambling son," his father fessed up. "Some things are hard as hell to admit . . . to accept. You are a father, and I'm very proud of you. But you know it's hard being the perfect parent or admitting your shortcomings to your children."

He was about to turn the bottle of cognac up again, but just looked at the bottle. He looked at his son with sad eyes. He liked the way the conversation was going. He liked his rambling. He had never been described as a talkative man. He was a king in his world and kings didn't need to be talkative, just heard.

That was his son's role, to listen. It was as if they were having a normal conversation. But like they were in a game of five-card stud, Sylvester's impatience had called his bluff, and now he had to fold or show his cards.

In a perfect world, he would fold and table this conversation for another day. The world he lived in wasn't perfect. He didn't choose to show his hand, but circumstances dictated his decisions.

"All the kids who attended the Herbert Brutus School were fathered by me," he had quietly, slowly, ensuring he pronounced every word meticulously.

Sylvester's mind was spinning. He had thoughts. He knew what he wanted to say, but he couldn't will his mouth to move.

"Over a hundred kids attended that school over the years Conrod," Sylvester finally managed to say.

"Yeah, I know son," he replied weakly.

Sylvester stood and looked down on his father. He was disgusted and disappointed. Actually, he didn't know what kind of mood he was in. In his mind, he had unrelenting questions he needed answered. He knew the man had children outside of his marriage. Hell, it wasn't a secret in Hollywood and it certainly wasn't a secret in their household. Ever since he could recall, his father spent more time in his penthouse than he did in their Beverly Hills home.

Life could be an unkind morsel to deal with, a foul ingredient to digest. It was hard for a son to wrap his head around his father birthing well over a hundred children—and that was the number he had read somewhere. He didn't truly know the correct number.

He didn't say anything else. He couldn't say anything else.

He threw the manila folder on his father's lap, and then proceeded to the patio door.

Conrod Bach heard the doors to the elevator close as he continued to look at the manila folder.

He knew the true meaning of the word *bastard*. After all, he created *bastards*.

CHAPTER 41

OFTEN TIMES THE MIND NEEDS A VACATION MORE THAN THE BODY.

I needed a reprieve. I still couldn't put my hands on what it was about Millie Dalbert. She looked familiar, but I couldn't place her face. I was pissed at myself. I was doing a shitty job. My focus wasn't completely on this one case.

I had allowed the Code of Colors investigation to steal my focus. I gave a lot of props to detectives like Clayton Melvin who could juggle five or six cases at a time. Clay had told me once that the top two cases always outweighed the others, but it was about prioritizing.

As a new agent, working at the regional level, that was the protocol as well—multiple investigations, but usually no more than three. I was out to make a name for myself, so I put in eighteen-hour days and many times I slept in the office or even in my car, staking out crime scenes. My success helped me move up fast, but I think a lot of that had to do with Elliot. He was my regional chief on two occasions and taught me the ins and outs of being a special agent.

Focus. That was Elliot's key lesson. "Stay on point," he would say. "And know the who from the what and the why from the how."

That was on my mind as I drove to my dad's house. I had dropped Paula off at the hotel. She had homework to do. I actually offered her to tag along, but she decided I needed family time. I wasn't sure she was right about that, but my mind really did need a vacation. I couldn't get Millie Dalbert and the thought I was being played out of my mind. Conrod Bach wanted me on this case. I couldn't prove it, but one thought kept creeping into my thought pattern—the attack on Stevie's school was about me. I didn't know why and didn't know if I was paranoid or making any sense. I felt as if someone was calling the shots and they needed me on this case. Maybe the diversion would draw my attention away from the Code of Colors investigation, enabling them to succeed in their mission. All of this was conjecture on my part.

My thinking could have been completely off—I felt my thought pattern was crazy. The attack happened before Patrick or I was assigned to our respective investigations. It was just strange for Conrod Bach to request me for this case. Did I think Bach was connected to the Code of Colors case? Not at all. However, deep down, I couldn't help to think there was a connection between the Code investigation and Jet Pack Eight investigation.

The screen door was unlocked and the big door was wide open. Although the street and neighborhood had changed, some things hadn't. Many older folks who had lived in the community for years still opened their doors on nice days like today. I wanted to say to allow the sunshine in, but that wasn't the reason. It was to see what was going on outside. To see who was walking up or down the street. As my mother used to say, being nosey, in other people's business.

I heard voices coming from the dining room, and then my father called out, "Who's in my house?"

"It's me, Pop, your son," I answered back. When I turned the corner from the living room to dining room, Howard Carson was sitting at the dining room table on his cell phone.

"Ok, lil' lady, we'll talk later and I love you," he said into the phone.

We shook hands and hugged when he got off the phone. "My granddaughter said hello and be careful," he said.

"I like that, your granddaughter," I replied. "How you doing, old man?"

"Doing good young buck, doing good. How in the hell are you?"

"Doing good as well Pop."

He stepped back and held me at arm's length, looking me over. The smile across his face was genuine. He and I had had our moments over the years. For most of my life our relationship could be defined as somewhat tumultuous. Since the death of Alyse, we had mended our relationship. For the past three or four years, we could be called father and son.

"I smell food," I said. "And it smell like barbeque, chitterlings and greens."

"That's all you smell."

"Come on now, Pop, I'm sure you have spaghetti as well." He laughed. Howard Carson was one of the best grillers I knew when it came to cooking ribs or anything else on a grill. And in Memphis, if you had barbeque, spaghetti, pork chitterlings, greens and grilled corn on the cob were a part of the meal.

I went into the kitchen and made me a plate, and returned to the dining room table. I ate while we talked. I actually felt good. It was nice being home again. It sounded funny—home. I thought about my mother, but put those thoughts to the side. I didn't want to mess up the moment. We were having a good conversation.

It was nice to get my mind off the case for a minute or two.

Pop told me how the family was doing. He was the oldest of eight children, five boys and three girls. Three of his siblings were dead. Two other brothers lived in other states. He had two sisters who also lived in Memphis. They were as close as brother and sisters could be.

After I ate, we moved the conversation to the living room. Our conversation stayed on family and that was a good thing. It was good catching up. Both of us were in this place—a good place, a well place.

I don't know when I fell asleep.

Somewhere in the deep crevices of my head, my mind was thanking me for giving it a break.

Often times the mind needs a vacation . . .

CHAPTER 42

THE PERILS OF LIFE START WITH FAMILY . . . AND A GOOD
ASSWHIPPING.

I smiled at that statement. That was my mom's saying. She used
to tell me that my father and I would be okay . . . as long as we
kept our distance. I know I wasn't the only one who felt that way.
I could never verify or validate the theory, but something told me
Pop thought the same.

After waking up, I had a helping of banana pudding. My father
was a damn good cook. He wasn't mom, but he knew his way
around the kitchen. I was shocked when I found out he was the
baker in the family and not my mother. She was a great cook, and I
always bragged about her desserts. As I enjoyed my second helping
of banana pudding, I shook my head at the irony.

"So, how was the interview?" my father asked me as he flipped
through the channels. He was sitting in his favorite recliner, with
his feet kicked up.

I was laughing inside. The old man had actually pulled out his
laptop computer and was playing solitaire. Even more crazy to me
was the simple fact he had a laptop computer. When Janessa told
me she bought him an Apple MacBook, I think I hurt my side
from laughing so much. But he had Yahoo, Hotmail and Gmail
accounts that I knew about. I didn't want to think about what
other accounts he probably had.

"It was okay," I said. "Millie Dalbert, the post office manager who opened the container with the head of one of the actors, I think she's hiding something. It has been in the news and definitely on the Internet, so I'm sure you are very versed in what's going on."

He laughed. "Of course. So I take it she didn't tell you anything helpful?"

"Not a damn thing, Pop. I got the feeling she was holding something back, but truthfully, I'm not sure what."

"Well, I'm sure it was an awkward meeting."

I had just stood up to get some more banana pudding when he said that. I didn't get the statement. Instead of letting it go, my curiosity got the best of me. "Why do you say awkward?"

"Millie Dalbert?"

"And?" I still didn't get it. My father had me stumped.

"KC, you act like you don't know Millie. Hell, son, you forget all of the women you had sex with?"

I sat back down. "Pop, what in the hell are you talking about? I don't know Millie Dalbert, and what makes you think I do?"

For Howard Carson, our conversation had been a nonchalant event for him. He hadn't looked at me during our conversation. His eyes and focus were on his computer or the television. But now his attention was on me.

"Son, you do know who Millie Dalbert is."

"Evidently not. Why don't you tell me?"

"Mikki Lanay."

I was glad I was sitting down. My mind had taken a quantum leap back to my days in California when I was playing for the Raiders and enjoying the party scene. A time when I was also partying at the same locations as eight kids known as the Jet Pack Eight.

Mikki Lanay was a teenage singer, entertainer and actress. To the world, she was a sweet girl with a golden voice and a bright future as a singer and actress. Her talents included dancing as well, and man, could she dance. But as fast as she came on the scene, she disappeared just as fast.

But I still didn't get it. How in the hell was Millie Dalbert and Mikki Lanay the same person. They looked nothing alike.

And that was the question I asked my dad.

"After she left Cali, she moved down here with her uncle, Jimmie D," my father began his story.

"Jimmie D? Your old friend Jimmie D?" I interrupted before he really got started. "The old dude you used to drink with, who used to tell the dirty stories on the porch all the time?"

He laughed. "Yeah, that Jimmie D. Millie is his niece. She grew up in Kansas City. But after she left the business, she came here instead of moving back to Kansas City and facing the people she grew up with. Didn't want to be judged.

"Jimmie told me Millie was tired of the fast life. That's why she left the madness in Hollywood. Put her old life behind her. Got a serious makeover too. Nose job, lip job, boob job. You name it, she got it done."

My dad couldn't help but laugh at himself. And truthfully, I was smiling. Just the way he said it made it sound funny. I was flabbergasted. I did know Mikki, or Millie. It was Mikki when I knew her. And Pop was right, we did have sex. But it wasn't just she and I, it was a threesome with Trinidad Capture, the third female member of the Jet Pack Eight.

But more importantly, Millie Dalbert, aka Mikki Lanay, owed Special Agent Coker and me another conversation.

I was so happy, I got both my Pop and I another helping of banana pudding.

CHAPTER 43

TECHNOLOGY IS THE CRIMEFIGHTER'S MODERN DAY COLT 45.

Captain Cary Chin had only been in the Air Force for eight years. She considered those years to be glorious. She had been to places she had never thought she would ever visit in a thousand lifetimes. She briefed people who had titles she'd never heard of, or even thought existed. All of that paled in comparison to where she was today and whom she was briefing.

She was stationed at the U. S. Cyber Command headquarters at Fort Meade, Maryland. She held the duty title of Deputy Chief of Air Force Cyberspace Division. She was the only lowest ranking officer who ever held that position, which was usually reserved for a lieutenant colonel. That how well received she was in her position. She hadn't been stationed to a desk in a couple of years, but she was among the best of the cyberspace operators when she did man a station, or led a cyber mission team.

Occasionally, she would jump on a desk station to see if she still had it. She knew the FBI was trying to track down leads on the Code of Colors. Her command was just one of several agencies the FBI had reached out to assist in their efforts to locate something on the group, preferably a known location or an upcoming operation.

Those unfamiliar with the art of seeking intelligence didn't know all that went into trying to find or boil down that information. That's what made Captain Chin one of the best at her profession.

She had come up with several computations to see if she could find something on the group. It also meant monitoring numerous networks to include landlines, or traditional phone lines, cell phone conversations, the Internet, various social networks and infamous dark nets. And that was her specialty, knowing the ins and outs of the dark net.

After building her computations, she put her system on surf and went about her business doing work. An hour and a half later when she came back to check on the system, she was blown away at the number of hits she had received via the dark net and text messaging. She immediately investigated every hit, downloading information, cutting and pasting, surfing every hit on social networks, and finally, gathering all pertinent information and accomplishing a worksheet.

When she presented her worksheet to her boss, the information flowed up the chain of command rapidly. When the top Air Force brass in her chain of command, Brigadier General Mickens, came to her office and told her to get whatever she needed to make a quick, informal, but formal, presentation to the FBI, she was shocked.

Two hours later she was sitting in the executive assistant's office to the director of the Federal Bureau of Investigation.

"Captain Chin?" the slender, tall, nicely groomed man said in the form of a question. He held his hand out to shake hers. She returned the gesture. "Supervisory Special Agent Patrick Conroy."

"How are you doing sir?" she politely asked. For Cary Chin, everyone was tall to her five four frame. She estimated Supervisory Special Agent Conroy was at least six foot one or six two.

"First, I want to thank you for possibly breaking this case for us," Patrick began. "Secondly, no reason to be nervous. Believe it or not, Director Lucas is just like you and I, puts his pants on one leg at a time and as cordial as any so-called bigwig you will ever meet."

She didn't know if that supposed to put her at ease, but she shook her head in the affirmative and followed the agent into the Director's office.

When she walked in, she was surprised at how large the office was. But what really caught her attention was the man himself— Director Elliot Lucas. She was a fan. She had followed his career, and unbeknownst to anyone, she had also worked up several worksheets of her own on Director Lucas.

"Captain Chin, so nice to meet you," Director Lucas stated as he walked from behind his desk to greet her. The man was truly big in size. Cary Chin was very good at estimating heights and weights. She estimated the director stood at least six five and probably weighed in the range of two-hundred-fifty, give or take a couple of pounds. Plus, she had never shaken anyone's hands that were the size of his hands.

The other agent in the room was introduced as Special Agent Maxwell Pack, Chief of the Criminal Investigative Division. She was led to a small, round table and she and the three agents took a seat.

"Before we begin," Director Lucas said. "The FBI and myself want to thank you Captain Chin, for the service to your country. It's because of military professionals like you that we enjoy the freedoms that we do."

"Thank you sir." For Cary Chin, this was the highlight of her life. She had briefed the Secretary of Defense and Chief of Staff of the Air Force on two occasions, but for her, nothing compared to this moment.

Director Lucas said, "When I heard you had personally retrieved this information, I was impressed. I was told you came up with your own algorithms and formulas, set the parameters, and solved our little problem."

Captain Chin liked the fact the director was smiling when he said all of this. The ironic thing was everything he said was basically true. "Well, it wasn't quite like that sir. I like a challenge and this was a good one."

Director Lucas wanted to know how she was able to get the information in such a fast manner. She explained everything she did as she passed out individual folders to each person in the room.

Maxwell Pack said, "The bottom line is, we are expecting two attacks in Georgia by the Code of Colors and possibly two abductions tomorrow."

"Yes sir," Cary Chin answered, although the comment wasn't directed at her.

"How did you know to connect the attacks with the abductions?" Patrick asked.

"I didn't, at first," she replied. "When I was going through the information I gleaned on the dark net, there were back and forth comments about M.Y. and T.P. being thrown to the wolves, and since I had been following the Jet Pack case as well. I just put two and two together. I also went back through some of the history and saw that a lot of the events coincided with each other."

"Pretty impressive," Director Lucas stated. "Captain, you think you might be able to retrieve other information on our Jet Pack investigation?"

"I can try sir. Everything I have found is in the folders, including everything on the Jet Pack. But I will continue to monitor."

Director Lucas shook his head. Everyone seemed please. Then Cary Chin dropped the bomb. "Honestly, Director Lucas, this information was very easy to retrieve. If I didn't know better, I think someone intentionally put this information out there. And the reason I say that is the various internet protocol identifiers and website addresses were meticulously masked."

"Meaning?" Maxwell asked.

"Meaning," Elliot responded, "whoever was behind this wanted us to stop the attacks, but let us know they were not helping us stop the abductions of York and Parkins. Right, Captain?

"That's correct sir."

CHAPTER 44

THE REALISM OF ACTUALITY IS THAT MEMORIES AND NIGHT-MARES SHARE THE SAME SPACE IN THE BRAIN.

"Thanks for stealing my line," a younger Brian Dye stated as he looked at Conrod Bach attempt a twenty foot putt on the artificial green on the balcony of his penthouse.

"Your line or Dyson's line?" the Hollywood exec asked facetiously.

"I gave it to Dyson," the bartender and student asked with impatience in his voice.

"Why should I give you ten million dollars to start a business, plus open up my Rolodex to give you business?" the exec said to the bartender. "Or better yet, why should I give you money and make calls on your behalf."

"Because you owe me sonofabitch!"

Conrod continued to play his game on his three-hole putting lawn. He had a good four to five inches on the former child protégé who chose bartending, then school, over being an actor and screenwriter. He knew the kid had talent when it came to the pen and creating stories. He had a great imagination and Conrod heard it come alive on the mike when he deejayed. He even heard that women hired him as a deejaying stripper on more than a few occasions—during those times, his imagination came alive.

It was never his intention to keep track of the young man. It just happened. His mother was the exec's personal nurse for over fifteen years. They had an on-and-off relationship for ten years, which resulted in two sons. Brian was the older of the two. He was also the only one still living.

"Brian, I don't owe you anything. The five million I gave you years ago, you have never touched. Your mom left you another four million when she—"

Conrod couldn't finish that thought. Didn't want to complete the thought. "You can say it, motherfucker! When she died! Why in the fuck is that so fucking hard for you to say?"

Father looked at son, son looked at father. It was a relationship they had never truly had. Brian knew he was an afterthought and one of many after thoughts with Conrod Bach. The only saving grace for him was he truly disliked and hated the man. And the exec knew how his son felt about him.

Their relationship was based on lies.

And this was the first time son had ever asked his father for anything.

"Brian—"

"Don't fucking Brian me, Conrod! Give me the fucking money, make the fucking connections, and once again, I will be out of your fucking life. That's the least your ass could do for killing my brother and my mother!"

"I'm going to give you the money, Mr. Dye, or White Sexual Chocolate, or Whup Dat Ass, or whatever fucking name you want to go by," Conrod said in a very mild tone. "But you little fucking asshole, if you ever say I killed someone again, I am going to kill someone, *your* fucking ass.

"And, if you ever come in my place or even see me on the street or any fucking where, and talk to me like I'm some fucking asshole you met at a club, I promise you, son, I will kick your little disrespectful ass. I didn't kill your brother, or your mother. I loved them both. I was sad at Jacob's death, just like I was sad at the other five deaths. But don't you ever put that on my table again. You understand, shithead?"

Brian was a proud man. A respectful man. That was a quality he inherited from his mother. He missed her . . . just as much as he missed his brother, who was three years younger. The thought of both of the people he loved most in life made it a lot harder to suck up his pride, trek out to Beverly Hills and go through the security obstacles of seeing the man who gave him life.

"Yes sir, I understand," he said. "Thank you."

Conrod Bach didn't say anything in return. He turned back around and returned to his putting.

He hated that memory. It was one of several memories that kept him upright for most of his life. It was one of several memories that kept him focused, made him the man he was today and the man he would be in the future.

Brian Dye was a creature of habit. He loved what he loved and he wasn't ashamed to admit it. He loved the taste of a good cognac or any good spirit for that matter. He loved trying anything once and that really did include any and everything, except sleeping with another man. And that came to his last love, enjoying the company, the taste of a good woman.

The good woman he really loved was the one he had almost killed—Lydia Smithers.

As much as he loved her, he hated her.

After all, they did share . . . the same father.

CHAPTER 45

THE ABSENCE OF SANITY BREEDS A CERTAIN DISTASTEFULNESS OF MADNESS.

I gave Paula a call at the hotel and told her I would pick her up in an hour. In the meantime, I told her to surf the Internet for Millicent Lashell Tucker, and download everything she could. Additionally, I wanted her to contact the Bureau and have them do a detailed background check on Millicent Tucker. As detailed a check that could be completed in one hour.

Sometimes in an investigation, you need something to pique your interest, excite your senses and get you engaged. I was reeling at the fact that Howard Carson, my father, was the one who provided me the vital information to connect the dots and get a better view of a big picture that was still forming. I had direction now that hopefully led to certain clarity. Killing the Jet Pack Eight for sport didn't make sense. But changing your name and appearance to step away from the past, then become involve in a crazy scheme like this made even less sense.

When I pulled up to the hotel, it took less than ten seconds for Paula to come out. I laughed to myself. She was indeed FBI. She was a professional and I thought she was trying too hard to impress me. She was trying to make up for betraying me. She was officially on my probation list, but I like the way she was meeting the challenge.

For some reason, I thought about Paula Coker at the Academy then, and the woman getting in the car now. She was wearing a black sports coat and black slacks, neither did her any justice. With her outfit, a little makeup and her short dirty blonde hairdo, she looked the part of a very serious FBI agent. An agent, I felt, was void of fun in her life.

"Talk to me, what you got?" I asked Paula as I pulled into traffic.

"Millicent Lashell Tucker, aka Mikki Lanay, was a singer and actress twenty years ago or so. She started acting at the age of eight. She did movies, got a couple of permanent jobs in short-run television series and even released a couple of albums in her teenage years."

"How about movies with Wash Tunnell?"

"I was thinking about that when I looked at her Wikipedia page. They did a couple of movies together."

Immediately, my mind went to a hundred and one different reasons Wash's head was sent to Millie Dalbert. I was so deep in thought I didn't hear Paula talking to me.

"KC?"

"I'm sorry, Paula, had something on my mind."

"Can you tell me where we're going?"

"Millie Dalbert's home," I replied. I forgot this was Paula's first time to Memphis and I was driving as if I knew where I was going. In a way, I did. I knew the area we would be visiting, but not the exact street. GPS would give me better direction once we got in the general area.

"Why? She knows this Millicent Tucker person?"

I glanced over at Paula and her face was buried in her laptop. She had photographs and plenty of narrative on Mikki Lanay, but she hadn't put it together yet.

"Millicent Tucker, aka Mikki Lanay, aka Millie Dalbert."

She looked at me with bewilderment in her eyes. Or maybe it was her proof that I was going crazy. "I'm sorry, KC, I don't see it. Ms. Dalbert's nose is bigger, wider, cheekbones are lower, forehead is more protruding and she is at least two shades darker."

I laughed. "Yeah, that can happen to us black folks as we get older." Paula didn't laugh. Yep, she was too serious at times. "Trust me on this, Paula, she is. Just follow my lead . . . and, let me be the lead. But bring your laptop."

Millie Dalbert lived in the Walnut Grove area of East Memphis. I didn't know this area didn't have a community name like Binghampton, Orange Mound, Walker Homes, Whitehaven, etc., as other parts of Memphis. It had always been the Walnut Grove area. When I was a kid in Memphis, this was one of the money areas in Memphis—or as my parents or other black folks would say, one of the rich white areas. I didn't know how rich or wealthy any of the residents were, but the houses were still very nice and affluent looking.

Millie lived off Walnut Grove, not far from Mendenhall and Walnut Grove, which indeed was an affluent part of the area. We drove deep into the neighborhood, before we came upon her street. Her home was the biggest house in the middle of the cul-de-sac. Her driveway was semi-circle that spanned from one end of the house to the other.

The right side of the driveway led to an oversized, two-car garage. Both garage doors were open. I angled my car to block both of the cars that occupied the garage, a Mercedes sedan and a Lexus sports coupe. The trunk of the Mercedes was open.

"Hey, what in the hell are you doing?" came the booming voice of a Caucasian man, with jet black hair and a finely groomed mustache, trimmed thin, but hairy thick. We stood around the same height, six-one, but he had a barreled chest and donned a tight tee shirt that accentuate his chest. He was pulling a suitcase.

"Move your car and get out of here, this is private property." His trademark was intimidation and control. Internally, I smiled. On the gridiron, I used to love playing against assholes like this. He was probably Millie's boyfriend. The sad thing for her was fools like this usually had more than one woman.

"We're here to see Ms. Millie Dalbert, is this her residence?" I asked politely, already knowing the answer.

"Who wants to know?" he said in the form of a demand.

I pulled out my ID and badge. "Supervisory Special Agent Carson," I stated as I flashed my credentials. "This is Special Agent Coker."

"I don't give a damn," he replied. "You guys have talked to her twice now. If you guys don't have the information you need, tough shit."

"What's going on out here?" Millie Dalbert said as she came out the door that provided entry from the house to the garage. "Samuel, what's going on?"

"I was just telling these agents to get the hell out of here," he responded.

"Ms. Dalbert, from where I stand, within one minute, both you and your boyfriend will be handcuffed and headed to a federal lockup," I volunteered as both Paula and I entered the garage. "You, for being a person of interest in the killing of three people, and your boyfriend here for interfering in a federal investigation."

"That's bullshit!" the man named Samuel emphatically stated. "I'm her attorney and she doesn't have to talk to you again."

"On what grounds she doesn't have to talk to us?" Paula chided in.

Samuel was dumbstruck. He had hurt in his eyes as if he wanted to hurt someone. "On the grounds you don't have any evidence that she was involved with any death in this investigation."

"Just out of curiosity, who in the hell are you?" I asked.

"Samuel Cottam, attorney at law. I represent Ms. Dalbert."

"I doubt that," I replied. "You guys are probably seeing each other . . . but I don't give a damn about that. We need to talk to Ms. Dalbert and as *her attorney,* you can sit in." I placed emphasis on her attorney, letting both know I didn't believe it.

"W-W-What do we need to talk about?" Millie stuttered.

"About your past, about Wash Tunnell and the Jet Pack Eight," Paula clarified. I looked at her. I told her I would be the lead and my look let her know I wasn't happy.

"I didn't know the man, I told you that earlier!" Millie was overexcited. I could see the fear in her eyes. She didn't know what we knew. Uncertainty could be a killer and a game changer. Millie didn't want to be on the losing end of that equation.

"Why don't we go inside and have this discussion," I suggested.

"Yes. Yes. That would be a good idea," Millie agreed.

As we made our way to the door, Millie said, "Samuel, please stay out here."

Without hesitation, Samuel answered, "No way, Mill, I'm coming in."

"No, Samuel. No. Please stay out."

"I told you I'm coming in, so stop fighting me on this."

"Dammit Samuel!"

The comment surprised the attorney. However, he was stubborn and a man used to calling the shots. As he kept walking, I stood between him and the door.

"I beg of you, Mr. Attorney," I began. "Please honor the woman's wishes."

"Get out of my way, Agent." Then the attorney did something stupid, he tried to push me out the way.

I grabbed his arm and in one motion, I twisted it and turned him around. Paula gave me her cuffs and I put one on his right wrist and the other on the door handle of the Mercedes' driver side.

"Mr. Cottam, you sir, are an asshole," I began. "I don't want to arrest you or have you arrested. I really want to kick your ass and I'm willing to take these cuffs off if you want to go a couple of rounds. Trust me, this is for your own good. However, if you want a fight, I can give you a fight and if you kick my ass, I won't even arrest you, and secondly, we won't question Ms. Dalbert."

"No, please let him go KC," Millie stated. "And please allow him to go."

"Fuck him, Mill, I will fuck him up!" Attorney Cottam excitedly clarified.

"No, Samuel, KC is a former football player and a top notch agent. This is as good a time as any for us to go our separate ways."

The two people exchanged gazes. Hell, I didn't know anything about their relationship, but something told me they had been dating for some years and Millie Dalbert wanted to end this a long time ago.

"Let me go agent," he said. "I will come back and we can talk later."

"Paula, please take Ms. Dalbert into the house," I interrupted. Special Agent Coker looked at me, then did as I asked. When they were out of sight, I pulled my phone out and called the Memphis Field Office. Told the office chief to send a couple of agents out to arrest Samuel Cottam for interfering with a federal investigation, and that they would find him handcuffed to a car.

"I can sue you motherfucker!" he screamed. "Matter of fact, I plan on suing you!"

I resisted hitting the man in his face. Instead, I surprised him with a knee to the groin.

It was stupid.

And I was sure the man would seek to sue.

At that moment, during that quick exchange, I was thinking . . .

. . . *let me give you something to sue about.*

CHAPTER 46

WHO SAYS YOU CAN'T CHANGE THE HISTORY OF MAN?

I followed the voices as I entered the house and joined Mille Dalbert and Special Agent Coker in Millie's living room. The house was filled with Victorian furniture. The sofa she and Paula sat down on was cream, trimmed with cherry wood. I sat in a matching chair that sat two to three feet away from Millie's position.

"Can we cut the charade and call you Millicent or Mikki," I threw it out there. Before the incident in the garage, it would have been nice to see Millie's reaction, just for shock effect. Even after the incident, Millie Dalbert still tried to play dumb.

"W-W-W-What you talking about?" she stumbled over her words.

"Listen, Mikki, I need you to call the number you called earlier today after we left you," I said.

She gave me a sideways look. She was nervous. I was sure the wheels in her head were spinning a thousand revolutions per minute. Her failsafe wasn't so safe after all.

"I don't know what—"

I interrupted her before she could complete that thought. "Mikki," I put one finger to my lips, "shhh." She had tears in her eyes. "Dry your eyes. You called me KC when your dumbass of a boyfriend was flexing. One thing is still the same about you, dumbass boyfriends.

"So stop the shit. Thanks to your boyfriend my patience is short. Call your friend and tell her I know who you are. Then ask her if you can trust me and if I will treat you right."

I was really rolling the dice on this. If I was right, Millie, aka Mikki Lenay, was going to pick up her cell and call a burner phone. That burner phone would belong to a woman named Trinidad Capture, and Ms. Capture will tell her to tell me anything I wanted to know.

Mikki closed her eyes and put each index finger on the inside corners of her eyes and gave each a rub. Then she stood and took her phone out.

"He's here, at my house and he knows who I am. He told me to ask you if I could trust him." That was all we heard as she walked into another room.

Paula was about to get up and go after the woman, but I gave her a hand signal to calm down and sit back down.

"Who is she talking to?" she asked me.

"I will tell you later," I replied.

It didn't take long for the woman with three names to return. Her eyes were lit up, but they weren't watery with tears. She had a look of indifference on her face. I think she wanted to get this over with, whatever this was.

When she sat, I said, "Well?"

"Do you remember me?" she asked.

"Yes. Yes I do," I replied immediately. "You have changed some things, but your lips and eyes are the same."

"Do you remember everything?" she asked shyly.

"Yes I do. But that's in the past. Let's deal with the here and now."

She shook her head in the affirmative. "How did you know?"

"About your secret?"

"Yes."

"My dad is very good friends with your uncle, he told me."

"Mr. Howard is your dad?"

"Yep. Howard Carson. The one and only."

She halfheartedly smiled. "I never knew his last name. He has been a very good friend to my uncle. I think they have been friends for like thirty or forty years."

"Tell us about Wash Tunnell," I changed the subject.

She didn't immediately say anything. She was looking down. I was sure a lot of old thoughts were running through her head. I did remember everything now. Wash was not the nicest guy in the world. He was arrogant, cocky, a royal pain in the ass. He didn't know how to treat women. He made it a point to embarrass them in the public eye. He and Terrence Parkins were the biggest drinkers and druggies of the eight actors.

"He stole my virginity when I was twelve years old," she began. She had raised her head. Her voice was even. I think she really was happy this day had come. "He raped me. That was the first time, but he had raped me three other times before I was fifteen. It didn't help that we did movies together."

Once again, she was quiet. I understood. She had to get her thoughts together. Many male law enforcement types didn't always get the total violation of women when it came to rape. It was a very invasive, demeaning and degrading crime. For many women, they tried their best to completely forget the violation they went through. However, for many of them, they could never shake the thought or the humiliation.

I was a man. I felt bad for the women who couldn't press on with life. I took my proverbial hat off for those that could put it in the past. Something told me many women were similar to Mikki Lenay, it didn't make a difference how old the crime, just the thought was very painful. And I felt bad for taking her through the worst violation of her life.

"He was only four years older than me, but I thought he was the nicest boy I had ever met. But I was wrong. He and Terrence were pure evil. They lived to wreak pain and hurt on others."

"Mikki, why you?" I asked. "Why send you Wash's head? I hate to sound crass, but you couldn't have been the only one he raped?"

She looked at Paula first, maybe feeling Paula was a kindred spirit, someone who could identify with what she went through or was going through. I really wasn't trying to be insensitive. I knew what she went through was a traumatic event. But we needed answers. The faster we received those answers, the faster we could let Millie get back to her life.

She kept her focus on Paula as she began talking. "Yes, he did rape more women . . . more girls I should say. We were young, pre-teens or teenagers back then. Why send the head to me, KC? I don't rightly know. Maybe I was the first. Maybe I was raped the most. Who knows?"

"Do you know all of the girls he raped?"

"Some of them. I could make you a list, but I promise you, it probably would only scratch the surface of all the girls he raped."

"Damn, did anyone in authority know about this?" Paula emphatically questioned. I could tell this was getting to her, maybe from a female perspective. "Did you guys tell anyone, report him to the police, security or authorities at the studio?"

"Oh, yeah, I told some people, Agent Coker. I told those responsible for us, the counselors at the school, security and even . . . the great Conrod Bach. But still, it didn't help me . . . or others. Those assholes were so off the chain, it was a shame."

"What assholes?" I asked.

"The good old Jet Pack Eight or Malibu Eight or whatever you wanted to call them." She snorted at her comment.

"What?"

"You know what we called them?" We had eye contact. I didn't say anything, my eyes answered for me. "The Chosen Eight . . . and even that wasn't true."

"What you mean?"

"Six of the eight were pure rotten. The other two were very cool, great people, decent people."

"Which two?" Paula asked.

"Trinidad Capture and Dyson Ryker," I answered for Mikki.

She smiled. "Yeah. You were always pretty observant." We exchanged gazes. "You were a protector as well. FBI makes a lot of sense for you."

"Thanks . . . I guess. Not to downplay your plight, Mikki, but what I don't get is why cut up the body? It would seem that if Wash was a rapist, his penis would be cut off. I get that. But it had to be something else, something more sinister."

Mikki didn't say anything. For whatever reason, all three of us looked at each other. I wondered what Paula was thinking. I was hoping this was not too much for her. Not only was she seeing another part of Hollywood, but she was also seeing another part of me, my past.

"Mikki, how involved are you in all of this?" I could tell the question surprised her.

"Funny, only our friend and my uncle still call me Mikki," she said. She looked at me. Her eyes were gentle. I think we both were remembering a different time, a different place. For me, life was good—until Lydia. For Mikki, I don't know if life was ever good.

"I promise you, I have nothing to do with this," she said. "I got a phone call out the blue. The number came up unknown. I only answered because I was at work. The caller told me not to hang up. If I hung up, he was going to out me. Let the world know who

I am . . . or who and what I used to be. Then he told me happy birthday.

"That was it. I promise. That was a week before my birthday. A week before the container came. It never dawned on me that the container was from the caller. Me passing out was the real thing."

I was searching my mind, trying to figure out what I was missing. And I was missing something. I had no idea what, but it was something. Mikki was telling the truth. As much as I shouldn't be sure, I was. I saw it in her eyes. She wanted this to be behind her, to carry on with her life. She didn't say anything. I knew she was wondering if she could continue on the path she was or if she had to start anew.

I put her worries to rest. "Don't worry about the future, Mikki. You can stay Millie Dalbert, post office manager. The Bureau will not out you. Put your bags up. Don't run or hide. No need to go on vacation. I think you still have bad taste in men, something that evidently hasn't changed."

She realized there was more I recalled than I would ever admit to, or she would ever want to know. She had been a lost sheep once and managed to reinvent herself. I think the only bad part of her then, and now, was the men she chose. I wasn't positive, but I think Wash Tunnell probably had more to do with that than she would ever admit.

"What am I missing, Millie, what aren't you telling me?"

"Nothing, KC, I promise you," she responded immediately. "I answered every question honestly. Ask our friend." That got me a look from Paula. "Who is also expecting a call from you."

I said. "Can I get a number?"

"I thought you had the number?" The inquisitive look on her face was real. "You played me?" Her tone was softer. She didn't smile, but I could hear it in her voice. "How did you know I called her after you guys left?"

"It made sense. You guys were always close. I just took a shot."

I rose to leave. Paula followed my lead. Mikki and I were still looking at each other. I wanted to wish her well. There was no use. She would be fine. She was a survivor.

"Ms. Dalbert, if you don't mind me asking, why did you leave Hollywood and change your name." Paula's question was out of the blue. It was a good question.

Then Mikki surprised us when she said, "Sit down."

CHAPTER 47

I KILLED MYSELF TO DIE ANOTHER DAY.

I smiled. I knew the phrase, the quote. It was from a movie called *I Died to Live Again*. Mikki had a small part, but it was Trinidad Capture's best movie. I loved the movie. I had seen it at least four times.

Mikki was smiling as well. It was nice to see that smile. Even with surgery, she still had that smile. It used to light up rooms whenever she entered.

"What's ironic is I wasn't the first or the last to kill myself to die another day," she said. Mikki paused and looked to be in thought before continuing. "I was disgusted with my life and I didn't know it."

I could see her mind working. She was looking for the right words. I took this opportunity to tell Paula to release Samuel Cottam and inform him that he had about five minutes to leave before the Memphis agents arrived. I also informed her to move the car to allow him to leave. The truth of the matter was, I called Julia instead of the local office. I was sure she would ask me about it later.

As soon as I heard the door open, I took the opportunity to ask Mikki about Trinidad.

"TC is TC, you know that KC." Then she laughed.

"What's funny?"

"I noticed that, TC and KC." She smiled. "You know she loved you, right?"

"No, I don't think that's the kind of relationship we had," I replied with probably more curiosity in my voice than anything else. I knew my answer lacked surety.

"Believe me, she did. She wasn't the same after you guys broke up. She really wanted to kick Lydia's ass. What she did was purely out of spite."

I was lost. I wasn't sure what Mikki was referring to. "I don't get it, what was out of spite?"

"Lydia saying you raped her. You didn't pay attention to her, you didn't try to fuck her. You were into Trini and Trini was into you. This was Lydia's way of getting back at both of you. After everything went down, Trini told Lydia to leave the country, and then told her to get comfortable, she would let her know when she could return."

"That's hard to believe." And it was hard for me to believe any of this. At best, Trinidad and I had great fun together. She got me. I think I got her. Yeah, she was always on my mind, but I wasn't sure I was always on her mind.

At that moment, I stopped thinking. I was glad when I heard the door open and Paula Coker rejoined us. I reminded Mikki what she was talking about and she picked it up from there.

"I can remember after a wild night of drinking, drugs and sex, me and a couple of others went to an Asian restaurant. There were two girls in front of us, placing their order. They ordered a two item meal and had asked the server how much a third item would cost."

She shook her head as if she was back at that fast food place. She was an actor and she was in the moment.

"The server told them it would be an additional eight ninety-nine if they ordered the third item separately, but just another dollar if they added it as a third item. I think these girls were high school juniors or seniors and they just didn't get it. As much as he tried to explain to them, they still didn't get it. And I just watched all of this unfold. So they get the third item separately, and when they get to the counter and he tells them the price, they exploded. And I just shook my head.

"But then I realized something. I was so much like these dumbass girls, except with fame and money. I had just had sex with, I don't know how many people, both men and women. And when I got back home, I looked at myself in the mirror and I didn't like what I saw.

"Agent Coker, the person I saw in the mirror made me puke. Hell, at one point, I was fucking princes from Middle Eastern countries at a million dollars a pop. I did disgusting things that no woman she should be doing for money. I had no self-esteem. I didn't like myself. So I did the only thing I could do, I called Conrod Bach and told him that was it, I wanted out. I know he had done the same thing for others who wanted out. So he made it happen."

I sat back down. "What do you mean, he did the same thing for others? He is the one who set you up with another identity, made you disappear? What else did he do? And how many others?"

This was the *what else.* I knew this was the missing piece of the puzzle.

"Yeah, others who wanted to leave the business, Conrod created a new identity for each of us and gave us five million dollars to start over in a new place, with a job and new face for those of us who wanted to look different. It was as if our old selves had died and disappeared forever."

"You have any regrets?" Paula asked.

"No, I thought it was the best thing for me at the time. If I hadn't reached out to Conrod, I would have been dead within six months, I was sure of that. Sometimes it takes decisions like this to save your life. I wanted to live, Agent. I choose life over death.

"In the movie I mentioned, *I Died to Live Again,* which was the point of the movie. Sometimes it's about walking away. Cutting ties and walking away. Forgetting about the madness, whether it be revenge or sticking around, hoping things will change. So many of us were afraid of change—Conrod made that change easier. He made walking away from the business easier. Could he be downright dirty and a sonofabitch? Yes and yes. But he believed in second, third and fourth chances."

"Millie, you think Conrod Bach had anything to do with this?" I don't know where the question came from, but it seemed the man's fingerprint was on everything, why not the deaths of his chosen ones?

"No, it wasn't his style. He had enough people to do his bidding for him."

"How about your new identity, did he personally handle everything surrounding your new identity?"

"Of course not. I'm sure he used his connections, but his wife, Linda Smithers, handled everything."

Paula and I looked at each other.

I had to ask the question. "Is Lydia his daughter by marriage or by blood?"

"By blood."

What the hell?

CHAPTER 48

Stupid is the heart, crazy is the mind.

Supervisory Special Agent Patrick Conroy was shaking his head at the irony in the case. Not the nuances of the case, but the fact an Air Force captain was bringing it home, being the closer. As much as Captain Chin had pointed out that the assailants had made it easy to be caught, Maxwell Pack and Elliot Lucas knew her expertise is what had led her to the information, whether it was hidden in plain sight or not. The NSA and other agencies had been unsuccessful in finding any relevant information. But it took the captain less than two hours to find what they needed.

Patrick was leading two teams down South to stop potential attacks from the Code of Colors. He was personally leading the charge to a small town in southern South Carolina not far from the South Carolina—Georgia state line. The second team was headed to Warner Robins, Georgia, the location of Robins Air Force Base.

Captain Chin had shared a series of conversations on the dark net. Elliot was impressed with how she solved the garbled mess considered to be chat room fodder. To Patrick, Maxwell and Elliot, it looked like pure garbage. But she had deciphered the question of the day, *whr wl da nx C sq tak occ?* The decipher translated to, *Where will the next C square attack occur?* C square was the dark net code name for Code of Colors.

How in the hell she was able to decode that language, Elliot didn't want to know. Which meant Patrick and Maxwell didn't want to know either. Not now anyway. Patrick had made a mental note to pick the captain's brain sometime in the near future. There were over one hundred fifty suggestions for the next attack in the dark net chat room. Patrick still didn't know how the hell she was able to decipher all of this crazy, garbled information in less than two hours.

Patrick was impressed with the captain. She was smart. Probably one of the most intelligent women she had ever met. Plus, she was very pretty. She stood about five-feet-five, her body was slender, fit like a runner. Her battle dress uniform, known as BDUs, fit her well. Even in uniform, he could tell she had a nice ass.

Patrick forced his mind to return to business. What Captain Chin gleaned from two of the one-hundred-fifty or more messages was that there would be an attack in Clarice, South Carolina at the Clarice School of Academia at the school's sports banquet. And the other attack would be at a theatric play at the Houston County Preparatory School, which was a one of two schools that children of military personnel stationed at Robins Air Force Base attended.

The captain said of all of the messages on the board, only two really got into specifics. For the captain, this was her world. The information was too specific. Everything else was conjecture, guesswork. Players, as they were known on the dark net, were purely guessing in generalities where the next attack would be. Most mentioned cities, other states or certain cities' government facilities or tourist attractions. Then someone mentioned the Clarice School and the sports banquet, followed by the mentioning of the Houston County play. Other players followed these suggestions on the board mentioning various cities and events, turning the board into a game of follow the leaders.

This was a different operation. The captain had made a suggestion that they needed to be careful with communicating their intentions. The dark net was infamous for finding out information. Captain Chin had developed several computations in an effort to find out which government employees were regular members on the dark net, releasing government secrets. She had had moments of success, discovering the identities of six government employees. But she had to change her computations at least four times.

Patrick and his team had worked through the night to prepare for the mission. He had arranged for transport, but not on trackable Bureau transportation. Instead, he had procured a cargo transport from KC's company, CarsonOne Productions. They had flown to Savannah to rendezvous with the other team. A team put together personally by Maxwell Pack. They weren't sure about the information on leaks in the federal government system, but why take chances when you didn't have to?

It was a nice Saturday afternoon in Clarice, South Carolina. SSA Conroy took a deep breath, gave a sigh. That morning he had briefed his teams and provided instructions. A team of twelve agents was situated in Warner Robins, Georgia. His team of twelve was situated within the confines of Reginald Convention Center, the banquet cafeteria hall on the Clarice School campus.

Patrick couldn't help but think . . .

. . . *how crazy was this, and how stupid were these kids?*

CHAPTER 49

THIS IS JUST A HARBINGER OF WHAT'S TO COME.

Terrence Parkins smiled as he heard the words of Conrod Bach. The words were in his head. It was a different time, a different place. It was the beginning. His first movie. He was the director, the producer . . . the man.

He was still hiding out. He was afraid. He didn't want to die. So why make himself an easy target? This was his life. People didn't take his life. He took their lives.

Dyson had set him up.

He had written some of the best damn screenplays known to man. The man was a genius. What he could do with pen and paper was amazing. And his biggest accomplishment—convincing Terrence he could do it. He could be the man. Responsible for his own success, accountable to dollar signs and fame.

He had a love-hate relationship with Dyson. The man was a model citizen, always doing the right thing, being in the right place, at the right time. He cared about people, especially family and friends. He believed in the good of people, and believed in others more than they believed in themselves.

And Terrence was in that category. He was beholden to Dyson, and that was his reasoning for loathing the man. Regardless of his success, Dyson's success made him look like a failure. He hated that about himself—which was one of a number of things he hated about himself.

The worst is the drinking.

He laughed at that thought. He wished he could laugh his problems away.

He had been dozing on and off for most of the night . . . or was it morning? He didn't know, and he didn't care. He had lost track of the day. He didn't know what day of the week it was, and in his current position, he didn't even know what the month was. He just wanted the world to stop—he wanted the killing to stop.

He could only imagine what his best friend, Wash, had been through. Getting his body cut up, like a B-rated horror movie. They were Hollywood royalty, above the fray, above others, even above the law.

And now this. And why? Because six teenagers, unfortunately, did what teenagers did—made a grave error in judgment many damn years ago.

What ever happened to forgive and forget?

He was watching an old movie. He loved the adorable boy in the western garb. It was him. *Death is the result of a challenged life.* He couldn't remember the name of the movie. But he knew the person who wrote it. The person who should be taking the blame for all that was wrong in their lives, and all that was wrong in Hollywood—Conrod Bach.

He thought he heard something. Maybe he was hearing things. Maybe it was the movie he was watching.

He was in his favorite chair. He loved this chair. He had it shipped from California. He remembered his grandmother sitting in this chair with him on her lap, enjoying seeing him on television.

Terrence didn't know if he was dreaming, having a nightmare or going crazy when the needle in his neck alerted his senses. He opened his eyes, and in front of him were Jimmie and Wash. He tried smiling.

Then the other man appeared.

"I-I-I know you," he managed to say.

The man smiled . . .

. . . then Terrence Parkins' world faded to black.

CHAPTER 50

Do the young die internally first . . . before they go to hell?

Patrick had done plenty of ops before and this was just another notch in his belt. His ducks were in line. He was expecting the usual eight assailants—six shooters and two videotaping. This was more aggressive, more daring.

Patrick knew that.

Maxwell Pack knew that.

He was missing something. He didn't know what it was. Of course, what he knew about the Jet Pack case and its connection to the Code of Colors case. That meant one of the Jet Pack actors was being snatched up today. Since there was to be two possible shootings today, did that mean two actors were in trouble?

That was a thought for another time. He had scoped out the complete building, from looking at the blueprints to doing a complete walkthrough the whole building. That walkthrough turned into three walkthroughs. He was being thorough, clandestine, trying to keep a low profile. His team consisted of three agents who looked young enough to be students or teachers, surveying the immediate area outside the banquet hall.

They had spotted two males, a well-groomed Caucasian and a studious looking African-American. Both were trying their best to conceal any interest in the happenings occurring at the banquet hall. Their surveillance skills were not the best. Patrick could only smile at this. Of course they weren't the greatest, they were kids playing grown up criminals, so basically they were low budget lookouts. It was a Saturday and they had backpacks as if they were going to class or to the library. A library that was on the other side of the campus.

Reginald Convention Center was a two-story red brick building. The facility had two double doors on the front of the building, an entrance on each side of the facility and two doors on the back. On one of the doors out back was the entrance to the kitchen and the second door led to a hallway adjacent to the kitchen. Three staircases led to the second floor. One staircase led from the first floor to the second floor kitchen, and the other two staircases were in the front lobby room, one on each side of the foyer.

Patrick and his team were not dressed like a FBI SWAT team. The team as a whole was conspicuous, wearing dark blue or black suits with hidden weapons on their person, no dark shades. This wasn't television. Dark shades and visible earwigs were always a giveaway for security personnel or law enforcement types. Regardless of how unsophisticated or stupid the criminal, certain things made it easy to spot the so-called incognito Five-0 asshole.

Patrick checked his watch. It was twelve fifty-eight. Two minutes before show time. All the athletes were in attendance inside the dining hall. Local law enforcement, in plain clothes, had been detailed to keep other students from this area. Patrick had requested the county sheriff's office provide their youngest looking deputies—and no hotheads. Although it was probably an idle threat, hotheads looking to be heroes would be arrested if they intervened.

Beautiful dark green grass covered the area from the parking lot to the convention center, as well as two sidewalks that stretched from the parking lot to the facility. The parking lot was thirty yards from the convention center. There was nothing to conceal anyone from approaching the building.

Patrick thought that was a godsend. His idea takedown was to have no shots fired. He had two agents outside in the back of the building ready to take down the two lookouts. In the lobby, four set of double doors led into the banquet hall. He had an agent at each door, ready to enter the lobby as soon as they got the word. Another two agents were in separate men and women restrooms on each end of the lobby, also ready to enter the lobby when they got the word. Then he had an agent on each staircase. He and one other agent were in the lobby, on opposite sides, awaiting the Code of Colors assailants to enter. The last two agents were in the banquet hall, just in case they missed something or someone.

"Coming your way," the local county sheriff stated in Patrick's earbud.

The game plan was to capture all except the lookouts in the lobby.

"How many?" Patrick asked.

He wasn't sure, but he thought the lookouts would be the ones responsible for recording the events inside the banquet hall.

"Six," the sheriff replied.

"We have two dressed in all-blue with video cameras heading towards the kitchen entrance," one of his agents said.

"They are about to enter the building," the sheriff added.

"Take down the cameramen before they enter the building," Patrick said to his agents in the back of the building.

As soon as he did, the other six assailants burst through the front entrance to the building. The lead was in white, followed by five others dressed individually in all-black, all-red, all-burgundy, all-orange and all-yellow.

"Go! Go!" Patrick said.

At that moment, eight agents were in the lobby area, surrounding the six Code of Colors members.

"F-B-I, don't move, weapons down!" Patrick shouted.

Although the assailants had on masks, they were shocked. It wasn't supposed to go this way. Every member looked around . . . looking at each other, and at the agents. Equally, in those split seconds, they were trying to gauge what their leader, White, would do.

"Weapons down!" multiple agents were shouting at them.

Patrick put up his hand and everyone shut up. "Listen to me," the assailants all turned around and looked at him. "We don't want to hurt anyone. I need you guys to put your weapons down. And please don't do anything stupid. It's dumb for anyone to die today."

Burgundy was the first to bend at the knees and place his weapon on the floor. He was followed by Red, then Black. Orange and Yellow were looking at White, who was still looking at Patrick.

He suddenly made a move to lift his weapon, a modified Heckler & Koch G36 assault rifle. Before he could, he felt a gun at the back of his head. The agent ordered him to the ground. He complied. He saw the same was happening to his other two comrades. The agent who was doing the talking, the one he assumed was in charge was speaking. Then local sheriffs came through the front doors.

"All secure in the back?" Patrick asked as he walked towards White.

"All secure, two taken down," was the reply from his agent.

He pulled the mask off White. He was shocked to see a young African-American male. As the others were de-masked, Patrick didn't say anything. Three Caucasians, two African-Americans and a Hispanic.

He picked up his phone and hit a number.

"All well?"

"Took them down at their house, as soon as they pulled out of the driveway," the male agent on the other end said. "Two vans, one white, the second black, both with dark tinted windows. Eight assailants, no casualties, no weapons fired. Turned over to the Georgia Bureau of Investigation."

"Copy, see you soon," Patrick said.

He dialed another number.

"All good down south," he stated to Maxwell Pack.

The silence on the other end of the phone worried Patrick. "Sir, you still there?"

"Yeah, Conroy, I'm still here. Unfortunately, all is not good down south."

Part Three

RECKONING

CHAPTER 51

THE STORM WAS THUNDEROUS, LOUD . . . AND HARMFUL TO THE SOUL.

Quiet before the storm was a lie. Our storm had hit like a two hundred mile per hour hurricane, hard and fast with plenty of power.

The Code of Colors was purely a smokescreen. I wasn't sure if the final act would be the abduction of Terrence Parkins, who was hiding out in a house in Georgia, or Mitzy York, who was going through drug rehabilitation in a self-admitted rehab facility in Santa Monica, California.

While the Bureau was stopping attacks in Warner Robins, Georgia and Clarice, South Carolina, Parkins was being abducted at the midway point between the two cities. The call went out to the local sheriff's department thirty minutes before the scheduled time of the attacks. The sheriff called the Bureau's headquarters in D.C. instead of the nearest office in Atlanta. By the time Maxwell Pack was contacted, he had taken action to find out what was going on, sending agents from Atlanta to the scene and even checked on WMT's flight out of Atlanta.

It was a fucked up situation, great planning on the abductors' part . . . and the criminals telling us they had the upper hand, that they were calling the shots and there wasn't a damn thing we could do to stop them.

Mitzy York's abduction was a different matter. It actually occurred Friday night, the day before the Parkins' abduction. Two security guards called in sick at the Lynwood Medical Center in Santa Monica, which was strictly a rehab center for drug and sexual addicts, and alcoholics. The two male guards were roommates and hung out together. When one called in sick, the other one always did the same. Usually, two other guards on the Center's payroll filled in for the two. That didn't happen this time. There were two new security guards.

The security cameras on Mitzy's floor were inoperable the entire night. The two substitute security guards were not at the Center when employees arrived on Saturday morning. The last time the nighttime nurse was on that floor was around one o'clock Friday night, into Saturday morning. She just walked the floor. Everything seemed normal, nothing seemed out of place. Because of this, there was never a reason to check Mitzy York's room.

The computer system logged Mitzy's door opening around three a.m. and the front door opening soon after. I was sure whoever abducted Mitzy left at that time, and the abductees might have been the substitute security guards. The only bad thing was that we had no camera feeds or photos of the guards. Additionally, a few of the Center's staff that actually saw the guards, only got a quick glance. Their shift started at eleven at night, and these people were dying to get home. The incoming staff just gave a head nod as they were buzzed through the door. Some of them didn't even acknowledge the guards. A couple asked about the regular guards, but it wasn't a long conversation. That was the couple our agents were questioning, trying to get a sketch of the guards.

The regular guards were at their apartment tied up and gagged. They were no help. Both had been drugged. How ironic. One remembered picking up a woman at a local store and bringing her back to their apartment, but that was it.

Two abductions. Great planning. The Bureau had mud on its face.

The storm was sudden. It was real. And we had no choice but to face it head on.

In every investigation against a person, you have this crazy thing called victimology. You have to take a look at the victims and hope like hell they're not as bad as the person or people you may be chasing. In our investigation, we were on the wrong side of victimology. Our damn victims, the actors who once made up the Jet Pack, might be killers themselves. From all indications, we had too many damn *coincidental* crimes occurring in areas the actors had been filming movies or TV shows.

I fucking hated *coincidences.* I was upset—I was swearing too much.

"In four locations where movies were being made, there were at least two similar killings," Paula Coker was briefing the team, specifically Jo Jo Sanu and Blane Taylor. I had heard and reviewed all of the possible crimes by the Jet Pack crew. Paula had already briefed us on the crimes possibly committed by Terri Wenthill, Jimmie Claymore and Wash Tunnell.

"Terrence Parkins was either directing a movie or playing a part in a movie," Paula continued. "The killings usually consisted of a couple being shot in the head, either while having sex, or naked in a bed, lying next to each other. Unfortunately, in every situation, there was no video or photos or anything. And, no one heard anything, even though a couple of the killings occurred in a hotel or motel."

"Are we sure about all of this?" Blane asked. "Fuck, KC, we are talking about fucking Hollywood elites. Why in the hell would they kill like this? What would be the motive?"

I cut Paula off before she tried answering the question. "Maybe it all was coincidental. Maybe someone besides the actors was committing crimes where these guys were, one big set-up. Who knows? However, before I allow Paula to brief you on Mitzy York and Derrick Paine, I need both of you to know that all of this may have started years before when these assholes were young. Supposedly, they committed some type of crimes back then, and this may be about vengeance. Unfortunately, we don't know what crimes or what they supposedly did."

"In other words, these actors who people have loved for years, decades even, may have been killing folks for a long time, or committing crimes and graduating up the ladder to bigger crimes such as killing folks in hotels and shit like that."

It was an astute statement by Blane in his Louisiana tongue. He was right. Either they started out this way decades ago or they progressed to bigger crimes. It wasn't something new with criminals, starting small and gradually moving up the criminal ladder. Taking more chances, becoming bolder as they grew older.

"You may be right Blane," I said. "You may be right."

Paula jumped in immediately. "Mitzy York may be the worse of the group," she stated. "Thirteen kills. Nine men, four women. All had one-on-one contact with a female . . . who happened to be caught on video numerous times. Every location, Mitzy York was in the area shooting a movie, filming a commercial or conducting business. If it was Ms. York who committed the crime, she did a great job of disguising herself.

"Sometimes she was caught on film wearing large black sunglasses with a hat and blue hair. Other times, it was a hat with traces of pink or gold or orange hair. A couple of times when she looked directly at the camera, it was dark sunglasses, a big floppy hat like you see in hippie movies and different hair color. During one killing, the female's hair color was actually blue, purple, pink and gold."

"Well, if she was caught on video on numerous occasions, how about the female's height?" Blane asked.

"From the few recordings we have looked at, it's possible," I stated. "However, the lady had on various sized heels. Let finish this up. Paula, last victim."

"Derrick Paine!" she damn near shouted. "Four killings in four consecutive nights, five years ago in—"

"Baton Rouge, Louisiana," Blane answered. "I was a new detective. It wasn't my case, but I remember it well. Every killing was performed in a different way—one was knifed to death, another was shot, the third overdosed, and the last was beaten to death with a baseball bat. Another interesting thing about all the deaths, the murder weapon was left at the scene along with a DVD of the victim's last breath.

"One witness, an older female, saw a possible suspect leaving the scene of the crime of the third victim, a Hispanic female, who lived in an apartment complex near LSU. She described him as a white male, six feet tall, maybe taller, with thinning black hair. She said she thought he had on a fake mustache and beard, because the mustache looked like it was crooked, wasn't normal. She thought he was medium build.

"That was on day four. On days one and two, he killed an African-American female student that attended Southern University, who lived in an apartment closed to the university, and killed a white female who lived in the downtown district. He took day three off, before killing a Hispanic female on day four, and lastly, on day five, he killed Officer Alley Suitland."

"What were the circumstances of Officer Suitland's death?" Jo Jo asked. I think it was an effort to let his partner know he was concerned, and his former fellow officer was important. Sometimes as law enforcement, we work cases, investigate people we don't know, and we forget that lives and families are affected. Although we see the emotions of loved ones, we try our best to stay indifferent and don't allow the case to become personal.

"She saw someone she thought looked suspicious, like the suspect in an apartment close to the scene of the first murder. When she followed the man into the apartment complex, it looked as if she surprised him. There was a bruise on her hand that the medical examiner thought he may have hit her, knocking the gun out of her hand. Then he proceeded to beat her to death."

"What was her nationality?" I asked that question.

"She was Caucasian as well, KC, but the woman who lived at the apartment Alley was killed was Asian-American."

No one said anything. Blane looked intense. This was personal. Officer Alley Suitland was not only a fellow officer, but a childhood friend, his best friend. I learned this when he was at the academy. They graduated high school and college together, and went through the Baton Rouge police academy together. She was also the one who convinced him to become a police officer.

"You have anything else, Paula?"

"No sir."

"Ok. It's time to solve this case. If we are fortunate, we'll find the victims before they die, if they're not already dead. But that's our priority, putting this one to bed."

I didn't have to say anything else. Jo Jo, Blane and Paula were professionals, they knew what they had to do. I kept my eyes on Blane as he walked to his desk station. He was motivated. I was sure we all had a little more motivation, knowing if we found the victims before they were decapitated like the previous victims, then we could possibly bring Derrick Paine to justice.

Victimology was about studying the victims of crimes, knowing what may motivate the criminal element to commit a crime against them.

Attorneys strongly disliked victims who were scum. Over ninety percent of cases that went to trial where someone was considered scum, the verdict came back not guilty. In most of those cases, the suspect was more than likely was guilty.

You hoped your victim was never as bad as your unsubs. Our victims may have been the *Hollywood* scum of the earth, and our unsub, or unsubs, may have thought they were doing the world a justice.

This wasn't just a storm, it was a shit storm . . .

. . . and the stink was getting worse by the day.

CHAPTER 52

Headaches, body aches and pain . . . oh my.

Static. That what it was. Static. Loud static. That's what woke Mitzy York out of her stupor. She didn't have a clue where she was, or how long she had been there. Her body ached, her head ached . . . hell, even her fingers and toes hurt.

The white noise had to be the reason her head was hurting. She tried to move. Then it hit her. She was tied up, bound or something. She wasn't sure what. She couldn't even move her head.

What the fuck is going on?

She wished she could answer her own question. She was discombobulated. She didn't have a clue what was happening. Her mind was racing a thousand miles per second.

The static, the white noise, it was loud. It wasn't helping. She was afraid to call out. She had to calm down. She felt a panic attack coming on. Not now. "Don't do this to me," she said to herself in a very low voice. So low she wasn't sure if the words actually escaped her lips, or if it was just in her mind.

She felt the tears rolling down her face. Worse, she could feel more tears sweltering in her eyes. She needed to let the tears flow, and then get her shit together. If only it was as easy as it sounded in her head.

She closed her eyes and tried to tune the white noise out. She had to recall her last memory. She made sure she only tuned out the white noise and not the world she lived in. She saw herself lying in bed with a man, and not just any man. It was her Stephen. To the world, he was known by his nicknames, Doc or Sin. She never liked either name. Yes, he was a doctor, one of the country's top neurosurgeons, and Sin was an abbreviation of his surname, Sinatra. But for her, Stephen was her favorite name.

A tear rolled down her cheek. She was getting mad at herself. Although she saw her and Stephen together, she lying in his big and powerful arms, it was impossible. She hadn't seen or been with Stephen since they were teenagers. In her dreams, they weren't young. It was the Stephen she knew today, the one she had followed for years. His thick, black mane all over his head, the facial hair, the wonderful mustache and sideburn. All slick black. No gray. He was heavier than their younger days. He was all man.

She could feel his lips, and recall their conversation.

"Hey, beautiful, how you doing?" he said in his silky, sweet Italian voice. He wasn't related to Frank Sinatra, but he was just as smooth. She recalled the days when that voice would automatically make her panties wet. She couldn't be sure, but she thought her panties were wet from just thinking about it.

"Steve, is that you? Is that really you?" she recalled saying. She touched his head, held him tight, pushed away and looked at the man. He was dressed like what he was—a doctor. And she was dressed like what she was—a patient in a rehabilitation center. But he wasn't a mental health professional, that wasn't his specialty, he was a neurosurgeon. She didn't get it. Then it hit her, he was there to do what he did, rescue his damsel in distress.

"Yeah, pretty lady, my little selfish Mitzy, it's me, in the flesh." She hugged him once more, not willing to let him go again. The last time she released her grip on him, the world went crazy . . . and she went with it. In an indirect way, he was the reason for her mental issues.

He kissed her. A French kiss. Internally, she smiled. The French had nothing on her Italian American lover. His lips were soft, his tongue hot and sensual. It made her body burn and lust for him. Inside, her body was on fire, tingling, betraying her in a good way. Truthfully, she didn't know if she was dreaming or having a moment, an actual moment, a physical moment. Did she and Stephen actually hook up the night before? She didn't know. She didn't care.

Real or not, she felt good. Reliving the moment . . . or dreaming the unbelievable. She felt good.

Had reality completely escaped her? She wasn't sure. If it was a fantasy, it was the best she had ever experienced. Her Stephen did that to her. She dare not open her eyes. No way she would allow the moment to escape her.

Their dalliance moved to the bed. It wasn't your typical hospital, twin-sized cot. The bed was a full size, definitely big enough for the both of them. Her mind was immersed in anticipation. Unfortunately, she had only had sex four times in the past with Stephen and the past was twenty years ago, when they were children. Even then, Stephen was as experienced as the several men she had been with. She couldn't imagine all he had learned over the past two decades.

She wasn't surprised he still did what he did, which was nibbling her earlobes and sticking his tongue in her ear. That always turned her on. Stephen was the first man who ever did that to her. And to think . . . he was only a boy then. His lips explored her body. His mouth was a fiery inferno of guilty lust. With every touch of his mouth, the occasional flicker of his tongue, she could feel her pussy get wetter.

That thought put another thought in her head and she smiled more. The first time they did anything, she asked him if he wanted

some of her love nest, and he replied, "No, I want some pussy."
That was the moment she fell for the Italian American, the day she
realized his dark personality complemented his dark complexion.

The memories were coming hard and fast, and yet, she could
still feel the moment from the night before. And no, she still didn't
know if it was real . . . or not, but something inside of her said it
was, and that was good enough for her. The soreness of her body
was a distant memory now. At this moment, her body only felt
pleasure. Dream or nightmare—it didn't matter. Only the moment
had credence. She made a point to keep her eyes closed as she
relived the night before.

She was oblivious to the white noise.

She and Stephen were in a spoon position, her back against his
hairy chest. He always liked it when she guided his penis into her
pussy, and if she were in a court of law, she would have sworn that
it was bigger now than it was when they were younger.

She could remember him always saying, "You want this guided
missile, don't you?" But she would never answer. Instead, she would
grab it and guide it herself. And that's what she did last night. Or
that's what she thought she did. And Stephen did what he was
so good at doing, fucking the shit out of her. She couldn't help
but smile and laugh to herself. The only time she talked dirty or
allowed dirty thoughts to occupy her mind was when she thought
of this madman—Doc, Sin, Stephen or whatever name came to
mind.

She even smiled and laughed at that thought. She was the one
who gave him his nicknames. Doc and Sin were her doing. One
had nothing to do with medicine, and the other had nothing to do
with him being a sinner in the traditional sense. He was her doctor
of love, her doctor of pleasure. And everything he used to do to her
was sinful. *Just like he did last night.*

Her body screamed with pleasure. He was a miner drilling for his pot of gold. And she enjoyed every thrust.

Then it happened, he screamed out, "Fuck, Mitzy! You crazy bitch! I have missed you!"

Her eyes opened. The white noise was back. It was a TV monitor. She was indeed tied down or in some kind of binds. Her body did ache. Her headache had returned.

"Fuck!" was the only word she could voice.

"Mitzy . . . Mitzy . . . is . . . is that you?"

She knew the voice. She hated the voice. But she knew the voice. Then she couldn't control herself. She screamed . . . and screamed . . . and screamed.

Her nightmare was real.

And it had a name . . .

Stephen Sinatra . . .

Doc . . .

Sin.

And this time . . .

. . . he was sinning in the traditional sense.

CHAPTER 53

. . . And the sun doesn't always shine.

"They're all dead," his best friend, Brian, stated weakly. His voice was barely audible, and Steve Sinatra couldn't make out what he said.

His friend was sitting on a cushioned bench in the lobby of the Rustic Building, one of the buildings on the campus of the Herbert Brutus School for Gifted Students. The building was the medical facility for the school, which included rooms that served as sets for movies and television shows.

Brian's right hand was wrapped in multiple bandages. His eyes were blood red from crying and weeping. The young Brian Dye was stricken with grief, heartbreak and fear. Tears still rolled down his face. And worse, hope had departed his soul.

"Brian, what did you say?" Sin asked as he kneeled down in front of his friend.

"They're all dead," Brian repeated himself. His voice was still weak. "All of my friends, they're dead."

Over the years, Sin didn't know how many times he had recalled the worst day of his life. It's a day that even then, twenty years ago, he knew he would never escape. Some things stay with you forever. Unfortunately for Steve Sinatra, the death of multiple friends can brand a brain forever.

This year was the twentieth anniversary of his worse day, of his heartbreak. The day was still a fiber of his life that he would never forget. But he knew one day this day would come. The day they got revenge. The day they provided peace to those who lost their lives, their souls and their spirits that dreadful night.

He was numb at the thought.

On that day, he and eight other students of the school were visiting the Port Hueneme Naval Base. Herbert Brutus School had an agreement with the military installation to conduct field trips to their advance construction facility. The Naval facility was known for training Seabees and other naval personnel on building airfields and facilities for scratch, at bare base locations. For some at the school, this was a big deal. Not every student would become the next great actor. Some would become good directors, producers, set designers, screenwriters and secure other jobs in the movie industry that made this field trip instrumental.

For Sin, that's how he saw his future—as a screenwriter, director and producer. He had been acting since age five and at the ripe old age of seventeen he had already been in eight movies, and a regular on two television comedies. The Herbert Brutus School was eight years old and he had been a student every year since the school was built. It was located in the Oxnard Dunes, not far from Channel Island, not far from the naval base. For potential actors and kids interested in various facets of the movie industry, the field trip was worth its weight in gold as they learned how to build sets, making a set staged in California look like it was a building in New York City in the middle of winter.

The school was founded and built by Conrod Bach for young actors, ages six through eighteen. Although some of the students had aged out of the school, they still attended on an occasional basis, especially during the summer sessions. The school was year-round, with more field trips and less classes during the summer. The school, as a whole, had approximately one hundred twenty students. Like Sin, many of the students had attended the school since its opening.

His day had started great. He had had sex with the luscious Mitzy York, and although he was seventeen and she was only sixteen, he thought they were in love. When he and Mitzy were together, he felt as if he was in another world. She put a smile on his face, made him a nicer person, a better person. He was a protector and unselfish, always being there for others. Mitzy made him want something, want someone—her.

The trip to Port Hueneme improved on a good beginning. Plus, his favorite teacher and the school's headmaster, Miss Linda Smithers, was on the trip. The Naval unit had a policy of no cell phones and beepers. Back then, cell phones weren't as prevalent or streamlined as they are today. In 1996, he owned a flip phone, a big flip phone. But the phone and his beeper were in the van.

Ironically, he still had the beeper and the cell phone. He didn't know why he kept the old devices. Maybe, they were mementos. They had to be. He didn't need anything to help him remember that day.

Additionally, there used to be a time when he could smile when he thought about Mitzy, but that feeling, that emotion was void to him now. It became void that night.

That was what *nostalgia* could do to you. Bring up thoughts you didn't want to think about.

So he missed the distressed messages Dyson Ryker had sent to his beeper. Dyson had used their made-up emergency code, double nine-one-one. He had three messages from Dyson. Two were their regular emergency and the third was a triple nine-one-one code. His heart dropped. *What in the fuck is going on?* was his first thought.

He was in a van sitting next to Miss Smithers, as he drove the van back to the campus. He tried calling Dyson's cell phone. No answer. He then called Dyson's beeper, in hope that he would call back. He searched his mind for others he knew had a cell phone and/or beeper. He called three other numbers. No answer. He was mad at his best friend, Brian, for not having a cell phone or beeper.

Then he called Mitzy. She answered, "Hello." But before he could say something, he heard a male's voice say, "Hang up the fucking phone." Then it went dead.

Miss Smithers saw his angst and wanted to know what was going on. He told her about Dyson's messages, and she gave him her phone and beeper that she hadn't turned back on. When he powered up both devices, Miss Smithers had multiple messages on both.

Within minutes they were back on campus, and that was exactly what it was, a campus. The Herbert Brutus School was just as large as most colleges with thirty facilities on the campus, occupying most of the livable area around the Oxnard Dunes. The school was less than a quarter mile from the beach and Pacific Ocean. The younger students resided in dormitories, while the older students lived in apartment type facilities, which were located closer to the beach.

After dropping the other students off at the student union, which was located in the center of the campus, Miss Smithers and Sin drove to the Rustic Building. Neither said anything. Miss Smithers had made one call without saying a word. Whoever was on the other end had done all of the talking. When she got off the phone, and Sin asked her what was going on, she still didn't speak. He didn't press her. He knew it wasn't good.

When they reached the Rustic Building, he ran inside and saw Brian sitting in the lobby of the building, looking like he was the victim of a fresh apocalypse. His eyes were red, tears were flowing down his face and his hand was bandaged.

Brian said something as soon as he saw Sin. Unfortunately, Sin didn't hear him. He kneeled in front of his friend on the cushioned bench he was sitting. "Brian, what did you say?"

"They're all dead." he heard Brian say. "All of my friends . . . they're dead."

CHAPTER 54

DEATH COMETH TO US ALL.

That's what his mind was telling him. However, for Terrence Parkins it wasn't that viable at all. The man was afraid. His last thought was being in the living room of his hideaway home in Georgia. Sleep was calling his name, but he was trying his best to fight it. He was watching old movies. Movies he and his friends had been in years ago. Movies that were made even before they were known to the world as the Jet Pack.

"Please, Mitzy, if that's you, please say something," Terrence said.

One second he blinked, he could see his seven-year-old self with a cowboy suit on—cowhide vest, checkered shirt, jeans, cowboys boots and a two-gun gun-belt on. The next second he blinked and he saw three men, two with masks on, playing a crude joke. The masks were of Jimmie Claymore and Wash Tunnell. The third man wore no mask. He knew the man. He couldn't remember his name, but he knew him. He was a bartender back in the day.

Worse, he knew his friends, Brian Dye and Steve Sinatra.

The billionaire and the doctor.

The oddball and the cool kid with blind loyalty to the misfits of the Herbert Brutus School for Gifted Students.

Misfits like Brian Dye.

"Mitzy, please talk to me," he begged. His body was bruised. He was sure he had broken ribs, two black eyes, a busted nose, a fat lip and worse, a broken spirit.

"Terrence, stop your fucking whining," Mitzy York finally replied. "Stop being the spineless, little bitch you've always been."

"I'm s . . . s . . sorry, I'm scared," he said. He paused for a reply, which didn't come immediately. Then he said, "I'm not afraid to say I'm scared, Mitzy."

She heard the fear in his voice. She, too, was afraid. Really, she was beyond fear. She knew she was dying this day. If not this day, tomorrow . . . or the next day. And she knew why death had chosen her number. As much as she wanted to think otherwise, she couldn't. In many ways, she knew she had died years ago. She was known as one of the world's top ten, maybe even top five, actresses. She earned that title—because with every film, she acted as if it was last performance. She acted as if she would never be in front of a camera again.

Her thought was, one day someone would finally arrest her for being a serial killer. And she was a serial killer. She couldn't help herself. Dressing in disguise, picking up a man or woman for a night with the promise of a blissful time, and then boom, she made her move. She wasn't positive how many people she had killed over the years. She was confident she could kill forever. She wasn't America's sweetheart, but she was one of America's treasures. She was a member of the Jet Pack Eight—eight of the nicest kids to ever grace television and movie screens.

If only people knew how screwed up they were. Then, and even now.

Now, that day had come. And she was at peace. She had to be. After all, her death would come at the hands of the man she had always loved. Til' death, do us part. It was her destiny. She wasn't fighting destiny.

She was just amazed at the irony. To die for a crime she wasn't really responsible for. But she participated. All who were there participated. She used to wonder if Dyson and Trinidad were there, if they would have participated.

"Terrence, remember when they first started calling us the Jet Pack Eight?" she asked. She didn't know why she asked the question. He didn't answer right away. So she continued. "I thought life was great then. To think, most of us were twelve or thirteen years old and it seemed like we had it all. You remember the movie, *The Educated Adolescents?*"

She stopped talking as her mind went back and forth through the various memories of her life. For Mitzy, she considered this to be the best time of her life. From day one, she loved being in front of the camera. She loved proving show after show, movie after movie, that she was the best. When media types talked about the future of the film industry, she wanted to be a central figure in those discussions. That was her desire ever since she could remember.

At her lowest, she was still the best. That's why she could still get the parts. When it came to her craft, she could stop the drinking and drugging while filming, while performing. But when the camera was completely off and the project was over, she went right back to her weaknesses, the things that killed the pain—drugging, drinking and killing.

The killing was what should have bothered her most. But it wasn't. She was sick that way. They were all sick that way. She remembered as if it was yesterday, the eight of them getting together and talking about the best way to kill someone. Dyson would never speak, while Trinidad would always change the subject after enough was enough.

She was oblivious to the silence. If Terrence was talking, she had tuned out everything. As much as she wanted to be in another world, she couldn't be. She was in the here and now. And it was only right that she was in the here and now with the person who got them to this point.

"We're in the O-R, Terrence, in the Rustic Building," she clarified. It was similar to other operating rooms in teaching hospitals and there was an observation deck that overlooked the room. Students of Herbert Brutus School had observed many of scenes in that O-R. Now, Mitzy York felt like this was her last stop.

"Where it all began, Mr. Parkins. Where you set the world on fire and killed off the Jet Pack forever. In our minds anyway. To the rest of the world, we grew up. In our world, you, Wash, Derrick and Jimmie killed us. Terri and I were there for the ride. But who would have thought we would like it as well. We didn't want to be what we called the other kids, oddballs.

"Instead, we became known as something else . . . killers and murderers, Terrence. The only thing . . . only a select few knew what we did."

"I . . . I . . . I did what I did for you, Mitzy," Terrence stuttered. As much as he tried to sound confident and assured, he wasn't. And Mitzy knew he wasn't.

"Keep lying to yourself Terrence," she responded. "You were afraid of Sin then, and you are afraid of Sin now. And you should be. I'm afraid too, Terrence. I loved the man then, and I love him now. And guess what? He is going to kill me without reservation, just like he is going to kill you. And sadly, Terrence, we both deserve it. We even deserve to die together."

Terrence Parkins tried moving his body. His movement was minimal. He ached all over. His body had taken a serious beating, and he didn't understand. It wasn't from the kidnapping. When he tried to get up from his recliner, the former bartender stuck him with a needle. Within seconds, he was out like a light. So he didn't understand how he had sustained so many bruises.

Had Sinatra and his friends beat him up? That had to be it. In his mind, he looked at Sinatra as being a coward. In his heart, he knew better. The only time the two had mixed it up, Sinatra had kicked his ass like he had stole something from a handicapped newborn. After that, he was afraid of the man . . . or afraid of the boy back in those days. Soon after, Mitzy embarrassed him by hooking up with the kid known as Doc.

"He would never kill you," Terrence said. "I'm sure your body is not as sore or hurt as my body. I don't know what they did to me, but somebody beat my ass while I was out."

"You remember that day you went crazy with jealousy, Terrence?" Mitzy paused again. Her thoughts were steady, not jumping all over the place as they had been doing. She was actually coherent now. It was as if the burden of dying was a relief and she suddenly had clarity.

Terrence didn't answer her, so she continued. "I saw Stephen when I was getting in the car. As much as Conrod was trying to get us out of there before he and Miss Smithers came back, it didn't work. The way he looked at me, I thought I was dead.

"And I did die that night Terrence. I think as much as you don't want to accept it, a major part of all of us died that night. And it sucked when I ran into Sin a year later at a nightclub. He looked straight through me. I know he had told you and Wash that one day, whether it was a year, ten years or a hundred years, that he would get revenge for his friends we had killed or hurt.

"Ironically, that day is upon us Terrence. You and I weren't the first to die, but we are the last. And we get to die together. I don't know if any of the others died together, but it's fitting we do."

The television monitors suddenly shut off. Darkness fell over the room. Neither Terrence or Mitzy spoke a word. Memories of a day twenty years ago created tension that filled the air. The silence spoke volumes.

For Mitzy, one thought weighed heavy on her mind.

A thought from the night she was in the embrace of Conrod Bach.

He said, "Don't fret, young lady, death cometh to us all."

CHAPTER 55

THERE IS A THIN LINE BETWEEN RESTLESSNESS AND STUPIDITY.

Derrick Paine had reached his threshold of restlessness and it was driving him crazy. He did what he wasn't supposed to do—go out into the community. For the past three days, he had gone out to eateries, convenience stores and gift shops in the downtown Ruidoso shopping district.

Ruidoso was a resort town in the mountains of the Sierra Blanca and Sacramento mountains. The town was known as one of New Mexico's tourist areas. Cabins dominated the area. The population was over eight thousand, five hundred. Old town and Native American culture accounted for the attraction of New Mexico, western Texas and southern Arizona residents. The biggest attraction was the Inn of the Mountain Gods casino.

This time of year brought in another two thousand tourists per week. For Derrick, that meant possibilities. Hiding out—laying low meant a kind of restlessness that brought out the evilness in him. He had donned a disguise. He was a redhead now, with a red mustache and goatee. He still had hair that covered all of his head, but he was thinning badly. Comb overs were a must for him these days. In the week or so he had been hiding out, he had lost at least fifteen pounds. He never complained about losing weight from the usual two hundred thirty-five pounds he carried.

For years he had quelled the urges of being what he referred to as beastly. The desire to kill, to see if he could get away with murder. It added to his storytelling, his writing. He was convinced it made him a better director. He hadn't only gone on one killing spree. In many ways he was happy he ran across the cop. In other ways, he was sad. He felt a certain power being in his beastly mode. That five-day stretch of killing reminded him of the day he had ultimate power. The day he got his friends to do the unghastly, the unforgiveable and certainly, the unforgettable.

That's why they were in the position they were in today. He had set the chain of events in motion. He loved being the mastermind, the puppet-master behind the madness. It was truly his first job as a director. The first time he was the boss, he called the shots, he bent the will of other actors and they responded to his voice, his power of suggestion.

That day had led to this moment . . .

. . . had led to him hiding out . . .

. . . had led to his desire to kill again.

To feel the adrenaline of taking another life was powerful. It had always been the driving factor behind so much he had done in life. Dyson had made his imagination real on the big screen. He had fed the man his dreams, his nightmares—shared the deepest darkness of his imagination. And, in turn, Dyson Ryker had soothed his soul by returning a work of art, in the form of a beautifully written screenplay.

He loved Dyson. The man was always there. Saving him. Making him do the right thing, think the right way. He recalled when he was writing a book based on his Baton Rouge killing spree. He allowed Dyson to read it, actually the whole idea was for him to proofread and review it. But Dyson returned three days later and asked him if he wanted to go to jail or just wanted him to kill him. Derrick understood. Writing a book with all the details of actual killings would certainly land him in prison. He knew he would have been dead within the first week of stepping foot in any prison in America.

He had donned his red haired disguise because she was redhead. He had moved three times, in three separate cabins since he had escaped to Ruidoso. He was supposed to move the day before, but he couldn't. He had spied on the redhead two days now. She was staying in a cabin across from him, past several huge trees, with nice greenery and big branches, and a paved road curved between the cabins. She had been shopping the past couple of days and today, he made it a point to follow her.

She was there alone. And that was a good thing.

They had passed each other on the streets of the shopping district in Ruidoso. Additionally, she had waved at him a couple of times when she was leaving her cabin, as he was standing on the porch of his cabin. He considered this to be a good time to formally introduce himself.

It was nightfall.

He had done his homework. The cabins on both side of her were vacant. The closest was on the backside and at least a good eighth of a mile away. Considering the season and the number of people he had seen touring in Ruidoso, he was surprised they still had vacant cabins in the area. The only other cabin that he could see was empty. This was perfect.

He knocked on the door and was surprised when she was almost immediately answered.

"Hi," she said in almost a whisper. Her features were soft and Derrick could see the flaming red, mixed with the dark red hue of her hair. He loved it. He was instantly turned on.

"Hi, yourself," he replied. "My name is Derrick. Derrick Paine. And I thought I would come over and introduced myself." He liked giving his real name. He had tried it with his second victim in Baton Rouge years ago. He was shocked at how easy it was to break the ice. After all, he was famous.

"Yeah, right," the redhead said. "Derrick Paine the director?"

"Yes, seriously, I'm Derrick Paine," he responded. "Usually, people refer to me as Derrick Paine, the actor, not director. But I'm glad you got it right." He smiled and she seemed to light up. His confidence rose. He had been told on numerous occasions how his smile was infectious and relaxing. And that was his goal—to relax his target.

"Well, I'm Melinda," she said. "Why don't you come in for coffee? I actually just put on a fresh pot."

Derrick gladly accepted. He was achieving his goal. She was so easy at putting her guard down. He knew he was to blame for that.

She moved from the door and walked farther into the living room. As he came in, he looked back to make sure no one was around. Her back was to him. He closed the door and reached his right hand behind his back for the knife. Then out of the peripheral of his left eye, he saw the man behind the door.

He felt the needle in his neck.

Then blackness ruled his world.

CHAPTER 56

Life is about a bunch of twists and turns . . .

. . . that leads you from point A to point Z. The thing is son, if you turn before twisting, you may miss the point."

Those were the words of my father, Howard Carson. I was a teenager, still mourning the death of my mother. Today, just like then, those words didn't make a bit of damn sense to me. But for whatever reason, they suddenly resonated in my head.

Damn you, Howard Carson.

"It's up to you to make heads or tails of the direction, to provide the navigation to how it best fits you as a person, as a man," I remembered my father saying. "And along the way, a ton of obstacles will appear. You will encounter bumpy roads, and sometimes foggy, rainy and snowy days as well as a host of other obstacles. But, young man, on your road to manhood, it will be up to you to determine how best to reach your destination."

My father surprised me with that spiel. However, I appreciated the advice. I was headed to Nashville to live with my brother and complete high school. My father couldn't convey to me how he felt about me leaving—but that was my traveling advice. I didn't completely get it at the time . . . nor did I want to get it. However, it was great advice that stayed with me forever. Regardless of how estranged our relationship was, it took me years to realize how much I hung on to the great advice he provided me.

It was day two since the abduction of Mitzy and Terrence. Was the Bureau feeling the pain? It really was an understatement. The media was having a field day with our so-called blunder of the Terrence Parkins abduction. It wasn't my job to feel bad for the Jet Pack Eight. My task was straightforward — catch the abductors and killers, prevent any other abductions and make sure justice was served. There was a possibility Derrick Paine was still alive and breathing, and if so, our job was to save him before he became *another victim.*

The odds were not in our favor—not in his favor.

We really were behind the power curve. *Clueless.* I wasn't sure that was the appropriate word. We weren't clueless in the aspect that we didn't have a working idea of what was transpiring. But clueless in the aspect that we had no clues whatsoever to proceed from. I think every member of my team realized the quagmire we were in. This was a true maze and we needed the one thing we didn't have, a GPS for solving ridiculous cases.

Ridiculous because the Jet Pack Eight could have pissed off a ton of people before they grew up and lived a so-called decent life. The information we had gleaned thus far on the public and private lives of these people when they were kids was appalling. As crazy as it sounded, someone should have kept a belt or switch in their hand at all times, and beat the meanness and nastiness out of these spoiled brats.

We knew about their past—their individual pasts, not their past together. Six members of the Jet Pack had probably done something that was getting them killed, one by one, three by three. That was pure speculation on my part. And speculation had never made an arrest that I knew of.

What did we know? Usually crimes of this nature, so personal and gruesome, were based on the revenge factor. Unfortunately,

Elliot had made that a specialty of mine. Of course I knew revenge was very personal. I had been there and back, bought several tee-shirts and didn't want to go back. But that's why I was here, racking my brain, trying to figure out what these superstars did when they were younger.

It always came back to the victims.

Victimology.

Then it hit me.

CHAPTER 57

THE NECESSITY OF THE FOOL IS TO WIN AT ALL COSTS.

And I wanted to win. I didn't know why I was pissed. It was an investigation. I had been a part of many investigations. I could blame it on familiarity. Maybe that was or was not the truth. I didn't give a damn.

I was in Maxwell Pack's office with Maxwell and Patrick Conroy. He had already called the meeting before I had a revelation. I had entered the room and Maxwell automatically knew I had something on my mind.

"We go on the attack, we throw out our Hail Mary and put everyone else on the defensive," I stated.

"What do you have in mind?" Maxwell asked.

"Chief, you know we were in Houston interviewing Pat Boldin when you told me about the Parkins's kidnapping." Boldin was Patterson Boldin, another former actor who was working for the federal government, who had also received a severed head—Terri Wenthill. "I got him to open up by telling his ass if he didn't cooperate, you would leak it to the press that he had something to do with the kidnapping and deaths of the Jet Pack members. And because they were so loved, he would be a piranha, looking for a place to hide.

"We need to go back to everyone who received a body part and throw out the same threat, and make them talk to us. And hell, if they don't cooperate, then we leak some information. I'm sure this would make others open up."

Patrick looked at me with a smirk. He knew me. Maxwell was familiar with me, but didn't know the nutty side of me. I was used to throwing junk out there to see what stuck, and what slid off like he was stick to Teflon. And I didn't give empty threats. Hell, the Bureau was full of attorneys. Someone had to give them something to do. They weren't crazy about me, but I kept them employed.

"Let's do it," Chief Maxwell Pack emphatically stated. He had a tinge of excitement in his voice. I think he was ready to get this over with as well.

No one outside the Hoover Building knew of the connection between the Code of Colors investigation and the Jet Pack case. Closing out the Colors case should have bought us a moment of good will with the media and a level of confidence with the public. That didn't happen. The Parkins's kidnapping killed whatever momentum we had gained. This was the lifeline Maxwell was looking for.

Maxwell asked, "What's the most expedient way of doing this?"

"We use Patrick and his team to accomplish the interviews. New blood. Agents none of the recipients have met. Plus, we treat them as hostile witnesses. Read them the riot act. I think they can hit everyone in a couple of days at the very least."

"What are your plans?" Patrick asked.

"First, take another look at the interviews of the assailants from the Code of Colors."

"Then?"

"Track down that fucking Brian Dye and make him tell me his role in this shit."

CHAPTER 58

Vengeance occupied a dark space in the mind.

It created everlasting demons that ate at the fiber of the soul. I didn't wish vengeance on anyone. It made good men bad, and bad men worse. I wondered if the abductors were satisfied with the chaos and sadness they had created.

Some would say it was presumptuous to accuse members of the Jet Pack for possible crimes I wasn't sure they had committed. But as agents, we had experience and knew something about crime. Good agents didn't need to be a member of the Behavior Analysis Unit to know when and why something was amiss. In this investigation, we possibly had bad players on both sides of the aisle. It would have been nice to really paint the Jet Pack in a good picture. But we couldn't. Whoever we were dealing with was waiting on us, the FBI, to release something positive and in admiration of the Jet Pack. Then they would drop the bomb—the individual past of each member.

"That's it," I said aloud. Paula and I were in our conference room, reviewing recordings of the interviews.

"What's it?" Paula stated as she place a video she was watching on pause and spun around to look at me.

"I know these kids did something when they were younger, Paula. But guess what? This is about more than just whatever act they did back then. It's also about the shit they have done since then. I can't explain how I know this right now, I just do. Just call it a gut feeling for now."

Paula didn't immediately say anything. From the look on her face, I knew she was thinking. She was a special agent and behavior analyst. Wearing both hats meant knowing what, how and when to say what was on her mind. She needed that pause before jumping in. I noticed how she did busy work to give herself some time to think this out.

She was going to be a damn good agent, and after this case, I had plans on recommending her to be on a BAU team. That was her calling. She would do well.

The Good Lord laid claim to an eye for an eye. But the reality was, not many people paid attention when that lesson was taught on Sundays. My mind was working. I was focusing on one person I was sure was involved.

"What are you thinking?" Paula Coker broke my deep thought.

I said, "Victimology."

"Victimology?"

"Yeah, you're a profiler, so follow me on this. In victimology, our job is to ask the question, 'What makes these victims the focus of a crime?' If there is more than one victim, we want to know the connection, the similarities."

I had Paula's attention. She rolled her chair closer to mine. "Our attention has been focused on the members of the Jet Pack. They were truly the victims in all of this craziness. And as much as we can't prove it, we know they were involved in something that got us to this point.

"But I think we are focused on the wrong victims, Paula. I think the victims we should be focused on are those who were victimized by the Jet Pack."

"It's easy to see these are crimes of a personal nature, and full of venom and hatred,' Paula added. "And I like the strategy, KC, but we don't have anything on any other crime that these selfish assholes committed. I think we all know we are missing something . . . and something big."

"Care to elaborate, ma'am?"

"I'm not sure yet, KC. Something strikes me as odd. I know Hollywood is brutal, and can create strange bedfellows. But in doing a mental make-up of all eight actors, there is no way these eight individuals should have meshed the way they did. I can understand Dyson Ryker and Trinidad Capture being the Alpha and Beta. They were the oldest and from all indication, probably the more mature of the bunch. I get the feeling it was their job to keep the other six out of trouble. The reason they may have gotten in trouble, assuming they did, were because the two of them weren't around.

"When you look at the other six, the only real thing they had in common was being Hollywood royalty. They all had famous parents. Yeah, they worked together, but their best work was when they weren't on the screen together. Out of the six, Mitzy York and Terri Wenthill had the true talent. Jimmie Claymore wasn't too far behind. But acting wise, the other three were good actors, even as kids. I get that Derrick Paine and Terrance Parkins excelled behind the camera . . . but I don't understand the role of Wash Tunnell."

Now my mind was wandering. Paula had brought up a great point. I didn't care why these kids hung out together. However, that was the major point. Why in the hell did they? It was as if Conrod Bach was obsessed with having his own Brat Pack. So why not make one? And who better to babysit them than two around their ages, but a little bit older and a lot more mature.

"Paula, you just may have something there," I stated matter-of-factly. "You ready to solve this case?"

I could see the beam on Paula's face. This was a moment for her. "You're damn right I am."

The twists and turns of life included strange bedfellows. That even applied to the good guys.

"What are you thinking?" she asked.

I said, "I know the key. Something happened that triggered a certain kind of madness in our Jet Pack Six, and we're going to find out what."

My confidence was high. With every thought, I knew I had the next clue.

"Well, how do plan on figuring out the trigger?"

"Brian Dye."

CHAPTER 59

Urgency in the mind has never equaled weakness of the heart.

That's what his mind was telling him. However, for Terrence Parkins it wasn't that viable at all. The man was afraid. His last thought was being in the living room of his hideaway home in Georgia. Sleep was calling his name, but he was trying his best to fight it. He was watching old movies. Movies he and his friends had been in years ago. Movies they had made even before they were known to the world as the Jet Pack Eight.

He thought his man-servant was reporting to work. He forgot what day it was. Saturday. He didn't work on weekends. The needle was jabbed in his neck before he could get off his recliner and find out who had entered his sanctuary.

In his dream, he was a man on a mission. And his mission had a name—Conrod Bach . . . and a title—father. He was a younger version of himself. As a boy, he was considered pudgy. As a teenager, the pudginess turned into a hard body. Now, as a man, his medium built body consisted of a pouch midsection and balding hair.

In his younger version, he was once again a hard body snaking through the B&B Productions building, in search of his prey. He was shirtless, but he had two bullet belts crisscrossing his torso. He also had on a gun-belt with 9mm Glocks on each side. He was pointing a semiautomatic assault rifle and shooting anything that got in his way.

Those trying to prevent him from reaching his prey were people he knew. People he had known for years. People he called friends. More importantly, people in another life he should be calling brothers and sisters.

These people were now his enemies and they too, donned weapons. But he would be the victor. He killed before he was killed. Jimmie Claymore, Terri Wenthill, Derrick Paine, Mitzy York, his best friend, Wash Tunnell, and numerous others he knew were his brothers and sisters—killed at his hand.

Then it reached the next to last level, as if he was playing a popular interactive video game. This was the level where he encountered the two bad asses of the Bach family—Trinidad Capture and Dyson Ryker. The Alpha and Beta of the Conrod Bach children. He was out of bullets. But he had a machete. It was a dream. It didn't matter where the machete came from, as long as he had it. His adversary, Trinidad, was an expert in the use of double blade ninja swordplay. Terrence wasn't an expert in any kind of sword play, including the machete he was wielding.

The battle was intense, but in the end he was the victor. That's the way it should be. It was his dream . . . his fantasy. Next, was Dyson. As he turned to face his biggest adversary, he saw the blade out of his peripheral vision. His eyes stayed on the man who hands gripped the sword that would cut his head off.

And it wasn't Dyson.

The scrubs meant he was a doctor.

The smile meant Terrence Parkins was a dead man.

CHAPTER 60

SUICIDE IS A VIABLE OPTION.

The electrical charge felt like a heavyweight boxer had hit him with a punch of a lifetime in the middle of his back. He tried to rise up, but the restraints kept him bound to the cot, bed, table or whatever he was lying on. He knew the charge was computer-generated. He knew because Dyson Ryker had presented him a script with a kidnapped victim confined to a casket type contraption, and computer-generated charges attacked the victim's body. In the script, the charges felt like real punches that left real excruciating, painful bruises.

Another scene in the script included strobe lights with a kaleidoscope effect that attacked the victim's face, leaving the person partially blinded and disoriented. Additionally, the lights made him feel as if he had a tanning light burning a hole in his face. He tried protecting his eyes by closing them, but that didn't stop the effects of the lights. He even thought what little hair he had left would catch a fire at any moment.

The cushion in the casket was semi-hard or semi-soft, however you looked at it. He was uncomfortable and he wasn't in a position to get comfortable, even if that was possible. He knew he had let out a yelp when he was electronically hit in the back, but simultaneously, Mitzy had let out a scream as well. He wished he could be a comfort or a knight in shining armor for her, but that wasn't happening. They were both in the same position.

He was true to the meaning of selfishness. He had never thought about how he would die. In his mind, he thought if it ever entered his head, it just might come true. But if he did have such thoughts, no way he would have thought it would end this way. Being bound in a fucking casket or whatever it was, and being tortured the way Dyson had wrote about all those years ago. And as much as it pained him, he didn't want to think that Dyson was a part of this.

In his dream, Dyson was supposed to be his next adversary. However, the man in the scrubs was Steve Sinatra.

Dr. Sinatra. The man's nickname was Sin . . . and he was committing the biggest *sin* of all—murder.

His mind was on overload. He really didn't know his head from his ass. He didn't have any idea what time it was or how long they had been there or if he had even gotten a good three or four hours of sleep. It seemed that every time he was lights out, an electronic punch would bring him back to the here and now. He wished he had read Dyson's screenplay to the last page. It was unrealistic—or so he thought.

"M-M-M-Mitzy . . . Mitzy, you awake?" She was also on his shit list. The ninth step of sobriety is admitting your sin, claiming up to your misgivings. Although this wasn't Alcoholics' Anonymous, the last thing Terrence Parkins would ever do would be admitting fault on his part. Regardless of what actually happened twenty years ago, in his mind, it would always be Mitzy's fault. She had sex with the enemy . . . the one with the appropriate nickname.

Sin.

"Yeah, didn't you hear me scream?" she said with attitude.

"I'm not the one you should be pissed at . . . it's the love of your life who put us in here."

Neither said anything. Both were thinking about the past. One wishing he had killed the one he was really pissed off at on that dreaded day. The other wishing she had made a concerted effort years ago to right the wrong that happened on that day.

"I think Dyson has something to do with this," Terrence stated.

"Why you think that?" Terrence could hear the fear and sorrow in her voice. One part of his brain was happy she was going through this. Primarily because she wasn't being beaten up the way he was. The other part of his brain wished they both were somewhere else—anywhere but here.

"What's happening to us," he said. "Dyson gave me a screenplay years ago with this exact scenario, a victim was being attacked by a computer while tied down in a casket-like box. A husband was seeking revenge for someone killing his wife."

"Fuck!"

"Yeah, fuck," Terrence said in a low voice.

"How does it end?" Mitzy asked.

"I'm sure it ends with our deaths. But I'm not completely sure, I didn't finish the script."

"Why not, it wasn't good?"

"No, because it was great," he replied. "I thought it was unrealistic though. Computers were getting better and better, but I wanted to be thought of as a great screenwriter and director. This was too unrealistic."

"Terrence, correct me if I'm wrong, but you have never written a single fucking word or single script in your life. Dyson or someone else has always written work you took credit for."

"How in the fuck do you know that?" he said excitedly.

"We all knew that Terrence!"

The sudden display on the monitors over each casket popped on. It caught the attention of both Mitzy and Terrence. The person on the operating table was Wash Tunnell, and a voice said, "This is the first of three videos. Enjoy."

Next, four people in scrubs appeared on the screen, looking down at Wash. The camera then zoomed in on the primary medical person, on his face. Next, the camera zoomed in on the faces of the other three possible medical personnel.

Neither person said a word. If they could see each other, both Mitzy and Terrence would have seen tears flowing down each other's face.

CHAPTER 61

DREAMS ARE WHAT DEFINE THE SOUL OF MEN.

That was the line Elliot Lucas had told me.

I had just buried my brother, Steve, and I felt the weight of the world was on my shoulders. He was the backbone of the family, and he was leaving behind a wife and three kids. Although our father was still living, I could only recall him being a father to Alyse. My sister-in-law, Denise, was very distraught at Steve's death, so the responsibility was all mines.

I had conveyed my fear to Elliot and told him I had dreams, possibly nightmares of failure. "The strong man can distinguish between nightmares and dreams," he told me. "And he can listen and find meaning in his dreams."

I was still in the NFL when he told me that. I don't know if my dreams led me to the Bureau. However, Elliot's speech stayed with me. Growing up in Memphis, years before riverboat casinos popped up in Tunica, Mississippi, Memphians gave their money to the dog track in West Memphis, Arkansas. My father was a frequent patron to the dog track. Sometimes he would tell my mother about his dream and ask her to look the subject up in her *dream book.* Hell, I think in the 'hood, at least one mom on every street had a dream book. On McAdoo Avenue, it was my mom.

I didn't have a dream book to realize Elliot was right. I had to make sense of the thoughts that occupied my mind every now and then.

In my dream, I was revisiting my days of old in Los Angeles, when Brian Dye was a DJ and members of the Jet Pack were regular patrons of the club scene in those days. I saw all faces of the Malibu brats and many other familiar faces. I couldn't recall names. Different clubs . . . different venues . . . one deejay.

The troubling thing was the faces. So many familiar faces. I wish I could say men and women, but the Jet Pack were teenagers, maybe young adults at best. I was sure the only two over twenty-one were Trinidad Capture and Dyson Ryker. The kids were famous . . . or maybe infamous and famous. They were Hollywood royalty. They owned the city, probably the damn state. I needed names. I needed . . . more than familiarization.

My mind kept coming around to the same thing—familiar faces with no names. The Jet Pack Eight were the known ones. But the true Jet Pack consisted of many faces. All young, all foolish, out to have a good time—whatever a good time meant to them. And one man was always the center of attention—DJ White Sexual Chocolate, Brian Dye.

The man was a womanizer, a man whore. I never saw him without a woman or two or three by his side. In another life, he was probably my hero. In many ways, Brian was a tall, lanky, shy kid. But in his deejay persona, he was transformed. Spinning records, alcohol and women were his security blankets. *Or maybe blanket.* He couldn't have one without the others.

I didn't want to call him Dr. Jerkyll and Mr. Hyde. No. He was Brian Dye, the good guy, and DJ White Sexual Chocolate, the man whore in sheep's clothing. Brian, the shy kid, became the billionaire. Something told me his deejay persona was still the monster within.

It was hard for me to believe. Brian was the centerpiece, the cornerstone behind the madness. My eyes were open. I needed to close them to get a clearer picture of what was what. I needed to place names on the faces, not familiarization. The familiarization phase was over.

The faces were many. They all started out as actors, entertainers. All chasing their dreams. Familiarization. They all knew each other. Partied together. Spent time together. Worked together. Drawn to each other. Probably spent more time together than they really wanted to.

Interesting.

It didn't make a difference, nightclub or the venue, there was one commonality—the deejay. He was probably destined to be the one.

I was awake. I kept my eyes closed. I needed to see the visions. I needed to make the connection.

Fuck!

I needed to take a leak. I was human after all.

Fuck!

Eyes open, visions and connections lost.

After we became friends, Brian revealed to me he had four regular women he spent time with. I didn't know if the four knew about each other, or if they did know, if they gave a damn. That was his brand during his deejaying gigs—to be a player.

It was strange thinking of those days. I had my moments as well. But Brian was the sexual predator. Women were his weakness, his kryptonite. Even when we got together to watch basketball or football games, he would have a woman on his arm.

I was wide awake now. My visions and connections were lost for now.

Damn, I needed sleep badly.

CHAPTER 62

Each given day is a harbinger of what's to come.

I had this big idea to confront Brian—actually to surprise him and take him out of his comfort zone. Too often, many ideas never come to fruition. The man was elusive. The Bureau's IT division as well as CarsonOne's information security specialist had been very unsuccessful in finding the whereabouts of the man.

Something told me Brian's technology footprint had changed drastically since this whole ordeal began. And I thought it was very intentional. The business and personal cell phones he used on a daily basis had been used intermittently at best for the past three weeks. The past week he hadn't used either one. I was still convinced the man was using other company phones or a burner or two.

I knew Brian was involved in this. The churning of my gut told me it was probably deeper than I had imagined. Initially, I was sure it was more than just providing the use of his company jets. But the more I thought about it, the more I was convinced he had a deeper involvement.

I was kicking myself. He once told me how he lost use of his right hand. He could do some things with it, but an accident or maybe an intentional act, took away the complete mobility of the hand. I couldn't remember and that was bugging the hell out of me.

I didn't know what time I finally dozed off. It didn't matter. My stupor didn't last long. At 4:10 in the morning, I received a text:

FOCUS.

If I hadn't looked at the phone number, I would have thought it was Julia. She knew me like a book. She knew how to reel me in and keep me on track.

The sender once knew me just as well.

Since our discussion with Mikki Lanay, I had called Trinidad at least ten times on the number Mikki had given to me. She never answered or responded to any of my voicemails. I don't know how long I stared at the text.

GLAD YOU'RE STILL LIVING STRANGER.

I was wondering if I would get a quick reply. It was only 1:30 Pacific time, three hours behind us early dwellers on the East Coast.

WHEN ARE YOU COMING TO CALIFORNIA? THIS IS WHERE YOU SHOULD BE. THIS IS WHERE YOUR INVESTIGATION SHOULD HAVE STARTED & ENDED.

I didn't know if I should touch that comment or not. This was Trinidad's way of telling me the only way to solve the case was to be in California. None of the crimes occurred in the Golden State. However, all of the victims lived in the Los Angeles area.

Before I could send another text, Trinidad beat me to it:

FOCUS.

Only a fool doesn't listen to the words of wisdom. I could be a fool at times.

WE NEED TO TALK. I WILL BE THERE TODAY. HOPEFULLY. NO LATER THAN 2MORO. LOOKING FOR YOUR HUSBAND. I NEED TO TALK TO HIM.

I wanted to see how long it would take her to answer the question. It was also my way of letting her know that he was our number one suspect. How true that was, I wasn't sure. I knew Trinidad. Her answer might tell me what I needed to know. Did Brian commit the crime?

LANDS AT DULLES IN HIS PRIVATE JET AT 7 YOUR TIME. WHAT YOU THINK YOU KNOW, YOU DON'T KNOW. AMAZING WHAT A FOCUSED SOUL CAN DO.

I was used to Trinidad's cryptic messages. She was good for telling you what you needed to hear, as long as you could decipher the message.

I could.

CHAPTER 63

A THRONG OF SUPPORTERS ARTIFICIALLY BLESSES THE WICKED AT HEART.

Mitzy remembered the days when she used to do her own stunts. Excruciatingly painful. That was her most memorable thought. She wished her mind was groggy with nonsensical thoughts. That wasn't the case. Her mind was clear. Too clear.

She and Terrence were sitting down in chairs side by side. Their restraints were gone. But neither one of them was in a position to make a run for it. She wished she could say both of them had been beaten from head to toe. She had been beaten from the base of her neck to her ankles. However, Terrence had been beaten from head to toe. His face was swollen. One of his eyes was closed. He had a busted lip, but he could still speak.

They both had viewed the murders of Terri, Wash and Jimmie. Every single beating, every surgical laser cut, and even the process of placing their body parts into cryogenic freezer units. And lastly, they had viewed each individual sitting down as they were now. There was one exception—the sound was turned off.

The lights came on. And sitting in front of them were three men and a woman. All were dressed in scrubs. Mitzy knew each individual.

She said, "I guess the chickens have come home to roost." She cracked a smile. It was genuine. She had lost. It wasn't a game she knew she was playing. "Or is it the hen coming home?"

"No, bitch. It's the rooster coming home to roost," the lone female corrected. "But something tells me you knew that."

"Of course I knew that Mikki," Mitzy responded. "This is funny. I can't speak for Terrence, but I never thought it would be you three. Mikki, Patterson and Drake. It just never dawned on me. It makes sense. But I didn't have a clue. Sin I get. But you three, I never imagined."

"In case you don't recall, Terrence, let me introduce you to my team" Sin said. "Mikki Lanay. Patterson Boldin. And Dr. Drake Devlin. Of course I don't have to introduce the team to you. Your face have been instilled in their brains for twenty years."

"Sin, why now?" Terrence mumbled. It pained him to speak. And not just his lip. His whole body ached. He was just waiting to die now.

"Why now?" Sin stated. "Why not now? I mean, legally, there is no specified time limit on murder. Plus, in renegade justice, we the jury consist of those seeking justice for those who aren't able to seek their own justice. Mikki's brother, Patterson's brother, Drake's brother and sister, River Gillard's brother—you remember good old River, don't you? You know, the guy who wrote several screenplays for you. The same River that took his own life because he couldn't handle it anymore. And of course, my youngest sister."

"It wasn't my fault, Sin," Terrence replied. "It wasn't."

"Yep, the same thing Terri said," Mikki added.

"And the same thing Wash said," Drake stated in turn.

"As well as Jimmie," Patterson chimed in.

Two victims, who could be considered assailants, exchanged gazes with those who might be cutting them up soon. Four judging two.

It didn't surprise anyone seeing the tears flow down Terrence's cheeks. It also didn't surprise anyone that Mitzy didn't shed a tear.

Sin said, "This is how this is going to happen. The reason your friends died is because they lied to us. Each and every one of them lied. It only took one of them to tell the truth and all three would have lived. But it didn't happen. They were too used to lying. So, this time, we are interviewing both of you together to see if you guys can tell the truth. If you do, your lives will be spared."

"What truth Steve?" Mitzy asked.

"What happened that day . . . from beginning to end."

CHAPTER 64

A DEFECTED HANDGUN IS AN INVITATION TO DIE WHEN BATTLING A BIG BAD SHARK.

Elliot told me the story about him tracking down Big Pauly Giacuomo, the biggest crime boss in New York, to the North Shore beach area in Honolulu, Hawaii. Big Pauly had been a crime boss for fifteen years and had laughed and boasted about the FBI's incompetence in convicting him. The man had been tried three times on various charges with no conviction. This time, Elliot knew he had him. While he was waiting on the beach for Big Pauly to finish his swim, he watched as the mobster tried his best to fight off the shark that was attacking him. He witnessed the notorious crime boss try to fire the handgun, but was successful. That same afternoon, the Coast Guard removed Big Pauly's dead carcass and his defected handgun out of the water. Evidently, someone had removed the firing pin on the weapon.

Since he wasn't arrested, Elliot viewed that as the big score he allowed to get away.

My big score was deplaning one of his company's Learjets. I had nine agents with me. Special Agent Paula Coker was with me in the limousine awaiting Brian Dye and his bodyguards to get closer to the car. The driver had been removed and retained. He wasn't officially in custody, but removed for his own safety. I was sitting in the back of the limo. Once Brian and his two brawny bodyguards were ten feet from the limo, both Paula and I would exit the vehicle, and the remaining agents would converge on the car.

This wasn't an arrest. Just a show of force. A scare tactic for a man we probably couldn't scare.

As Brian and his bodyguards approached the limo, Paula and I exited the car as planned. My own entourage of three black Suburban SUVs sped towards our location. Then the damnedest thing happened. Brian's biggest security protection specialist charged at me with his head down. I was exiting the back passenger door of the limo. The man had to be at least six-six and weighed about two hundred eighty pounds. He was African-American, with a baldhead, very broad shoulders and I was sure he had less than ten percent body fat.

I sidestepped his attack in the nick of time, and rammed his baldhead into the side of the limo. Then I went for what I considered to be the weakest part of a person's body—I stomped on the outside of the man's left ankle. The instant break confirmed my suspicion, it was the weakest part of his body. I followed that up with a hard right to his left cheek. His face was hard, but the hit was solid. So solid, I was sure I would be icing my hand on the plane ride to Vegas.

I heard Paula call out, "Not another step!" to the other bodyguard. "Hands up!"

I wanted to make sure my attacker was down for good. He was. I turned around and the other security protection was a bit smaller than his co-worker. He was also African-American, standing about six-three, maybe two hundred twenty or two hundred thirty pounds. He was lean. If I was worried, he would be the one I would be worried about.

Brian didn't have his hands up. He was a billionaire and his status gave him that privilege. I was sure that was his mentality. He was once the coolest, nicest guy I knew. Now he was an arrogant prick.

My people were surrounding us, with weapons drawn. I took the steps needed to close the gap between us. Then I did the unexpected—I grabbed the billionaire by his collar and dragged him to the limo.

"Arrest this asshole and get him medical assistance," I said. My statement wasn't directed to any one specific person.

I pushed Brian into the back of the limo, following directly behind him and closing the door behind me, all in one motion. When the door closed and Brian turned around, I punched him hard in the middle of his chest.

He moaned loudly as he fell back and reached for his chest.

"Fuck KC, are you fucking crazy!"

He was on the back seat. I sat directly across from him. "Am I crazy?" I said. "Seriously, Brian, that's your fucking statement, am I fucking crazy?" I looked at my former friend. I was beyond pissed off. In my mind, I had to count to ten. *One thousand one, one thousand two, one thousand three . . .*

"I will have your badge for this dammit!" Brian stated before I could complete my count.

"Shut the fuck up!" I yelled. "I should kick your ass, you lying sack of shit! You used to be a stand-up guy, good fucking people. Now you are a piece of shit! I know money changes people, but damn, dude, you are a complete asshole now. What the fuck, Mr. Dye?"

We exchanged gazes. No words had to be spoken. Maybe Brian was doing what I was doing, remembering days of old—a time when things were simpler. Or so I imagined. I could be spending my time in jail for a crime I didn't commit. And who knows what Mr. Dye could have been doing.

I was waiting on the magic words, "I want my attorney." But the words never came. I saw something in Brian's eyes. Maybe a trace of the old Brian. Maybe something else . . . like fear.

"I really want to kick your ass," I said in my calmest voice. "You lied to me dude."

Still nothing.

I said, "Tell me your part in all of this . . . and Brian, if you lie to me, I promise you, I will give you something to take to Director Lucas."

"W-W-W-What do you want to know?" he managed to say.

"Tell me about your involvement in this mess."

"I have friends who needed to use my aircraft and equipment. I didn't ask questions. They are people I respect, love and care about. I was happy to help."

"What friends?'

"Friends you know."

"What is all of this about?" I thought I would throw Brian off his game. I knew the man. He was trying to calculate my next question. Actually, trying to stay a move ahead. I knew the game.

"KC, honestly, I don't know. I'm only extending a friendly gesture to friends."

"You know I could arrest you for being an accessory to a crime."

"Arrest me then."

I didn't expect this. So I had to do something he didn't expect. In one quick action, I pulled my weapon and shot at the man's head. Not directly at his head. I made sure my round was an inch from his head.

The look on his face was priceless. The blood left his face. He looked white as a ghost. I saw tears in his ducts, just waiting to be released. I think he really did see his life flash before him.

The door suddenly opened and it was Paula Coker with her gun pulled.

"Close the door!" I screamed. And Paula did as I commanded. My reaction caught her off guard.

"Who were you so generous to, Mr. Dye?"

"Drake." His voice was weak. Fear had gripped the billionaire. I made it a point not to look at his genital area. Something told me he may have pissed himself.

"Drake?" I put my gun up. Now I was the one whose blood had probably left his face. Drake Devlin. A friend. My friend. "You're a fucking asshole, dude. I want to kick your ass more now than I previously did."

"You wanted to know, I told you."

"Who else?"

"I'm don't know."

"Why would Drake do something like this?"

"Because the Jet Pack took his twin brother and his youngest sister."

"When?"

"Twenty years ago. Before we met you."

"Why now?"

"River committed suicide over the holiday season."

I felt like dirt now. River Gillard and Drake were best friends. River was one of the top screenwriters in Hollywood. He was quiet, meek. The complete opposite of Drake. Additionally, Drake had told me he lost his brother and sister to a boating mishap some years ago. His doted on both his twin brother, Duncan, and his youngest sister, Desarae. He always talked about how much smarter they were than he. It was hard to believe. Drake had an IQ of one hundred and ninety-two. He was the real most interesting man in the world.

Drake had won an Oscar at age fourteen, and was a prime reason the four movies he starred in were in the top ten highest grossing movies in the nineties. He became a doctor because of Duncan and Desarae's desire to be doctors.

Dr. Drake Duncan was one of the top surgeons in the country. Forget specialties—he was highly qualified as a surgeon in over twenty of them. And more importantly to me, he was a good friend. He was the only one from that crowd I actually kept in touch with. We made a promise to each other after I left the NFL, we would attend two sporting events per year. Plus, Drake helped me get security contracts with medical facilities throughout the country when I started CarsonOne Productions.

I broke our promise last year. I was too busy to attend any events with Drake. I also failed to call him back when he caught me in a meeting three months ago. Yeah, feeling like dirt was being disrespectful to dirt. I had let a great friend down. He had been there for me, and three months ago he probably needed me.

"Tell me what happened," I said to Brian. He was no longer holding his chest and seemed to be more relaxed now. That was a good thing. I think he knew he had stunned me.

"I don't know what happened. I just know the Jet Pack killed them. There was no boating accident. Wash, Terri and the rest killed them . . . along with several others."

"Where is Drake, Brian?"

"I truly don't know, KC. He needed my aircraft. I made it happen. When I was starting out in this business, it was Drake who put me on the map. He turned people on to my business. He guaranteed medical professionals throughout the world that I could deliver the goods. He made me."

"Does Trinidad and Dyson know what you told me?"

"Which part?"

"All of it."

"They know more about what happened to Drake's siblings than me. As far as endorsing the destruction of the Jet Pack, no, they didn't know. This was the time to do it though."

"Why do you say that?"

"Dyson has been out of the country for the past six weeks," Brian replied. "If he is in country, no way this happens."

"I threatened to kick your ass, Brian. Dyson and Trinidad will probably do it."

CHAPTER 65

FEAR IN THE FOOL, RUNNETH THE MOUTH OVER.

"While you were busy fucking Mitzy, I was busy getting fucked up with Terri, Jimmie, Wash and good old Derrick," Terrence explained. "Good old fucking Derrick."

Those words hung in the air. Steve, Drake, Patterson and Mikki knew what they meant. Even Mitzy knew what it meant.

Derrick was choirboy by day, the devil's number one son at night.

"It was after midnight, and we were already a little frosty by the time Derrick came with his concoctions. He had a mixture of alcohol called Satan's Potion, and another mixture of capsules with who knows what in them. But the effects were fucked. Our heads hurt. Caused us to have headaches and hallucinations—hell, I thought ghosts came alive.

"He didn't tell us what he gave us, but it was potent. And dangerous. Even more dangerous considering Derrick was being Derrick, the storyteller. Always with the great tale. And he had a doozy this time.

"He told us every damn person in the schoolhouse had the same father. Good old fuck 'em all Conrod Bach. And that there was a rebellion brewing . . . Conrod's other children against his favorite children—us, the Jet Pack Six. He then told us Dyson and Trinidad were the outsiders. That both of them knew the truth about *our* father, and they would lead the rebellion against us.

"Honestly, Sin, we were so fucking out of it with the drinking and drugging, we didn't know our ass from a whole in the ground."

"You are saying you guys had no culpability in any of this?" Steve asked. "That none of you take responsibility for any of this?"

"No," Mitzy chimed in. "He is telling you what happened. How things got carried away. Why events occurred the way they did."

"Shut up, bitch, you weren't even high or drunk!" Mikki interrupted. She had venom in her voice. The women exchanged looks.

Mikki played along with this charade, but she knew she and Terrence were dead after this. At that moment, she felt bad for Terrence. He was telling the truth, in hopes that truth would set him free. But only in his mind. She speculated that mental freedom was better than no freedom at all.

"Continue," Drake said to Terrence.

"Derrick got to us. We were getting high in Exam Room 3 of the Rustic, when Derrick made the statement there were students, the children of the devil, in the O-R."

Terrence stopped. It wasn't a pause. He needed to gather himself. His one good eye was filled with tears, while his swollen eye leaked tears. As much as he had thought about that day, this was the first time he had to recount it all—blow by harmful blow.

"Continue," Drake repeated.

"Be patient, Drake!" Mitzy screamed.

Patterson shot Terrence with a quick jolt of the taser. The man screamed as the sudden, unexpected shot caused him to fall back and hit the floor. The device could deliver up to fifty thousand volts, but the average jolt was usually over twelve hundred, which by Terrence's reaction, still could knock you on your ass.

"What in the fuck is wrong with you Patty?" Mitzy excitedly exclaimed.

Both Drake and Sin helped the man back up, sitting his chair upright and helping him into it. Terrence was still visibly shaking from the twelve hundred volt jolt. Regrets were on his mind. Regrets he could never share with this group.

"Patterson, don't do that shit again," Drake stated. "Get yourself together Terrence. We want to hear the rest of the story."

Terrence shook his head in the affirmative. He was still shaking. He looked fragile and frail. For many, the delivery of that kind of electrical charge, for even a few seconds, could put one in medical danger, especially if delivered near the heart. Patterson had aimed the taser at Terrence's stomach, center mass. When Terrence suddenly vomited, it didn't surprise anyone. He, nor Mitzy, hadn't had anything to eat for what seemed like a week. In actuality, it was two days.

Steve said, "Pick up the story Mitzy."

"I can't," she said with bitterness in her voice. "Remember, I was fucking you. Or was it you fucking me? I forget."

"I-I-I-I'm okay," Terrence's voice was weak. "We . . . we . . . we went into the O-R, and there they were. Nine of them. And I swear, I don't know where all the tools and equipment and stuff came from. One minute, we were in the exam room, and the next minute we were two hallways over in the O-R with knives, hammers, drills and whatever else we had."

"It was Derrick," Mitzy added. "He had a bag over his shoulder like he was fucking Santa Claus. He gave everyone some kind of tool to use as a weapon while they were in the exam room. I was supposed to have been in the O-R that day. I met the group as they were entering the hallway of the O-R, and Derrick told me what he had done. I was flabbergasted, but before I could really do anything, they had run into the room and started the craziness.

"Terrence had the drill and he attacked a couple of kids. Terri and Jimmie were the real crazy ones. Terri had a hammer and

Jimmie had a small sledgehammer. Between the both of them, I think they hit every person that wasn't a part of the Jet Pack upside the head. That made it easy for everyone else. Wash had a knife in each hand, and he knew what to do with them."

Tears were flowing down Mitzy's cheeks. The same could be said for Terrence, Mikki and Patterson. Drake and Steve continued to listen attentively. Both had shed their tears years ago.

"Then three others came in the O-R and tried to stop us," Terrence stated. "Brian was one of them. Jimmie hit him in the back with his sledgehammer and when he fell to the floor, I drilled a hole in his right hand. And truthfully, that's my most vivid memory of the whole day. That's the memory that stayed with me forever. The rest of it kind of came back to me over the years."

No one said anything. However, the silence was golden. This was the fourth time Steve, Drake, Patterson and Mikki had heard the same story. Only one time did they hear a different version, and that was from Terri Wenthill, who traded roles with Mitzy York. But it clear to the four of them, Terri lied.

And each time they heard the story, it was the same result—Patterson and Mikki couldn't hold back their emotions or tears, while Drake and Steve listened intently.

"Why did you all stop?" Drake asked.

"Because I sprayed them with the fire extinguisher in the room," Mitzy answered. "And I even hit Terri and Jimmie upside the head to get them to stop."

"And why did you do that?" Steve added.

"Derrick was busy cutting up a couple of people with an ax he had," Mitzy stated sadly.

"Six dead, six others badly injured," Drake stated.

"And no jail time or death penalty for anyone," Steve added his thought.

"Until now," Mikki closed the door on the discussion.

CHAPTER 66

LIGHT LOVES THE INTENT OF DARKNESS.

My three team members and I were flying in one of the Bureau's learjets on our way to Los Angeles. My right hand was sitting in a bucket of ice. It wasn't often I used the Bureau's aircraft. I usually commandeered one of the company's, CarsonOne, aircraft. We had a few aircraft on the ramp, but they were receiving preventive maintenance or being used by training personnel. I was in the back of the plane, contemplating life and past endeavors, adventures and friendships, while my team was in the front of the plane talking and getting to know each other.

River had committed suicide by shooting himself in the head, leaving behind a wife and four children. Drake was the pseudo uncle and brother-in-law, but I was sure the family was financially set. Reading the information I gleaned from the internet, River's brother had died on the same boating accident as Drake's brother and sister. I knew that to be a lie now.

I was recalling the times the three of us had had years ago. But my mind was more reminiscent of the times Drake and I had hung out over the years. I could remember him telling me that Trinidad Capture would like to meet me one day. To me, that was great to hear. But he wouldn't introduce us. He told me that when the time came, it would happen. He didn't lie about that.

When we touched down in L.A., it was noon. A UH-60 Black Hawk helicopter was waiting to take us to the B&B Productions building in downtown L.A., where Trinidad was awaiting my company. And that was what I told my team when we arrived at the airport, I was attending this meeting by alone. They weren't happy, especially Paula Coker, but I was the lead and this was going to be an awkward situation as it was. I knew Trinidad. She would talk to me. There used to be no secrets between us. I was hoping that still held true.

The ride was quick. On the side of the building and a football field length away from the parking lot was the company's helipad. There were a couple of technicians to greet us, but neither said anything to me as I deplaned from the helicopter. I made it to the lobby of the building and told the security specialist Miss Capture was expecting me.

"You know where to go," was the only thing he said.

I didn't say anything. He was right. I did know where to go. I walked down two corridors, entered a door that said Private, and took the first of three elevators that took me directly to the seventh floor, the private office of the Vice President of New Films and Shows—Trinidad Capture.

When I got off the elevator, I knew where I was. In the center of an overly spacious office that had two other rooms—a full bathroom and a bedroom fit for a queen. And the queen beckoned me to come have a seat on her brown soft leather sofa.

I was greeted with a hug—a long hug—as Trinidad put her head on my chest. I knew what was up. It was the embrace, the feelings, the togetherness we relinquished when I was falsely accused. No words were necessary. We would eventually discuss business—probably even discuss old times. For now, we were content with the here and now. This was different. We were catching up on a lost moment.

"How you be woman?" I finally asked.

"Seen better days, but I'm say fair to middling Mr. Special Agent. How you be?"

Damn. She could always get me with that voice. Every word was laced with a silky soul and sultriness that made grown men weak in the knees and women weep with jealousy. Trinidad had a model's body—she was five ten barefooted, looked like she was around one hundred twenty to one hundred thirty pounds, curves still in the right places. She wore her hair in a short bob and she always had terrific breast.

In my forty-four years, she was on my list of seven or eight women who I considered to be the epitome of pure sexiness. Of course, Julia was at the top of the list.

"You do know this is about business?" I said, as we were still in our embrace.

"Shut up. We'll get to business. This is fourteen years overdue, so you owe me. After all, after this day I will never see you again."

She had a crack in her voice. And I was sure I had tears on my shirt. I didn't say anything. She was probably right. The next time we would probably see each other was at a funeral, one of us lying in a casket, waiting on the curtains to fall forever.

Lives can be affected by the damnedest of things. Lydia tried to send me to jail for helping her out. I took out that betrayal, and my anger, on the one person who truly loved me back then. If I had swallowed that anger and gave in to my desires, who knows—Trinidad and I would have possibly been married today, and she and I may have had children together.

But that was the past. And it didn't do any good to go down that path. Sometimes life threw you lemons . . . and you just had to throw them away.

"I know Julia is a good woman, and I know you two are great together," Trinidad said. "But I wish I had her life."

"You have three wonderful sons and a husband who loves you."

"Brian doesn't love me, KC. My marriage to Brian was one of convenience and power. We helped each other. Plus, I was in a bad place for a long time."

She stopped talking. Her mind went to another place, another time. I knew—because my mind had been to those places.

"I'll make a deal with you," she said.

"What kinda' deal?" I'm sure she heard the trepidation in my voice.

"You let me keep holding you and I will tell you anything you want to know."

I pulled my head back and looked at Trinidad. Fuck! She was still as beautiful and warm as ever. "No shit, you will tell me whatever I want to know, no holding back?"

She didn't say anything, but I saw it in her eyes.

"Conrod Bach?"

"He is my father and the father of all of the members of the Jet Pack . . . and he has over one hundred other children."

I was still looking at Trinidad. "Say what?"

"Yes, KC . . . I have over one hundred twenty siblings. And yes, that's why Jimmie, Terri and all the rest are dying."

I'll be damned.

CHAPTER 67

THE HUBRIS OF THE HAVES, CAN BE THE DEATH OF THE HAVE
NOTS.

In my mind, I was twelve again and sitting on our porch, listening to my father and his friends. It was smack talk, which they called talking *cash shit*. The best at talking cash shit was Mr. Bud. He lived directly across the street from us and was Howard Carson's primary drinking partner, and best friend. Besides my father, the other smacktalkers went by the name Naked Head, Big Man, Mr. Kid and Shorty B.

"You know what the most powerful thing in the world is?" Mr. Bud asked, not directing the question to one specific person. I remember hearing answers such as a Mack truck, airplane and a locomotive train.

Mr. Bud then answered, "Pussy!" And that answer and lesson was directed at me. "Boy, that little area between a girl's legs drive sane men crazy and bring powerful men to their knees. And you know what, Lil Kenny, some men call it the pussy's brew. Because some women's pussy is so good, you think there's a spell put on you. And boy, believe me, if you live long enough, you hope you run into that pussy's brew at least five or ten times in your lifetime."

As much as all the men on that porch laughed, all of them voiced or nodded their head in agreement.

I had been a victim of that brew on several occasions, and ended up marrying the best of that brew. The second best was the woman I was hugging now. She was telling me a tale of a man she called father, who had probably been the worse victim in mankind of pussy's brew. He was so hooked on the stuff, and the spell was so powerful, the man had procreated over a hundred and twenty children. And that procreation had turned children into monsters, and monsters into demons. And they went by the moniker Jet Pack.

I initially felt a sense of guilt hugging Trinidad, until I realized this wasn't about love—at least, not present love anyway. This was about past love and more importantly, Trinidad not being able to look me in the eye was due to the sins of her father. She was an actor, and had always been in the business and she was always truthful with me. Now, I wasn't so sure.

I was still trying to wrap my head around Conrod Bach's misgivings and what Brian had told me earlier. And that was the give and take in our discussion, I told her what Brian had relayed to me earlier, which was followed by her telling me another fantastic tale.

This one was the story of six famous kids learning about that their benefactor, a man they loved and thought was doing the best for their career—only to learn he was actually their father, and wanted to build a Hollywood empire with those who shared his blood. And the unbelievable star of this tale was Derrick Paine, the Jerkyll and Hyde of the Bach clan.

Trinidad began by saying, "Everyone knows Derrick was a natural at directing and even telling a story, but the one thing not many knew or know about Derrick is that he loved biology and chemistry, and he was just as natural at coming up with crazy liquid concoctions. And supposedly that's what happened—Derrick drugged everyone except himself and Mitzy. But hell, Mitzy was already bat shit crazy."

She continued to tell me that by the time the carnage was over, six students were dead and another six were seriously injured at the Herbert Brutus School for Gifted Students. She described the madness that happened at night with members of the Jet Pack being mad out of their minds due to drinks made by Derrick. Then he supplied weapons in the form of hammers, knives and drills.

I was trying to maintain a bit of objectivity, but it was the wildest, craziest story I had ever heard, and it was coming from a person I knew to be very stable and grounded.

"I know, KC, it sounds crazy," Trinidad said, justifying what she had told me.

"Where were you and Dyson?" I asked.

"Conrod was in town, and that day we were having brunch when Dyson got a phone call from Brian."

"Did you know Conrod was your father then?"

"Yes, at that time, his three kids by his wife knew, and Dyson and I knew."

I pulled back, so I could look at Trinidad's face. "His three kids by his wife. Who was his wife and what three kids?"

"Sylvester and Lydia Smithers, and Derrick Paine."

"What? Derrick has the same father as Lydia . . . and Sylvester?"

"What about Thurmond Paine and his wife? He was just as big an executive in Hollywood as Conrod Bach."

Trinidad smiled. "No, sweetie, no one is as big an executive, or mover and shaker as Conrod Bach. But I never knew the set-up with any of the couples who had Conrod's children. I talked to my mother, but she was a single woman. She used to be Conrod's secretary . . . I know right, typical. But it was the same for Dyson, single mother, and his mother also worked for Conrod. But the rest of the so-called Jet Pack had two parents, and they were people with some status in Hollywood.

"And I definitely have no idea why Derrick would take Thurmond Paine's name versus Conrod's. I do know the Paines couldn't have kids, but I thought that was after they had Derrick."

I was dumbfounded. Was this the truth? Or was I being fed a fairy tale? Was the pussy's brew affecting my right mind? It's the history that clouds our present and future at times.

"So, Brian didn't lie to me, but he didn't tell me the whole truth, like he was there and he was a victim?"

"They call that shame, KC. Although he got there late, he tried to play the hero but he failed. Even now, that day still haunts him. Not what happened to him, but what happened to the others."

"How in the hell could you sleep with and marry your brother? You have to explain that TC, because I don't get it. And frankly, it makes it hard to believe any of this. You're not the kind of girl who marries her brother, or have babies with her brother."

"It's complicated, KC. Very complicated."

I let go and stepped back. I didn't know what to think. I saw sadness in Trinidad's face, and I was sure she saw disappointment in my face. I couldn't pass judgment, but that was what I was doing.

She didn't say anything. She walked to her desk, picked up a manila folder and gave it to me. Her eyes said a lot. One, that what she had just told me was the truth. Two, she was sadden by my reaction. Once in our life, she was the one who couldn't do any wrong. Lastly, her eyes said she still loved me and wished things could be different.

"I'm sorry," I said.

"Why?"

"For overreacting to Lydia's accusations," I replied. "I never wanted to say I was arrested for anything, including a minor traffic ticket or a false case of identity. But I was arrested—for rape. It affected me."

"I know it did," Trinidad said. She cracked a halfhearted smile. A smile of concession. Trying to keep the best memories we had wrapped tightly in a nice package, never to be broken or disturbed.

"I wish you would have relied on me versus calling your brother or Elliot Lucas. I could have taken care of the whole thing."

"TC, I didn't know then, what I know now."

The room was filled with silence and a bit of tension. I didn't want this. I was probably wrong for coming by myself. Truth be told, I didn't want Trinidad implicating herself or getting closed-mouth on me. I loved Julia and she would always be my life. It hit me that Trinidad was and would have been my life if not for her sister, Lydia Smithers. And that even sounded strange in my head—her sister.

"What's in the folder?" I asked.

"The scene I just described and a written explanation of everything, including my father's involvement."

I was so consumed, I completely forgot over half the questions I wanted to ask, like what was Conrod's involvement.

The second question, I had to ask. "Tell me where to go, TC?"

"Oxnard. Herbert Brutus School for Gifted Students. Rustic Building."

"The O-R."

"The scene of the crime—then . . . and now."

CHAPTER 68

AND THE WICKED SHALL DIE . . . AN EVIL AND HEINOUS DEATH.

Derrick Paine had endured the mental anguish his captors tried to behest on him. He had viewed video after video of his friends being tortured, confessing their crimes, begging for their lives and ultimately, dying for crimes then, and now. He had viewed the O-R scene from twenty years ago three times.

Internally, he laughed at it all.

They didn't know he still considered that to be his finest work. Hell, the three times he had viewed it since his kidnapping, only added to the other two or three hundred times he had viewed it in the privacy of his home. He couldn't count the number of times he had masturbated to the film . . . or the number of times he had drawn inspiration for his next screenplay. The film was motivation to him.

Just thinking about it now got his penis hard.

He always considered himself to have a good side and a bad side. Now, the good side had died. He was what he was, an evil genius who could take the vile parts of him and transfer them to the big screen. He was one of the best because he truly lived his life on the big screen. His stories stopped him from being the serial killer he easily could have been.

Dyson knew that. That's why Dyson reviewed all of his screenplays and made the needed changes, the required adjustments.

Dyson stopped the insanity from being viewed by the world. Only the sane versions of his stories made it to the screen. And that, in itself, was crazy enough for the audience.

His four captors were sitting in front of him. He knew each and every one of them. He was sure he was the only one who knew each of them. Yes, everyone knew Drake and Sin, but he was sure Mitzy and Terri didn't recognized or remember Mikki Lanay, especially since her surgery. And none of them probably remembered Patterson Boldin—because he was a forgettable guy.

But he remembered them all. He kept up with them all. They were all a part of his success. Every screenplay he had ever written and movie he had ever directed was with his brothers and sisters in mind. They motivated him, inspired him to be the best. He could visualize killing them all. He wished he had killed all twelve of the kids at the O-R twenty years ago, instead of the six. That was okay though. He was the director. And that was when he knew, he would be one of the world's best directors.

And it ending this way, was icing on the cake for him.

No words were spoken. They observed him. Waiting on him to break. He was sitting on a chair. It was a specially modified chair. He liked it. His chair was pulled forward, in a clamped down, head-restraining contraption. Both of his arms were pulled back and stretched out, while his wrists were strapped in and connected to a pole that was eight inches away. Both of his ankles were strapped to the back legs of the chair. Since his head was pulled forward, his whole torso was in the same position.

He was naked. And the thought in his head was one that made him smile. *I came in this world naked, and I will leave it the same way.*

"I remember hanging out at Dyson's place and seeing a draft of one of your screenplays," Drake said. His voice was slow, methodical, and very deliberate. "It was a couple of years ago. The screenplay was actually in the trashcan. I picked it up and flipped through the pages, and I was fucking shocked at how damned dark it was.

"But I saw the similarities to this very room, the infamous O-R. And I read about the killings. Then there was a scene when the head of the medical school lied to family members about how six students had died on a boating accident. Drowned and lost at sea."

Derrick smiled. "What, am I supposed to be sorry? Feel some kind of remorse for your brother and sister, Drake? Hell, they were my brother and sister too!" This was followed by laughter.

Then, out of the blue, Mikki Lanay grabbed the small sledgehammer and swung down his left arm at the elbow. Derrick yelled in excruciating pain. This was followed by a vicious attack by the other three members of the team—Drake, Steve Sinatra and Patterson Boldin.

If Derrick could, he would laugh. He was a bloody, black and blue mess. He had been beaten, stabbed and cut. He had cried out repeatedly in pain. A pain he had never felt before. A pain he was sure no one had ever endured before.

When he was young, he was called nerdy, geeky, odd and strange. After orchestrating the death of six people, he was said to be on the edge, crazy, mad and full of anger. He was diagnosed as being bipolar, borderline schizophrenic. He always laughed when he thought about that. He knew he had a split personality. He embraced the good and the bad.

Do it motherfuckers! Do it! You will never break me!

He was defiant to the end.

And the end came when Sin hung the axe at the base of his neck, simultaneously when Drake came down hard on his head with the swing of a bigger sledgehammer.

After that, Sin continued to chop, while Drake continued to swing.

And the wicked did die . . .

. . . an evil and heinous death.

CHAPTER 69

THE JET PACK SAT ON A GREAT WALL, THE JET PACK HAD A GREAT FALL . . .

. . . and Conrod Bach couldn't save them. Not one . . . not all.

Our mission consisted of saving the last three members of the Jet Pack, and hopefully, arresting the unsubs. I didn't know if unsubs was the right word to use. At least one was no longer an unknown subject—that one being Dr. Drake Devlin.

Prior to departing the B&B Productions building, I called my team and told them to deploy the first team to the old Herbert Brutus School in Oxnard, the Rustic Building, via UH-60 Black Hawk helicopter. That team consisted of Special Agents Jo Jo Sanu and Blane Taylor, along with two other special agents from the Los Angeles Field Office. I had two other teams deploy via two suburban vehicles. I had Paula Coker wait for me.

En route to pick up Paula, I viewed the contents of the manila folder I had received from Trinidad. I'll be damned. The folder contained an iPad, a compact disc, two thumb drives and a eighty plus page document. Upon my initial glance at the document, it looked as if it was the Cliff's notes version of Conrod Bach's life, and it included the Jet Pack's history.

I had just started viewing the iPad when we picked up Paula. *What the fuck?*

The picture was as clear as day. And the scene was unbelievable. I fast-forwarded the video. I was watching a snuff film. This was depravity at its worse.

I couldn't speak. I just watched. No emotions.

But I finally understood.

Paula was perusing the document when she said, "I think this is Conrad Bach's manifesto."

Before I could respond, a transmission came through my headset. "Raven Three-Two to Raven Three-One, over."

It was Jo Jo. "Talk to me Three-Two."

"How far out are you Three-One?"

"Two mike." That meant two minutes.

"Over."

From Jo Jo's voice inflection, I knew the verdict. From looking at the video, even fast-forwarding trying to view the whole thing before we landed, I knew what to expect. Three more dead bodies. Three more dead superstars.

We were greeted by a fellow agent regurgitating in the lobby of the Rustic Building. Hell, I thought his face was as green as a Martian. I was surprised the smell, or the sight, of the agent didn't affect Paula.

As soon as we made our way to Operation Room One, Jo Jo and Blane were processing the scene. Throughout the room, there were approximately fifteen to twenty cryogenic containers. From first view, I was sure those freezer units contained the body parts of Mitzy York and Terrence Parkins.

That was my thought because I was two hundred percent sure the mangled mess of a body against the far side of the room was Derrick Paine. I should say the mangled separated head was Derrick's. The rest of his body was cut up and beaten badly. I couldn't describe it. It was personal . . . it was pure rage . . . it redefined overkill.

"Paula, have agents from the Field Office pick up Conrad Bach," I said.

"For questioning?"

"No, for murder and accessory to murder," I replied. "Also, have them put out a nationwide bulletin for Dr. Drake Devlin."

"You good?" Jo Jo asked me.

"Yeah, I'm good." I looked around the room again. Taking in the scene. "I was just thinking about Humpty Dumpty."

"Humpty Dumpty?"

"Yeah, all the King's men couldn't put him back together again either."

CHAPTER 70

HE WHO HAS THE BRICKS, BUILD THE FOUNDATION.

"Conrod told me every time he heard someone say, *'the house that Michael or Payton built,'* he would smile and laugh to himself," Elliot said. "He would tell me that not only did he build the house, but he lived and played in the house. He was the King of Hollywood. When Michael and Payton were blowing snot from their noses, he was building empires and destroying companies. He became a savior for an industry, in turn, he became the foundation of the industry."

I had just briefed Elliot, Maxwell Pack and Patrick Conroy on what happened in California. It was the next day. My team and I were back at the Hoover Building, and had reviewed everything I received from Trinidad. Paula was right—it was Conrod Bach's manifesto.

Of course, he knew all the secrets. He had the biggest secrets. From multiple children to covering up the original crime in Oxnard twenty years ago, Conrod had put everything on paper. The iPad, compact disc and flash drives all included one item—Derrick Paine's first film, the original killings at Herbert Brutus School for Gifted Students. I think he would have taken those secrets to his grave.

"Good briefing, Carson," Elliot stated. "So, what's next? Where do we stand?"

"Warrant out for Mr. Bach," Maxwell said, before I could get a word out. "Another one for Drake Devlin. With everything we have, we have no idea how many partners the doctor had working with him, or the connection to Code of Colors."

"Additionally, for the other alleged crimes committed by the Jet Pack, we have agents questioning the law enforcement officials who conducted the original investigations, and seeing if we can connect those crimes to members of the group. In Bach's papers, he did a good job of connecting the crimes, but his answer for everything was paying the families. Except in this case, it was handled a little different. Those families were told that long lost relatives had left them money. There was no admission of guilt. And of course, what family is going to complain about receiving a check for two or three million, or more?

"Thus far, we know three families were paid huge sums of money from relatives who died, and either they didn't know the relative, didn't know the relative had a will, or even had money."

"I get that," Elliot said. "If I was presented with over a million dollars and I didn't have much or had been working all of my days, I would jump on it too."

"Sure you would," Maxwell joked.

When the door to Elliot's office opened suddenly, and his executive secretary stuck her head in, we were all surprised. "Sir, all of you need to get down to the lobby. Dr. Devlin and two others are turning themselves in."

No one said anything. Instead, we all followed Elliot's lead and followed him to the lobby.

"Looks like you may actually be closing another case Carson," Elliot said sarcastically, while we were riding down in the elevator. Elliott and Maxwell were in the front, and Patrick and I were behind them. Sometimes I wished I could just hit him in the damn face. Patrick and I exchanged gazes and he had a smile on his face. In the history of smartasses, he had to be the biggest.

When we reached the lobby, you would think we had walked into a three-ring circus. We had uniformed agents on the outside of the building, controlling the press from entering the building. We had other uniformed and plain-clothes agents with their guns drawn, pointing at three assailants—all three on their knees with their hands behind their heads.

Two Caucasian men and an African-American woman.

Dr. Drake Devlin, Patterson Boldin and Mikki Lanay.

I took the lead and told everyone to put their guns down. I signaled for all three to get up.

I got toe-to-toe with Drake. "Supervisory Special Agent Carson, my name is Drake Devlin, and today, me, Mr. Patterson Boldin and Miss Mikki Lanay are turning ourselves in for the murder of Mr. Derrick Paine."

Drake and I looked at each other. As much as I wanted to be disappointed, I was probably more upset.

"Why didn't come to me Drake?" It was the only thing I could think to say.

"This was bigger than you KC," he replied in a low voice that only he and I could hear. "We have a friendship. I wasn't trying to get you involved. It was a spur of the moment thing."

"That's bullshit Drake," I tried to say in an equally low tone. I don't think I succeeded. "We have always had each other's back. And you know there is no limitation on murder. I could have jailed all six."

We continue to look at each other. Cameras flashing and red recording lights were not lost on me. However, it took Patrick leaning in and prompting me to press on.

Before I could say another word, Drake said, "Our attorneys are in the crowd outside. Could you please allow them to enter before we proceed?"

Patrick went to the door, and returned with two elderly men in high priced suits.

Then once again, Drake repeated what he had said earlier, "My name is Drake Devlin, and today, me, Mr. Patterson Boldin and Miss Mikki Lanay are turning ourselves in for the murder of Mr. Derrick Paine."

The attorneys didn't say anything.

I said, "Put the cuffs on them. Dr. Devlin, Mr. Boldin and Miss Lanay, you are under arrest for the murder of Mr. Derrick Paine, and the suspected deaths of Miss Theresa Wenthill, Mr. Wash Tunnell, Mr. Jimmie Claymore, Mr. Terrence Parkins and Miss Mikki York."

I then proceeded to read them their rights. As we were about to lead the suspects to the elevator, one of the suits gave me a flash drive, while the other attorney walked over to Elliot and handed him another flash drive. Then the attorney leaned in and whispered something in Elliot's ear.

As Patrick and I were leading Drake and company to an elevator three hallways away from the lobby, Drake said to us, "SSA Carson, we are only admitting to the death of Derrick Paine."

"I know that Drake, that's why I read the charges the way I did."

"Well, the flash drive will confirm we did the one crime. The other crimes we are not responsible for."

"Drake, shut up until we get to the interrogation room and your counsel is present. You are the smartest person I know, don't get dumb now."

Once again, Patrick and I were gazing at each other in an elevator. This time I wanted to hit Drake, Patterson and Mikki in their faces. And I didn't know if I was mad because they turned themselves in, or how they turned themselves, or maybe I was mad that they didn't allow me to bring the others to justice for them.

CHAPTER 71

THE TWISTS AND TURNS OF LIFE CAN BE AS TOXIC AS A
HAZARDOUS WASTE DUMP!

*First, on behalf of the B&B Productions family, I want to offer
our condolences to the families of the students who died at the Herbert
Brutus School for Gifted Students twenty years ago. As a former student
of the school, and a former member of the Jet Pack, I, along with
Trinidad Capture, had no idea any of this had ever happened.*

*Four days ago when the news broke that this madness had happened
years ago, followed by the news that three of our former classmates had
killed the other members of the Jet Pack, it saddened both Trinidad
and I. This happened on our watch and we had no idea.*

*For me and my family, all of this has been overwhelming. Today,
my siblings and I had a home-going ceremony for our father, Conrod
Bach, who died several days ago. Today, he was cremated and that was
followed by a celebration of his life.*

I, like so many others throughout the nation, was viewing the
telecast from Los Angeles, specifically, downtown L.A., on the steps
of the B&B Productions building. It was subtle, but the African-
American man conducting the press conference, representing B&B,
had just dropped a bombshell. Dyson Ryker, the Chief Operating
Officer, was also Conrod Bach's son. I don't think anyone saw that
one coming.

Sylvester Smithers flanked him on his right, and their sister, Lydia Smithers, on his left. I could only shake my head.

Dyson was being as calm and cool as he could. He had stopped talking. I wondered where his mind was at that moment. I couldn't remember the last time we saw each other. He had picked up some weight, but he still looked to be in football shape—offseason football shape. During the first month of the off-season, you could eat what you wanted and didn't have to worry about working out, being at practice or meeting weight requirements.

I knew he was the chief operating officer at B&B Productions, and this had to be one of the hardest days of his life. I could tell by the tears he was trying his best to hold back.

I must say, the company's attorney as well as my own personal attorney did not want me to do this press conference today. However, I felt compelled to face the world and say, I'm sorry for what happened twenty years ago and I'm sorry for what recently happened to my friends. And yes, I still call the Jet Pack my friends. You can condemn me for that. I loved them just as much as I loved my father. At one point in time, we were closed friends . . . and we were family. Somewhere, things went awry for them.

I didn't know if Dyson was acting or being real. He looked emotional, as if he was trying his best to keep it together. I was cynical. Much like with Trinidad, I didn't know what to think.

Conrod Bach died of pancreatic cancer. He actually died several days ago. The same day my former classmates turned themselves in to the FBI. I'm not going to make excuses for my father. He wouldn't want me to. He lived his life. He made mistakes. Yes, he knew what happened twenty years ago. And, in his mind, he tried his best to make good for all that transpired that dreadful night.

Because of confidentiality and nondisclosure agreements, I cannot discuss the terms of what settlements were made years ago. But over the years, my father did his darnedest to make up for that night in other ways. And yes, those ways were financial, from giving billions in scholarships to providing various grants and donating to numerous charities to a ton of other venues. And I know it's no solace, but when he died, he felt as if he didn't do enough, and he wished he could do more.

Think what you will of our father. He was a man, a mere human. He had flaws. As I stand up here today to announce he was not faithful in his marriage. A marriage that most of the world didn't know about. A marriage that lasted over thirty years. And yes, he had children out of wedlock. But I, and others who call the man father, we loved him. And that love is everlasting.

With that, Dyson turned and walked away, and Lydia and Sylvester Smithers followed him. I'm be damned. Dyson was the leader of the pack. I didn't know if that meant he was responsible for the killings of his friends, and this was all about vengeance for he and Trinidad, or if he really knew about the original killings years ago in Oxnard.

"Helluva thing, helluva man, huh," Elliot Lucas stated. He had summoned me to his office before the press conference. He and I were watching his big screen television. I wasn't sure this was why I was here. Maybe he wanted company. Maybe he was in mourning himself. I, like much of the world didn't have a clue Conrod Bach was dead.

"I guess it all depends on your perspective, Director," I replied. "Hell, I have more questions now."

"Don't worry about it, the case is over. Ended with the three turning themselves in."

"I think it was more than just those three."

"Maybe. But they took the fall. And the attorney general will cut them a sweet deal. That's one reason Ryker did the press conference. They will do time, but their attorneys, who all probably works for B&B, or better yet, the Bach family, will make this too good to be true. They will point out the holes in the case and the fact that their clients talked to us when they were still represented by counsel.

"Plus, in case you didn't know, they only confessed to one crime, Derrick Paine. Their fingerprints were not on any of the cryogenic freezer units. We only had circumstantial evidence against Dr. Devlin. That wasn't by chance. They did that on purpose. If Brian Dye was pressured, I'm sure they discussed him turning on the good doctor. And they probably had already discussed the three martyrs. It all points to one big collaboration.

"And we just saw the ringleader."

Director Elliot Lucas never ceased to surprise me. He knew more than he was letting on. I didn't understand how any damn cases in America occurred without this man knowing something about it.

"Elliot, bet you a thousand dollars Conrod Bach didn't die from pancreatic cancer. And another thousand that you knew he was dead and what he died from."

He smiled. "Sorry, Carson, I love my money."

"Can you tell me how he died?"

"Sure I can," he replied. "Pancreatic cancer . . . I assure you that's what the death certificate states."

I half-heartedly smiled. The man was full of riddles. I think it was just a natural thing. I wasn't sure he was even aware that he talked in riddles as much as he did.

"KC, one thing I have learned in my six decades plus of living is that life is just a series of twists and turns and you hope you twist and turn the right way. I looked at Mr. Ryker and I have to take my hat off to him. He sent the world a message today. He is B&B Productions. He is definitely the shot-caller."

"Do you think he had a role in all of this?"

"I can't prove it, KC, but yeah, I do. Like I stated, he is the shot-caller. I know you think Brian Dye was the man behind this elaborate scheme. I think Dye was the executor, but the mastermind behind the plan was the man you just saw walk away from that podium with all his minions following behind."

I looked at the television. Of course, there were pundits on the screen trying to dissect and analyze Dyson's press conference. He wasn't the greatest professional football player, but he was a leader. He was the one other players looked to for leadership and motivation. And he delivered. Unfortunately, due to a couple of injuries, his career didn't last long. But it was long enough for him to make an impact on those who graced his presence.

"Interesting speech," I stated. "Probably opened the company up to a ton of lawsuits."

"From who?" Elliot retorted. "I don't know for a fact, son, but I'm sure Conrod paid the families handsomely for their losses years ago. Additionally, all of the kids who were killed were his kids. *Too many secrets.* Secrets I'm sure Dyson Ryker doesn't mind exposing. Secrets the families probably don't want released more so than Dyson.

"He made his point in his speech. He made sure the world knew he was doing this press conference at the objection of his attorneys. That was the operative statement. His father had issues. He wasn't a perfect man. Dyson threw that out there. Hell, the families of the Jet Pack members can't sue without exposing their loved ones as killers and not without exposing the fact that Conrod was the father to all the students of Herbert Brutus. And, as you know, you can't broker a deal if you have nothing to offer in exchange.

"Anyone who tries to sue needs evidence, some kind of viable proof. And think about it, son . . . Lydia Smithers had proof of the crimes her six brothers and sisters committed. Believe me, KC, she didn't collect that information. She loved her brothers and sisters. I believe she didn't keep in touch with each of them on a monthly basis like she stated. I wouldn't be surprised if Dyson, or maybe Trinidad, collected the articles or kept track of their fellow Jet Pack members' wrongdoings. They were the two oldest of the group. If they had been there that day, the killings never would have happened."

"Trinidad, why Trinidad?" I asked with plenty of doubt in my voice, and I was sure Elliot could see the doubt in my eyes as well.

"When Ms. Smithers accused you of rape, I went to Conrod's office. He introduced me to his daughter, Trinidad Capture, and told me he was sorry his other daughter, Lydia, had accused you of a crime you didn't commit. I couldn't help myself, I asked him how he knew you didn't commit the crime. Trinidad intervened and told me you two were together the night before, and she is the one who gave me the tapes, pictures, recordings and letters of Lydia's misgivings. Then she told me Ms. Smithers would be taking a long trip aboard and you wouldn't have to worry about anything like this again.

"I didn't question their motive, or her authority. It was clear to me Conrod was the present Alpha. However, Trinidad was the future. Watching the press conference today, I realized one thing, KC . . . with Dyson and Trinidad, there is an Alpha A and B."

As I got up to leave the room, Elliot said one more thing. "Conrod put a gun to his head and pulled the trigger."

I didn't say anything. I thought about what Elliot had just shared. In a way, my mind was blown—on so many levels. Dyson. Trinidad. Lydia. Conrod Bach. Brian Dye.

And then there was Elliot.

I marveled at how he approached business and life. Sometimes he allowed the cards to randomly drop. Other times he manipulated the deck. Even when you didn't think he was in the loop, you slowly learned that he was always in the *loop*.

I smiled and shook my head as I left the room.

In my mind, after Elliot had delivered his latest oration, I envisioned him dropping the mic.

He had been given a special gift—to control the twists and turns of life.

CHAPTER 72

THE ENDING IS NOT ALWAYS EPIC!

"We did it, Doc!" Ray Reynolds shouted as Dr. Steve Sinatra walked through the front door of his Malibu home. The house sat on a rolling hill in a gated community. The bottom floor of the two-story house was lined with a wall of floor-to-ceiling windows that provided a breathtaking, unobstructed view of the Pacific Ocean. The second floor housed four bedrooms, a floating-style staircase and catwalk. The walls weren't as prevalent with glass as the bottom floor, but it still afforded a great view.

"Fuck! We kicked some ass, Doc! We did the damn thing! You hear me! We did the damn thing!"

Although Sin wasn't as exuberant as his partner in crime, he was indeed happy. He sat the bag he carried in his left hand on the island in the kitchen as well as the pizza he held in his right. The bag contained two six-packs of beer, chips and salsa.

"Yes, we did do the damn thing, Ray, we did indeed," Sin said in a calm tone. The two men gazed at each other. One was overexcited, while the other resonated with the moment. It was as if his ship had finally come in. For him, his heart was at rest, his mind at ease.

Sin said, "I told Brian I would come over and celebrate with you when this shit was over. And thanks to you, it's over."

The two men shook and embraced. Ray was along for the ride. But he realized how important this was to his two friends. He and

Sin had never been the best of friends. Brian was their bond. The one who held the glue together. Helping with their ordeal, Ray got it. Damn, did he get it.

They settled in the great room, watching Ray's eighty-inch television with surround sound. His favorite team, the Lakers were on, struggling through another game. The food and beverages had been transferred to the coffee table that sat in front of them. The list of beverages included two bottles of cognac, a bottle of gin and a couple cans of soda.

Sin was a lightweight when it came to drinking. He preferred soda with his hard liquor, but his drink of choice was beer. Whereas, Ray was a man with a strong conviction when it came to drinking. He preferred his whiskey or gin straight up, refrigerated cold, no ice.

"Doc, I'm sorry, man, for all the shit I have given you over the years," Ray said. "I can't believe you and Brian lived with that shit for twenty fucking years. Damn, that would have messed me up inside."

Sin didn't say anything. His mind was in another place. Internally, he felt he had died ten times over. At one point in his life, he didn't know the meaning of a good night's sleep. Three or four hours—if he was lucky. When he was in med school, he had a built in excuse for not getting enough sleep. But he knew med school was nothing compared to what he had went through in his life.

He wanted to be a director and producer. He wanted the film industry to be his life. But after his friends were killed and others seriously injured, he lost that luster, that desire to be one of Hollywood's biggest assholes.

Ray was still talking. Sin didn't catch everything he was saying. However, he liked that Ray could be sympathetic to their history.

"You know, I became a doctor because I wanted to save people," Sin stated, although Ray was in mid-sentence. He was drunk. Better yet, he felt good. "Ray, it was good doing good for others. Saving lives, ensuring loved ones didn't have to make funeral plans or bury their sons, daughters, parents, friends, whatever. I did it because it brought me joy. Made me a person."

"I know, Doc. You and Brian are great people."

"No. No we're not, Ray. We killed people. We killed people who we once thought of as friends."

"Only because they killed your true friends, Doc."

"Yeah. That may be true. But Ray, killing is killing. I see that now. We killed."

"It's the alcohol talking, Doc. Everything will be good. Tomorrow is another day, a better day."

"Yeah, maybe so."

"What you think about Dyson's press conference?" Ray popped open another can of beer, and immediately took a deep swallow. He wiped his lips. "That's a pretty deep dude."

"Now, that's good people" Sin stated. "He's the real fucking deal." His words were coming out slurred. His thoughts were slow. He couldn't remember how many cans of beer or how many shots he had had. "We all owe the world to him and Trinidad."

"Fuck, can you imagine how much money they will be paying out?"

"No money. Conrod Bach paid off everybody years and years ago. The families got up to ten million each, and that included families of the kids who were hurt like Brian. Plus, Brian and the other five got five million as well."

"Damn. At least the man had a heart."

"No . . . he didn't. He had a dick, he used it. Made a ton of babies, probably holds the world record for the number of kids he had. But the motherfucker had one thing."

Sin poured himself a shot of cognac. That one was followed by another.

Ray didn't say anything. He was fascinated. The stories of the rich and famous always enthralled him. That's why he worked as a bartender. He sucked at acting. The best he could do when he came out to Hollywood was a couple of very low-rated softcore porn movies. But this kind of stuff he lived for.

"Dyson Ryker. That's what he had . . . Dyson fucking Ryker. Well, two things. Trinidad. They kept him honest. Made him do the right thing. They were the two kids he always wanted. The two he doted on. The two with all the common and book sense."

Ray was mesmerized. Hollywood was full of crazy tales. To him, this was the craziest. And even more crazier than that—it was the best kept secret in Hollywood. He knew Conrod Bach was probably the most powerful man in Hollywood. But he didn't know how powerful until he went down that road with Brian and Sin.

"Who is that?" Sin asked.

"Who is who?"

"Your doorbell rang," Sin answered.

"Oh, did it? Brian told me to expect a package today. I'll be right back."

"Cool, you do that, and I will hit the head."

Ray felt good as he whistled and occasionally clapped his hands on the way to the door. He was still excited at their perceived victory—the victory of killing six people.

When he opened the door, the woman with the flaming red hair surprised him. They say the brain can process an image within ten to fifteen milliseconds, a split-second, which is considered a fraction of a second. In those milliseconds, Ray Reynolds saw a face, flaming red hair and a gun with a silencer attached. The double tap action both hit him in the left section of his chest, his heart.

Death came fast. His life was gone before his body hit the floor.

The female moved through the house, towards the sound of the television. She had both hands on her weapon, arms extended, gun ready to fire. Her haberdashery was about distraction—black thigh-high boots, tight-fitted black leather pants, black gloves, a lightweight burgundy jacket and a white lace push-up bra that showcased a nice pair of size thirty-six double D breasts. *Distraction.*

She didn't see anyone in the great room with the television. However, she did pick up on the noise coming from the half-sized bathroom in the hallway not far from the great room. She stood ten feet from the door, in a ready-to-shoot stance.

When the stood opened, Steve Sinatra was looking down as he took his first couple of steps. When he looked up, his split-second never formulated. The first shot hit him in the heart, followed by a second shot to his throat.

She laid the gun down on Sin's torso . . .

. . . and left the way she came in.

CHAPTER 73

LOVE IS NEVER LOST ON THE TRUE AT HEART . . . ONLY THE
STUPID.

It's over!

Brian Dye watched as Dyson Ryker walked away from the
podium and into the B&B Productions building, followed by
Lydia and Sylvester. He had mixed emotions. They were a screwed
up family. And by *they*, he meant all of them, to include himself,
Sin, Trinidad and the other one hundred half-brothers and half-
sisters he had.

He felt his existence was one big lie, fairy tale and nightmare
rolled into a mess of a quagmire he called life. He remembered
Conrod telling him, "The perplexity of Brian Dye is Brian Dye.
You were served lemons, son. But instead of making lemonade, you
want to make a ten course meal with the finest wine and richest
dessert."

He hated when Conrod called him *son*. The truth of the
matter was he was another one of his father's bastards. As much
as he wanted to hate the man, he couldn't. He was standing as
Dyson gave his speech at the podium, then he said Conrod had
died and they cremated him. His father was dead. And the man he
had openly hated for so many years now brought tears to his eyes
because he was gone.

He knew Conrod didn't know how to be a father, but the
sonofabitch tried. He built the Herbert Brutus School for Gifted

Students to keep his children in one location and to get to know each other. The purpose of the school was to be the daycare center, place of learning and performing arts academy for his offspring. Unfortunately, the one thing the great Conrod Bach didn't count on was the sexual desire of boys and girls.

Brian Dye shook his head as he rode down the elevator and entered the black Mercedes Benz limousine. He was flying out of Dulles Airport today, and he was looking to the drive on Interstate-66. He knew he wouldn't be coming back to the nation's capital for a while.

He was putting the city behind him for now, just like he had to put his father's life and death behind him. After all, the old man was right, he did want his ten-course meal with the best wine and dessert. He thought that was Trinidad Capture. He was wrong. It was Lydia Smithers.

The sad thing about it all . . . they were all half-brothers and half-sisters. And they did love each other, as much as half-siblings were capable of loving. Just not the way their dad wanted them to know or care about each other.

He wanted to smile and shake his head at the craziness he called his life. Unfortunately, he couldn't. He was a billionaire, with a great wife and three terrific sons, and still, he wasn't happy. He should have been happy . . . spearheading the killings of those who caused him and his friends pain for so many years, he was supposed to be happy.

Now, the showdown. Dyson told him to stay away from the Jet Pack. To leave it alone. He didn't have the blessing of the next King of Hollywood. He still couldn't smile at his thought. Dyson was that quiet warrior who carried a big stick and when he said no, he meant no. But Brian defied the next king. Even at the behest of his wife, he said *fuck it.*

"Billionaires don't take orders dammit," he said to no one in particular. The partition separated him from his driver. "I'll deal with Dyson when I see him."

He was a man trying to convince himself he was stronger and braver than he actually was. He knew Dyson and Trinidad calmed the beast they all knew was their father. They were the ones who rebuilt the company and made it more majestic than it used to be. No one knew the true power of Dyson Ryker, but he did. As much as he loved the man, more as friend and businessman, than half-brother, he was equally afraid of the man.

He answered his cell phone on the first ring. "Hey, baby, how are you doing?"

If his wife could see his face, she would see angst, disinterest. He loved her, but their marriage was one of convenience, one of business. His love for Lydia was dominating his mood. He wished he could turn back the hands of time to the day before he lost his brother and his friends, and complete function in his right hand.

"I'm on the way to the airport and should be home in three or four hours." He rolled his eyes at her reply. "Love you too."

He hated himself. His mind was elsewhere. His love was elsewhere.

The perplexity of Brian Dye is Brian Dye.

His father was right. And he still missed the sonofabitch.

He was so deep in thought, he was surprised when the partition came down, realizing they had pulled to the side of the interstate. When the driver turned around and he saw the gun, Brian did what he hadn't been able to do—he smiled.

"Just one question, who ordered the hit, Dyson or Trinidad?"
"Yes."

His death was quick. One shot.

The driver departed the car . . .

. . . and walked back to the car parked behind him.

CHAPTER 74

Hey lover.

"Lover? You must have the wrong number, Madame, I'm a happily married man," KC responded with a smile on his face.

For Julia Carson, it was a reply that put a smile on her face. "Well, I may say, your wifey is a very lucky woman to have such a loyal husband."

"I think she is, but if you tell me who you are, I will tell her to expect your phone call and you can tell her that for yourself."

"Well, tell me sir, what makes you so special, and how you know your wifey is not out there playing the field?"

I laughed out loud and I could hear Julia doing the same. If we were together at that moment, I would have answered the question with a laugh and a kiss, a kiss that would have led to something more.

"First, I'm a damn good looking guy and she would never be able to find anyone as good looking as me. Two, I'm a terrific lover and I know all of the right buttons to turn her on and then some. And lastly, on top of that, I'm rich."

Julia laughed again, but it was as if she was stifling her laughter. She was on a job, she wasn't in a position to openly laugh or display any kind of emotion, not the emotion she wanted to release. That would be unprofessional and more importantly, compromising. Even calling me while she was still undercover was a no-no. But this wasn't the first time she had disregarded the Bureau's or CIA's procedure. However, something was different. I could tell in her voice. The last time we wee together, I could tell something wasn't right. Maybe she missed her family. I know we always missed her whenever she went away.

I knew her assignment was unsanctioned. It wasn't information I was supposed to know. She didn't tell me that information. The one person I thought would be in the know, wasn't either. And it was unusual for Elliot not to be in the know.

That why I was worried.

"You're a fool, you know that right?" she jokingly bantered. "So, four turn themselves in, then a billionaire and his two best friends are killed. Sounds like an interesting ending to an interesting case."

"I don't know how interesting it really was," KC responded. "There was no need to create a Code of Colors and kill innocent kids, and if they wanted revenge, fuck, why go through all the shit they went through? If it was Brian and his friends, they could have found a way to kill the Jet Pack assholes without the dramatic adventure."

"Damn, lover, it sounds like Mr. Dye got your goat on this one."

I smiled. "You are stupid, you know that right?"

Something told me she was probably smiling back.

"I miss you woman," I replied in a serious tone.

"I know. I miss you and the kids as well."

The proceeding silence said a lot. It verified something wasn't right, but I treaded lightly. "Everything good?"

"Everything's good. Heard our song today and got a little sad that I was in one place and you were in another."

Our song was Maze and Frankie Beverly's *Happiness*. I could hear the slow and mellow melody in my head. The song was heavy-handed for us. It was playing the first time we made love . . . and damn was it so appropriate. I think from the first beat and first line, we knew it applied to us.

She gave me happiness and I, in turn, would like to think I gave her happiness.

Yeah, heavy-handed indeed.

"Have to go, see you soon," she said. "And Kenny, know this, I love you."

"Love you more, Julia. Love you more."

CHAPTER 75

AND THE COAT OF THE RAVEN WAS BLACK, BOLD . . . AND ITS STRENGTH WAS ALL POWERFUL.

Julia wished she could sit in darkness. But that was impossible. She had observed and studied her subject for two weeks and tonight was the final phase of her mission. He expected the lights to be on. The man was a victim to routine and regularity. One day, the lights would be on downstairs, another night, all of the lights in the house had to be on, and the third night only the lights upstairs were on.

There were other subtleties that he was sure that only he and his mistress, Tabitha, knew. But he was gravely mistaken.

Regardless of her title with the Bureau or family status, Julia Carson knew she was more assassin than executive assistant, mom or wife.

This was her world, her livelihood. As much as she had tried to move away from her true love, she couldn't. On several occasions, both she and KC had tried to walk away from the Bureau and just be entrepreneurs and parents. Some things never worked out as planned. She knew that fact only too well. The assassin in her also knew all too well.

She looked at her watch. Two minutes out. She turned on the shower. Hot. Smoky hot. Although the man was in his early sixties and a victim to routine, he was still a freak at heart. She knew he would think Tabitha was in the shower and he would voluntarily join her.

She heard the garage door go up. She looked at her watch.

Right on schedule.

He never disappoints.

The kitchen door that connected to the garage didn't open immediately. Julia instinctively knew something was wrong. He truthfully was a man of routine. He would only break that routine if something was indeed wrong, or not right in his eyes. She couldn't think of anything she may have missed.

She was in the spare bedroom closest to the master bedroom. That didn't make a bit of difference because the spare bedrooms were around a corner from the master. The staircase led directly to the master bedroom.

She made a quick decision. Get the hell out of the room and make her way to the garage. She couldn't run though. She had to be quick, but quiet.

She opened the door and made her way to the hallway. As soon as she peeked around the corner, she saw her target rapidly ascending to the top of the staircase, with a gun in his right hand and looking at the phone in his left.

He fired his weapon as soon as he spotted her, but in one motion, she quickly took cover behind the wall, squatted, rolled and double tapped on her back.

The first shot hit the man squarely in the middle of his neck. The second shot almost, simultaneously, hit him in the middle of his forehead. She knew if he wasn't looking at his phone, he probably would have killed her.

She didn't want to kill him that fast. She needed information from him verifying what Tabitha had provided to her.

Julia picked up his phone and saw what he was looking at on his phone. It was a view of the hallway. She knew if she played with the phone, she would probably see a view of every room in the house. Knowing Nicholas Holt, Chief of the Counterterrorism Division, the way she did, she was sure these views were displayed on his dashboard display in his vehicle. Views he probably looked at on his ride home every single day. She wondered if he had cameras in the master bedroom, or maybe motion or heat detectors she may have missed.

She was mad at herself. She missed this. Although she had placed a mini spy camera in the dashboard of his car—unfortunately, it wasn't in a position to see anything on the display. Anything he was privy to see. It almost caused her death.

She was even madder at herself. She needed to know who the mastermind behind the plan to kill Raven was. When she asked Tabitha this question, she replied after some convincing persuasion, "Your husband."

It didn't make sense. She needed verification from Nicholas Holt.

In the world she lived in, she could never fathom or imagine her husband, Kenny Carson, would ever want to kill her uncle, the director of the FBI, Elliot Lucas.

The Raven.

ACKNOWLEDGMENTS

Sending love to two of my boyz, Steve "SIN" Sinatra, for providing me a title and letting me run with it, and Brian Dye, for sharing your great stories as a deejay, paying your way through college—I wish everyone knew your real backstory, the things you have overcome to become the great success you are. Additional thanks for allowing me to use your names as characters. I hope you both like the final product.

To Steve and Mary Wooden, I couldn't ask for a better brother and sister-in-law. In my time of need, you guys didn't me the opportunity to say no. You both dropped everything, and came by my side and made sure I lived to see another day. Love you both!

To Yolanda M. Johnson-Bryant, Literary Wonders Media Group and Bryant Consulting—thank you for being in my corner and the tough love. Additionally, thanks for the great editing job and being a royal pain in the butt, which in this case is a good thing.

To Melissa Forbes – one of the best freelance editors in the business. Please forgive me for never giving you your props. You always make my stories sing.

Special thanks to my friend of thirty years, Clayton Melvin, as well as Mrs. Paula Coker-Albert and Blane Taylor for allowing me to use your names as characters. I hope you all like the final product.

To my fans and audience, Thank You for supporting me, reading my books and recommending my books to others. I write because I love the art of storytelling—and I'm always amazed at how my words and stories resonate with others.